River Card

A NOVEL BY
JOAN DESTINO

River Card is a work of historical fiction. Apart from the well-known actual people, events and locales that figure in the narrative, all names, characters, places and incidents are the products of the author's imagination or are used fictitiously. Any resemblance to current events or locales, or to living persons, is entirely coincidental.

Copyright © 2013 Joan Destino
All Rights Reserved

ISBN-10: 061580702X
ISBN-13: 9780615807027

To

Colonel Donald Daniel Vol Janin, United States Army, Retired
and
Eleanora Shifren Vol Janin

Gratitude

Writing the story of Georgia Alexandra Kassov Cates has been a part of my life for more than twenty years. John W. Bakaly, PhD, helped me to organize my own mind. Lisa Mitchell taught me to write fiction and in the process became a lifelong friend and literary mentor. Randy Benjamin put my cover design image on paper. Jacque Hallstead, Nancy Leibowitz and Sarah Lindsey read the early drafts, shared their suggestions, and gently but firmly prodded me to finish what I had started so long ago.

My family is my center, the source of my energy and my wellbeing: -- My son, Donald Daniel Destino, his wife, Darien Elise Lindsay and their children, George Morgan Destino, Bennett Eli Destino, Theodore Beck Destino, and Louise Lenore Destino -- My daughter, Cassandra Susanne Destino and her husband, Matthew John Petty -- David Andrew Destino, my husband of forty-eight years, my true love and enduring partner.

WHEN I FIND A WELL-DRAWN CHARACTER IN FICTION OR BIOGRAPHY, I GENERALLY TAKE A WARM PERSONAL INTEREST IN HIM, FOR THE REASON THAT I HAVE KNOWN HIM BEFORE—MET HIM ON THE RIVER.

— Mark Twain

Prologue

**December 26, 1997 – Almost Midnight,
the Mirage Poker Room, Las Vegas, Nevada**

It really wasn't about winning money. Playing seven-card stud was what she wanted to do, or so Georgia Cates had been telling herself since the first time she had sat down at a casino poker table. Now a little less than a quarter-million dollars in chips and paper money lay on the green felt in front of her. She casually riffled a stack of white five-thousand-dollar chips. Never mind that this money was all that was left of the $500,000 she had started with a few hours ago, and never mind that the entire half million was not hers in the first place and that she could go to prison for a very long time.

She had perfected her poker face, and the eight carats of diamond rings on her fingers sparkled, but not because her fingers were trembling. No one could guess that the elegant, perfectly composed woman in the Jil Sander suit was about to throw up. She tried to swallow, but her dry throat convulsed, and she coughed to cover up the gag impulse.

Who was she trying to fool? Herself? A little late for that. She had to win; her survival depended on it.

Chapter 1

Georgia
June 26, 1998

It was like trying to hurry across a frozen lake in four-inch sandals. She forced herself to slow down as she made her way along the marble thoroughfare that spanned the Bellagio Casino.

"I will not slip, I will not fall," she intoned, very aware of the several curious glances she got. But vocalizing her thoughts, transmitting them via her vocal cords so that the vibrations were sent to her eardrums and the neural message delivered to her brain, validated the reality of her existence. Talking to herself was the only way she knew to keep focused. So what if she was acting loonier than a bag lady?

"Think out loud," she commanded herself. "I am Georgia Kassov Cates, poised and elegant, strolling along in my perfect clothes, great haircut, makeup subtle but effective. But can they see my lips moving? Do I care?"

Trying to imagine what she must look like on a casino surveillance camera, she concentrated on a nonchalant but brisk stride, doing her best to edit out the throngs of tourists, many with necks craned and fingers pointing. At her? No, of course not. This was Bellagio, and there were thousands of reasons to crane necks and point.

Right before she reached the massive revolving front door, Georgia opened her purse. A huge rubberbanded wad of hundred-dollar bills fell out and hit the marble floor with a thud. She bent down quickly and grabbed the money.

"Don't panic," she whispered to herself. "Keep cool. Think! Think about every move you make. Talk yourself through this."

She stepped into a corner and tucked the cash deep into her black leather Fendi handbag, then unzipped a compartment in her wallet and removed the envelope that she had kept there since that afternoon weeks and weeks ago. She didn't need that photograph anymore. Knowing more about what had happened to her when she was six years old would not change anything. Now it was about the future, and she wanted to go there—and only could if she convinced herself that she was real and being Georgia was her only option. And being her was good. She just had to get away from here for a while. Get away from the fear.

"Now put the wallet back," she coached herself. Holding the envelope in her teeth, she zipped up the purse and placed the strap on her shoulder.

Georgia entered an empty section of the revolving door, and by the time she emerged into the Las Vegas night, the envelope and its contents had been ripped into tiny pieces, which she dropped into an ostentatious faux verdigris receptacle—a Bellagio trash can.

Four cabs were filled before it was her turn. As she slid into the back seat, her heart slammed against her lungs as she pictured the ragged pieces of envelope and photograph lying amid the other debris that filled the trash can. That's all those random shreds of paper were now: a bit more detritus to be hauled away and annihilated, burned to ash and dispersed into the soil or the oceans or the atmosphere. Gone, evaporated.

In a moment they were passing by the Bellagio fountains that spouted and swayed to Frank Sinatra's "Singing in the Rain."

"Hi, how ya doin'?" the cabby said perfunctorily. "Where to?"

His slick black hair was pulled away from his face, a mass of greasy curls, caught up in a rubber band, lumped at the back of his neck. He looked up into the rearview mirror as he spoke to her, and all Georgia could see were dark shadows beneath darker eyes. The picture on the dashboard, clipped to his taxi company ID, showed a gruff, thin-faced man in need of a shave—no humanity, no goodwill, but then, Georgia reminded herself, those photos were not supposed to be character studies.

When she didn't respond right away, he asked, "Are you okay, lady?" The tone of voice had much more to do with his liability insurance than anything altruistic or chivalrous. Georgia nodded, looking into the reflection of hard, black eyes.

She felt herself caroming off Earth again. As though she were merely another weightless shred of ash, less insignificant than any single molecule. She forced herself to focus on the cabby's stare, which was riveted on her. Those dark circles—were they proof of fast living and mean spirits or evidence of trouble and pain? This anonymous man who looked back at her from the rearview mirror, did he possess a soul? And if he did, by recognizing her as another soul, was she rescued from oblivion?

"Could you just start driving?" Georgia managed to get the words out, but to her they sounded like she was six years old.

The driver pulled out into traffic, repeating flatly, "Where to?"

"I'm not sure. Could we just drive?" Her little girl voice again.

"No way," the driver said, braking and pulling back to the curb. "That kind of crap always means trouble. Either tell me where to take you so I can call it in or get out and find some other place to get your shit together."

Mean spirits, she thought, and no soul. Georgia was cornered in some remote part of her mind again. Trapped.

"Lady," the cabby said with exaggerated patience, "what you wanna do?"

"I don't know," she whispered. The ache in her throat paralyzed her vocal cords. Georgia reached into her purse, fumbled a twenty-dollar bill out of her wallet, and thrust it toward the driver.

"You don't need to do that," he said gruffly.

As Georgia opened the car door, his cheeks puffed out with a loud sigh. "Stay put. I'll drive."

Georgia slumped back onto the seat, pulling the door closed as they merged into traffic again, heading south on the Strip. So maybe, she thought, he wasn't soulless. Neither one of them spoke for a few minutes.

She was exhausted. How easy it would be to drift away…as Marsha had done.

No! She forced herself to focus on the pulsing, brilliant scenery as they passed Tropicana Boulevard with its astonishing quartet of fantasy panoramas. On the northwest corner was the skyline of New York, New York, encircled by a rumbling, stomach-wrenching roller coaster that brought a King Kong perspective to the cityscape. Directly east, on the other side of the Strip, at the entrance to the radiant blue edifice of the MGM Hotel, a classic sculpted lion, massive and majestically gold, faced southwest as though he were contemplating the turrets and peaks, festooned with medieval flags and undulating spotlights heralding the magical kingdom of Excalibur. And across from the medieval pageantry, on the fourth corner, was the incongruous equatorial splendor of the high-rise Tropicana Hotel. Only in Las Vegas.

And that was where she was now…only in Las Vegas. Not in some abandoned wasteland of her soul. She was here, in Las Vegas, now. And this was where she had to stay. This was where she had to rescue herself. Here. Only in Las Vegas.

Inside the cab, silence was replaced by the crackle of the two-way radio as the dispatcher droned on to other drivers. She looked forward and found those eyes in the rearview mirror. She noticed how deep set they were. They moved back and forth, monitoring the traffic and her as well.

"So…" the driver said, as though that was enough to elicit a response from his passenger.

Georgia cleared her throat, trying to relieve some of the tension that had accumulated in her neck. She coughed. He waited for her to catch her breath. They had passed all of the hotels by now and were on an open part of Las Vegas Boulevard that paralleled the freeway. He pulled into the empty parking lot of a huge discount mall.

"So," he repeated. "You lost?"

Now there was a phrase with at least a triple entendre, Georgia thought.

Unable to find her way home? No.

Lost money? Yes.

Lost in time and space? That was not an option, not anymore.

"No," she answered out loud, "I'm not lost."

"So tell me where you're supposed to go."

"I'm not sure."

He pulled out on the street, heading back the way they had just come. A few minutes later, they were back at the intersection of the Strip and Tropicana Boulevard. The light was red.

"Look, lady," he said with a new softness in his voice, "you don't look like you're down and out, but I know that doesn't mean anything. Maybe you're in big trouble, but I'm not the guy to help you. All I can do is move you around the city, and if that's not what you need then you're probably wasting your time and your dime."

"Bellagio. I have to go back to Bellagio," she managed to say, still having trouble with her voice.

"Bellagio," he repeated. "You sure? You weren't too happy when I picked you up there. Maybe you should go somewhere else and try your luck."

Georgia swallowed hard, willing herself to seem in control. "I have to go back to Bellagio," she said with more strength in her voice than she expected.

"You sure you want to do that? Back to Bellagio?"

"Yes, I'm sure, and you can just let me off in front of Bally's. I'll walk the rest of the way."

This time he accepted the two twenties she handed him. She was back on the sidewalk and now she started to run. Clutching her purse close to her side, she concentrated on the feel of each footstep, reminding herself each time her foot hit the ground that she was attached to Planet Earth. She was as susceptible to the laws of gravity as every other person she passed. They all moved with an innate confidence, each knowing he or she existed and would not float away.

Georgia reached the next corner and there, first in line at the red light, was the same taxi she had just been in moments before. Did the driver see her and smile? She wasn't sure. But it didn't matter. She didn't need to be seen to be validated.

The light changed, and the traffic began to move. With an undeniable recognition of the truth, whether that cabby had seen her or not, whether she existed in the cabby's consciousness—or anyone else's, for that matter—Georgia Kassov Cates knew she was a full-fledged, card-carrying member of humanity, and she waited for the walk sign with the rest of the crowd. She too shared the collective consciousness of mankind. She was real, she was consequential, and she persevered outside the dimension of her own isolated fears. And now Georgia could get on with her own new life, the one that she had tiptoed into six months ago, only to be catapulted into a free fall. Now, finally, she had been able to pull the rip cord and land on the ground.

Chapter 2

December 2, 1997 – Six Months Earlier

She was on her way. Escaping. Squeezing up the rabbit hole just as Wonderland imploded.

At a little before eight on an overcast early December morning, Georgia pulled into the gas station. All she needed now was a full tank of high test and she'd be on her way. She was going AWOL! Off to Vegas!

The car phone rang. As she reached for it, she watched the attendant jog over from the service bay. He had recognized the white Jaguar with the vanity plates that read "4GCATES." He waved, and she gave him the thumbs-up sign for "fill it up" while she answered the phone.

"Good morning, Mrs. Cates, this is Elizabeth Peterson." It was Jeff's secretary, overly cheerful and obnoxiously condescending. "Hold for your husband, please."

One heartbeat later, she heard another voice, this one deep, steady, and threateningly familiar.

"When will you be back?" Jeff Cates never believed in preliminary amenities, even under the most pleasant of circumstances, and this was definitely not one of them.

Georgia's pulse sped up as she automatically went into defensive mode. "I told you when we discussed it yesterday," she said, annoyed that her words sounded so unsteady. "I'm not sure."

The pause that followed was perforated with tiny electrical sound impulses, like nettles in her ears. She tried to wait him out but gave up as usual. "Everything is ready for the holidays," she said, trying to control the little girl whine. Another silence. This one lasted less than five seconds. "And I've cleared my business calendar…and everything's been taken care of for the open house…and I'll decorate as soon as I get back."

She clamped her teeth together to stop the babbling, holding her breath for several more seconds of chilling silence, but that was all she could stand. *She was such a wimp!*

"Jeff, there is just no reason why I shouldn't go," she said, fighting the dread that was coiling up in her stomach, hating the way her tense vocal cords made the words sound so squeaky.

Jimmy, the gas jockey, was cleaning the windshield. She smiled at him through the window. At least this could look like a normal conversation. Maybe she could convince herself as well as Jimmy.

"Besides," she continued, "you're leaving for Seattle today. You won't even miss me." Missing her was never the issue, she knew that.

"You just went to Vegas." Jeff's voice transmitted an insidious combination of patience and fury.

"That was almost two months ago." *Damn! Squeaky and now whiny too.* She cleared her throat with a silent gulp.

"Be back by the end of the week," he said and hung up.

Georgia pushed the button to lower her window. "Hi, Jimmy!" Friendly, cheerful, composed. Boy, she was good! Not a hint in her voice of how fast her heart was beating or how many butterflies were dive-bombing at her stomach lining. "Would you check the tires today?"

"Sure, Mrs. Cates. That must mean you're off to Vegas again."

She nodded and looked away, pretending to search for her credit card. She couldn't handle any more chitchat right now.

As Jimmy walked off to process the sale, Georgia watched the early morning commuter traffic, a solid mass of vehicles flowing in both directions past the gas station. Everyone in Southern California was up and moving. Some were taking kids to school or going to the office, the supermarket or the dentist, or would spend the rest of the day pumping gas and cleaning windshields. But she, Georgia Cates, knew of Elysium or, as it was referred to here on Planet Earth, the Mirage Hotel and Casino, and had given herself permission to return there. Once again she had extricated herself from purgatory and would soon be indulged by the gods.

Gas tank filled, windshield cleaned, credit card receipt signed, she was off.

At the freeway entrance, she merged with traffic and slid an audio tape—a gift from her son, Mike—into the cassette player. A Mozart concerto was replaced by the Grateful Dead, and she raised the volume to just below pain.

> "…Since it costs a lot to win and even more to lose,
> You and me better spend some time wondering what to choose,
> Goes to show you don't ever know…"

The car phone rang again. Grateful Dead put on mute. Another call from Jeff's secretary. "Mr. Cates would like you to phone him this evening at his hotel in Seattle." Georgia made all the correct "uh-huhs" then reached over and flipped the phone power switch to "off."

Back to the Grateful Dead.

> "Goes to show you don't ever know…
> You watch each card you play and play it slow.
> Wait until that deal goes down…"

How had she missed this music when she was younger? The melodies, the rhythm, the poetic lyrics—had she even been conscious in the '70s and '80s? Not really.

Maneuvering in and out of the fast lane, Georgia felt the tension in her throat and chest ease as she passed those who drove so righteously at sixty-five or even seventy-five. She saw the sign, "Barstow and Las Vegas – Exit Only." Now she was really on her way.

The farther out she drove, the higher was the percentage of those headed for Vegas, and she joined in the fellowship. Gaining speed, she navigated toward the mountain straight ahead. As the road angled sharply to the left, she soared up the first ascent into the Cajon Pass, making the subtle corrections needed to spurt by all of those who were underpowered.

Less than an hour later, she passed the halfway point, a large heart-shaped sign. "Jenny Rose Cafe – Five Miles Ahead" and 131 miles from either edge of the spectrum that charted her life. On one end was the gated driveway of her Creste Verde home, where she consistently and efficiently performed life's duties; on the other, the immense, lavish portico of the Mirage Hotel and Casino, where it was the duty of others to serve her every whim.

The next milestone was the sign for Zzyyxx Road. Did the road named by the end of the alphabet lead to the end of the earth? She'd never know. Car and soul were committed toward their predetermined destination, resolutely, inexorably.

The road between Barstow and Baker was straight and monotonous; another audiotape reduced the tedium, and Georgia sang along.

> "Masquerade, hide your face so the world will never find you.
> Masquerade, every face a different shade.
> Masquerade, look around, there's another mask behind you…"

She passed through Baker at her cruising speed of eighty, happy to have several compatible drivers in her caravan. Now another mountain range appeared. Time to insert the tape she always saved for this final stretch, the climax of her journey.

George Michael crooned, "…you must have been kissing a fool."

She felt the first twinges. Charging down the slope of the second mountain range, she saw a group of shimmering dots appear and then meld into the neon signs for "Whiskey Pete's" and "Prima Donna."

Nevada!

She and her entourage, those now doing eighty-five-plus, made the final dash for Vegas. The image of the lady in the luxury car belied the atmosphere inside—the music and the pleasure were for her alone. Her spasms intensified with the beat of George.

"I want your sex!"

Her breath was shallow as she struggled to keep the upper portion of her body still while contracting thigh muscles to sustain the feeling. Only an innate survival instinct held in check the impulse to close her eyes. She kept the car on the road as a potent force drew her north.

Between a set of low rolling hills, the Vegas skyline erupted in full size like the inside of a giant pop-up greeting card. Mandalay Bay was the closest golden edifice, but in the distance—beyond the Luxor pyramid, Excalibur's turrets, the New York, New York skyline, the grandeur of the yet-to-open Bellagio and the Romanesque towers of Caesar's Palace—was the Mirage. Somehow, it seemed more sumptuous than all the others, as though it had been molded out of solid gold while the others were merely veneered with gilt.

"I'm here," she whispered. "I'm back."

Merging into local traffic, she exited at Flamingo Road, glad for the long red light at Las Vegas Boulevard. She breathed deeply, flexed and relaxed her leg muscles, and turned off the tape.

Georgia smiled patiently as the bellman gave her the speech about how she would not see him again because someone else would deliver her luggage to her room. He got his five dollars. Carrying her purse and a small tote bag, she followed a group of Japanese tourists, nodding her thanks to the gentleman who held the door open. The arsenal of photographic equipment hanging around his neck twisted and jangled as he bowed.

She walked into the lobby with confidence and style. The façade was in place, and she had mastered the act. She was a player, a VIP. All those who noticed her would assume that this was the most elegant, sophisticated, self-assured, admired and adored woman who had ever walked on these marble floors.

Check-in took only moments because she stepped up to the "invited guests" window. While her credit card was processed, she watched several species of miniature predators glide by in the enormous seawater shark tank that loomed over the front desk.

"How have you been, guys…miss me?" said Georgia. The clerk smiled tentatively, not sure the greeting was for him or the fish.

Room key in hand, she turned back toward the lobby, where there were always hundreds of people rushing by or gawking at the scenery or searching for a lost companion. The inhabitants might vary from minute to minute, but to Georgia, they were always the same beings whose single role in life was to populate the lobby of the Mirage Hotel and Casino.

She followed a narrow path along the edge of the carpet, avoiding the route through the tropical rain forest, where first-timers shuffled along, nudging their companions and pointing to the waterfall whose eternal rush was a veil of white noise, subtly muting the ordinary clang and cacophony of the casino. She could smell and taste the spicy air, a combination of liquor and cigarette smoke mixed with the dampness from the rain forest and the universal aroma of thousands of people converging.

Jackpot bells on fertile slot machines were a familiar and intimate welcoming chime. She strode by dozens of gaming tables: roulette, craps, blackjack and pai gow. She charted an efficient course, sometimes darting between rows of slots but always aiming for the express elevators. Inserting her room key activated the button for the twenty-fifth floor; seconds later, stepping out before the doors were completely open, she knew instinctively in which direction to turn.

Georgia unlocked the door and called out softly to the empty room, "Hi, honey, I'm home!" Pulling back the drapes, she kicked off her shoes, yanked off her silk trouser socks, and sank her bare toes into the plush carpet. The view was to the south, past the dazzling intersection of Las Vegas Boulevard and Flamingo Road. Two long blocks east, she spotted the dimly lighted sign: "Best Value Motel." Georgia and Jeff had stayed there in 1979, when she was six months pregnant with Sonnie. She'd spent one whole afternoon trudging through drugstores and gift shops, searching for rubber beach thongs to wear in the slimy shower stall. A year later, the Cates had returned to Vegas and checked into a motel unit attached to the Dunes. They walked through the employees' parking lot and passed by the kitchen to get to the casino, but the tile in the shower had been clean.

By the early '80s, the "Special Spectacular Weekend Holiday" coupons were no longer necessary; they could afford slightly better accommodations. In 1985, Jeff established a line of credit at Caesar's Palace and the Golden Nugget. Their reservations were handled by casino hosts. Now, at the end of 1997, Georgia was a VIP at one of the finest hotels in Las Vegas.

A bellman knocked on the door. Another five-dollar bill elicited thanks from this liveried body builder who hauled suitcases to pay the rent.

Usually when she traveled, she fit everything into one carry-on suitcase. But coming to Vegas was different. She'd perfected her packing technique many trips ago, and although it meant checking luggage, taking enough clothes for changes in mood—and her moods did vary—was important. Sometimes a cashmere sweater and well-tailored jeans were right; she also liked soft linens and knits. These were her Vegas clothes. The jeans were a little tighter than what was acceptable in Creste Verde; in fact, jeans of any style were rarely acceptable in Creste Verde. The Vegas knits tended to be a bit more revealing, just a dash more provocative, and she'd chosen corals and plums instead of her usual breakfast colors: the classic tonal creams, wheats and oatmeals.

She was forty-two years old and her waist was less than an inch larger than it had been at twenty-two. She could thank her years of aerobics classes and tennis as well as a few good genes for that. Her bust line was quite a bit fuller after two kids, but the weight lifting that had accompanied all the workouts had paid off in muscle tone.

She never wore glitz. Rhinestones and sequins were the neon signs of the tourist, as was the jacket that proclaimed "Lady Luck!" in red, white and blue stones and gold studs.

Oh, Shirl, that will be just perfect for Vegas!
Never.

Each time she arrived, Georgia's system of check-in, unpacking and dressing—the entire process—would ultimately land her in a seat at the poker table. The very sameness of the drill intensified the strong sense that Georgia Cates was supposed to be here. How else could she explain the delight, the contentment, the profound rightness that she felt every time she arrived? And the feeling never dissipated while she was there. She was home again, where she belonged, where she was happiest, where she was in control.

In less than an hour, Georgia was ready to leave her room. She should probably put in a call to Jeff in Seattle, but she couldn't remember the name of his hotel. Anyway, he knew where she was. She reached for her purse, making sure that her room key was tucked in, and returned to the elevators, inspecting herself in the floor-to-ceiling mirror. The tangerine cable knit sweater over white, slim-fitting serge slacks was perfect for her mood—vibrant and contrasting. She ran her fingers through her hair, pulling strands of ash and golden highlights out from the rich brown, making it fuller, more spiky, as if she'd been out in the wind—not exactly elegant, but a bit more uninhibited than her usual look, and maybe a little more interesting.

But it wasn't just her appearance that pleased her. What was this odd little giggle that seemed to want to escape from her? Was it because she was defying Jeff by not calling? *How adolescent!*

Chapter 3

Georgia swept through the casino, deftly sidestepping those who had nothing better to do than stroll along. "Out of my way, honey," she murmured to herself, maneuvering past a large woman with a Siegfried and Roy shopping bag.

The noises of the casino retreated to an inconsequential hum as she made her way through the "railbirds," that curious flock of onlookers, either too broke or too intimidated to venture inside, who stood at the edge of the poker area, craning to see the action.

She tuned in to the unique sounds of the card room. No slot machine bells tolled in here. The dominant theme was provided by three competing microphones, paging various players.

"Ed M., five-ten stud!" Followed by, "Andy for ten-twenty hold 'em!" And then, "Montana Jones, you have a phone call on line four! Pauline, one-to-five stud!" Once again, "Ed M., five-ten stud! Ed M.! Final call for Ed M." Three seconds later: "Barney for five-ten stud!"

The chorus was provided by the dealers as they called for chips and new cards or announced that a seat had been vacated.

"I need a fill on fourteen!" or "Setup on twenty-two!" or "Seat on eleven!" Their random keys and pitches provided an aggressive contrast to the monotone loudspeakers. And beneath the entire oratorio, like thousands of thriving crickets, was the constant trill of the chips—the organic pulse of the poker room.

Murray Janson was the day shift brush for the low-limit games. The maître d' of the poker room, the "brush" in poker parlance, keeps track of open seats, escorts the player to the game, and literally brushes up cigarette ashes from the felt-covered tables. Short and stout, Murray balanced on tiptoes as he spoke to a tall woman with long, lush blond hair. When he spotted Georgia, he called out, "It's the lady from LA!"

"Hi, honey," Georgia repeated her private joke. "I'm home."

"Georgia," Murray said, "have you met Melanie? Melanie, this is Georgia Cates. Melanie came in for the poker lessons this morning; now she's ready to play." Murray addressed one woman then the other, as though he were playing tennis with himself, lobbing the ball high into the air then running around the net to return the shot. "Melanie's gonna start at twenty-forty," Murray said, winking at Georgia.

"Hi," Georgia said, somewhat startled as she made eye contact with the beautiful woman who stood next to the counter. A black spandex jumpsuit fit her perfectly proportioned body all too well. Dozens of gold bangles chiming from her wrists glimmered along with large gold disk earrings. What was it about this woman? She was probably in her early forties. Her outfit and accessories were far from elegant, certainly not in any sense classic, hardly even tasteful, and yet the entire effect was knockout.

She had been gazing at Melanie for longer than was comfortable for either one of them. "Well, good luck to you," Georgia said.

Melanie nodded with a smile and then walked away.

Georgia turned her attention back to the brush.

"What's new, Murray?"

"Not a hell of a lot. Mostly the same old stuff. Same bosses, same locals, same tourists. Then you show up again and bring some real class to this place."

Georgia grinned. "You know no one makes me feel as special in here as you do, Murray, and I could stand here and let you elaborate for hours, but the local piranhas will be so disappointed if I don't join one of their games. They're probably waiting for me before they start their Christmas shopping."

"The word is that you can hold your own with those guys. Maybe it's time to step up in limits."

"Not on your life," she said, laughing. "Whoever told you that isn't paying much attention. I get lucky sometimes, but most of them can play me like a fiddle."

The truth was, she thought, her confidence in the game was growing all the time. Maybe Murray was right; maybe it *was* time for her to move up to another betting level. *Well, maybe sometime soon, anyway…maybe.*

Murray picked up the loudspeaker to announce open seats in the three-six hold 'em game. Georgia saw Melanie sitting at a table on the other side of the room but could not decipher the look on her face. Was that a slight smile? For some reason, this piqued Georgia's curiosity. Was Melanie really timid, or was that look more evasive than shy? She kept the woman in her peripheral vision as she made her way toward the brush with the middle-limit stud lists.

After adding her own name to the appropriate waiting lists, Georgia found an empty table and sat down. It wouldn't be a long wait. There were several live games in her range of stud limits, and she was third on the ten-twenty list, second on the fifteen-thirty.

Georgia closed her eyes a moment. Meandering through the poker room babble were hundreds of voices. As snatches of conversations wafted by, Georgia tuned in. When she looked again, two men stood nearby, one looming almost a foot over the other. Both were wearing flak jackets over drab, worn-out tee shirts; both needed a shave and haircut. They were exchanging "bad beat" stories.

"…so I pop him back and then he pops me again. Now I have to figure that he puts me on my two big pair. He paired his door card, so I figure he's tripped. I fill, and guess what the son of a bitch catches on the goddamn river? Fuck'n quads! Four fuck'n fours!"

"Tough beat," the big guy said, shaking his head. "Last week I get quads and get cracked by a shitty six-high straight flush. Cost me my engine overhaul, and my car is gonna croak out any minute." Both men lit cigarettes and, empathizing with each other's misfortunes, strolled out of the poker room.

A man with a gray knit hat covering his head so that his ears and face glowed pink beneath it sat down across from Georgia. He called to a passing waitress to bring him a cup of hot water with lemon. His thermal-knit turtleneck sweater was tucked into warm-up pants, which disappeared into thick wool socks and low-cut rubber rain shoes. All of the clothing was gray, except the rain shoes, which were neon orange, like the ones worn by road laborers. He had days and days of stubble on his face. That kind of beard always made Georgia wonder what had been the occasion sometime in the previous week that was important enough in the man's life to have called for a shave.

"Good afternoon," he said in Georgia's direction.

"Hello, Mr. Kruikshank," she said, smiling. She'd played with him many times, and he often pushed past eccentric and was well on his way to weird. She picked up the latest edition of *Card Player* magazine and began to read an article. But as minutes passed, Georgia couldn't ignore the fact that Mr. Kruikshank was staring at her.

Suddenly he spoke as though they were already in the middle of a conversation. "Yes, yes, precisely," he said, nodding. "In this room exists the entire galaxy." Now his eyes seemed focused somewhere between Jupiter and Mercury.

Georgia forced another smile. She wanted to stand up and walk away but was trapped by her good manners. She dug into her purse in search of nothing. Then another stud player pulled out a chair at the table. Georgia had met Milt Braverman at the ten-twenty table many trips ago. He had broad shoulders and a very flat stomach for a man probably in his late forties, about six-two, with light-brown, karakul-curly hair trimmed close to his head. His face was a series of angles formed by a combination of a strong jawline, high cheekbones and a patrician nose. Today he had on a camel hair jacket over an open-collared blue dress shirt.

Great look, she thought.

It was okay to be attracted to him, Georgia had reminded herself a couple of times. Just attracted, nothing more. He was very generous about giving her valuable playing tips. Not everyone did that. He told her that he was a private investigator, working for insurance companies, and played stud to augment his income. Several times, after all-night games, they'd eaten breakfast together in the coffee shop, always conducting a thorough postmortem on the latest poker session.

"Hi, Milt," she greeted him enthusiastically as he sat down. She was being rescued from the uncomfortable clutches of the bizarre Mr. Kruikshank.

"What's up, Mr. Kruikshank?" Milt asked as he winked at Georgia.

Without acknowledging the salutation, Mr. Kruikshank continued to extol on his theory. "Each table in here is an entity, and in these worlds, catastrophes and epiphanies occur with equal consequence. Red, green and black tides of chips ebb to and fro. Some inhabitants on these planets of cushioned felt barely survive the droughts, while others prosper from the floods, but each in his own time moves on."

Georgia pursed her lips to control a giggle. Glancing across at Milt, she quickly looked away as he winked at her again.

Mr. Kruikshank sat up straighter in his chair. "And the cocktail waitresses," he proclaimed, "move about the planets, delivering the fuel of existence, the lifeblood of creation. These gorgeous androids make no judgments. They have no concern for the height of the stacks in front of patrons as they place a glass or cup on the requisite cocktail napkin, hand held out an extra moment to receive a tip. Their long legs propel them while their strong arms bear trays of beverages, a few nurturing, others merely hydrating, and some numbing and sedating."

Georgia could see from the corner of her eye that Milt was grinning at her, daring her to look at him and keep from cracking up.

"Ah, yes, the floor men," Mr. Kruikshank went on. "The dispute resolvers, the galaxy police. They meander about the space between tables, waiting to become indispensable. Only they have the power to adjudicate a disputation, and only they have the authority to call forth the green-jacketed, behemoth security guards who escort the uncooperative to the ends of known existence, setting them adrift in the outer spheres of the casino."

Georgia cautiously looked at Milt, who was surreptitiously tapping his temple. Quickly she went back to searching the depths of her purse.

Mr. Kruikshank continued to communicate from orbit. "I would aspire to be a comet…the kind who streaks in with three stacks of redbirds, either loses them all in twenty minutes or wins a couple of big pots, grabs a chip rack, fills it, and vanishes in the direction of the cashier's cage. I always wanted to be a comet," he said with a deep sigh, "but I'm more like a moon…just hanging around."

Squeezing lemon into his water, Mr. Kruikshank gazed into the cup, as though seeking some mystical information in the liquid. Suddenly he looked up toward the ceiling, and his voice sounded genuinely anxious. "Primordial gases spew forth from the air conditioning ducts," he announced with great alarm. He covered his ears with his hands. "And the intercom system reverberates with pulsars and quasars. Their waves will mutate the neuro-processors in our brains and our heads will implode, and every one of us will become a supernova, a black hole for eternity!"

Over the loudspeaker, Georgia's name resounded among the pulsars and quasars. Instantly she was up, amazed as Mr. Kruikshank smiled sweetly and acknowledged her departure, never removing his hands from his ears. "Be very cautious, dear Georgia," he said pleasantly. "You too are susceptible to the outer forces of the universe."

Mildly surprised that Mr. Kruikshank had used her given name, and avoiding even a marginal glance at Milt, she uttered a lame, "Sure."

Georgia slipped into the two seat at one end of the ten-twenty table next to a plump, gray-haired woman with pretty, soft brown eyes. "Georgia! My favorite tourist!" She reached out and patted Georgia's arm.

"Hi, Marsha. How are you?"

"Fine, fine," Marsha said absently. Cards had been dealt, and Marsha's focus was back on the game. Amy, the chip runner—who had to be twenty-one to work in the poker room but looked like she was not yet sixteen—took Georgia's three hundred dollars to the cashier and returned with red chips. Georgia pulled a five-dollar "redbird" off the nearest stack, asked the dealer for change, and handed a blue one-dollar chip to Amy.

"Thanks," Amy said. "Good luck."

A tall, gorgeous cocktail waitress appeared. Her name tag said "Mindy, Davenport, Iowa." "Hi, Miss Georgia," she said, grinning. "Nice to have you back in town. A Perrier as usual?"

"Yes, please," said Georgia.

Mindy, Amy, Marsha and Milt, even Mr. Kruikshank, faded from Georgia's thoughts as the sensation of becoming a spectator of one's own experience took over. The video recorder in her mind began filming and playing back this scene simultaneously. She indicated to the dealer that she was not yet ready for a hand.

As the game proceeded without her, Georgia concentrated on squeezing the reality of the moment directly into her soul. Every time Georgia sat down at a poker table, she could unwrap the package of her own existence. And she had to remind herself that life had to be more than the mere exercise of cautiously mining one's own memories, both short term and long term, and she had to be more than a mere tally of what she remembered, but still, her recollections were her only measuring tape. She drifted away from the moment again as her mind culled through her ten years of playing casino poker.

Chapter 4

December, 1987

It had been another Christmas season, ten years ago, when Georgia had first become a railbird. She and Jeff were in Vegas for three days, and he was winning. She had sat behind him the first evening as he rolled over a ten-twenty hold 'em game. The next day, three thousand dollars ahead, he had gotten hot at craps and tripled that. All of this made him very magnanimous.

"Go shopping," he had decreed as he headed for a hundred-dollar blackjack table.

Instead of browsing the hotel boutiques, Georgia spent her time leaning on the rail that surrounded the poker room. She studied the process of how the cards were dealt and how the betting proceeded. She was very intimidated by what she saw, but it also excited her in a way nothing ever had. Why? She wasn't sure.

The Golden Nugget card room offered several different poker games, including Texas hold 'em and Omaha, but neither of them appealed to her. In those games, bets were made with a minimum amount of information. It was like gambling out in the pit where the fast-action games were played. It was Jeff's kind of game.

Georgia couldn't predict or influence the roll of the dice across the craps table, the turn of the wheel of fortune, the bouncing lead ball on the roulette wheel, certainly not the capricious combinations of the slot machines, or what card the blackjack dealer would turn up, or, for that matter, what the hold 'em or Omaha dealer would flop. The action player—which Georgia knew she was not—puts money into the slot or on the table then crosses fingers. The hope is always that some perfectly timed miracle, a propitious roll of the dice, or turn of the wheel, or flop of the cards, will beat the odds. Control is sacrificed for excitement, and action is the goal. This *betting on the come* was not for her.

Seven stud seemed to be her kind of game. She watched the hands develop, saw the "up" cards, paid attention to the betting, and, by process of elimination, calculated how one hand compared to the others. Part of the challenge was to be able to read the other players, to add to the information base, to predict how each of them would play their cards. Poker: the only game in Vegas with a human factor and the chance to manipulate other players. When to call, raise, reraise, or bail out and fold—there were choices, and choices meant control.

Georgia had read several books on playing casino poker, memorizing the glossaries. Now she knew that the "door card" was the third card dealt, and it was faceup like the next three cards, and that the "river card" was the seventh card dealt, and it was facedown.

She was a better-than-average bridge player and assumed that her card sense increased her understanding of the statistical probabilities of how poker hands developed. Now she focused on the rhythm of the betting and the gestures that were the silent signals for words like "check" and "raise."

Impressed by the experienced cardplayers who riffled their chips, she took twenty one-dollar chips back to her room to practice. After Jeff was asleep, she had covered the round glass table with a towel to absorb the noise. Using only one hand, she stacked the chips, split the stack in two, and shuffled the two stacks back together. After an hour, it got easier. After two hours, it became second nature.

It was the last full day of their trip. Jeff's rush continued, and he was as mellow as he could ever be, happy to float between the pit and the sports book, reaping the returns of his amazing lucky streak. He wouldn't go into the poker room anymore; there was much more action for the Master of the Gaming Universe in the other parts of the casino. Georgia was free to do as she chose.

She was back at the poker room rail again. She had read, she had watched, she had listened, and she could riffle the chips. Now it was time to play. She walked up to the counter, where a gentleman in coat and tie, the brush, kept a list of games in progress.

She waited while the brush attended to an irate customer. It seemed that the old guy had requested a table change and that someone else had moved before him. The brush checked his clipboard and then spoke into his microphone.

"Hey, Benny, your new player in the six seat is supposed to be Clyde. He's on his way over."

From across the room, Benny looked up from dealing and nodded acknowledgment. Clyde, his seventy-plus years etched into a dried mushroom of a face, made his way to table two, mumbling to himself. The brush turned to Georgia, eyebrows raised expectantly. Suddenly the culprit who had usurped the six seat at table two shouldered Georgia aside. Pounding his fist on the counter, he raged through clenched teeth, "What the hell is going on? You told me I had the next transfer! Now I lost my seat!"

The brush, serene and dignified, turned to Georgia. "This gentleman apologizes for his rude behavior, ma'am. Doesn't he, Jake?"

Jake got the message. Without turning toward her, he muttered a tepid, "Sorry."

"Now, young lady," said the brush, "what can we do for you?"

Georgia chose to ignore both the lackluster apology of the player as well as the patronizing tone of the brush. "I'd like to play some one-to-five stud."

"Of course, my dear. Follow me, please."

The brush walked briskly to a nearby table, pulling out a chair for Georgia. Then he returned to the counter, followed by Jake, who was obviously determined to be the next order of business.

Georgia's heart was pounding, and she could feel her pulse in her forehead. She reached into her purse, pulled out a one-hundred-dollar bill, placed it on the table in front of her, and waited while the dealer finished the hand that was in progress.

Then "Loretta" from "Fresno, California," or so it said on her dealer's name tag, counted out forty blue one-dollar chips and twelve red five-dollar chips. She pushed them toward Georgia and tucked the hundred-dollar bill in her tray. As Georgia pulled the stacks toward her, they fell over and she smiled, hands trembling. The chips felt heavy, much more substantial than the ones she had used to practice with in her room, although they were identical.

"This is the first time I've played poker in a casino," she announced.

She took a quick inventory of the responses. Three players ignored her, two smiled thinly, and a Gabby Hayes look-alike drawled, "Well, come on in, honey, the water's fine!"

A heavyset lady at the other end of the table said a sarcastic, "Oh, swell."

"Welcome to the game," said Loretta. "Do you know the betting structure, or would you like me to explain it to you?"

"I think I know how it goes," Georgia said, "but I can ask questions between hands, right?"

"You can ask all the questions you want." Loretta was Poker Dealer Barbie. Long, false eyelashes swooped over soft blue doll's eyes. Her tiny face was barely visible under a volume of shoulder-length platinum hair, teased to an astounding height. She was friendly, patient, efficient and, as far as Georgia was concerned, the kindest dealer in Las Vegas.

Loretta dealt two cards down to each player. Georgia bent over the table, cupping her hands to shield the cards and lifting the corners as little as possible. She saw two jacks, and when she looked at the table, a third jack slid in front of her. She was rolled up! Her forehead throbbed, her dry throat got drier, and her fingers shook. No way could she handle this. She threw all three cards facedown into the center of the table.

You folded three jacks! What the hell are you doing?

Georgia took in deep, deliberate breaths, willing her pulse to slow. She shifted in her chair, sat up straight, and placed her hands firmly on the table. *One more hand. I'll try one more hand. Maybe I won't get good cards and I can fold again.* Suddenly three more cards were in front of her. Her hole cards were the ace of clubs and the king of clubs. Her up card was the queen of clubs. She realized, with a chilling fear, that she had to stay in this, the second hand she had ever been dealt. She called the dollar bet, and then, with a growing sense of dread, called the two-dollar raise. Five players received a second up card. Hers was the jack of diamonds.

Keep a poker face, she told herself over and over. She held her breath and kept her eyes down. She was sure the ace and king of clubs were flashing in them like the jackpot row lit up on a video poker machine. The young man to her right bet the maximum five dollars. She had to call. *Why did she think she'd enjoy playing this game? This was agony!*

Four players were left to receive the third up card. Georgia's was the nine of diamonds, now positioned next to the queen of clubs and the jack of diamonds. Everyone checked. Salvation! She was going to get a free card. Her fourth card up was the ten of clubs. She had a straight to the ace.

Loretta Doll announced that Georgia could have a possible straight. Georgia fought hard and barely won stifling the giggle that tried to escape. Now she prayed that everyone would check, allowing her to pull in her very first pot, totaling about fifty dollars. Instead, the stout lady in the eight seat shifted her mother-of-pearl cigarette holder from one side of her large, scarlet mouth to the other and reached for a red five-dollar chip. It made a tiny thud as it fell near the tremendous pile already accumulated in front of the dealer.

How could this woman with her jack, ten and nine of hearts and three of diamonds have the audacity to bet into Georgia's obvious straight? And then the kid with the Metallica tee shirt and portable tape deck, who had been undulating to the mysterious music that was being transmitted via headphones directly into his psyche, threw in two red chips.

Calm down and think! Georgia's mind ground out the possibilities. *The heavy metal fan raised. The best he can have is a king-high straight. I can beat him. But what about "Chunky Woman" and the man on the other side of me, with his pair of tens, who has yet to act? But if I* get another club, I'll have an ace-high flush, and I know Chunky Woman could only have a king-high flush because the guy with the pair of tens is also showing the ace of hearts. But maybe he has two pair. But I have a ten and an ace, so he probably doesn't, and even if he does, he's not going to get a full house.

The other players began to shift about in their chairs or drum their fingers on the leather rim of the table. Georgia knew that her beginner's dispensation had ended. She threw in ten dollars; the pair of tens folded. Chunky Woman raised another five dollars.

For God's sake! Georgia wailed in her mind. *Have you no mercy?*

"See y'all at the river," Metallica said as he flipped his red chip in a high arc. It bounced once on the table and then landed in the pot. Loretta pulled it out and placed it between the kid and the gargantuan pile of chips, waiting for Georgia to add her own chip, reraise or fold her cards. Georgia pushed the chip out in front of her. She had to call; she'd come too far to give in now.

The last card slid across the table at Georgia, and she caught it with trembling fingers. *What good is a poker face*, she complained to herself, *if your hands are broadcasting in Morse code?*

Chunky Woman didn't even look at her seventh card, the river card. She shoved a red chip toward the dealer. Metallica spent some time shuffling his three down cards and then slowly fanned them, an inch in front of his nose. He called the five-dollar bet.

Oh shit, thought Georgia, *I have to figure out what's going on. They know I have a straight, but they don't know how high. Chunky Woman probably has her flush. The kid is spitting into the wind; his last card couldn't have helped him much or he would have raised.*

Turning back the corner of her river card, she first saw that it was black then the three little petals of the club suit emerged. She had her ace-high flush. It took a couple of tries for Georgia to grasp the two red chips. She knew she had to toss them out simultaneously or say she was going to raise. If she silently threw one chip after the other, it would be considered a "string bet," and the raise wouldn't be allowed. And the chances of her vocal cords producing anything more than a croak were nil.

Chunky Woman's eyebrows, applied with black Magic Marker, came together in a frown. She bit down hard on her cigarette holder then looked at her river card. Whatever she found there added no joy to her life. She threw in a red chip with a disgusted grunt. Metallica had come to play, so his red chip followed.

"Okay, let's see 'em," Loretta said, and all the hole cards in the three remaining hands were flipped faceup. Georgia's ace-high club flush beat Chunky Woman's jack-high heart flush. Metallica's two pair came in an anemic third. Loretta pushed an eighty-dollar pot toward Georgia. Georgia pushed three blue chips back to Loretta.

Slow, deep breaths, she told herself again. *In through the mouth, out through the nose. How embarrassing if I fainted!*

"Thanks, sweetie," said the dealer, depositing the tip in her shirt pocket. "See how easy it is?"

"Nice hand," mumbled Chunky Woman. "Caught the club on the river, didn't you?"

"Yep, but what a draw she had," said Gaby Hayes, who had folded his first three cards way back at the beginning of the hand. "Nice playin', honey."

Two more cards had already slid toward Georgia before she could stack up all of her winnings. She stopped organizing and paid attention to the new cards. The queen of spades and six and two of hearts were tossed back to the dealer without a moment's hesitation. Now Georgia had some time to process that last hand. An exquisite sensation began to build. She had attained this incredible thrill because she had joined the game. The exhilaration was more delicious because all of the sensation was masked by her poker face. It was hers alone and more intense because she sat at a table with eight other people. Fear and trepidation were replaced by a voracious need to play more hands. She had found a way to pleasure herself in public!

That had been almost ten years ago. She'd learned a lot about poker since then, and every time she threw chips into the center of the table, she was reaffirming her independence. One of the cardinal rules of casino poker is that there can be no discussion or coaching while betting is progressing. "One player to a hand" is the adage, and this had always appealed to Georgia. No one could tell her what to do. The chips in front of her were the symbol of her autonomy, and only she could decide how to play them.

Every time a pot built up and Georgia's cards held up, the undulating sense of pleasure would take another delectable journey through her mind and body. It was very addictive, and she had known from the first time that her need to discipline these cravings was great. Eventually she'd considered playing at escalating stakes, but assured herself that going to the fifteen-thirty or twenty-forty tables was for the challenge of competing against better players. The size of the pot was not important.

**

"Are you gonna join us any time soon?" asked "Lance" from "Pittsburgh, Pennsylvania." He was one of her favorite dealers, and she had told him so many times. It wasn't just because he was movie star handsome or even that she had won some very large pots when he dealt. He could snap those cards out faster and more skillfully than anyone else in the room, and he never rose to the bait when disgruntled players blamed their bad luck and/or poor playing on him.

"I don't grow 'em; I just deliver 'em" or "I'm only the mailman." And he ignored all dirty looks, even the occasional menacing evil eye. But he always had a friendly wink for Georgia. In fact, they had shared a few poker sessions when he was off duty. Lance was one of the dealers who spent a large part of his life in the poker room. He played stud the same way he raced his Kawasaki: tearing full speed ahead, offsetting the probability of disaster with an abounding self-confidence.

So now Georgia switched off her mental video recorder and pushed her ante out in front of her. She peeked at the cards that she had been dealt, turning them up just enough to see the corners. A quick and practiced glance around the table to make note of all the other up cards, and the mental process of deciding whether to call, raise or fold became her sole focus. The rhythm of the game took hold of her, and she was caught up in the enchantment of each developing hand.

Finally, as Georgia folded a hand and lifted her arms to stretch, she touched something and turned to see.

"Stephanie! How long have you been standing there?" Georgia said, smiling but a bit startled.

"Long enough to watch a pro in action. You know, you can't be called a tourist anymore. You play like a local."

Georgia grinned. "Well, maybe a commuter."

"Come to my office. I've got some paper work for you to sign."

Georgia knew that the "paper work" would be a batch of comps, which were tickets for free meals in the hotel eateries. She had first met Stephanie soon after the Mirage opened, when Jeff had established an impressive line of credit in the casino. It became apparent, to those whose job was to pay attention to such things, that Georgia spent most of her time in the poker room while her husband often took breaks from his high-limit hold 'em and Omaha games to indulge in the activities out in the pit, where the casino would inevitably make a profit. Mr. and Mrs. Cates were added to the VIP list and thus fell into the domain of Stephanie Bellamy, assistant to the poker room manager, Edward Patrone. Her primary responsibility was the care and feeding of potentially lucrative hotel guests, specifically the ones who frequented the poker room.

Georgia referred to Stephanie's business card when she called to make reservations. No long waits on hold for the "next available representative" to tell her that the Mirage was booked full for every weekend through the second decade of the twenty-first century. Stephanie, an early-'90s Vassar graduate, as efficient and no nonsense as her well-cut black jacket and slacks, always had rooms available at casino rates and could also make dinner and show reservations.

Occasionally Stephanie would receive a clever greeting card from Georgia, including the fifty dollars that many of the poker room patrons tipped for the extra attention. But Georgia always added some personal touch, like a decorated tin of hard candy.

In the last couple of years, Georgia came to Vegas much more often than Jeff did, and she had established herself as a poker room regular. The VIP treatment continued, and sometimes the two women took a break together for coffee. Their discussions usually centered on the poker room and its colorful inhabitants, like "Ratso Rizzo." His real name was Davey Stein, and he held the record for number of times he got paged. He was a frenetic little man, about five-four, with thinning hair, black and greasy. He popped in and out of poker games, always attending to some piece of business or dashing to answer a page. He seemed to know everybody and was always calling across the room in squeaky Brooklynese. Georgia had tagged him with the name of the Dustin Hoffman character from the movie *Midnight Cowboy*. She remembered when it had won the Academy Award. When Stephanie saw the movie on video, she had called Georgia in Creste Verde to tell her how right on she'd been. Stephanie had said that she had never known anyone as old as Georgia whom she could talk to so easily.

Swell, Georgia had thought. As old as what: Stephanie's mother? Methuselah?

Today, when the two women entered the poker room office, Edward Patrone, impeccable in an expensive dark gray suit, leaned on the edge of the desk, talking on the phone while studying his manicured fingernails.

"Of course, Mr. Cranston. Anything you need, you just let me know." Patrone looked up, but his expression remained blank. "You bet, Mr. Cranston." He reached for a piece of paper and wrote quickly. "It'll be taken care of. You have my word as poker room manager. We look forward to…" He put the receiver back on the cradle.

Stephanie mimicked a western drawl. "Brady Cranston's comin' to town. Lock up the money and hide the women 'n' chilern."

No smile from Patrone as he handed her the note. "He wants show reservations. Make sure everything is done right." Then, with a curt nod to Georgia, he left.

Not exactly Mr. Warmth, Georgia thought. Patrone had seemed distracted when Stephanie had first introduced them, and Georgia always had the feeling that he never placed her, even though she had reintroduced herself a couple of times.

"Who's Brady Cranston?" asked Georgia.

"A real pain in my derriere. He won the World Series of Poker a couple of years ago. Not that the million-dollar prize was more than chump change to him. Anyway, he's at the top of the high-limit poker heap and gets the royal treatment because, when he plays here, his games get major press, not to mention that he always brings several juicy high rollers along with him. The Mirage will do anything to keep them all happy and free of any distractions. They're here to play poker, but they wander out to the pit once in a while, and that's what this place is all about."

"So what kinds of things are you expected to do for Mr. Cranston?"

Stephanie leaned back in her chair. "The real stuff?" She didn't wait for a reply. "Okay, the real stuff. Sometimes this glamorous, high-paying, fulfilling and exciting occupation of mine includes a few chores not specifically mentioned in the job description. I can handle most of it without taking it personally, like when a high roller tells Edward that his kids need to be kept busy. I'm the one who calls their room to find out when they want to go to the water park, or Grand Slam Canyon, or the movies. I find the baby-sitter to keep an eye on them at the pool, or arrange for a driver to wait for the darlings while they hang out at the mall. Another time I might have to go to the mall myself to look for some warm-up suits for a big-time player who doesn't like what he saw in the hotel boutiques. I shop, I bring the stuff back to the poker room, and I return what he doesn't want. So much for professional job skills."

Stephanie reached for a small acrylic card file. "This is where I keep all the stuff about who wants what when, how much and what time." She scanned the file and extracted a card with Brady Cranston's name on it. "Needless to say, I'm not supposed to show you any of this, but…let's see," she said as she read her notes. "Ah, yes. Mr. Cranston must have use of a Nordic Skier, which I rent and have delivered to his suite. Item two: I have to make sure his bar is stocked with New Orleans microbrewery beer. He doesn't like any of the twenty-six brands that are always available at the Mirage. And then there's item three: he always has his luggage sent ahead and expects to find everything unpacked and stored away by the time he's checked in. Housekeeping always gives me a hard time on that one."

"What other kinds of things do high rollers ask for?" Georgia leaned toward the desk to get a better look at the file cards.

Stephanie pulled out another card. "Here's a good one. Hassam Agrevi. He wants his bed made up in black satin sheets—a reasonable request," she commented dryly. "He always brings a companion." She rested her chin on two long, slender fingers. "You know, now that I think about it, he never brings the same one twice. Guess he likes variety. Or maybe it's just that once they get a load of the S and M paraphernalia that we store here for him between visits, they choose not to accompany him again. You'd think he'd find some pros who are into that stuff, but maybe that's how he gets his yahoos, from initiating the uninitiated."

Tracy, the poker room receptionist, knocked on the open door. "Edward said he wants you to sign these comps. He doesn't have time."

"Thanks, Tracy," Stephanie said as she was handed the stack of forms. Tracy smiled pleasantly and left. "I've got to do these right away. Edward should have had them ready—now everybody is waiting for them." She slipped Hassam Agrevi's file card back in the box and reached for her pen.

"Can I look at some more of these?" asked Georgia, indicating the file box.

"Yeah, but don't let anyone else see you and just be careful when you put them back. I hate it when they're out of alphabetical order. And obviously don't spread the word that Stephanie Bellamy opens her card file to any and all."

"Of course." Georgia culled through the file. "Now here's a change of pace," she said, scanning a card. "Phillip Vance. He gets a villa suite, and a limo is to be available for him, his daughter and her bodyguard at all times. Does he stay here often?"

"He's been here for months with his little girl, no wife or girlfriend that I'm aware of. He's this very suave English guy, a pal of Steve Wynn's, and he's developing another new casino resort. I don't know too much about that, but as you can tell by that card, he gets just about anything he wants; in fact, sometimes it's like he runs the show in the poker room too."

Stephanie went back to signing vouchers, answering her phone simultaneously. While she spoke into it, Georgia stood and mouthed, "I'm outta here." Enough poker room miscellany. It was time to get back to the game.

Chapter 5

Georgia returned to her seat in time to watch a giant pile of chips accumulate in the center of the table as four players raised and reraised each other. The hand was won by a studious-looking young man with close-cropped red hair and steel-rimmed glasses.

An elderly woman who had contributed about a fourth of the seven-hundred-dollar pot smiled and clucked, shaking her head as she spoke. "Such a hand you have. Congratulations!"

The winner, concentrating intently on stacking his chips, did not acknowledge the comment. The woman went on. "Do not be embarrassed that you stayed in such a pot with fives and sevens to catch a full house on the river. So what that you were against aces up in four cards? You are a very brave young man to put that much money into the pot with such poor odds. Yes, yes, such a brave young man."

Georgia, as well as several other players, grinned at the woman's less-than-subtle sarcasm. Zivah Koski had only begun to come into the poker room this past year, and she had made an astonishing initial impression, although no one had smiled then.

That first time the elderly woman had approached the table where Georgia was playing, she had asked timidly, "Is this seat empty?"

"It's yours now," the dealer had said.

A one-hundred-dollar bill was pulled from a worn leather purse, and the dealer pushed a stack of twenty red chips toward her. As the old lady reached for them, the sleeve of her sweater pulled back to expose a thin white arm. The numbers were the same color as the dozens of blue veins that traversed the papery skin on the underside of her wrist. A "four" and a "two" were perpendicular to her hand, but the "three" that followed floated slightly above the first two numerals and was tilted away from them. Then a "four" and an "eight" were haphazardly placed, a little larger and skewed in opposite directions as though the tattooer had been in a great hurry.

Everyone but Georgia had quickly redirected their focus. Several players began counting their chips while others scanned the room, ostensibly in search of the cocktail waitress, murmuring to each other about the poor service. Coincidentally, two others had found hangnails and were in the process of making sure that the condition was not life threatening, and the dealer was concentrating on every shuffle of the cards, as though his entire professional future was at stake.

"My name is Zivah," she announced as she looked around the table.

Only Georgia stared. The woman made no effort to pull down her sleeve, and after a moment, Georgia's gaze left the indelible numbers and found the clear, gray eyes twinkling with amusement. Obviously Zivah was not afraid to evoke an immediate response from those around her.

"My name is Georgia."

After that, whenever Georgia returned to the Mirage, Zivah was in a ten-twenty game and always had a warm greeting for her. Once, when the two women had shared a table in the snack bar, Zivah had succinctly summarized her experiences as a girl during and after World War II.

"Officially I was never in a concentration camp. Still, I am a Holocaust survivor because I am the only member of my family who was not sent to the ovens. My family fled to Poland from Russia, but then my mother and father and both my sisters were taken away, and only I was hidden in a shack in the forest. I lived through the war, and then, when I was sixteen years old, I was given papers, copies of records from Auschwitz, proof that the rest of my family was dead. So that I would always remember them, I have my mother's concentration camp serial number printed on my arm."

Georgia's breath caught in her throat. Zivah saw the reaction. "Ach, I should not speak so much about such terrible things."

"No, no," Georgia said, quickly regaining her composure as she realized that the older woman had misinterpreted her response. "I'm not offended. It's just that I have a memory from when I was a very little girl of someone else with numbers tattooed on her arm."

In the following months, Zivah attached herself to Georgia whenever possible, inviting her to a small apartment near the airport for a homemade dinner of roasted chicken with kasha stuffing and piroshki. Georgia had not tasted those things since her own Grandma Genya had died more than twenty years ago. Zivah's version of the Russian comfort food was exactly as Georgia remembered. Zivah's living room also reminded Georgia of Grandma Genya. A red paisley gypsy shawl was draped over a dining table, and dozens of silver-framed photos left no room for dinner plates. They had eaten on a tiny patio table, sharing a half bottle of claret while they watched the sun set over McCarren International Airport.

After dinner, as Georgia walked through the cramped living room, she glanced at the many old sepia portraits and a few snapshots on Zivah's dining room table. Zivah had never mentioned having any children, and Georgia knew better than to ask. So who were all the people in those pictures? Were any of them still alive? On a small tea wagon next to the sofa, atop a starched and ironed antique antimacassar, stood a single photograph of a pretty young girl leaning against a tree.

"This is me," Zivah said, caressing the frame gently.

"You were very lovely," Georgia said.

Zivah continued to run her fingers over the ornate frame. "Another time, long ago."

That had been several months and several Vegas trips ago, and now, as Georgia settled into the two seat, Zivah whispered to her, "This is a good game. Those two," indicating two young cowboys at the other end of the table, "don't know how to fold."

Time evaporated in hand after hand. When a player at the other end of the table filled two racks with red chips and left, a muscular man in a Fila warm-up suit sat down. His fine, light-brown hair was streaked with blond stripes, and his tanned, handsome face made him seem more like a tennis pro than a poker pro. He smiled at Georgia in recognition as he pulled five hundred dollars out of a packet of bills clamped together with a horseshoe-shaped silver money clip. His name was Nick Loggin. She often saw him up in the top section, that cordoned off and slightly raised portion of the poker room where the highest-limit games were played. But it seemed he only hung around, talking to some of the high-limit players. She'd only seen him sitting in middle- or lower-limit games.

Soon after, Mr. Kruikshank also joined them. He hadn't yet returned from some distant galaxy and sat in the seven seat, staring at his chips. Milt was playing in another game but kept looking over at Georgia's table, greatly amused by the exasperation that Mr. Kruikshank began to cause as soon as he entered the game. An hour passed, and every new dealer had to slow down to accommodate Mr. Kruikshank's eccentric style of play.

"The bet is ten dollars," the dealer said in Mr. Kruikshank's direction. No reaction. The dealer leaned closer. "Ten dollars?" Another pause. Now, with a little less patience, "Do you wanna call the bet, sir?"

No answer.

Sitting in the eight seat, next to the dealer, Nick Loggin slammed his fist on the table.

"Call the floor man," he bellowed. "I've had it with this asshole!" Nick had lost almost a thousand dollars in the last hour.

Ying, the inscrutable dealer from Taipei, yelled, "Supervisor on seventeen!"

Georgia sat very still, happy to have perfected her poker face. The day shift assistant manager was there in seconds. He put his hand on the back of Ying's chair and leaned over the table. Nick and Ying spoke simultaneously. "Hold on, sir," the assistant manager said to Loggin and then to Ying, "Okay, dealer, tell me what's going on."

Before Ying could speak, Nick Loggin banged his fist on the table again. "Never mind the dealer. I'm the one who knows what's going on here! This jerk," he said, gesturing toward Mr. Kruikshank, "is holding up the game!"

Ignoring Nick's outburst, the assistant manager repeated, with a little more emphasis, "Dealer, tell me what's going on." When Nick started to speak again, he put up his hand to make the point that it was the dealer to whom he would listen first.

Nick stood up, batting the man's arm away, and roared, "Don't put your hand in my face!" The din in the entire room immediately dropped many decibels.

"I did not mean to put my hand in your face," the assistant manager said in measured tones. "I am following poker room procedure, which calls for me to get the initial information about a table dispute from the dealer."

"Bull crap!" Nick slammed the table again. His stacks of chips shifted and fell over, some spilling into Mr. Kruikshank's pile, which wasn't stacked at all. When Mr. Kruikshank started to separate out those chips that had just landed on his own, Nick jabbed him in the shoulder, yelling, "Get your fucking hands off my chips!"

By now, other poker room personnel and many players had gathered around the table, some gawking, some snickering, while others watched from behind their own poker faces. Edward Patrone, the poker room manager, arrived at the table just as several security guards entered the room. Mr. Kruikshank sat rubbing his shoulder, his expression turning to mild puzzlement, as though he couldn't understand where the pain had come from.

Patrone stepped between Nick and Mr. Kruikshank. "Settle down," he said to Nick, and then to Mr. Kruikshank, "Are you okay, sir?"

Nick had spotted the security guards, who were now standing nearby. "Yeah, yeah, he's fine," he said. "I didn't hit him hard." Then in an even more conciliatory tone, he added, "Guess I lost my temper, but that guy shouldn't be allowed to play in here."

Patrone turned to Mr. Kruikshank. "Sir, we've had several complaints about how slow you play. Now, this player is out of line," he said, indicating Nick, "and I'll deal with him in a minute. But you can't continue to slow down the game."

Mr. Kruikshank nodded amicably.

"That's it?" bellowed Nick. "That's all you're gonna do about this? Shit!" He wiped spittle from his chin with the sleeve of his Fila jacket. "Talk to Pat Kelly, or Schultz, or McGann. They all complained about him too."

Patrone signaled to the security guards as he put his hand on Nick's arm. "Let's finish this discussion at the cashier's cage. I'm sure you agree there's no need to hold the game up any longer."

Nick pulled away from Patrone. "So I get kicked out while he goes on playing? That's bullshit!"

Two security guards came up next to Nick, one on each side. Just then, a distinguished-looking man wearing a very expensive, exquisitely tailored sport coat stepped out of the crowd that had gathered around the table.

He was not too tall but with a posture and bearing that added inches to his frame and an aura of authority to his presence. "Edward." He spoke to Patrone in deep, resonant Oxford English. "Mr. Loggin certainly has a bit of trouble with his temper, but perhaps we can reach a mutually satisfying resolution to this dilemma without any more inconvenience to your other patrons."

Patrone bowed his head slightly. "Of course, Mr. Vance."

Zivah whispered to Georgia, "That is Mr. Phillip Vance. So much for Mr. Big Shot Cardroom Manager."

Georgia smiled at the remark and then glanced up to see that Phillip Vance was looking directly at her. She lowered her eyes as an image of his face was filed in her brain, like a piece of clip art downloaded from the Internet. Vance's nose was thin and straight, but his lips were full, and all these features seemed slightly uneven, Picassoesque. Sleek black hair was combed back from a high forehead, and his eyebrows, not nearly as dark as his hair, were a little too thick, but wire-rimmed glasses softened the effect.

"Mr. Vance?" Patrone inquired.

Phillip's gaze was still focused on Georgia as he said, "Mr. Loggin is ready to retire from his gaming endeavors for the time being." Then his eyes harpooned Nick Loggin as he continued, never altering his composed, urbane tone of voice. "When he does return, he will never lose his composure again because he appreciates the dire consequences of such a lapse. He realizes that he would henceforth never be permitted to play poker in this room. Not ever."

Nick was mumbling to himself, but he sat down in his chair, reached under his seat, and retrieved an acrylic rack, into which he began to place the remainder of his chips.

Mr. Kruikshank pushed eight red chips toward Nick. "I believe these are yours," he said pleasantly. Nick added the chips to his rack, ignoring Mr. Kruikshank. The floor men went back to their respective sections of the room. The noise level began to rise as conversations resumed and games continued.

Nick picked up his rack of chips and, without a word, walked to the cashier's window. The security guards sauntered toward the poker room entrance, and Patrone returned to his own office.

Ying, the dealer, asked Mr. Kruikshank once again if he wished to call the ten-dollar bet. Mr. Kruikshank folded his cards, and Ying swept them in, pulling Nick's hand into the muck as well. Zivah called the bet, and Georgia folded.

Mr. Kruikshank was nodding again. "Yes, yes, yes," he confirmed to no one in particular.

Georgia watched Phillip Vance as he returned to the top section. He leaned down to speak to the man who sat in a chair next to his. As he did so, he glanced back at Georgia and smiled. She looked away, but a moment later, involuntarily, her eyes darted back in his direction.

Oh, swell, he probably thinks I'm deliberately trying to keep his attention.

Am I?

The dealer asked for her ante, and as she pushed the chip out in front of her, Zivah leaned over, patting Georgia's arm again.

The older woman hadn't missed a thing. "Interesting man, yes?" she said, gesturing toward the top section. She smiled enigmatically at Georgia before peeking at her own hole cards. "I can introduce you. I sometimes baby-sit his daughter, Livy."

"I'm married, remember?" Georgia said as she tossed her chips in to call the bet.

"So where is your husband?" Zivah asked. "You come here without him all the time, yes? Such a wonderful marriage you have?"

More of Zivah's quirky sarcasm, Georgia thought as she watched a five and a jack fall in front of other players. When someone with a king showing raised, she folded her two jacks with a five kicker, but she didn't answer Zivah. She didn't have an answer for Zivah.

Chapter 6

Now, with the interruptions and distractions over, Georgia joined the action, and the hours flew by. About nine o'clock, Zivah asked Georgia to join her for a quick break. The two women bought yogurt and soft pretzels at the snack bar and strolled out to the Habitat, where Siegfried and Roy's famous white tigers were on display.

A huge pool with white rock ledges, waterfalls and jungle vegetation was displayed behind a fifty-foot-long glass partition. On the casino side, crowds of tourists walked by as they entered and left the Mirage via the moving sidewalk to Las Vegas Boulevard. There were always a number of people leaning against a rail that prevented anyone from touching the glass. The size of the gawking crowd was always an indication of the activity on the other side of the glass. If the resident white tigers were playing in the pool or batting at each other like gargantuan kittens, it was almost impossible to get anywhere near the rail. If the big cats were dozing, fewer people stopped to watch. Tonight, three tigers were curled up on different levels of the habitat, sound asleep, or at least obdurately ignoring their audience.

"Zivah! Zivah!" called out a pretty little girl about nine years old who sat sidesaddle on the very broad shoulder of a man in a three-piece suit. She seemed quite at ease, obviously familiar with this setting and very comfortable on her perch above the rest of the crowd. The child reached down and patted the top of the head of the man who stood next to them. He looked around to see who the child was hailing, and Georgia recognized Phillip Vance. The no-nonsense bodyguard, from whose shoulder the child had just alighted, shuffled along directly behind her as she skipped up to Georgia and Zivah, greeting them with a quirky kind of enthusiasm, half curtsying, half bouncing. Her soft brown curls bobbed up and down.

"Olivia! My favorite customer," Zivah gushed. She reached out and put her arms around the little girl, hugging her affectionately.

"Who's this, a friend?" asked the child, indicating Georgia.

"Mr. Vance, Olivia Vance," said Zivah, "I introduce to you Georgia Cates, a lovely lady and an excellent cardplayer."

"Zivah calls me Olivia the way my daddy does, but most of my friends call me Livy."

"Then so shall I," Georgia said.

"How do you do, Georgia Cates?" Phillip Vance said with British resonance. "I am most pleased to make your acquaintance. And may I begin with apologies for the inappropriate behavior of some of those unruly poker room denizens? That was hardly a pleasant encounter we had earlier; a formal introduction is an imperative." Then, as an afterthought, "And may I introduce Wilbur Robles?" Both Vance and Robles bowed.

"Wilbur is my bodyguard," Livy added helpfully. Wilbur gave a sparse smile then stepped back a bit.

"Do you play cards in the Mirage often?" Phillip asked Georgia.

"Yes, I do," she replied. "When…"

"Astonishingly," Phillip interrupted, "I can't imagine never having noticed someone as lovely as you before today."

"This mystery I can solve," said Zivah. "She is not what you call a 'local.' She is from California. So, Mr. Vance, maybe you will help me. We must make her want to come back here many more times."

"I should like to make it a top priority," Phillip replied, looking at Georgia as he said it.

"Me too," chimed in Livy.

Zivah grinned at Livy and her father as though the three of them had just accomplished the intent of their conspiracy.

"So you see," Phillip remarked, "father and daughter are committed to making you feel like a *local*, to use Mrs. Koski's term. How serendipitous."

Livy reached down and tugged on one leg of her bright pink tights, pulling it up under her denim miniskirt. "Are you and Zivah best friends?" She tilted her head as she looked up until her ear almost touched her shoulder. "Zivah's one of my best friends."

"Zivah is my dear friend, and I guess that makes you and me friends too."

"Do you come here to see the tigers every day?" asked Livy.

"When I'm in town, I do. I stay right here in the hotel, but I live in California most of the time."

"I went to California last summer." Livy was tugging at her tights again. "Daddy took me to Disneyland and Knott's Berry Farm. I liked Knott's best 'cause Disneyland was too much like Disney World, and I've been there lots and lots of times."

Now Zivah spoke up. "Olivia, my darling, forgive me for interrupting, but Georgia and I, we must go back or we will lose our poker seats."

"Of course," Livy said with precocious aplomb. Then her huge fawn-brown eyes encircled by thick lashes the color of butterscotch looked up at Georgia. "Will you still be here tomorrow?"

Georgia saw a need, a yearning deep in those eyes. "Yes, I will," she said, "and then you and I can continue this conversation. Okay?"

"Okay!" Livy replied. "It's a date! Right here, at the Habitat. What time? Say two in the afternoon?"

Phillip cleared his throat and said, "Ah, my Olivia, you are a most persistent young lady."

Livy reached for Georgia's hand and shook it. "We've got a date, right?"

"Right," Georgia replied, laughing as the child bobbed a little curtsy.

Zivah and Georgia stopped in the ladies' room on the way back to the poker room, and as they washed their hands, Zivah asked, "So what do you think of Mister Charming Phillip Vance? Handsome man, yes?"

"Yes, Zivah, he's a handsome man."

"So?"

"Zivah, remember, I'm married. Don't make trouble."

"Trouble? I never make trouble. But I will make the truth again. I said it before and now I say it again. How do you say…I can be sarcastic. I see how much in love with your husband you are. How you never leave him for a minute, never go anywhere without him. How he is always right next to you whenever you come to Las Vegas. Why should I make trouble?" Zivah smiled innocently.

"Besides," Zivah continued as she patted her nose with a small powder puff, "I only ask do you think Mr. Vance is handsome. I think he is, and he is a very important wheel around here. I see that in the poker room, and Wilbur, the henchman or bodyguard or whatever he is called, told me that after Bellagio opens, Mr. Vance is going to build a brand-new casino someplace else in Nevada."

"Really?" Georgia was happy to focus on something other than her reactions to the man.

"Wilbur tells me that it is going to be only for the rich rollers, like Bellagio, but far away from Las Vegas, out in the desert. No families, no tourists, just millionaires. He will have many helicopters that will take the rich rollers back and forth to Las Vegas." She was shaking her head. "To tell you the truth, I don't think there are enough people with so much money to open such a casino, but Mr. Vance is a very smart man, so he must know."

Georgia looked at herself in the mirror, using her fingers to arrange her hair. "Yes, Phillip Vance is a very interesting man."

"His wife died, you know," Zivah said, obviously encouraged by Georgia's response. "Wilbur told me that Livy's mother was a show girl, you know, real glamorous. Livy was born right after they got married, and then the mother got sick." Zivah uttered the next word like someone who never swore but had to speak an expletive. "Cancer," she said. "She died before Livy was one year."

"Why do they live here at the Mirage?"

"Wilbur says that they have traveled most of the time, to where Mr. Vance has businesses. But Mr. Vance likes the poker, and I think he is a good friend of Steve Wynn, so now they live here. Wilbur takes care of Livy most of the time, but I come so he can have time off or do something for Mr. Vance who is very busy getting money for his new casino. It is fine for me because I can come and go from my poker game."

They returned to their table, and Zivah was immediately dealt three very promising cards. Her dissertation on Olivia and Phillip Vance was over.

Chapter 7

At one in the morning, Georgia's chips totaled more than twelve hundred dollars. Now she was on a rush. This was the most fun poker could be—when cards that had potential at the beginning of a deal consistently developed into the winner on the river. In poker, timing is everything, and this was Georgia's magic time. Everything worked in her favor. Two pair or even one big pair held up; nobody got cards to beat her. Tonight she was the only one at the table who had been sprinkled with fairy dust, so no one else improved their hands if she didn't. But then, when her pair turned into trips or even a full house, several other players invested heavily in her pot, hoping to catch a straight or a flush, and even if they did, Georgia's hand would get better. She had tripled her original buy-in, and then the poker fairy closed up shop and Georgia's cards went cold. Deal after deal yielded three anemic discards. Her thoughts floated away from the poker table. Time for another break.

Sitting on one of the upholstered stools in the soft-hued, opulently lighted Mirage ladies' room, Georgia pulled out her makeup pouch and began to apply blusher. In the mirror, she saw the reflection of tall, beautiful Mindy Cameron. She had changed out of her cocktail waitress uniform and now wore an off-the-shoulder pink angora sweater, black leggings, and four-inch high heel mules. She bent over at the waist, flipped her thick, long, lush blond hair forward, and pulled a brush through it. Then she straightened up quickly, flinging strands away from her face and finishing the tussled effect with her fingers. Her expression said it all. Perfect.

The only other person in that section of the ladies' room was a petite woman in a poker dealer's uniform who sat up on the counter next to Mindy, knees drawn up, smoking a cigarette.

"Georgia!" Mindy squealed, her mules clacking on the marble floor as she scurried over to hug one of her favorite customers. "Rita, it's Georgia!" she said as though the other woman were blind. Rita and Georgia exchanged grins as Mindy continued to talk, tossing her hair back and forth as she watched her own reflection.

"You're right," Mindy said, as though Georgia had been present for the entire conversation, "I'm probably gonna regret it, but I can't figure out how to say no to any of them." Then as an aside to Georgia, "Men, that is." Just in case it wasn't clear what they were discussing.

"Exactly how many of them are there?" Rita asked, meeting Georgia's gaze in the mirror. Both women pursed their lips and rolled their eyes.

Mindy didn't notice. "Well, let's see," she said and began to keep a tally with her fingers. "Of course there's Nick, although after the scene he just pulled in the poker room, I probably should just meet him at his apartment. But then there's the Japanese guy, Zenri. He has this amazing sexy way that's so different from the all-American boys. And I still haven't figured out how to break it off with Harold, the guy who deals in diamonds, you know, the big-time Omaha player. And then Lance, the dealer with the big pecs. See, I can count them all on one hand and still have a finger left over." She looked at Georgia for a reaction. Georgia hoped her smile was ambiguous.

"Mindy," Rita said, shaking her head in amused disbelief, "you can't date four different guys who spend most of their time in the same casino."

"I know," Mindy whined, "but I just can't miss what any of them has to offer me. I mean, it's not like I date every guy who hits on me." Strands of blond hair took wing again as her head jerked back and forth. "I'm being selective. The diamond guy and the Japanese guy have bucks and pull and give me presents and show me a good time. I've been to the best restaurants, all the top shows, and the swankiest homes in Vegas. And Lance, the dealer, is one of the most gorgeous hunks I've ever laid eyes on. I love sitting behind him on his motorbike, and even though Nick Loggin never has any cash, he knows where all my buttons are; he can turn me on just by looking at me. And he's got connections too. You know he's like some kind of assistant to Phillip Vance. He's always going places for him, and sometimes he gets to go to shows or restaurants with him, and sometimes he brings me along."

"Do what you have to do," Rita said. "And I hope I don't need to keep saying, 'I told you so.'"

"I'm outta here," Mindy said. "I told Nick I'd meet him in the Rain Forest Bar. The Sports Bar is just a little too close to the poker room."

As Mindy checked herself once more in the full-length mirror, Georgia's and Rita's reflections made eye contact again. Back at the Golden Nugget, before the Mirage had been built, Rita had dealt Georgia her first four-of-a-kind hand. Rita had been the mother of two back then but now had eight children, including one set of twins and another of triplets. She'd told Georgia that she and her husband had thought that they would even out their brood of five to a neat half dozen and ended up with the triplets to make eight—and without fertility pills!

"She's trouble waiting to happen," Rita said when Mindy was gone.

Georgia nodded in agreement. "Sounds that way."

Rita slid off the counter and sat on a stool next to Georgia. "I've seen a lot like her lately. They remind me of lemmings; they just follow each other out to Vegas from all over the country, and most of them end up falling off the cliff."

Georgia's and Rita's reflections continued their conversation. "She's so young and gorgeous," Georgia said. "I guess sometimes that can be trouble."

"With a capital T! It's weird how many of the healthy ones, I mean the ones from, you know, from mainstream, middle America, like her—the kind who come from what the magazines call a 'highly functional and productive family'—move to Vegas looking for excitement and a new lifestyle. She's a college graduate, raised in Iowa, homecoming queen, good grades and plenty of self-confidence. She has it all, and now she's supporting herself exceptionally well with the tokes she gets." Rita shook her head sadly. "That kind just can't seem to leave well enough alone. Mindy says she's looking for the highs and rushes. Whatever happened to plain old happiness and fulfillment?"

"Maybe she wants it all," Georgia said. "Maybe we were the ones who sold short. When I was her age, my definitions of highs and rushes were about altitude and being in a hurry."

"Well, she's really a nice kid," Rita said as she stood up, adjusting the black dealer's tie that had been loosened at her neckline. "I just hope she doesn't pay too much for 'having it all.'"

When Georgia came out of the ladies' room, she wandered over to the lounge section of the Baccarat Bar, stepping into its relative tranquility. No walls separated it from the surrounding casino, but the deep-pile carpeting and the soft lighting in the lowered ceiling produced a subtle haven. The comparable serenity of the bar was in degrees only. Here was a slight respite from the din, ring and clatter of the slots, the incessant paging system and the discordant shrieks of those who had won twenty dollars or twenty thousand. The low tables were surrounded by chairs, softer and much more comfortable than blackjack stools or poker seats.

Georgia sat down and ordered a Perrier. She never drank any form of alcohol when she was playing poker; even one glass of Chardonnay made her sleepy. She settled into the comfortable leather chair, happy to be alone and anonymous, happy to amuse herself by studying the other groups sitting in the bar.

Nearby, a passionate couple, unable to refrain from foreplay, were either too drunk or too libidinous, or both, to bother finding a more private setting. She licked his mouth then his jaw and Adam's apple as he reached inside her low-cut dress, extracted a handful of breast, and manipulated it like a wad of Silly Putty.

Three older couples sat at a table to Georgia's left. Four of the six were engaged in an energetic conversation, while one very exasperated wife kept nudging her torpid husband, who was losing the battle to keep eyes open and chin off chest. A little farther away, several women were laughing loudly, making sure that everyone within hearing distance knew that the girls from Bakersfield were here on their yearly Vegas fling.

Then she spotted the two men at a table in the corner. Phillip Vance sat across from another high-stakes player who had answered to the name Montana Jones when he was paged in the poker room. Montana looked like he could star in a Wild Bill Hickok review. He wore jeans, boots, a plaid western shirt and a cowboy hat, but they were all merely background for several pounds of silver decoration, including the hatband, the huge bola tie in the shape of a scorpion, the silver-studded belt with the buckle designed like a charging bull, and the silver-toed boots. This gentleman must have invested heavily in silver polish. Montana's face was permanently tanned, except where wrinkles had shielded the skin from the sun, and his shaggy, thinning white hair lay over his collar like sun-bleached straw.

He held a glass containing something dark brown and undiluted by ice cubes in one hand and a cigarette in the other. Taking a drag followed by a sip of his drink, he exhaled the smoke through his nose into the glass. Then both men stood up, shook hands, and Montana walked out of the bar.

She'd guessed when she'd been introduced to Phillip Vance outside the Habitat that he must be about five-ten, a few inches shorter than Jeff—probably more comfortable to dance with. *Now where the hell did that thought come from?*

Vance's sport coat was a soft tweed—cashmere, no doubt—over a cream-colored dress shirt and dark, forest-green slacks. No tie. He did have excellent taste in clothes. *Does he realize the color of that jacket is heather?* she wondered to herself. *And that Venus, the goddess of love, whose origin was in the fields and forests, was often associated with heather? And what the hell does this have to do with anything, huh, Georgia?*

Georgia had been staring at him for several minutes, her mind floating off into a soft, foggy place. She tried to sip her empty glass and was startled by the slurping sound. Leaving a tip on the table, she walked out of the bar, trying not to seem hurried, keeping her eyes focused straight ahead, praying to God she wouldn't trip on anything.

It was late in the evening. Georgia was back at the poker table, and deal after deal went by without yielding a promising hand. A misty sleepiness began creeping into her brain, shrouding her concentration. She stood up and went to the counter to get three acrylic chip trays. Returning to her seat, she began to fill the trays with hundred-dollar stacks of red chips. As she did so, Zivah, who always kept her chips racked and ready to go, bid everyone a "good evening" and left.

"Not bad for a night's work," said Marsha as her short, chubby fingers carefully pried up the corners of her down cards and then reached for enough chips to call the bet.

Georgia gave her a friendly smile. "Thanks, Marsha."

"You should invest those profits in an elegant piece of jewelry," Marsha advised. "I'd love to help you pick something out."

"I know! I know!" Georgia said, still smiling. "A woman can never be too thin, too rich or have too much jewelry."

But Georgia knew exactly what she'd do with this money, even though she'd never hurt Marsha's feelings by discussing it with her. She knew how much more fortunate than Marsha she was in so many ways. For one, Georgia's winnings were used only to buy more red and green chips. Sometimes the tractor pulled up and shoved all of her money around the table. Then she'd dip into her reserve; that was the only thing poker profits were for: to replenish her stash.

Marsha had switched her attention to the cards on the table, and Georgia continued to count down her chips and place them in the racks. Georgia never wanted to be forced to leave the table because she'd reached her loss limit. Nothing was more important than playing. Fortunately she had a wide margin in which to operate. Every so often her stash had been depleted. Then she'd had to write a check on the tax account that she and her mother shared, but the money was always replaced before the next statement came. The several lines of credit she'd opened lately did concern her once in a while. It was just so easy to get them. But one way or another, she was able to keep everything in place, and the couple of balances on those credit card lines would get paid down as soon as she went on a major rush at the table.

Once or twice she had borrowed from her business account. Depending on how many fund-raising projects she had going, she could have as much as several hundred thousand dollars at her disposal. And on a few occasions, her balance had been as high as a half million before she transferred the profits from a benefit project into the organization's account. So a thousand here or there was hardly ever a problem. The most she'd ever withdrawn for her poker needs was three thousand dollars. True, the money might disappear at the poker table, but she knew that she and Jeff had plenty of accounts into which she could dip to replace what she had lost, and if not, she had the credit cards. She'd always been able to cover these transactions by laundering them in and out of their joint checking account, her mother's account and the credit cards, but she knew there would be a gargantuan interest fee to pay if Jeff ever caught on. Although she'd convinced herself that she was willing to chance that possibility, once in a while the thought of actually experiencing those consequences sent a chill of dread through her. But then she'd remind herself that, one way or another, she could lose a great deal before she ever approached serious trouble.

Marsha had stayed in the hand to the sixth card but then folded, never showing what she had in the hole. The worst kind of poker, Georgia thought sadly—calling every bet, hoping to catch up to the better hand, not having much of a chance then giving up at the river. And the poor old woman never seemed to catch on. As Marsha reached out to place her next ante, she turned to Georgia. "Well, goodnight, dear girl. You sleep well."

"I will, Marsha, and you take care too."

Well into her sixties, Marsha had a penchant for novelty sweaters, and the one she wore this evening was embroidered with gray kittens frolicking across her chest. Another size larger would have been much more flattering.

Marsha had told Georgia her whole sad story.

Marsha and Martin Kulick had enjoyed two great years retired in Vegas before he collapsed one morning in the shower. Marsha had been in the kitchen, wondering why he was taking so long in the bathroom. Finally, after calling him several times, she had gone to check. She had turned off the water and covered him with his terry robe before she called 911. She knew he was gone.

She had moved twice in the past three years. Selling the three-bedroom condo made sense. Her husband had died, and she didn't need all that room. Her son and daughter both hated Las Vegas and had been true to their vows never to visit if their parents chose to retire there. And they hadn't relented, even when she became a widow. Someday she would go to visit them in Cleveland and Fort Lauderdale, as soon as she could save the money for airfare. The small profit she had made when the condo sold had been depleted before the first anniversary of Martin's death. She had moved again a few months ago from the security apartment on the west side to a cheaper place nearer the Strip. Now she was well on her way to finishing off his life insurance.

Marsha pulled out her ATM card and caught up with Georgia. At the poker room cashier's counter, Georgia waited while the man ahead of her was handed his safe deposit box. Expertly and casually, he counted the seventy-five one-hundred-dollar bills he had brought from the pot-limit hold 'em game, along with the stacks of pink five-hundred-dollar chips, then placed them on top of more cash and chips and locked the box.

Georgia's gaze strayed up to the balcony. Phillip Vance was observing her again. He nodded. She looked away, oddly annoyed at herself. With a knowing smile, Marsha also looked at Phillip Vance. "That's what I need: a big shot high roller who looks at me the way Phillip Vance looks at you." She gave Georgia another melancholy smile then turned away and headed toward the bank of ATM machines. Georgia never had the chance to respond to Marsha's remark. Just as well.

Chapter 8

When Georgia entered her room, the flashing light on the telephone made her scalp tingle. *Relax*, she reminded herself. If there was an emergency, she would have been paged in the poker room. The sense of dread that had nudged her when she'd opened the door now wrapped itself around her when she heard Jeff's recorded voice.

"It's a little after five p.m., and I have just been informed that my conference here in Seattle has been canceled. I'll explain later. You have to return to Creste Verde tomorrow. This is about the firm and extremely necessary. I realize that this is very short notice, but you probably shouldn't have gone to Vegas anyway. I'm on my way to the airport now. Will stop off in San Francisco tonight and be home tomorrow. I'll leave another message at home if I have time. Goodnight."

The sleepiness she had felt just minutes before in the poker room had vanished. She had been ordered home, and she would have to comply. Jeff had become more and more demanding over the years, but there was no denying his pragmatism. He would not have left that message if there were not a good reason for her to come home immediately. She knew that. But how infuriating that he didn't even give her the courtesy of an explanation. And worse yet, she realized her anger was suffocated under the inevitability of the situation. She could be as angry as she wanted; she still had to leave Vegas in the morning. It concerned Jeff's business, and if he needed her to be there then she would have to be there.

After changing into her nightgown, she pulled out her bags and began to pack. She switched on CNN and tried to concentrate on the news. No luck. The truth was she didn't want to go back to Creste Verde, for any reason. She took half of a sleeping pill, curled up under the blanket, and tried to float off to her safe and familiar, soft and foggy sea. Sleep finally came sometime after two.

Georgia was startled awake. For a moment, being conscious did not dispel the terror. Lying very still, she had to assure herself that she was safe and in control. The clock read 5:15 a.m. She showered and dressed, ate breakfast, and called for the bellman.

On some Mirage stationery, she wrote a note apologizing to Livy for not being able to meet her at the Habitat that afternoon and promising to be in touch as soon as she returned to Las Vegas. In the lobby, she handed the envelope to the concierge, asking her to have it delivered to Phillip Vance's suite.

By six thirty, she was out of the Mirage driveway, turning right on Las Vegas Boulevard. She put a recorded novel into the tape deck. Ten minutes later, after rewinding the tape for the third time, she flipped off the cassette player.

Concentrate, she ordered herself. *Be mature, practical. Deal with the here and now.* She was in her car driving south on her way back to Creste Verde and her other life. It was time to bring up the sense of duty, the spirit of the corps, the old rah-rah, the holiday spirit, the unbinding enthusiasm. Where was all that crap anyway?

She switched on the radio; none of her tapes appealed to her just now. Maybe an easy listening music station would help to focus on the near future and her immediate responsibilities, which were filed under the headings of The Husband and His Career, The Kids, The Mother, The Business, The House, The Holidays—not necessarily in that order. She'd start with her son, Mike; he was the easiest.

Sweet Mike. They'd never called him Michael, even though he'd been named for his paternal grandfather, who had always been addressed by his full, given name. Her son, on the other hand, had been

Mikey until first grade, and then he'd firmly announced that his name would be Mike from then on. Now her baby boy was pushing twenty-one, and Georgia had felt a few twinges of empty nest syndrome when he'd told her about the great opportunity to make "big bucks" over the holiday but only if he could work in Park City, Utah, for the entire Christmas break. "Oh, by the way," he'd added, his girlfriend, Krista, and her family were renting an A-frame there.

Mike had thought of everything. He'd get a red-eye on Christmas Eve and spend about six hours at home in Creste Verde before he caught another flight, which would get him back to Park City by six the next morning, in time for work. The exhaustion factor that Georgia had seen as only one of several flaws in his design had been gently and patiently dismissed by him. Neither one of them brought up the fact that the round trip airfare would cost as much as a week's salary on ski patrol. His father had a limitless supply of frequent flyer miles.

A commercial on the radio reminded her that there were twenty-three shopping days until Christmas. At least that was not her concern. Not only were all of her gifts purchased, they were wrapped, tagged, and ready for distribution. Otherwise she wouldn't have been able to go to Vegas. But there were still tons of things to do, starting with the open house that the Cates family hosted every year on the second Saturday in December. Harold, the best of the eight catering managers who worked for Cates, Gleason et Cie, Georgia's professional fund-raising firm, had assured her that the Cates Christmas party was his number one priority.

Her only responsibility was decorating the house. Every year she did something different, usually incorporating a unique color scheme that began at the front door and continued through the entryway into the living room, family room, dining room, billiard room, library, both guest bathrooms and the deck. She'd been thinking about royal blue and silver this year, but maybe she'd just use the same reds and pinks and purples from last year and pull out some of the gold ribbon from previous seasons. Then she wouldn't have to spend so much time running around matching and coordinating everything.

GEORGIA

As Georgia's car came out of the Cajon Pass and rolled into the LA Basin, she tried to plan her party menu, but nothing excited her; she'd tell Harold to decide. Then, just as quickly, she gave up trying to mentally rearrange the furniture for the holidays. Instead she would simply fit the Christmas paraphernalia here and there.

The mail truck was pulling away from the curb as she approached her driveway, where a giant privet hedge, nine feet high, shielded the grounds and house from the street. It was bisected by the east and west entrances to the wide expanse of herringbone brick pavement that curved from the sidewalk, past the front entrance, and around to the sidewalk again, fifty feet farther west.

The courtyard was filled with vehicles. At the front of the line was the housekeeper's car. Lena refused to park on the street, claiming someone had once broken her side view mirror. Georgia suspected that Lena thought leaving her car on the street was demeaning. As she'd often reminded Georgia, she was one of a very few Anglo-American domestics left in Southern California. Behind Lena's Camaro was the gardener's truck then a plumber's van, and the pool man's station wagon brought up the rear. Georgia parked on the street, pushed the remote to open the heavy wrought iron gate, and walked up the driveway.

Carlos, the gardener, turned off his blower and pulled down his gas mask. "Mrs. Cates!" he hailed in that definitive Southern California cadence that develops in the offspring of Spanish-speaking immigrants. "The cleaning lady said you were in Vegas again."

"I was, Carlos," replied Georgia as she walked toward the front door.

"I'm going to the nursery this week," he said, following close behind her, "and I need to know what kind of plants you want."

Georgia unlocked the door. "You decide, Carlos."

"But Mrs. Cates! I can get pansies, or primrose, or poppies, or begonias, or cyclamen, or…"

"That's fine," said Georgia as she stepped into the entry.

"All of them?"

"You decide," she repeated. "You know what will work. I trust your judgment."

She was about to close the door when he asked, "What about poinsettias? Do you want me to get you a case of them again this year? And do you want all pink ones again or red ones?"

"That's fine," she said and gently shut the door. Walking toward the kitchen, she was assailed by the clamor that always seemed to reach a crescendo just as she came home. A game show host was bellowing questions at his contestants from the TV in the kitchen as well as the one in the family room. Two televisions, the washing machine, dryer and exhaust fan were all in a battle of decibels but were losing out to the pipe-clanging plumber, whose legs and lower torso extended from under the kitchen sink.

Georgia called out, "Lena, I'm back!"

Lena peered around the corner from the laundry room. "What are you doing back so early? Is something wrong?"

"No, nothing's wrong. I just have a lot to do." She smiled pleasantly at the plumber, who had twisted around to acknowledge her before resuming his clanging.

Lena snatched several pieces of paper from her apron pocket. Georgia sighed deeply. This could only mean one thing. Lena's greatest pleasure in life was to be the bearer of bad news. And the anticipation in her Betty Boop voice did not bode well.

"Well, it sure has been crazy around here," Lena said. "Your answering machine tape is full already. I took a bunch of messages too. Two packages and a stack of mail are in your office, and some lady dropped off a notebook; it's with the mail. And then there's these." She brought a piece of note paper to within inches of her nose, pushing back tendrils of damp, peroxide-damaged hair as she struggled to read her own writing. At sixty-two, Lena still tried to be a blond bombshell.

"I'll start with right after you left. The carpet cleaning people came like they were supposed to, but their machine broke. They'll call when they can come back. The gardener has been bugging me about what kind of flowers you want. The lady came with the window shades for the bathroom, but they didn't fit. She said to tell you that she's very sorry and she'll put the reorder on rush. And then this morning I get here and find the kitchen sink full of disgusting goo. I tried to rinse it down the drain, but it was all clogged up, so I called the plumber. He's been here over two hours already; I think he's almost done now."

Georgia listened to this litany of household disasters and, one by one, mentally minimized their threat. The carpets weren't that dirty, and all the dozens of people who would be here for the open house would probably be standing on the couple of bad spots, and there would be more stains afterward anyway. She'd already dealt with the gardener. Hopefully the shades would arrive before next weekend, and if they didn't, so be it. And Lena had taken care of the kitchen sink.

"Anything else, Lena?"

"Well, what about all this stuff?" Lena was waving the small wad of randomly sized papers.

"Thank you for taking care of the sink. If you'd just sign the bill when the plumber is through, I'd appreciate it."

"Fine," said Lena curtly, handing over the notes.

Georgia walked to the bedroom wing and into the study that she had furnished for her own office. The desk and chair had been her father's, and she'd had them refinished in a soft ash varnish that blended with the gray carpet and the taupe walls. She eyed the stack of mail and the large black notebook that had been decorated with flower and butterfly stickers and was labeled "Women's Auxiliary Spring Fling Benefit." Sitting down at her desk, she pushed it all aside.

She stared at the phone for a long moment then reached for her master list of things to do for the holidays. It referred to several sub lists, such as "table decorations" and "holiday menus." She had to squint to concentrate, as though the ink had faded while she'd been in Vegas. She glanced at the messages that Lena had scribbled on random pieces of paper. Most of the calls were memos from her business partner, Andrea Gleason. *God bless her*, Georgia thought. Andrea was taking care of everything.

Georgia pushed the button on the answering machine. It took the tape its full minute to rewind. More calls about meetings and projects were mingled among messages from every member of her immediate family.

Her mother's voice had the customary undertone of bruised feelings. Georgia smiled. She guessed that Sonia Kassov assumed that her daughter should be waiting by the phone at all times, that Georgia's life was simply held in suspension between phone conversations and how very inconsiderate of her not to be there when Sonia called.

The message was cryptic. "Georgia dear, please call me." These were the only words she ever left on the answering machine, always refined yet obviously disappointed. The same words, in the same tone, had been recorded when Georgia's father had been promoted to full colonel and, years later, on the day that he'd suffered a fatal stroke. Today Georgia decided to interpret her mother's message as an invitation to chat and not a harbinger of momentous news. She'd call later.

Sonnie Cates's voice also had a signature tone on the message machine: a mixture of impatience and annoyance. Maybe she'd inherited that from her namesake. Sonia Eleanora Cates had many of her maternal grandmother's traits.

"Mother, you talk too slow, and you don't have to say you'll call back at your earliest opportunity; people assume that. Anyway, the reason I'm leaving a message is 'cause both my econ and history finals were rescheduled, and I'm through early so I don't have to hang around. I get into LAX at two something, and Billy's plane gets in at four, so we're gonna take a shuttle back to Creste Verde together. His parents don't get back from Europe until the day after tomorrow. If you're still in Vegas, I'll be fine, so don't get tense. Ciao."

"Right," Georgia said out loud. *Why should I get tense*, she thought, *just because two nineteen-year-old hormone-infused kids who haven't seen each other for six weeks are planning to spend a lot of time together in one of two homes, one of which is devoid of even a token of adult supervision?* For that reason alone, Georgia was glad she came back.

Next message: "Hi, Mom! This is your son, Mike." Georgia smiled. He always started that way. It was his perpetual joke, an endearing habit for an only son. "Just wanted to remind you that I'll be home today. No classes because it's the hundredth anniversary of the founding of the university. I'm going to skip the celebration so I can spend some time with Krista and also check out my skis; they probably need to go into the shop. I'll have to go back on Sunday, so don't plan on me for Sunday dinner…that is, if you were planning Sunday dinner. Anyway, hope you're around. I know Dad's in Seattle. If you're not around, I'll try to reach you at the Mirage. I need to talk to you and Dad about this great chance to make a bundle in Park City over Christmas vacation. Krista's family is going there too; did I already tell you that? Love you. Bye."

Her son was a junior in college, but he was still her baby boy. Her life had been calm those first three years of parenthood, before Sonnie had entered the world. When the children were growing up, she had referred to Mikey as "easy" while Sonnie was "challenging."

The next message was from Jeff. "I'm in San Francisco. Alan Berg had a heart attack and died. Everyone that was supposed to be at the conference in Seattle is going to be in LA because the funeral is at ten tomorrow morning. I assume that you will make an effort to be at home as early as possible today. I would find it most disturbing to return to…" The tape ran out. Georgia smiled again.

Next she dialed the local market and put in a grocery order to be delivered. Dinner would be cold cuts, bread and salads. She put her car into the garage and carried in her bags. After unpacking, she stowed the luggage away in her closet instead of returning it to the storage locker at the other end of the house.

Showered and dressed in comfortable slacks and a shirt, she glanced at her bedroom clock, annoyed at how quickly the day was passing and how little time she had left to herself. She wandered through the house, trying to sort through a puzzling blend of uneasy thoughts. What had happened to all of the concentration and energy that had always been focused on the house and the holidays and her business, not to mention her family, several of whom were about to arrive? No thrill from that prospect. Added to this was a sense of enmity and resentment. But for whom, or what, and why?

She wandered into the den, where, on a bookshelf, there were photographs of Georgia and Jeff from their college days, the wedding and twenty-three years of marriage. In every picture of the two of them, she was always looking at him, and he was always looking into the camera. Georgia had never noticed that before.

Jeff had been a handsome young man. His appearance, always a priority, was maintained with regular exercise, a healthy diet, and, when he was finally able to afford it, facials, manicures and haircuts from a Beverly Hills *stylist* who made office calls. In the last several years, the monthly bills for his wardrobe had been more than the mortgage payments on their first house.

Chapter 9

1962

Georgia had been nineteen that February in 1962 when she and her parents had been dining in the senior officers' mess at Fort Dix, New Jersey. Major General and Mrs. Hamilton Cates and their son, Jeffrey, were seated at the next table. Georgia was instantly attracted to the young cadet. Hamilton and Anne Cates, as well as her own parents, had encouraged the romance from the start. Jeff had just completed his third year at West Point and was expected to carry on a five-generation tradition of military service. Georgia was his perfect mate, an "army brat," the daughter of a career officer.

That fall, Georgia returned for her senior year at Wellesley College in the suburbs of Boston, but her heart and most of her conscious thoughts were at West Point. Jeff's phone calls were casual in attitude yet, due to their frequency, very encouraging. He invited Georgia to every West Point social weekend, including graduation, which both his parents as well as hers attended. Later, she met him in New York City, and he spent a two-week leave with her family on Cape Cod. Then he left for an overseas assignment. He would be attached to the military attaché in West Berlin.

Jeff's letters to Georgia made it clear that he prided himself on having the instinct not only to be in the right place at the right time but, more so, to never be in the wrong place at the wrong time. Serving as executive assistant to the commanding officer was not only a stroke of good fortune but a fertile opportunity to advance his own prospects.

He never proposed; he simply began to write to her about wedding plans. He had all the ideas. She always agreed.

"Whatever Jeff wants, Georgia wants, as long as Jeff wants Georgia," she repeated to herself, over and over. Nothing mattered more.

During the Christmas holidays of 1965, within days of returning from overseas, he gave her a one-carat diamond solitaire. On the second Saturday in May 1966, the chapel at Fort Belvoir, Virginia, was packed with friends and professional acquaintances of both families, most men and a few women in military uniform. The mother of the bride was lovely in her pearl-gray silk sheath with a lace coat to match. Jeff's mother was less striking, and the unfortunate choice of saffron-yellow for her fitted satin suit made her resemble a jar of French's mustard. Both fathers were exceptionally dapper in their full dress whites.

Georgia would have preferred a simpler wedding gown than the one that had been chosen for her. But her mother was the authority on fashion and appearance, and Georgia knew better than to argue; and the look on Jeff's face as she started down the aisle convinced her that she had been right to relinquish her own opinions. They did make a striking bride and groom, she in her clouds of satin and tulle, and he in his perfectly tailored dress uniform. Captain and Mrs. Jeffrey Cates spent their honeymoon in Provincetown, on the tip of Cape Cod. Arriving late on a Saturday night, they didn't leave their cottage until Monday afternoon, and then for just a couple of hours on the beach. Later, as they were dressing for dinner, Jeff wanted to talk about their plans for the future.

Georgia was sitting at the dressing table and he was standing in front of the mirror in the bathroom. "I've made a decision," he called out, his voice echoing off the tiled walls. "But we aren't going to tell anyone about it for a while, okay?"

"What kind of a decision?"

"Come in here so I don't have to yell."

She walked into the bathroom, seeing his face reflected in the circle he had cleared in the foggy mirror. "Sit down," he said. She sat on the edge of the tub, wishing that the room wasn't so humid. The lines in her pageboy would quickly disappear into strands and clumps of stubborn curls, and her half hour of blow-drying would be wasted.

"I've decided to resign my commission," he said as he applied shaving cream.

"Your commission?" She hadn't expected this.

"I want to make a lot of money," he told her. "And I can't do that in the army."

"How much money?" she asked. "Officers make plenty of money."

"Not enough for me." He kept his eyes focused on his cheeks and jaw. "In Germany I met a couple of guys who think just like I do. One went to Harvard and the other to Cal Tech, and we have it all figured out. All we have to do is put together winning combinations."

"Combinations of what?" She wrapped her arms around herself and watched him in the mirror.

"We'll put people with good ideas together with people who have lots of money to invest. Then we're gonna get a share of the action. But first we're all getting MBAs as fast as we can, and then we'll form the triumvirate of the century." He continued to shave. She wanted to ask him how long he had been making these plans without so much as mentioning them to her. Didn't her opinion have any value? *Look at me, Jeff,* she pleaded silently. He didn't. Why couldn't he sense her apprehension?

He rinsed off the remaining shaving cream then rubbed a towel through his hair and dried his face. "I didn't say anything about this before because I wanted to be sure that the other two guys were on board before I made the decision to join them. I didn't want you to worry about it until it was a done deal. We've already decided on the name of our company, the Venture Capital Group—succinct and precise. We're gonna combine the most promising new businesses with the most reliable sources of capital. Then we'll just pull in the payoffs."

He walked out of the bathroom and stood before the full-length mirror on the closet door, viewing himself from different angles. "You see, most guys who come from my background make a giant compromise. They convince themselves about wanting to serve their country and all that bullshit about the military being in their blood, etcetera. But that's because most of them are just basically realistic. They know their limitations, and a career in the military will give them that built-in cap of what they can achieve. Sure, they can be promoted, work their way up in command, even be a general or a chief of staff, but the pay level is set by Congress, and making any extra money is extremely improbable. I have more going for me. More brains, more balls and more ambition, and that puts me one up on most of the competition."

Georgia followed him into the bedroom and stood at the foot of the bed, still trying to catch his eye in the mirror. He turned to face her. "Look what's happening to me," he said, indicating his taut penis. They missed their dinner reservation and ended up calling room service for the third night in a row.

"Just remember, honey," Jeff said as they were driving back to Virginia after the abbreviated honeymoon, "we're not telling anyone about my plans to leave the army until I say so. I don't need my parents' advice on this…or your parents' either. Okay?"

Georgia readjusted her life. No officers' clubs, officers' wives' teas, generals' receptions. No living in junior officers' quarters, which usually included a cleaning service, nor would she ever need to use her legacy: an inbred mastery of the complexities of military protocol. Instead, the first few years of her marriage were comprised of a nine-to-five job with forays to the supermarket and weekend battles with washing machines and vacuum cleaners. They lived in a tiny studio apartment in Palo Alto, California, while all three of the "triumvirate of the century" attended Stanford Business School.

She worked for an insurance underwriter reviewing policies—not much more than proof reading. She spent most of her work days dotting i's and crossing t's. It was a dull job but necessary to pay the rent and buy groceries. Both General and Mrs. Cates, as well as her own parents, had expressed their profound disappointment at Jeff's decision to leave the army. Very little moral or monetary support for this alternate life plan had been forthcoming. Jeff and Georgia had to rely on government loans and her paycheck. Fortunately she didn't become pregnant until the second and final year of graduate school. Michael Peter Cates was born three weeks before his daddy's graduation.

Jeff passed out blue-banded cigars and gently rocked his baby boy, even changed his diapers. But his enthusiasm for becoming a father had not developed until late in Georgia's pregnancy. "How did this happen?" had been his initial response to the news that she was going to have a baby.

Georgia had asked herself the same question over and over. She knew she should be taking "the pill," but it made her feel so sick. The obstetrician had patiently explained how the diaphragm she'd used instead had probably failed.

"Usually when a woman gets pregnant while using a diaphragm, it's because she's had it in place too long and hasn't reapplied spermicide. Do you remember me warning you about that? It's also printed in the instructions."

Georgia had been careful, scrupulously careful, but sometimes Jeff would fall asleep before she came to bed. Then, the next morning, he'd wake her and want to enter her right away. And to be desired by Jeff was to be safe and secure. At that moment, nothing else mattered. She never knew how to tell him that he had to wait while she went into the bathroom to apply more spermicide. It was her own fault.

Georgia, Mikey, and Jeff moved from Palo Alto to an apartment complex on the west side of Los Angeles, near the beach. The young Cates family's living conditions in Santa Monica had been far from luxurious, but there were some pluses. Georgia enjoyed the camaraderie of the other tenants, mostly couples in their late twenties or early thirties. The men, for the most part, were beginning professional careers, having completed law, business or medical school. Georgia had thought of that apartment complex as a middle-class ghetto where everyone's lives entwined. Most of the women didn't work, so mornings were spent sipping coffee in one another's apartments, and everyone kept an eye on whichever little ones were about. Two-car families were rare, and carpooling to the market and the mall further reinforced the companionship. The swimming pool was the center of activity on every sunny afternoon. Children splashed in the shallow end, mothers lolled in lounge chairs, eyes riveted on the water, ears tuned to the latest gossip. Late afternoons were spent preparing dinner so that everyone was back for "happy hour" by the pool as husbands arrived home.

Six months after moving to Southern California, all three Stanford MBA certificates were hanging in a suite in the newest high-rise in downtown Los Angeles. Ten years later, the Venture Capital Group would occupy the top six floors, as well as an entire ten-story building in Pasadena.

Several times during those early years, Georgia had asked Jeff about buying a house. He told her that when he had the time to look around and to study the real estate market, they'd consider the possibility. When she offered to do some of the initial legwork, he'd said that she should just concentrate on her duties, which were taking care of Mikey and keeping house.

Mikey was eighteen months old when her duties were expanded. Sonia Michelle Cates was born just a little less than a year after Jeff had convinced Georgia that having two children close to each other in age would be the most efficient way to raise the perfect family.

When the Jeff and Georgia Cates did finally become homeowners, it was in Creste Verde because Jeff had determined that here was the ideal combination of prestigious community and excellent school system. They bought the house in one day. Jeff had seen the for-sale-by-owner ad in the morning paper. He had been mildly interested, enticed by the low price. He told Georgia to drive out to look at it. If he had time during the day, he would do the same. She had spent a total of ten minutes touring the house with the owner. The elderly woman in blue jeans and a bandeau top, revealing a flabby and puckered midriff, carried a wad of tissues, blowing her nose and dabbing her eyes as she pointed out features of the house. She repeated over and over how she'd raised her family here and never wanted to live anywhere else. Georgia's inquiry as to why they were selling brought on more tears.

"It's my husband's idea," came the explanation in a voice muffled by the Kleenex. "He wants to move to a condo in the Valley to be nearer his mother. She's ninety-six." Sniffles and snorts.

Georgia thanked the woman for her time and drove to the offices of a local real estate agent. She made an appointment to come back the next day to look at other houses on the market then she rushed back to Santa Monica to pick up Mikey and Sonnie from the next door neighbor who had been watching them all morning.

Jeff called her in the early afternoon. He had gone out to Creste Verde at lunchtime, taking along one of his partners who had become the real estate expert of the firm. They both concluded that Jeff should grab this house before the old couple realized how underpriced it was. Georgia had expressed her doubts. The house was shabby, in dire need of new paint and paper, carpet and tile. She'd hated the monotonous color scheme. And she knew that buying a home and redecorating it were two completely separate financial functions. Convincing Jeff to buy new carpet or to paint or paper—they were not do-it-yourselfers—was a remote possibility. She also dreaded dealing with the pitiful owner.

Jeff rebuffed each of these concerns and told her to get a babysitter and meet him back in Creste Verde at six. They were going to make an offer. Georgia sighed as she hung up the phone. Gazing around the cramped apartment, a pile of toys and a playpen on one side of the tiny living room, a desk in a corner of the dining area, and stacks of books everywhere, she told herself that any house was better than this place. And Creste Verde was the right community. But did the third bedroom have a closet? And wasn't there some strange Rube Goldberg contraption for locking the front door? Was there a dishwasher? Did the family room have an outside entry? Was the pool heated? She couldn't answer any of those questions because her interest in the house had been minimal and she'd left as quickly as she could. She called Jeff late in the afternoon and told him how many questions she had about the house.

"We just can't afford your dream house right now," he'd said. "If we're going to get into the real estate market, we have to start small."

Small was one thing, but dreary and decrepit? Georgia wanted to express more doubts, but whatever she had to say would sound like a spoiled brat, so Jeff must be right again.

After a few moments of silence, Jeff had said, "Look, honey, you really have absolutely no concept of real estate costs. I've got lots to do before I can leave today, so let's finish this up."

"But maybe we should just look around some more before we put the offer in." There! She was holding her ground, but why did she always get that ache in her throat that made her voice sound so whiny?

Jeff replied, "Right. We'll just let a terrific deal get away while you look for some kind of mansion that we can't afford. Georgia, honey, this place is gonna get grabbed. The price is way below market, and they don't know what the hell they're doing. And if we don't move on it, someone else will." Final nail in the coffin. "You do want a house now, don't you?"

And all those questions that Georgia had were answered with bad news. The front door locked only after it had been shouldered shut from the inside, making it impossible to ever leave the house that way. The family room did have an outdoor entry, which was not good. That door would have to be locked at all times because it was one more way that the children could get to the pool, which was not heated. No dishwasher, the kitchen tile was terribly chipped, the stove was broken, and the dining room led to the kitchen only through the service porch. All this was pointed out by Georgia and dismissed, one by one, by Jeff as "no deal breaker."

For the umpteenth time she asked herself, *Why am I such a wimp?* And the answer was always the same. It was etched into her psyche like grooves in stone that had been formed by eons of tiny drips of water. *You already have more than you deserve, so shut up and be grateful for what you have.*

They moved in two weeks before Thanksgiving. After everything had been unpacked, pictures hung, books arranged on shelves and kitchen cabinets organized, Georgia had to face the fact that she was lonely. This was a town where children attended preschool from age three, and mothers went to meetings. Afternoons were spent driving children to lessons and workshops or orthodontist appointments, and there was certainly no such thing as a late-afternoon "happy hour."

The loneliness subsided within the first year. Mikey was attending nursery school five mornings a week, and a woman came to the house three days a week to sit for Sonia Michelle, who by now was called Sonnie. Georgia's mother, who had been pleased to be her granddaughter's namesake, was annoyed by the nickname, but then Sonia was usually more often annoyed than pleased.

Georgia had joined the Women's Club Juniors, the Philharmonic Auxiliary, and was an officer on the Church of the Good Shepherd nursery school board. She and Jeff entertained several times a month. The guest list usually included business associates and current and potential clients.

When Sonnie was three years old, Jeff told Georgia to start searching for a larger house. His business was flourishing, and his optimism was reflected in his impatience with the tight quarters they now occupied. She was to look in the most prestigious areas of town and not to even consider less than four bedrooms, four baths, formal living room, dining room, family room and an expansive entry. Jeff also needed another room for his home office, and a spacious deck near the pool and spa were a necessity for entertaining. A tennis court, circular driveway, gated entry and guest house were optional but preferred.

Georgia found a property with every requisite and every option except the tennis court, but there was plenty of space on the lot to build one. Jeff approved. They moved in and were settled for Mikey's fifth birthday. By the time Mike was in high school, Georgia had been a PTA president twice, had chaired dozens of benefits, and had established a reputation as an expert fund-raiser. She had indulged her creative talents by focusing on the Christmas holidays, constantly adding to her Santa Claus collection and planning elaborate decorating schemes. Mr. and Mrs. Jeffrey Cates hosted several philanthropic Christmas events, as well as their own holiday open house, which had grown from an invitation list of fifty the first year to 350 last year.

Georgia's life, she often told herself, was full to overflowing, replete with righteous satisfaction. She had set goals and achieved them. She was the adoring wife; the loving, consistent and affirming parent; the devoted daughter; the perfect hostess; the efficient fund-raiser; the successful business woman, and she played a respectable game of tennis. The good little girl had become the good little woman.

Deep inside her, in a tiny, secret part of her existence, were the embers of dark memories. Once in a while they flared, inflaming a paralyzing fear that could only be controlled with her lifelong ability to tamp them down again. She kept her brain full with more nonmalignant recollections of a little girl growing up as an army brat. There had to be as little space as possible for those few rogue brain cells that contained the awful truth to function.

After several writing courses, she began to chronicle those more benign memories, which had been embellished with scores of family photographs, as well as the typical verbal history that every child absorbs. And then, little by little, as her confidence in her writing abilities had flourished, she'd added some of the darker events. But she'd never taken any of those passages to writing class. No one ever saw them.

Carefully culling through those early recollections, designing a fictional façade, she blended what she allowed her mind to accept as fact with her cautious but vivid imagination. The beginnings of a novel evolved, which she titled *Alexandra*. She had never finished it, but printed out a draft, hid it away, and deleted everything from the software on her computer. Maybe, someday, she told herself, she'd finish it.

Chapter 10

1997

For some time, Georgia had been staring at the framed snapshot of Jeff holding her hand on the beach at Del Mar. She glanced at her watch and calculated that her family would begin to arrive in a few hours. Hurrying to the front door, she was relieved to see that Carlos's truck was still in the driveway. "Carlos! Can you do me a big favor?"

"Sure, Mrs. Cates."

"I need help getting some boxes out of the storage shed."

"So I think what does Mrs. Cates keep in there?" Carlos followed her to the far end of the backyard, beyond the pool house and tennis court. "I think it must be important stuff, all locked and connected to the security system."

"Many precious things, Carlos. Not worth a lot of money but very important to me." Georgia turned the combination lock and disengaged the alarm. Carlos hauled four large packing boxes, one at a time, and Georgia carried a half dozen smaller ones. He would not accept the twenty dollars that Georgia offered him, and she made a mental note to add that amount to his Christmas tip. After seeing him to the front door, she went throughout the house, turning off the ringer on every phone. Hurray for message machines; hers had a newly rewound tape. She pulled two folding card tables from a closet and set them up in the middle of the living room.

All of the boxes, except one, contained her Santa Claus collection, and as she unpacked them, she greeted each one like an old friend, carefully inspecting them for any damage or decay that might have developed during their year in hibernation, indulging her childlike fantasies, whispering and humming softly, floating off into her own magic Christmas world.

Each box was labeled. "Tiny Santas" were wrapped individually and packed in a hatbox. The largest in this category was less than an inch high. The smallest, one of the most expensive, was the size of a pea, a porcelain rendition of a lilliputian Saint Nick, leaning forward to balance the sack of toys flung over his shoulder. Only with a magnifying glass—Georgia would place one next to the tiny Santa—could every detail of his jolly, whiskered grin and the minuscule but perfectly wrought collection of toys in his sack be appreciated.

From other boxes came the Santa with a patchwork robe, stitched in Appalachia, and the Norwegian Saint Nicholas, dressed in green velvet with a beard of white fox fur. A magnificent Greek Santa, wearing a coat of gold threads and silk tassels, had been discovered in a secondhand store in San Pedro. Georgia had painstakingly snipped the stitches from one whole seam of his costume so that she could pull it off and have it dry cleaned. Then there was the leather-covered Native American Santa, crafted on a Zuni Reservation in New Mexico, and a roly-poly stuffed version in parachute fabric. Packed separately was one of the largest members of her collection. He was fashioned out of a full-sized wooden ironing board, the tapered end defining his red fur-trimmed hat.

Another box was marked "Antiques" because each was at least fifty years old. Her only reason for going on those antiquing expeditions that her friends organized was to search for Santas. She had found several prizes, like the quilted one from West Virginia, circa 1900, and the hammered tin sleigh with Santa in place, circa 1880. Probably her most ancient piece was a primitive wooden Saint Nicholas dragging an evergreen tree. On the underside of the trunk was carved, "By SLH 1825."

The front door slammed shut. Georgia hadn't even heard it open. Mike appeared in the glass-domed atrium that separated the living room from the entry. He dropped two duffel bags on the marble floor and plopped his laptop computer case on a leather and iron bench then strode into the room, bent over Georgia, and kissed the top of her head.

"Just in time for Santa duty," Mike said. "I've missed that. When was the last time I helped you unpack these?"

Georgia stood up and embraced her son then stretched on tiptoes to kiss him on both ears. She leaned back and looked up into the face that so resembled the old sepia-toned pictures of her own father as a young man. There was the sandy hair, the natural waves gelled in a retro-trendy style, the same cheekbones and the full mouth.

"It's been a long time since you wanted to help. Seems to me it became uncool about the sixth grade."

"Funny how what was uncool in junior high becomes another poignant memory in college." Mike picked up a rag doll Santa with a white yarn beard. "I remember this one," he said. "Will you make some popcorn?"

"Sure," she replied, already heading toward the kitchen.

They were sitting Indian style on the floor in the living room, munching on popcorn and sipping cans of Diet Coke, when they heard the kitchen door open. Sonnie called out, "Hey, family, I'm home! And I've got company with me!"

"You know," Mike said conspiratorially to his mother, "that's her way of warning us to act normal in front of her friends."

Georgia chuckled. "I'm never quite sure what her definition of normal is. I usually get it wrong."

Georgia and Mike waited for Sonnie to come into the living room, but she didn't appear. Instead, a moment later, she called from the kitchen, "Who made popcorn, and where is it?"

"We're in the living room," Mike yelled.

Sonnie came through the dining room, towing a tall young man wearing a faded flannel shirt and denim overalls. "Heeeere's Billy!" she announced, Ed McMahon style.

"Hi, Billy, and hi to you too," Georgia said as she hugged her daughter. Mike greeted Billy with a handshake and Sonnie with a slap on her rear. She swatted him back. Her long, honey-and-cinnamon-streaked hair, hanging well below her shoulders and parted in the current zigzag fashion, fell into her face. She flipped her head to get it out of her way, and Georgia once more—as she had often been lately—was stunned at the lovely, button-nosed, sloe-eyed young woman that her little girl had suddenly become.

Then, as she took in the scene, Sonnie observed, "The bewitching Santas have emerged from their crypts, I see, like a pack of red-coated vampires. Only instead of skulking through the night in search of the pulsing arteries of innocents to drink dry, they bound about from rooftop to rooftop, slithering down chimneys and sucking up milk and cookies."

"Sonnie loves to add her own twist—I mean twisted interpretation—to honored tradition," Mike explained to Billy.

"Actually, Mike," Georgia interjected, "Sonnie got sarcastic about our Christmas traditions at just about the same age you were when you began to find them uncool."

"I'm not sarcastic," insisted Sonnie. "I just don't see the need to change everything in the house just because of some silly, over commercialized holiday. Dad agrees with me. Like on Christmas morning, when Mom comes in and wakes me up."

She was speaking to Billy, who seemed to be studiously scrutinizing each and every Santa Claus. "These days, it's the adults who are up early and all excited about opening presents," she went on. "And what is the reason we have to drag our rears out of bed at some ungodly hour, you ask? Why can't we have opened our presents in the peaceful quiet of a lovely Christmas Eve?"

Georgia looked at Billy and rolled her eyes. He smiled back at her tentatively, unsure on which side of this precarious family fence he belonged. Mike pointed to his temple, indicating his assessment of his sister's mental health. Sonnie ignored them.

"When Mom was a kid, one year her parents decided to open presents on Christmas Eve, a much more civilized tradition, if you ask me. But Mom hated it, got all depressed on Christmas Day, and vowed that when she had her own family, they'd never, ever open presents on Christmas Eve again. And here we are, still paying for the traumas of the last generation."

From the time Georgia was eight, her mother and father, as well as Grandma Genya, had opened everything under the tree before they went to bed on Christmas Eve. She had told Sonnie and Mike how she believed it took the joy out of Christmas morning, but she had never described how agonizing it had been. She remembered, but that was not to share with her children.

**

When she'd awakened that Christmas dawn of 1955, for an instant the anticipation had hung in the air above her like a bubble that had been blown from a magic wand. She was safe and snug in a soft, warm bed in a pretty bedroom with pink polka dot curtains in a gray house with large white columns at the front door. But most important of all, the frightened child she had been the year before, the one who had been called Alexandra, had been left in Germany. She was Georgia now, and Georgia was safe.

And yet, simply acknowledging that she used to be Alexandra evoked the cold, sharp, threatening shards of memories. The beautiful bubble floated away. She crept out of bed, down the stairs, and into the living room. Gazing at the piles of torn paper and tangled ribbon, she'd suddenly understood that it didn't really matter what was wrapped in all the boxes, or how many presents there were, or whether they'd been chosen from her own Christmas wish list. It was the packages themselves that were important, like going to bed on Christmas Eve and listening for the sound of reindeer hooves on the roof. Without the magic that thrived on anticipation, she was lost and adrift again in a cold, black universe of adult reality. She promised herself when she grew up, when it was her choice to make, she'd never open presents on Christmas Eve again.

**

Georgia gave herself a mental nudge. Her son, obviously relishing the role of troublemaker, had moved on from the topic of opening presents on Christmas Eve to other family legends.

"What was that story of Christmas in Germany," he asked with a wicked grin, "when Mom was a kid? All about how she put one of her shoes on the windowsill every night for ten days before Christmas and found a present the next morning?" Mike shook his head in mock consternation. "I never understood why she told us all about that and then didn't let us do it too. It would have been cool."

"That's what I get for trying to share my childhood memories with my own children," Georgia countered dryly. "Other kids were satisfied with opening a window in an Advent calendar, but my two darlings concluded that I was a neglectful mother because I didn't add ten more presents for each of them to the dozens that were always under the tree on Christmas morning. Besides, you might recall that Dad put a stop to that by explaining that the American Santa Claus came to our house just once a year, and all the packages and toys were delivered, via the chimney, after we had gone to sleep late on Christmas Eve."

By now Billy was back to a studious contemplation of the minute details of each of the many Santas, obviously intent on keeping out of the line of fire as each Cates lobbed veiled but unequivocal jabs at each other. Mike was grinning, and Georgia knew her son was enjoying all this, especially when he got a rise out of Sonnie.

"Next," he continued, "comes how Sonnie and I trimmed the tree in the evening and Mom took it all down the next day and redecorated it, and then we came home from school and congratulated each other on what a good job we'd done."

"Enough," Sonnie said. "That's plenty of cute little Sonnie-and-Mikey stories. Come on, Billy, let's make some phone calls and see who's around."

"Just one more memory," Mike said. He was on a roll. Grinning and winking at Billy, he said, "Mom, remember the year Sonnie had the flu on Christmas morning, and while we were in the living room waiting for you and Dad to get up, she threw up all over the Christmas presents?"

"Oh, fine," Sonnie said. "Why don't you just get out my naked baby pictures?"

Billy was headed for the hallway. "I'll use the phone in the kitchen and see who's pulled into town."

Sonnie punched her brother in the shoulder and hurried after Billy. Mike put his arms around his mother and sang softly into her ear, "Why can't they be like we were, perfect in every way..."

Georgia laughed, pecked him on the cheek, and said, "Get out of here, oh perfect son of mine. You've caused enough trouble for now."

Mike grinned back. "I'll be back for dinner."

"That'll be about seven," Georgia called after him as the back door slammed. Moments later Sonnie and Billy passed by the living room. "We're going over to Craig's," Sonnie said. "A bunch of the kids are over there."

"Dinner is at seven," Georgia repeated.

"We'll see," came the reply just before the door slammed again and all the clamor and chatter evaporated into the welcome silence of the empty house. Georgia returned to her place on the living room floor. Only one unopened box remained, and she pulled the tape away gently, then lifted out the manuscript of her secret novel and a figurine wrapped in a faded brown velvet storage bag. This was the Santa that she had owned the longest of all. Lovingly she rubbed the lustrous porcelain surface with the velvet sack. He was about ten inches tall and wore the red robes and headpiece of the traditional German Saint Nicholas. She had been four years old that Christmas in Germany.

Alexandra

A novel by Georgia Kassov Cates

I SIT BESIDE MY LONELY FIRE
AND PRAY FOR WISDOM YET—
FOR CALMNESS TO REMEMBER
OR COURAGE TO FORGET

FROM "REMEMBER OR FORGET"
CHARLES HAMILTON AIIDE, 1830–1906

November 1949 –
Brooklyn Naval Yard

The blast of the ship's horn made her ears ache. Alexandra Georgia Kassov was four years old and three feet high. Her view was limited to shoes, coat hems and suitcases. She clutched the thick, furry sleeve of her mother's Persian lamb coat. It was black with an exaggerated collar and cuffs of buttery soft mink.

Sonia Kassov, carrying a large carpetbag as well as a purse and a briefcase, her little girl clinging to her right sleeve, was doing her best to move through the dense crowd on Dock #6 at the Brooklyn Naval Yard.

Sonia glanced over her shoulder. "Mama!" she called to a frail, elderly woman who was struggling to keep up with her. "Please stay close to us. I can't see you when you are behind me."

"I try! I try!" the woman wailed.

Alexandra kept tripping because Sonia was unable to maneuver them both between the dozens of piles of luggage. Grandma Genya, who had insisted on accompanying them to the gangplank, kept slowing down to catch her breath or to comment to a stranger about the noise, the cold wind or the confusion. Sonia had tried to say good-bye to her at the taxi, but Genya had begun to sob, and so the inevitable was postponed at the expense of Sonia's frayed nerves.

Finally they reached a platform where documents were being processed. Alexandra had managed to haul herself up the high step so as not to impede her mother's progress. Genya was not as successful. She stumbled and would have fallen if not for a teenaged boy with an athlete's reflexes who managed to throw his arms around the helpless woman, grasping her and holding on until she had regained her balance.

What was left of Sonia's patience dissolved as she watched her mother's near catastrophe. Alexandra could not keep hold of her mother's coat sleeve as bag and briefcase were dropped and Sonia pivoted around to face Genya. Speaking in Russian, she firmly announced that it was time to say good-bye.

"Alexandra, promise me! You make your mommy send me a telegram as soon as you arrive," pleaded the anguished old woman.

"Kiss your grandmother," Sonia commanded.

Alexandra tried to put her arms up to be embraced, but her head was grabbed and banged against the belt buckle of her grandma's coat as the woman frantically sobbed.

"My baby! My baby! How will I live without my beloved baby, Alexandra!"

"Enough, Mama!" said Sonia. And then, a bit softer, "I've told you over and over, we'll be away only two years or less. Not a lifetime. We'll send many pictures, I promise. And I'll wire you as soon as we get there. Now please, leave the dock. This place is bedlam."

Genya was sobbing again. Then Sonia got an idea. "Listen to me," she said. "If you go back up the stairs, you'll be able to see us on the deck of the ship. We'll look for you up there by the taxi stand."

Reluctantly Genya hugged the top of Alexandra's head again then grabbed Sonia around the shoulders, frantically kissing ears and coat collar. She let out one more agonizing wail as she allowed herself to be helped off the platform by the same boy who had saved her a few moments before.

Sonia called out to Genya, "It might take some time for us to get up on deck so be patient!"

Crying and blowing kisses, Genya backed away, immediately colliding with another elderly woman. Some divine combination of opposing forces kept them both upright.

Sonia, mercifully, had missed this latest of her mother's misadventures. She had turned to retrieve the passport and official military papers from her briefcase and then queued up behind a dozen other women, each with one or more children in tow.

When Alexandra and Sonia reached the front of the line, a uniformed army officer sitting at a metal table studied the passport. He was about the same age as Alexandra's daddy—in fact, he looked like his pictures. But then so did most of the men in uniform. This one smiled at Alexandra and stamped the passport and papers. Alexandra returned the smile.

"You have a beautiful mommy, little girl," he said. "I hope you both have a pleasant voyage. You can board now."

He handed the packet back to Sonia, who ignored his compliment as well as his good wishes.

Alexandra peered up the length of gangplank, trying to see past the boarding passengers, searching for the top of this funny staircase that had no steps. She and her mother began the ascent, moving slowly up the incline, part of a long line of women and children. Alexandra thought they would never get to the top. Unable to see over the canvas sides of the gangplank, she had no way to measure their progress. Sonia peered ahead, lost in her own thoughts, and the child stayed quiet.

At last they stepped onto the deck of the ship, once again presenting papers and passport to another man who looked like her daddy. He too compared the picture of daughter sitting on mother's lap to the woman and child who stood before him.

They really did not resemble each other at all. Sonia, a slim five-eight, had lustrous natural jet-black hair styled in a magazine-perfect pageboy. She had a flawless, creamy complexion covering a bone structure to rival Garbo's and astonishing eyes, turquoise blue, made even more striking by perfectly trimmed chrome-black bangs.

Alexandra, at four, was still baby plump, with light-brown corkscrew curls and hazel eyes, a muted package compared to the spectacular contrasts of her mother.

After a moment, the officer handed Sonia back her documents and waved them on.

Sonia let out a deep breath and smiled for the first time all day. "We're finally on our way. This is the happiest I've been since before Daddy left for Germany."

Alexandra wanted to know when they'd be able to wave to her grandma, but before she could finish the question, Sonia cut her off.

"Alexandra, just be still now. I have to find our stateroom. Stay close to me. No, don't hold my hand. It's too hard to carry all of this stuff if I have to hold on to you too."

Sonia asked a sailor to direct her to stateroom D41.

A moment's pause. "Oh yeah, you mean 'troops quarters,'" said the ensign, pointing to an opening. "Take the gangway inside there down four decks."

Dodging those who were coming up as well as those who were hurrying past them on the way down, they descended into the depths of the ship. Alexandra wanted to ask why they had to go down so far, but the clang of high heels and combat boots on metal stairs made it impossible to be heard.

Just a few feet from the bottom step was the door they were looking for.

"Well, that's convenient," breathed Sonia. "At least we don't have far to go once we get down here."

They crossed over the bulkhead that rose from the opening. The room stretched away for hundreds of feet, almost a quarter as long as the entire ship. It resembled a concert hall, but instead of seats, there were rows and rows of three-tiered bunk beds interspersed by scores of lockers. Off to one side were a dozen metal sinks next to showers with canvas shower curtains and toilets with canvas partitions.

The combination of the high-pitched voices of excited children, their mothers calling to them nervously, and the constant reverberations of slamming locker doors was deafening. Added to this was a tinny, flawed recording of the Andrew Sisters singing "My Blue Heaven" interspersed with equally ear-jolting announcements made over the scratching, squealing and popping loudspeaker.

Just about every adult, including the officials in uniform, was smoking. Permeating the murky haze was the earthy smell of canvas, the acrid odor of disinfectant and the inevitable aroma of hundreds of anxious humans occupying a closed space.

Alexandra peered around, wide-eyed, then looked up to see how her mother was reacting. Sonia stared ahead, shaking her head in disbelief.

This time it was a woman in a dark blue uniform who asked to see their papers. She had extremely short, straight hair.

"Report to that table over there," directed the WAVE, pointing to yet another line.

Sonia's face was very pale. Her hands trembled. The well-worn papers were stamped again, and each piece of luggage was marked "D41-108,109." Sonia was handed a new sheaf of papers by another WAVE.

"Read these," she said. "Important safety regulations."

She leaned over the table and looked down at Sonia's fashionable platform heels.

"You better have some sensible shoes with you." The thought was kind, but the tone of voice was not. "Follow the numbers on the foot of the bunks until you find the ones assigned to you. The suitcases that you checked through should be standing by your lockers… next!"

Sonia had not uttered a word since they had entered the room. Slowly she walked to the first set of bunks and then moved down the rows until she found 108 and 109, a bottom and middle bunk. She opened a nearby locker and, after hanging her fur coat on a hook, tried to push in the largest suitcase. It wouldn't fit. Silently she carried it back to the bottom bunk and was about to shove it underneath when a voice came over a loudspeaker.

"No luggage may be stored under bunks! Empty suitcases are to be delivered to area C!"

Alexandra could see her mommy begin to shake before she heard the sobs.

"What's the matter, Mommy?" She tried to pull her mother's hands from her face, but Sonia turned away, her head falling on the bare pillow at the head of the bunk.

Two women, putting their belongings in lockers nearby, exchanged meaningful looks, and a girl about twelve years old peered at Alexandra and proclaimed, "That little girl looks like Shirley Temple!"

Sonia looked up to see who had made this adroit observation about her daughter. Only Betty Grable's image was more universally recognized than Shirley Temple's. And indeed, Alexandra did resemble the child star. It was the soft brown hair, in a tumble of corkscrew curls, and the tiny, turned up nose.

Several months ago, Alexandra had won the Shirley Temple contest at Radio City Music Hall. Although the real Shirley was no longer the four-year-old of "Good Ship Lollipop," that image was still potent and hearkened back to a more peaceful, happy time. Alexandra had been singing the song for most of her young life, always happy to accommodate her parents' request to perform, and she hadn't been frightened by the imposing stage or the hundreds of people that filled that vast movie palace. Pleasing her mommy was the goal, and this was a golden opportunity. She belted out the lyrics, free of any self-doubt or shyness. The judges loved her.

Sonia had beamed for days, telling anyone who would listen what a special child was her Alexandra. Copies of the pictures taken by the press and of every newspaper that had reported the contest were kept in piles in her grandmother's apartment. A packet had been prepared and mailed to her daddy.

Even Christmas morning could not come near to achieving the bliss that had accompanied those heady days after the contest. In fact, the holidays had been a very confusing time for Alexandra. Her grandma Genya and her great-aunt Rya had prepared all of the special holiday dishes, and there had been magic anticipation when she was tucked in bed after they returned from midnight mass.

She'd dreamt that night of the glistening gold in the brocade of the priests' robes, the tinkle of the tiny timpani held by the acolytes, and the pungent incense. The true Russian Orthodox Christmas would not be celebrated for several weeks, but the conventional Christmas Eve mass had nevertheless mesmerized Alexandra.

In the morning, the small fir tree, bare the night before, had been transformed, adorned with all of the twinkle and sparkle she could imagine, and underneath were the toys and packages. She fell to her knees and began to explore all of the treasures that had been miraculously deposited under that enchanted tree.

Sonia sat nearby, tears streaming down her face. She'd been that way for days. How she missed her Michael, she would say. How she wished that they could skip Christmas this year. It was so painful to be apart from him at this time.

And so instead of diving into the delicious pile of presents, Alexandra went to Sonia, put her arms around her neck, and whispered, "Don't cry on Christmas, Mommy. You told me we were supposed to be very happy because the Christ Child was born."

"You're so right," whimpered Sonia. "I'll be right back."

Sonia went into the bathroom and reappeared several minutes later, her face freshly made up, her hair brushed and gleaming. She and Alexandra stood by the tree, careful not to stand in front of the packages that had arrived from Germany. Genya took their picture then Sonia's tears began anew.

Now, almost a year later, they were on their way to be with their daddy, and yet her mother, who just a few minutes before had been glowing with joy, sat weeping.

One of the women who had been watching them approached. She was older than Sonia, about the same height, but thick through the waist. Hair that once had probably been sunny blond was now streaked with dull gray and pulled back in a no-nonsense ponytail. Her face, devoid of makeup, was lined and splotchy, but her voice was gentle and sympathetic.

"You're havin' a tough time, huh?"

Sonia looked up then sat up and reached in her purse for a hanky to wipe her eyes.

"I can't believe we're going to live like this for six days," Sonia wailed. "Oh, I knew that we'd probably have to share staterooms, but this is unbelievable!"

"I guess it would be kind of a shock if no one prepared you," said the woman. "My old man told me in his last letter to get ready for some basic military bivouac on the way over. My name is Margaret Cavenaugh, and me and my kids take up bunks one-ten to one-fourteen. So I guess we'll get to all know each other real good before this trip is over."

She beckoned to two boys, about eight and ten.

"Joseph and Patrick, you're gonna take this lady's suitcases over to that table for her."

Joseph and Patrick, a matched set of red hair and freckles, bounded over and snatched up the bags.

"Hold on, hold on!" their mother said. "She hasn't emptied them all yet." The boys backed away, giggling and whispering and shoving each other self-consciously.

"This is very kind of you," gulped Sonia as she continued to unpack. Alexandra wanted to help, but as she began to pull clothes from a suitcase, Sonia said, "Leave everything alone, Alexandra. You'll just make it harder for me to keep things organized."

Alexandra backed away.

"Hi," said the girl who had compared her to Shirley Temple. "What's your name?" She'd placed her hands on her knees so that her face was on the same level as Alexandra's.

"Alexandra."

"Mine is Mary Katherine. I'm named after my grandmother."

No reply from Alexandra.

"How did you get your name?" Mary Katherine asked.

Alexandra put her right index finger in her mouth and enunciated around it. "My grandma Genya said I got 'Alexandra' 'cause that was my great-grandma's name and 'Georgia' because that's the part of Russia my daddy's mommy and daddy came from."

"So you're Russian," Mary Katherine said. "I'm Irish."

Sonia had been listening to the two girls as she emptied the remaining suitcase.

"Actually we're all Americans," Sonia clarified in a slightly shaky voice. She cleared her throat and then said, "The name Mary Katherine is of Irish heritage and Alexandra's ancestors were White Russians."

"What other colors of Russians are there?" Alexandra asked.

"None," Sonia replied. "It's just a way to say we're not Jewish."

"Why aren't we Jewish?"

"Because we're not," replied Sonia impatiently. Then with a quick glance at Mary Katherine and her mother, "We're Russian Orthodox, and now enough of your questions. Let me finish putting our things away."

Once again the loudspeaker crackled. "Departure is at oh-three-hundred hours."

"That's in five minutes," declared Margaret. "Come on, kids—topside, now!"

"See you later!" called Mary Katherine as she and her family bounded toward the bulkhead.

Sonia jammed the remaining items into their lockers, turned the keys, and grabbed Alexandra's hand to rush out and up to the main deck.

Emerging from the stairwell, Sonia immediately realized what a struggle it was going to be to get to the rail. Everyone had the same objective. She grabbed Alexandra's wrist and pulled her along, hurrying down the deck, looking for a break in the jam of people at the rail. Finally, spying a small opening, she pushed Alexandra in front of her, and when they squeezed into the spot, she lifted her daughter into her arms.

"Help me find Grandma," she said. "Up there, by that line of taxicabs."

Alexandra locked one arm around her mother's neck and peered over the rail. The dock was still crowded with people, waving and shouting and crying. Some held signs that read "Bon Voyage" and others just stood sadly, looking up to the main deck. A military band played "Anchors Away." She scanned the area where Grandma should be. Sure enough, there stood the woman, brown coat with black fur collar and brass belt buckle.

"Over there, Mommy!" shouted Alexandra, pointing up and to the right.

"Oh, I see her!" shouted Sonia. "Wave, Alexandra, wave!"

Alexandra swung her arm in a big arc, but Genya kept peering back and forth, sweeping her eyes across the deck but never focusing on them.

Alexandra called, "Grandma! Grandma! Here we are!"

Sonia didn't yell but also waved frantically.

The ship's powerful horns erupted again, and Alexandra could feel the vibrations as though the sounds had been produced in her own body.

Suddenly the dock seemed to back away from them. The band picked up the tempo, and people yelled and cried. Another mighty blast of horn, and then there was water between them and the dock, and Alexandra knew it was not the dock that was moving but the ship.

Sonia and Alexandra waved a while longer as the tugboats began their mission of herding the giant vessel out of the port.

"I'm afraid she can't find us," said Sonia, her voice breaking. Her tears had started again. "This is just too much. I can't even wave farewell to my own mother!"

"Don't cry, Mommy." Alexandra's throat ached, and tears filled her own eyes as well.

Sonia put Alexandra down on the deck and slowly turned toward the door to the stairs leading down to the miserable place where they would have to survive for the next six days. Alexandra followed.

Chapter 11

1998

Georgia sat up on her knees and stretched. She has been sitting Indian style in the middle of the living room floor, clutching the porcelain Santa for a very long time. *Enough of this*, Georgia told herself. Time to deal with the here and now. Within a few minutes, she had selected all the Santas that would be displayed this season. The rest were put back into their storage boxes and sealed up for another year. The pages of her manuscript were put away as well.

Half an hour later, Georgia heard the airport limo pull into the driveway. Jeff was home. He came in the front door and walked back to their bedroom. Georgia had been laying out the suit and accessories that she would wear to the Berg funeral the next morning.

"I want you to get the pearls out of the safe." That was his greeting.

"And hello to you too, dear," Georgia said.

"Hello." Jeff flipped his briefcase on the dresser and took his carry-on into his dressing room.

No kisses or embraces for me, Georgia thought. *I've been a bad little girl; I went to Vegas without permission. Well, so be it.* And if he could be obstinate, so could she, or at least she could have a go at it. She hadn't had much practice.

"Actually the pearls don't go that well with this," she said, indicating the gray cashmere Ungaro suit she had just hung on the edge of the closet door. "The buttons are too ornate to add pearls." She knew what was coming.

"Then wear another suit," he said.

"Why?" she asked with an innocent lilt.

"You know why," Jeff said, coming out of his dressing room in a terry robe. He walked into the bathroom and turned on the shower.

Georgia followed him. "I honestly don't understand what you mean." She sat down at the inlaid antique dressing table she'd had built into the marble counter.

"Don't give me that bullshit. I'm too tired to play cute little games with you right now." He stepped into the shower and shut the door. It banged with enough force to swing open again. He pushed it again, holding his hand against it until the latch caught. Georgia got up and went back into the bedroom, smiling like the cat that just ate the mocking bird.

The pearl necklace with the diamond and ruby clasp had been purchased on a trip to Hong Kong several years ago. Jeff had given it to her one evening just before they were to have dinner with a group of Chinese businessmen.

"Let those slants take a gander at these," he had said as he fastened the clasp behind her neck then gently rotated the pearls so that the gemmed clasp sat just below her collarbone. "Fifty thousand bucks, and every one of them will know to the yen what it's worth."

That was why she was to wear them to the funeral tomorrow, because most of those who attended would also appreciate what they were worth. That was important to Jeff. She put the cashmere suit back into its storage bag and pulled out a black wool crepe dress. The pearls would just barely peek out from under the matching coat.

The following Sunday, the Cates 1997 Christmas open house was due to begin at five. Now the porcelain Santa Claus occupied a place of honor at the center of the wide rosewood mantle that ran half the length of the fifty-foot-long living room. A dozen or so of the more elaborate Santas were also displayed here. Of the hundreds of items in Georgia's collection, less than a quarter had been unpacked this year. The remainder would spend this Christmas season off duty, tucked away in their storage boxes.

Usually the fifteen-foot-high noble fir that stood in the front window of the cathedral-ceiling living room held scores of unique baubles and hundreds of feet of wired silk ribbon, a different color every year. A second tree in the huge family room would be trimmed with nothing but hundreds of Santa ornaments. Not this year. Selected Santas adorned the tree in the living room, and a combination of ribbons from the past years of red, gold and purple themes turned the massive tree into an astounding, immense, brilliant jewel.

Maybe a few astute guests would notice that this year the effort at decorating had been reduced. Still, thought Georgia, the results were sufficient. Carlos, the gardener, had arranged dozens of red poinsettia plants at the front door, set on two tiers of plastic crates to create a banked effect. Georgia had assured him that she was completely satisfied with his efforts. The gigantic spruce wreath, delivered every first of December by Air Express from L.L. Bean in Maine, was decorated with one large, red velvet ribbon and a few springs of holly. The effect was simple and elegant.

Although the guests were not expected for hours yet, by noon Jeff was dressed in his newest Versace sport coat. He annoyed the caterers with dumb questions and harassed the bartenders, who were trying to set up the three bar locations. Jeff took this party very seriously.

Georgia came into the living room at four, dressed in white silk: a man-tailored shirt and slacks and a slim leather belt, also white, with a rhinestone buckle. Her poise de soir pumps twinkled with crystals. White sapphire earrings, three carats each, brought a symmetry to the sparkle, while glints of red and green shot from the ruby and emerald dinner ring worn on her right index finger. Although she was only five-foot-four, the monochrome outfit made her seem taller, and another few inches were added by her dark brown hair, streaked with subtle shades of gold, brushed up and back from her lovely, if slightly too round, face.

She had just completed the final inspection tour, checking every room in the house. Georgia was pleased with the understated effect she had achieved. This had been her first "recycling" Christmas, and by using less than half the number of ornaments that normally hung from the tree, the contrast of ribbon and green boughs was very dramatic. It also took half the time to achieve. Instead of the substantial hours—and dollars—she invested in her table decorations, this year she had bought varieties of fresh squash, small pumpkins and artichokes, and had Lena spray them all with gold paint. When the caterers arrived to set up the buffet tables, Georgia showed them the boxes of golden vegetables and told them to arrange them with their greens any way they wanted. The result was terrific.

Just before the guests were due to arrive, the Cates family gathered for a picture by the Christmas tree. Georgia knew that this was one of the few times that both of her children would be dressed somewhat close to her own standards. As it were, Georgia thought that Sonnie's red mini chemise resembled a slip more than a party dress, and Mike would have been so much more clean cut without all the gel in his hair, but all in all, they looked pretty sharp.

The family portrait was taken by Simon DuVol, professional photographer. Then, when the guests arrived, Simon would spend the rest of the evening snapping candids with a Polaroid. His assistant put each shot into a Christmas photo frame, and as Georgia's guests departed, they were presented with a souvenir of the evening.

"It's nostalgia time!" announced Sonnie as she came into the living room. Sonnie's boyfriend, Billy, sat down on a sofa at the far end of the room. It was obvious from the way he kept tugging on his sleeves that he preferred worn-out flannel shirts and jeans to his gray slacks and navy-blue sport coat.

Mike and his girlfriend, Krista Ferraro, had just come in the front door. They had started dating the fall of their senior year in high school, and both chose colleges in the Bay Area, just five miles apart. Krista was pixie petite with cropped, spiked copper-red hair. Only a twenty-year-old body like hers could get away with wearing that black spandex miniskirt and white organza blouse.

"It's time for another addition to the family album," Mike said, winking at Krista and squeezing her hand. Then he hooked his arm around his sister's waist and propelled her toward the Christmas tree. "Someday we'll both be grateful that our devoted mother insisted on these photo opportunities."

Sonnie scowled at him but allowed him to escort her to the tree. "At least," she said, "she doesn't use pictures of us for a Christmas card to send to their five thousand closest friends. That is so lame!"

Krista sat down next to Billy on the sofa. Both of them looked a little nervous. Dealing with the entire Cates family at the same time was never a leisurely experience.

"Let's get this over with," said Jeff, who had also come into the room. He looked at himself in the mirror over the mantel, smoothing razor cut Beach Boy-blond hair behind his ear. "Let's get a move on. I need to be at the door when the guests start arriving. Are you ready yet, Simon?"

"Just about, sir," replied Simon.

Sonnie stood with her arms crossed in front of her, a world-weary, tremendously put-upon expression on her pretty face. As Jeff joined the group by the tree, he said to Sonnie, "Come on, princess, at least try to look like you are happy to be with your family at Christmastime."

"Sure, sure," Sonnie said in a resigned tone. Then to Simon, "You must so be getting a major dose of déjà vu. You've been photographing our Christmas party for as long as I can remember. Do you ever cease to be amazed at the consistent dynamics of this so yuppier-than-thou family? The wife is always dressed in white, serene and beautiful. The husband always checks his perfectly styled hair in the mirror and tells you to hurry up. The son is always so lovingly tolerant of his mother's wishes, and the daughter…that would be me…always makes caustic remarks about holiday traditions." Simon grinned silently as he affixed his camera to the tripod.

Twenty minutes later, the photographic equipment had been removed from the living room, and Georgia told the caterers to put out the hot food. Three young men, wearing short red jackets and bright green bow ties, waited in the circular driveway to park cars. Sonnie and Billy, Mike and Krista were inaugurating the bar on the tented deck.

Jeff stood by Georgia at the front door, greeting the early arrivals. By six, the house was filled to overflowing. It seemed everyone always dropped in at the beginning of a Cates Christmas affair, and few left until well into the evening. In Creste Verde, on the second Sunday in December, this was the place to be.

When Jeff's animation and charm went into overdrive, Georgia knew that Jim Fields had arrived. Jim was the chief rainmaker of Jeff's firm, the Venture Capital Group, and he was bringing a guest this evening who could be a possible major profit-making weather front all by herself. Jeff was anxious to offer her his utmost holiday hospitality.

Fran Fields had been a professional tennis player in her younger days, and she still dressed as though all social events were merely the rest breaks between important tennis matches. Her off-white wool pantsuit with the Wimbledon logo on the jacket reminded everyone that once Fran Huntley Fields had played in that most prestigious of all tournaments. The fact that she'd lost in the first round was not often discussed. She'd been there, and, as she pointed out to anyone who became ensnared in her repeated reminiscences, that was what counted.

After the prerequisite air kisses from Fran and the spine adjustment that Jim provided along with his hug, Georgia turned to greet their next guest.

"Melanie Nallis," Jim announced.

"We've met before," Melanie said softly.

"Of course," Georgia said, recognizing the mysterious woman she'd tried to chat with in the Mirage poker room.

"Melanie, welcome to our home," Jeff pronounced with more than enough savior faire. Melanie was close to six feet, with that combination of slimness, muscle tone and full breasts that most women would gladly exchange their entire heritage for. Her thick platinum hair swept over her forehead and then was caught behind her right ear. But it was the eyes, a combination of gold and silver flecks, like precious ore radiating with metallic glints, which catapulted her out of the ranks of even the most beautiful and into a realm of her own. Again Georgia was astonished at how truly amazingly gorgeous this woman was, albeit a bit over the top by Creste Verde standards. This time she wore a waist-cinching dark green raw silk suit, strands of emerald crystals that reached from earlobes to shoulders, and a pair of Hermès four-inch heels with a purse to match that Georgia knew had a combined cost of at least six or seven thousand dollars.

Jim Fields was talking again. "Melanie has some funds to invest, and I'm doing my best to convince her that our little firm can help her find just the right vehicle, probably something in Vegas; seems this pretty lady wants to get into the gaming business."

Melanie's voice was subdued and throaty, and its effect on the men was obvious. "Thank you both for including me," she said to Georgia and Jeff.

Georgia extended her hand. "Welcome," she said simply. "It's nice to see you again. How did you do in your first poker game?"

Jeff spoke up before Melanie could reply. "Enough front door small talk. The next order of business, and the most relevant, I might add, absolutely must be conducted in the presence of a bartender." He gestured toward the other end of the living room.

"I hope we'll have a chance to talk later," Georgia said to Melanie, rolling her eyes in mock annoyance.

"I'd like that," Melanie called back as Jeff guided her into the living room.

Georgia turned to hug her business partner, Andrea Gleason, who had arrived with her fiancé, Eric Solomon. Andrea and Eric looked like unisex twins. Both were dressed in black slacks and red silk shirts that looked perfect on their tall, tanned and angular bodies. Their curly black hair was worn at about the same length, just above the ear. They even had matching gold hoop earrings.

"Welcome," said Georgia, squeezing Eric's hand with both of her own. "I'm really glad you could come. My guess is that Andrea has had very little time for socializing these last several weeks. And I assume all is well since I haven't had any complaints from our clients."

"That's probably because I never give out your phone number," said Andrea, planting an affectionate kiss on Georgia's cheek. Eric placed a gift wrapped bottle of champagne on a marble table already laden with a wide variety of packages and bottles deposited by other guests.

Andrea and Georgia had known each other for several years before they formed Cates, Gleason et Cie. Georgia got credit for the original idea, but the success of the company was due to the perfect combination of talent, brains and savvy that had been generated when the two women pooled their resources.

Andrea had an established catering business with seventy employees capable of simultaneously handling weddings, benefits, dinners for eight and conventions for thousands. Georgia, in her capacity as chairwoman of numerous philanthropic events, had worked with Andrea many times. Andrea had immediately recognized the potential in what Georgia had proposed. They would combine catering with a complete package of fund-raising services and offer nonprofit organizations, as well as other businesses, the opportunity of generating money to serve their community and gaining invaluable public relations in the process, not to mention getting the most banquet for their buck.

Georgia did the research and put together a package that offered everything from preplanning, budgeting and creative ideas for unique events to insurance, permits, publicity and financial management. She worked out a simple but efficient strategy. For example, if the Do-gooders Hospital Auxiliary needed $250,000 to fund a renovation of the neonatal parents' lounge, they could hire Cates, Gleason et Cie. A deposit of $100,000 would net them a profit of $270,000. Georgia and Andrea would use the seed money to fund the event, which included cost of location, all catering needs, publicity, ticket sales and every aspect of managing the entire affair. Tickets would be priced at four hundred dollars per person, and five hundred guests would attend, plus another five hundred who would send patron donations, and dozens of ads would be sold to publish in the program.

Cates, Gleason et Cie retained 10 percent of the gross, not including the original seed money. Five hundred tickets would yield

$200,000, and donations and program ads would bring in another $100,000. Ten percent of $300,000 would be Georgia and Andrea's fee.

Both Georgia and Andrea had established reputations that proved to be exactly what was needed to convince organizations to invest in their services. Hard work, meticulous planning and a fair share of good luck provided success from the very first project, and the business had blossomed and expanded. Now Georgia had two assistants and a clerical staff of four, and Andrea's catering division employed a total of one hundred. Much was saved in expenses by keeping almost every aspect "in house." Within the last two years, they had added their own equipment rental division and a desktop publishing service, as well as a full-time florist and decoration designer.

When Eric and Andrea returned from hanging up their leather jackets, Georgia said, "There are bars in the living room, billiard room and on the deck. Go forth and imbibe."

"If you insist," said Andrea, grinning. "But I hope you'll have some time after this gala feast and jubilee to come into the office, not that there are any crises. I just miss you."

Eric added, "Andrea is like the Maytag repairman. You got all of the clients so organized there isn't much for her to do except sit around the office waiting for the phone to ring."

Georgia laughed. "That's a bit of an exaggeration."

"I'll say," Andrea concurred. "But those two assistants of yours really are a whiz with the clients. They get a straight A in hand-holding, troubleshooting and even psychotherapy. You've got them trained better than Seeing Eye dogs."

"I'll take that as a vote of confidence," said Georgia.

"But I really would like to talk shop with you sometime soon."

"The first of next week, I promise. Now go join the festivities. Remember, you're on a busman's holiday. Just enjoy yourself and stay out of the kitchen. Herald, your number one party manager, is on the scene, so you can relax."

Finally, with most of her guests having already arrived, Georgia recruited one of the catering assistants to stay at the front door and direct latecomers toward the coatroom and the bars. Now she could circulate. But first she slipped into the hall and hurried back to her bedroom. She'd kissed at least two hundred people in the last hour, and she was in need of some cosmetic damage control. As she sat in front of the mirror, reapplying lip liner and lipstick, she studied her hair and decided that the next time she went to Vegas she would go to the Mirage hair salon and have a lot more blond highlights added, especially in the front. The way her hair was right now was on the brink of matronly. "Not yet," she said to her image in the mirror. "I'm not ready for 'matronly.' Not quite yet."

Alexandra
A novel by Georgia Kassov Cates

November 1949

Within twenty-four hours at sea, mother and daughter both developed "sea legs" and were spared the agony and indignities of seasickness. Sonia had read all of the regulations, which included mess hall schedules. Breakfast: 0700:05 hours. Lunch: 1100:35 hours. Dinner: 1700:35 hours. Eating dinner at 5:35 in the afternoon made for a very long evening. Movies helped, and many women whiled away the time by doing each other's hair and nails. Sonia found fellow bridge players.

During the day, recreation was offered in the form of escorted group walks around the main deck, card games in the game room, and use of the ship's library (although it seemed to have a preponderance of male-oriented literature). "Briefings," as the army referred to the attempt to prepare these women for life in an occupied foreign land, were scheduled there for late mornings. It had been determined that these wives and mothers needed only the most basic explanation about the sociological situation and the political climate in Germany, so most of the lectures were about what could be expected in the way of shopping and homemaking needs, schools and medical services.

Some thought had gone into providing amusement for the children. Appropriate movies were shown almost nonstop, morning and afternoon. One rec room had been outfitted as a play area with wooden blocks and crafts and games. There was a nursery as well, for babies to eighteen months.

Life in D-41 was tolerable, if not comfortable. Mercifully, not every bunk was occupied. A group of fifty-five mothers and 135 children shared a facility capable of sleeping three hundred soldiers. The unoccupied bunks became the living room furniture, where groups gathered to chat or play.

And so Sonia and Alexandra Kassov became citizens of the seagoing village of D-41, an odd community comprised of mothers and their offspring. Alexandra spent much time observing the boys. She'd had very little exposure to males of any age, having lived a large portion of her first four years with her mother and grandma as well as Aunt Rya and Cousin Irina.

Mary Katherine was Alexandra's constant companion, mothering her, enjoying the senior status of an almost-teenager. Sonia never objected to this arrangement and spent hours sitting at a card table in the recreation room. She had been delighted to find that almost all of the women who knew how to play bridge were officers' wives. Sonia had no trouble chatting with them, discussing such relevant topics as what kind of facilities were available at the officers' clubs at the German military bases or how they would be able to travel throughout free Europe.

Mingling with the wives of the noncoms and GIs was another matter. It was unusual within the military for wives of officers to have such ongoing interaction with the wives of their husbands' subordinates. It was not that she disliked any of them but that they had nothing in common. Of course she was grateful for Margaret's kindness, but still she considered the woman crude and overbearing. When Sonia and her mother had sailed to Europe in 1938, they'd had a stateroom in tourist class. On the return voyage, the immigrants had been in steerage, which must have been something like D-41.

Margaret kept a keen eye on the girls, and Alexandra enjoyed becoming an adopted member of the Cavenaugh clan, although it was obvious that Joseph and Patrick merely tolerated her. Mary Katherine assured her that all boys acted as dumb as her brothers, and ignoring them was the best thing to do. Whatever the older girl told her Alexandra took as gospel. She dismissed the taunting and teasing because she was protected by her patron saint, Mary Katherine.

Mary Katherine's mother, however, was a puzzle to Alexandra. One moment Margaret was gruffly ordering the boys to desist from some annoying activity, and later she would take them, one at a time, onto her lap and speak quietly with them, nuzzling their ears and stroking their hair. Even well-behaved, responsible and mature Mary Katherine got a turn at being cuddled and caressed by her mother.

At dinner on the third night out of port, Alexandra sat contentedly next to Mary Katherine as the mothers at the table discussed their reactions to the voyage so far. Sonia had already voiced her disapproval of the traveling accommodations, and a few of the others had mildly, almost apologetically, concurred.

Captain Hillary Kincaid, thirty-six, single and a career officer, sat at the head of the dining table. She was one of the liaisons to the families aboard the *Utah*, and this was not turning out to be her favorite assignment. She had little in common with these wives and kids, but she would do the best she could to make them as comfortable as possible and to prepare them for life in Germany.

Captain Kincaid cleared her throat and spoke loud enough to be heard at the other end of the table.

"Did you know," she began, "that besides D-forty-one, there are five more troops' quarters, three decks' worth, on this ship?" She smiled tentatively, pleased that everyone had looked up at her.

"There are a total of three hundred and eleven women—only twenty-one of whom are childless—and seven hundred and twenty-one children, ranging in age from six months to seventeen years. And as you know, all of you have the honor of being among the very first group of dependents to join the troops in Germany."

She waited for remarks or questions. There were none, so she went on.

"But this is hardly a passenger liner, as you all well know," she said. "It's a troopship, and the task of transporting families on it is a new one for the military and, to be honest, only a secondary function."

"We're more than aware of that," Sonia said.

"Let me try to explain," Captain Kincaid continued. "You see, most of the men aboard are a part of the Fifteenth Battalion. They're on their way to Frankfurt to replace the Twenty-Second Battalion, which is ready to rotate stateside. They've been there since before D-day."

"So have some of our husbands," Margaret said.

"That's true," Captain Kincaid replied. "But your men volunteered to take another overseas assignment, and bringing you to Germany was one of the provisions that the army offered them to encourage them to stay."

"That's right," Margaret agreed. "My Jack figures he's learned his way around, understands some of the language, and might as well help out over there some more. Besides that, when would his family ever get another chance to live in a foreign country? He believes this kind of thing is good for kids—teaches them about life."

Another woman sitting next to Sonia spoke. "I'm not sure I understand this whole 'occupation' thing. What are American soldiers supposed to do over there now? The fighting is over."

Captain Kincaid remembered, almost to the word, the lecture given by the major in charge of personnel readiness during the two-week course at Fort Belvoir. Now she'd have to translate, exchanging military jargon for words that these women from all over the United States would understand.

"More than two years ago, the German people were liberated from Hitler but not from hell," she began. "The Germans who survived, and the thousands of refugees who fled from the unbelievable devastation all over Eastern Europe, are now trapped in a ruined land, barren and cratered." She paused. "Like the moon.

"You see, Hitler's 'scorched earth' policy was horribly effective. He decreed that nothing should remain for those who would survive the war because the best of the population, the Aryan elite, as he called them, would be annihilated in the conquest. The Allies should find nothing to redeem for their military victory."

"Enter the Americans!" proclaimed a young mother as she spoon-fed her baby boy. "Now our guys are supposed to watch over what's left of a pathetic country in need of total restoration and try to help out a nation that, just two years ago, was willing to kill as much of the population of the world as Hitler told them to."

"The fact is," Margaret Cavenaugh interjected, "that whether we agree or not, our men are going to stay in Germany. We might as well make the most of it."

Sonia joined in. "Most certainly! I understand that there will be a chance to collect porcelain, silver, jewelry, all sorts of treasures, for close to nothing."

The young woman who had been feeding her son gave Sonia a frosty look. "I'm from Ohio," she said, wiping her baby's face with a napkin, "a little town outside of Sandusky. We lost twenty-eight men and two women in the war, including my brother-in-law, my best friend's husband, and the guy I went to the senior prom with. It was hard to talk to my friends and family, in fact to anybody in town, about going over and living in the country and with the people who had just been on the other side of the trenches. I just kept saying that the most important thing to me is that I could be with Bill again and that little Billy would not have to turn two without ever having seen his daddy."

"Well, we might as well help them Germans out as long as we gotta be there anyway," Margaret said. "My Jack says in his letters that the place is a mess, the people are all sick and starving, and there's no government to get them back on their feet. It's gotta be done. The Americans might as well do it. Somebody has to."

On the fourth late afternoon at sea, Sonia and her new bridge friend, Candy Thurston, trailed behind the other women as footsteps and words ricocheted off the metal floor, ceiling and walls of the gangway leading away from the game room. They were returning to D-41 after a three-hour bridge session, where Sonia and Candy had handily beaten two full colonels' wives. Between hands, everyone had been buzzing about the rumored clandestine parties on the troop decks.

Sonia spoke to Candy in a low, confidential voice. "I am utterly in love with and absolutely devoted to Michael," she said. "But what could be the harm in having a beer and a dance with another man, or several men, particularly in a sociable setting?"

"Only getting your husband demoted," Candy replied sarcastically. "I've heard that's what happens to some men when their wives are found to be fraternizing and encouraging insubordination among the ranks. But then again, maybe the challenge of a little exhilarating adventure at sea is worth the gamble. Who's to say?"

"What do you mean?" Sonia asked. She'd slowed down her pace so that the rest of the women had walked beyond earshot.

"Anything you want it to, sweetie," Candy replied. "You're not going to get any advice on this matter from the likes of me." She grinned mischievously at Sonia as they stepped over the bulkhead into D-41 then she turned and walked off toward her own bunk.

Alexandra was still watching a movie with the Cavenaugh kids, so Sonia went off to shower in one of the inelegant canvas-enclosed stalls. Dried off and wrapped in a chenille housecoat, she peered into the tiny mirror hung on the inside of her locker door. Sonia smiled at her reflection as she brushed out her long, dark hair.

She continued to stare at herself for some time, widening her eyes, observing her face from different angles. She reached for the new bottle of Shalimar, which she had planned to open when they docked in Bremerhaven—the only perfume she'd packed because she would buy plenty more when they traveled to Paris. She opened it and put a drop behind each ear and between her breasts.

When Alexandra returned from the movies, she was listless and subdued, ate very little of her dinner, and put up no resistance when she was tucked in bed ahead of schedule. She was fast asleep when her mother slipped away. Several youngsters had been coughing and running fevers from the time the ship had sailed. On this night, a little over seventy-two hours into the voyage, many of the children of D-41 were very restless and cranky. They awoke crying, and mothers found it difficult to get them to calm down.

Alexandra was wrenched from sleep by a sharp pain in her stomach. As she lay there, she tried to find the place where her headache stopped and her tummy ache began. Her pajamas were clammy with sweat. She called out to Sonia. No one answered. Tears trickled out of the corners of her eyes, but her sobs were subdued because her throat was very sore. She tried to call out again, but when she took a deep breath, it produced spasms of hoarse, resonating coughs.

Someone sat down next to her and brushed back her damp hair.

"Jesus, Mary and Joseph! You're burning up, child!"

Her covers were pulled away, and strong arms lifted her up. She recognized the scent of Noxema.

"I want my mommy," whispered Alexandra.

"Mommy will be back very soon, darlin'. Meanwhile I'll stay here with you." Margaret Cavenaugh, cradling Alexandra, sat down on the bunk and leaned back against the pillow.

Alexandra sensed that it was very late, and yet there was a great deal of activity. A woman who was holding a redheaded baby girl walked by the bunk and spotted Alexandra curled up in Margaret's full, fleshy arms.

"Her mother off with the others?" the woman asked.

Margaret put a finger to her lips and nodded.

Alexandra must have dozed because suddenly she was being pulled from her warm, soft nestling place. The smell of beer, cigarettes and perfume filled her nostrils, and now her tummy hurt even more. The cold air made her shiver, and she struggled to find a way to rest her sore head and neck.

Sonia was talking as she placed Alexandra back on her bunk.

"Do you really think I should take her to the dispensary now? You can't get there without going out on deck, and it's so cold and windy. Shouldn't I wait until morning and see how she is?"

Margaret's voice: "No! You can't wait till morning! That's why Alice Rubio went to find you. The child is deathly sick. Here, wrap her in this blanket and get going."

Alexandra was cocooned in a khaki wool army blanket, lifted up, and carried out of D-41, up one flight of stairs, out on deck and then around the corner and into a long metal corridor whose walls clanged in time with Sonia's footsteps. Then they were in a room full of bright light with the smell that meant shots! Alexandra began to whimper hoarsely, feeling strangely weak.

Another voice: "We'll get to her just as soon as we can. Take a seat over there. What was the name? Kassov? Spell it." A young man dressed all in white was writing on a tablet.

Her mother's voice: "K-a-s-s-o-v. My husband is a major. How long do you think it will be?"

"Hard to say."

An hour later, Sonia tried for the fourth time to find out when the doctor would finally get around to Alexandra. The orderly tried to ignore her, but Sonia persisted, asking to speak to the officer in charge. An army nurse with captain's bars was called over. She informed Sonia that all of the children were in need of medical attention, and their fathers' ranks had no influence here. She did look intently at Alexandra, who gazed back sleepily. Then the captain walked away.

Sonia shifted about on the metal bench, trying to find a comfortable position. Her thoughts drifted back up the several flights of decks, where women shared swigs of beer and drags on cigarettes with libidinous young soldiers and danced to a barely audible Bing Crosby rendition of "Deep Purple," playfully wrestling with wandering hands and mouths. Yes, Sonia had enjoyed herself. Her dance partner was better behaved than most, and the two of them had put on an exhibition, circling the metal floor, spinning and dipping. Everyone had stopped to watch them, and she had spotted Candy Thurston, who was looking at her with open admiration and approval. Perhaps if Alexandra perked up, Sonia could go back there tomorrow night.

Light was filtering through the porthole when the orderly called Alexandra's name. Right there on a gurney in the waiting room, a doctor listened to her heart, looked in her eyes, ears and nose, felt her neck and under her arms, and pushed on her tummy. Then he moved to the next gurney. Sonia was at his side instantly.

"Well, how is she? How sick is she?" demanded Sonia.

The doctor began to examine a young boy who was breathing in short, tortured gasps. "Right now it's probably the flu. You better pray to whoever you pray to that's all it is."

The nurse who was attending to Alexandra motioned to Sonia.

"Okay, listen up," the nurse said. "Until we see signs of breathing difficulties or a lapse in consciousness, we'll assume your daughter has influenza. Take her back to your quarters, wipe her down with cool, wet towels, and make her drink lots of fluids." She pulled a small bottle out of her pocket. "Give her one of these sulfur pills, crushed in a teaspoon of sugar, every four hours."

Back in D-41, mothers took turns watching over each other's children so that some could snatch a few hours of sleep. Worry and fear were etched on the faces of all those able to comprehend the enormity of the threat. They were still three days from Bremerhaven.

Twenty-six confirmed cases of viral pneumonia had turned the voyage into a nightmare. The most critically ill were placed in the ten oxygen tents in the ship's infirmary. Others were helped to breathe with pumps that were manipulated by nurses, orderlies and mothers. Even some of the troops were called in to help. The elicit late-night parties came to an abrupt halt.

Then more devastating news. One of the giant turbines that powered the *SS Utah* malfunctioned and had to be shut down. This decreased the ship's speed by almost half. They wouldn't reach Bremerhaven for another six days.

Misery preceded tragedy. Two children in the oxygen tents, one girl and one boy, could not be saved.

Alexandra slept on and off, having lost all sense of day and night. Often she would awaken to find Mary Katherine sitting at the foot of her bunk. Although the older girl had been spared of any infection, her two brothers had become as sick as Alexandra.

Sonia would often fall so sound asleep that Margaret had to reach into the upper bunk and shake her, and even then she would awaken reluctantly, mumbling that sleep was the only escape from this miserable situation. She'd climb down and go through the motions of caring for Alexandra: helping her to the bathroom, bathing her with a cool cloth, feeding her broth and ginger ale, sitting and patting her aimlessly and muttering just loud enough for Alexandra to hear.

"How could this have happened to us? Why are we being punished? Wasn't it enough that I had to live through the war without Michael?"

After two days, Alexandra's head began to clear. Her body didn't ache so much now, and she was awake for longer periods of time, always grateful to have someone nearby. Her appetite began to return, and she asked for something besides juice, broth and crackers.

"That's all they ever deliver to D-forty-one," Sonia complained. "I guess I'll have to bring you back some cereal and fruit when I go to breakfast. No one cares if you get a decent meal around here. Thank goodness your mommy is here to take care of you."

On the sixth day at sea, Alexandra felt well enough to get out of bed and put on a shirt, overalls, shoes and socks. She had strict orders to stay very near her bunk. Mary Katherine tried to involve Joseph, Patrick and Alexandra in a game that would occupy them all at once. Margaret was scrubbing underwear at one of the sinks, and Sonia had gone off in search of a bridge game.

Captain Kinkaid had been nervously hovering over her brood since the crisis began. Although her nursing skills were nonexistent and she found no maternal instinct to guide her, she cared, and that kept her scurrying between bunk beds, wringing her hands a lot.

Finally all those who had only the flu began feeling better. She reported that the pneumonia victims were in the infirmary, a total of thirty-one, not counting the two who had died. Ambulances, doctors and nurses would be waiting at the dock in Bremerhaven to transport them to the huge army hospital in Berlin. Fathers had been notified and would be given leave to stay with their sick children when they arrived in port.

That last late afternoon on the open ocean, Alexandra knelt on the floor between two bunks playing with her doll when Candy Thurston walked over to chat with Sonia. Sitting cross-legged on an empty bunk, Candy lit a cigarette and offered one to Sonia, who sat down across from her.

"I can't stop thinking about those poor kids who are still really sick," Candy said, reaching for a metal ashtray from the bedside stand.

"Thank God this voyage on the sea of hell is almost over," Sonia said, exhaling smoke like an exclamation point.

"I can't even imagine what it must be like for the women whose children died." Candy shuddered. "You know, they were each given an officer's cabin for privacy."

"I know," Sonia sighed. "Maybe all of this misery and sickness could have been avoided if better accommodations had been provided for everyone."

"Well, this ship is what it is, a troopship, not an ocean liner. But the fact is that there was just no way to increase the ship's speed," Candy said. "Those poor, wretched women. The unthinkable happened, and they've had all these long, horrid days to wait until they can reach Germany, so they can be flown back to the US with their husbands to bury their babies."

Alexandra looked up at her mother and asked, "Why are they going to bury the babies?"

Sonia shook her head, patting Alexandra on top of the head. "Alexandra, this conversation does not include you. Why don't you go see what Mary Katherine is doing?"

"Mary Katherine said she had to help her mommy."

"I'm sorry," Candy said. "I shouldn't be talking about this in front of the child."

"It's okay," Sonia said. "She doesn't understand anyway." Then to Alexandra, "You know better than to interrupt. Why don't you see if there's another page you can color in your coloring book?" She stubbed out her cigarette and went on talking to Candy.

"I know we're supposed to feel terrible about all this, and I do. But I have to tell you that I'm also so incredibly relieved to finally be docking in Bremerhaven and escaping from all this disgusting depression."

"You're right," Candy agreed. "We should be very grateful."

"Never mind being grateful," Sonia said loudly so that other women nearby could hear. "As far as I'm concerned, the US Army as well as the US Navy, in fact the entire United States government, owes us each a profound apology, and I think we should demand it."

Chapter 12

December 1998

Bladder emptied, makeup refreshed, head cleared, Georgia opened her bedroom door and started back toward the party. But she wasn't in any hurry; in fact, the exhilaration that she usually experienced when entertaining on this scale was missing. She'd be glad when everyone went home.

The Mirage poker room—that's where she really wished she was right now. She had to face it. Georgia Kassov Cates of Creste Verde, California, had a major case of the "Been There, Done That" syndrome. Georgia Cates, the Vegas fifteen-thirty stud player was who she wanted to be.

As she came into the living room, Jeff motioned her over to a group standing by the fireplace.

"Well, here's our gorgeous hostess," said Jim Fields, circling her waist with his arm while the drink he held sloshed out of the glass and onto Georgia. He didn't notice.

Fran Fields proclaimed, "I was just telling Jeff how much you amaze me, Georgia. I simply can't imagine how you accomplish all that you do with such panache. Not only is your house utterly exquisite, but your holiday decor should really be photographed and written up in *Vanity Fair* or *Town and Country*. And then there's this incredibly fabulous party. I just don't know how you do it all, and run your business, and still stay involved with all of your volunteer work. You know, you really do put the rest of us to shame."

Melanie Nallis, who was standing next to Fran, caught Georgia's eye. They exchanged amused smiles. Fran took a sip from her glass of scotch then called out to a woman who stood in a group of people nearby, "Gloria! Come over here and back me up. I say that our hostess is just too good at everything she does. I think we should drum her out of the corps."

Gloria Marangi, dressed in Christmas plaid Pendleton, stepped over and pecked Jim Fields on the cheek. "Merry Christmas," she said as she gave Fran an abbreviated hug. Then, with a smile and a wink to Georgia, "You'd better be careful, Madam I-finished-my-Christmas-shopping-before-Thanksgiving. We don't take kindly to your type around here."

"Worse yet," Fran added, "when she's not consulting on charity events, or sitting on the board of The Children's Guild, or redecorating this palace, she's off to Vegas. I just don't know how she does it all."

Georgia saw a little muscle in Jeff's cheek begin to pulse, but before she could respond to Fran's and Gloria's teasing, Gloria's husband, Howard, joined in. "We all know what our Georgia does in Vegas," he said. "She fishes for card sharks, and when she gets one on her hook, she reels him in like a pro." Then to Georgia, "Larry Turnbull told me he saw you at the Mirage once and watched you play for a few minutes. He says you're way out of our league; that you play with the big boys."

"My wife's getting quite the reputation," Jeff commented blandly. His smile made the pulse in his cheek more noticeable.

Georgia made a self-deprecating curtsy. "Now please excuse me, oh powerful master, while I go to churn the butter and milk cows." Everyone chuckled, including Jeff, but the pulse in his cheek continued to quiver.

Georgia checked in on the caterers, and when she came out of the kitchen, Melanie Nallis was in the living room, standing off to the side, alone. Georgia went over to ask her if she would like to be introduced to some more people.

"Actually," Melanie said, "I'd just as soon to talk to you. I gather you spend some amount of time in Vegas. And obviously you're into poker." Georgia felt a light tap on her shoulder and turned to find several couples who had arrived recently. "Go do your hostess thing," Melanie murmured. "We'll get together again later."

By ten o'clock, Georgia was back at the front door full time bidding her guests good night and happy holidays. Fran Fields gushed, "What a delightful evening this has been, dearest Georgia. And best of all, now I know that we'll be seeing you very soon. I do hope you and Jeff will enjoy our little Crater Lake retreat. Christmas is very special there, sort of back to basics. We do our own cooking and just enjoy the wilderness and each other. I'll call you next week so we can plan out the details."

Georgia looked at Jeff, who had turned his attention to other departing guests.

"Until Christmas, pretty lady," said Jim Fields, kissing Georgia on her mouth with his wet lips open then turning to Jeff, patting him on the back, and saying, "Great time, Jeff, great time. And more to come. I'll look forward to our holiday together. I'd love to get this thing with Communicorp put to bed before the first of the year, and Christmas in Oregon might be just the ticket. The girls will be in touch and plan all the festivities. We'll make it a double celebration: Christmas and new business, all in one."

Melanie reached out to take her hostess's hand. "Georgia, I'll look forward to seeing you when you come to Vegas again. It would be fun to get together. Maybe you can give me a few pointers on stud."

"I'd like that," Georgia said. "I mean the getting together part." She grinned. "But poker lessons from me would hardly be to your advantage. Besides, I'm not sure when I'll get back there again."

"Not until after the first of the year," Jeff interjected, giving Georgia a look that left no doubt as to who made these decisions.

"Well, until whenever that is," Melanie said. "Thank you both for including me in your wonderful party."

Sonnie and Billy had bailed out hours ago, and Mike and Krista left right after the last guests. The caterers had cleaned up, and the house was in order. Jeff had gone to change into his robe and slippers. Georgia perused the dozens of hostess gifts on the hall table. She had promised Sonnie that none of them would be unwrapped until the next day.

As Sonnie had pointed out, "If I have to put up with all the traditions that annoy the hell out of me then we can also keep the one that I always liked the best: opening the stuff that everybody brings us. It's the only thing that makes up for all this phony social stuff."

Georgia went into the living room and turned out all of the lights except for those on the Christmas tree. When Jeff walked by on his way to the kitchen, Georgia said, "Please come sit in here with me for a few minutes."

"I want to catch CNN," he replied as she heard him open the refrigerator door. Then, "Where's all the smoked salmon? I never got any."

She heard him shuffle to the second refrigerator located in the butler's pantry off the dining room. Again he called out, "I can't find the smoked salmon. It isn't all gone, is it? That thing had to weigh twenty pounds!" No reply from Georgia. Now Jeff walked back to the living room. "Hey," he said, "what's with you? Where's the salmon?"

"I told the caterers to take it."

"What the hell for?" he roared. "You know that's my favorite thing. Shit! It must cost three hundred dollars! There was probably more than a hundred bucks' worth left. What were you thinking?"

"Will you sit down so we can talk? It's important," Georgia said quietly.

Jeff walked over to the sofa where Georgia sat and loomed over her. "I don't want to sit down!" he yelled. "I can't believe you gave all that salmon away."

"Don't sit down if you don't want to, but you'll have to hear what I'm going to say anyway," Georgia said, amazed at her own composure.

"I don't have to listen to a goddamn thing!" he shouted and began to pace back and forth in front of the tree.

Georgia watched him for a few moments and then said softly, "I won't be spending Christmas in Oregon."

He took a deep breath and blew it out through pursed lips. "Okay, okay," he said in his version of a placating tone. He had stopped pacing. "I know you feel like this idea came out of left field. Actually it all started last month, while we were working on the Communicorp thing. One day Jim gets this idea that we go to Oregon with them for Christmas. He's already invited the CEO from Communicorp. I said I'd check with you and then I forget all about it. The next week he asks again, and I tell him we're trying to work out the plans."

Jeff had been fiddling with the control on the light switch, brightening then dimming the room. "I just never remembered to ask you." Then accusingly, "Then you went to Vegas."

He waited for Georgia to say something, but she didn't. "Anyway, another week later, he wants to know if we're coming. I can't tell him that I keep forgetting to ask you, so I say we're just making sure that we're free for the holidays and that's why I haven't gotten back to him. Then today, when he brings it up again, I tell him that we can do it. I just couldn't put him off anymore. Besides, they said we could bring the kids and your mother. Fran's mother will be there too, so Sonia will have a pal. I figured that made us available."

His last words trailed off, but Georgia still didn't speak. She continued to gaze at the Christmas tree. She remembered the mantra she had pronounced to herself for so many years: *Whatever Jeff wants, Georgia wants, as long as Jeff wants Georgia.* It had lost its effect; in fact, now she could hardly comprehend how powerful that thought had once been and how much it had propelled most of her life.

Jeff, it turned out, could tolerate less than fifteen seconds of silence. "What the hell kind of games are you playing? You said you wanted to talk to me, so talk!"

Using the same tone of voice as she had before, she repeated, "I won't be spending Christmas in Oregon."

"Yeah, yeah, you said that. Are you trying to give me some sort of ultimatum or something?" This time Jeff didn't last five seconds. "Look," he said with practiced authority, "if it's important that we spend Christmas with the Fran and Jim Fields, we will. You know how important this Communicorp deal is."

Georgia's eyes moved from the Christmas tree to Jeff's face. As soon as he saw the cool glaze, he looked away. The pulse in his cheek was doing double time. "I'm going to bed," he said. "You'll get over this. I have enough other crap to deal with." He strode out of the room.

Georgia went into her dressing room, pulled out a nightgown and slippers, and walked back down the hallway. She slept in a guest room.

Alexandra
A novel by Georgia Kassov Cates

November 1949

It had taken a combination of smiling finesse and quick moves to make his way to the front of the hundreds of officers and enlisted men who had come to greet the *Utah* with its historic cargo of American women and children. Now Michael Kassov, major, United States Army, was standing at the chicken wire barrier, one hand holding the brim of his officer's cap, eyes squinting as he looked upward to search the decks.

The husbands and fathers waiting for the huge ship to drop anchor on this crisp December morning had all been informed of the virulent influenza and pneumonia epidemic that had struck just days out of New York. And then they had all endured the long days of delay as the ship followed its slow, torturous course toward port. The ambulances waited near the gangplank. And although those fathers whose children were the sickest, or worse, had been individually notified, every one of these family men had reason to be anxious.

Most were aware that whatever the age, any number of months produced a profound difference in a child—the more time, the more change—and so some were preparing to greet strangers. Many would see their children for the first time. These were the babies who had been conceived in the passion of the final hours just before their fathers were shipped out.

Normally Michael Kassov's primary expression was an engaging smile. His clever hazel eyes were as much a part of that smile as were his flawless white teeth. But at this moment, concentration sobered his handsome features.

His girls were finally here; he'd be able to hold them soon. For more than a year he'd had to be satisfied with letters and snapshots. His favorite picture was of Alexandra and Sonia standing in front of the Christmas tree. It had been taken almost a year ago, and their smiles had assured him that they were well and as happy as they could be without him. The smell of kasha and roast chicken, the sound of Christmas carols and New York traffic, Alexandra's healthy pink cheeks, Sonia's deep blue eyes and red lips all merged to soothe his loneliness—all this from a black-and-white snapshot.

But at night it was only Sonia's face that filled his dreams. Her portrait, framed in sterling, stood on the footlocker next to his bunk. He polished it daily, as often as he did his insignia. He always placed it in just the right position so that he could look at it when he was lying down.

Only on those most desperate of lonely nights had he sought relief from the overwhelming urges. And then that woman had come to apply for a job in the household he was preparing for his family. And had so devotedly, in her fledgling English, expressed her understanding of his situation. She said she'd never be in the way when his family arrived, but then had been less than stoic when he told her they could never see each other again and that she couldn't have the job as cook after all. It had been rather messy at the end, until she finally went away. But all of that had been just a physical thing—nothing to do with his consuming love for Sonia.

Now he could just make out Sonia's face beneath a maroon wide-brimmed hat as she started down the gangplank. And then, a minute or so later, she stepped onto the pier, and Michael caught his breath, trying to cope with the double shock of looking directly at the exquisite woman who was his wife and realizing at the same moment that his daughter was not beside her.

Sonia looked around, spotted him at the rail, and waved as she smiled through her tears. Then, as Garbo might have done, she pulled her fur collar up under her chin and continued through the line, showing her passport, completing the remainder of the entry procedure.

Michael stared at her, as stunned again by her beauty as he had been the first time he saw her at the party given by one of his Columbia classmates. But why wasn't Alexandra with her? And why was Sonia so calm about it?

It was half an hour later before the paperwork was completed and the luggage was extracted from the piles that lay on the pier. It had taken Sonia several minutes to explain to the lieutenant, who checked papers at the bottom of the gangplank, why her daughter was not with her.

Finally Sonia and Michael were able to run to each other, one of hundreds of couples reuniting on that day. She locked her arms around his neck, his six feet two inches barely providing him with a proportionate height advantage over her five-foot-eight-inch frame and three-inch heels. She kissed him, sobbing about how wretched she'd been without him, the nightmare voyage, and how she had barely survived the strain. He was lightheaded from the feel and smell of her.

"Where is Alexandra?" His mouth put the words directly into her ear as it absorbed the taste of her. She didn't respond but continued to chant her litany of miseries. He asked again. No answer. He reached behind his neck, pulled her wrists down to her sides, and looked directly into her eyes.

"Where is Alexandra?"

For an instant she hesitated, as if she was trying to remember, and then her deep-throated laugh brought forth the words.

"Oh, Michael darling! I'm sorry! She's fine. She's with a lovely family we met on the boat. I wanted to meet you alone. We'll join up with them this evening."

Her voice became a strident whisper. "I have to be alone with you. I can't wait until tonight. Take me somewhere now. Please!"

Michael stared at her. His anger at her decision to postpone the reunion with his daughter was vaporized by an electrified physical response to her.

He spotted a GI who had been assigned to help the officers with their families' luggage. He spoke rapidly, handing the young man the keys to his jeep. Then he grabbed Sonia's arm and steered her toward a line of waiting taxis.

The room in the small hotel just off the Greiserplatz was charming and meticulously clean. Michael and Sonia never noticed. Hours later, they were grateful that the room had a rare private bath.

Alexandra held on to Mary Katherine's hand. She was happy to be leaving the ship, especially since she did not yet have to say goodbye to her dear friend. Sonia had explained that first Daddy would want to spend a little time alone with Mommy. Margaret Cavenaugh had offered to take care of her for the remainder of the day.

Now, finally, Alexandra and the Cavenaughs were walking down the gangplank. Joseph and Patrick were trying their best to control their fidgeting because Margaret had made it clear that she would tolerate no high jinx at this time.

Their mother had been reminding them all morning that their dad would be waiting and that they'd better be prepared to curb their rowdiness. Staff Sergeant Jack Cavenaugh expected his sons to "follow platoon regulations." But that didn't stop them from getting in just one more disdaining jab at Alexandra.

"You know," said Patrick, doing his best to scuff the heels of Alexandra's shiny Mary Jane patent leather shoes, "our mom didn't want you to come with us. But she said that you were better off with us than if you were palmed off on someone else. She even had to lie."

"Yeah," said Joseph, climbing on the taunting bandwagon. "She said that she was going to have to tell everyone that she was taking care of you because your mom got sick."

Patrick's turn again. "Yeah, she was too embarrassed to say that your mom just didn't want you around when she met up with your dad."

Alexandra looked up to see Mary Katherine's reaction to this hurtful information, but the older girl was distracted by all the commotion and excitement of disembarking.

Jack Cavenaugh did not notice Alexandra in the first few moments of his family's reunion. Everyone hugged and kissed him, even the boys, and then Margaret introduced Alexandra. A look passed between husband and wife. Jack asked no questions.

"Okay. Troops, follow me!" He led them, in a marching cadence, to a jeep where he and the boys loaded luggage in the back and on the floor. Then everyone piled in, Mary Katherine sitting on Margaret's lap. Alexandra was directed to perch herself on Patrick's lap. Patrick was not happy but smart enough to know this was not a time to voice his protest. Instead he shifted his legs to make it as uncomfortable and precarious as possible for the annoying kid who sat on them.

They drove away from the harbor and toward the center of the city of Bremerhaven. Alexandra gaped at the dilapidated barns and pathetically lean cattle, the open fields pocked with giant divots caused by grenades and bomb shells. Everyone in the jeep stared out at the incredible destruction that met their eyes as they entered the city. They passed through streets lined with piles of plaster and bricks from which jutted skeletons of buildings. Charred frames sometimes defined what had been an apartment house or an office building. But mostly the avenues were banked with nothing but mounds of pulverized brick and mortar. These heaps of devastation were underscored by meticulously clean sidewalks and streets.

"The citizens of Bremerhaven don't have much to work with," Sergeant Cavenaugh remarked loudly enough to be heard in the backseat. "They can't get rid of all this rubble yet, let alone replace the buildings, but as you see, they sure know how to use brooms and shovels."

Alexandra's world to date had been the canyons of Manhattan, the lush greenery of Central Park, and the undulating beaches of Fire Island, none of which bore any remote resemblance to this place. She asked Patrick why all those buildings had been smashed.

Patrick answered, "Because our air force had to show those Krauts who's boss."

Alexandra did not know who the "Krauts" were, or why they needed to be shown who was boss, but she wondered where all the people who had lived in those houses had gone. She hoped they all had grandmas and aunts to visit like her Genya and Rya.

The Cavenaughs were going to spend the night on the base in the noncoms' guest quarters before driving the almost two hundred miles to Frankfurt, where Jack was stationed. Tonight they were having dinner at a Hofbrau house in the center of town, Alexandra included. Her parents would meet them later, back at the quarters.

Sonia and Michael left the hotel on Kleine Strasse and walked onto the Greiserplatz. It was after six, and traffic was heavy in the darkness of the chilly December evening. Sonia wrapped her coat tightly about her, sinking her chin deep into the warmth of her mink collar. Michael hailed a cab, and a shabby prewar Mercedes-Benz sedan with a new "Taxi" sign on its roof pulled over to the curb.

"The main gate at Bremerhaven Army Base," said Michael.

"Jawohl!" said the driver. "Nicht pay in Deutsche marks, jawohl?"

"Jawohl, American dollars," replied Michael as he helped Sonia into the backseat.

As they pulled into traffic, Sonia buried her face in Michael's neck and whispered, "I'm sore and I hurt all over and I want more and more of you."

He pulled her closer. "I can't wait to see Alexandra," he said. "Do you think she's okay about coming to Germany? How did she take going away from your mother? Genya's been part of her life for as long as she can remember."

"Your daughter is just fine," Sonia said. "She was excited about the trip and seeing you and living in a new place. And so was I! I didn't sleep well for weeks before we sailed. Either my mind was racing with all of the dozens of things I had to take care of: the bank, the military orders, the shots, the shopping and the packing…"

Now she put her lips next to his ear, breathing her words, "…or I'd lie in bed, sliding my hand over my nipples and pretending it was your hand, imagining what it felt like to you when they became hard.

And then I'd reach inside of me and pretend it was you getting me ready. And I'd rub that spot that you and I found together, and I'd feel the spasms and get wet and ache for you."

"No more aching," he said, his voice soft and deep, his mouth tasting her neck again.

As they approached the gate to the army base, an MP waved the taxi to the side of the road. When they were out of the cab, Michael leaned into the front window to pay the driver, who bowed his head and chanted "danke, danke schön" over and over.

Now Major and Mrs. Kassov were escorted to a military jeep. The driver gave a crisp salute, and Michael returned the gesture. They were taken to the noncoms' guest quarters, and Michael told the young GI to wait while they retrieved their daughter.

Alexandra was sitting in the lounge, legs swinging from a chair, listening to all of the Cavenaughs, who were telling their dad about their adventures at sea. Michael nodded and smiled at Margaret and Jack, but then his eyes found his own little girl with her soft brown curls and that tiny nose. He swallowed hard and knelt by her chair, gently placing his hand on her cheek.

"Hello, my beautiful princess," he said softly.

Alexandra slid off the chair and raised her arms. Michael lifted her.

She hugged his neck, feeling the scratchy fabric of his uniform and smelling the combination of cigarette smoke, shaving lotion and wool. After several moments she pulled her head back and put a hand on his cheek, looking directly into his eyes.

"I'm much bigger than the last time you picked me up, huh?"

"Oh yes," said Michael, his voice catching. "You're much bigger, and you're beautiful."

"Am I gonna go with you and Mommy now?"

Michael wrapped his arms tighter. "Of course you are! We're gonna be together from now on: you and Mommy and me."

Sonia had been standing in the doorway watching her husband and her daughter. Now she turned, extending her hand to Jack Cavenaugh.

"I'm Major Kassov's wife, Alexandra's mother," she said, emphasizing the "major" just a little too much. "Your wife and children were very kind to Alexandra during our dreadful ordeal on that hellish ship. And it was so nice of all of you to keep an eye on her these last several hours."

She turned to Michael, who was still holding Alexandra tightly. "Darling, we should compensate these people for their services. Could you write them a check for, say, ten dollars?"

Michael pursed his lips. Jack scowled, a red flush climbing out of his collar. Margaret responded by standing abruptly, blowing a kiss at Alexandra and saying, "Good-bye, Alexandra. I hope you enjoy your new home." Then she walked out of the room.

Michael gently placed Alexandra back in the chair and, clearing his throat, said to Jack, "My wife means well."

"Good luck at Herzo Base, sir," Jack said to Michael. "Kids, say a quick good-bye to Alexandra and come along." He left the room as well.

Joseph and Patrick spoke in unison. "Bye, Alexandra." They were gone before she could reply.

Mary Katherine knelt beside the chair, putting her arms around Alexandra. "I'll miss you, little one," she said. "You were fun to take care of. Maybe we'll be on the same ship when we go back to the States."

Alexandra put her hands on Mary Katherine's shoulders. "I wish you were coming with us and you could be my sister instead of Joseph and Patrick's."

"Maybe I'll send you a letter and your mommy can read it to you," said Mary Katherine. She stood up, turned to Sonia, and quietly said, "Good-bye, Mrs. Kassov." Then, blowing Alexandra one more kiss, she quickly walked away.

"Well, I'm not sure what the problem is," Sonia said with a shrug, "but obviously they misconstrued my gesture. They just don't think the way we do."

Michael took Alexandra's hand as she slid from the chair. "We'll talk about it later," he said.

The next morning, Michael, Sonia and Alexandra drove into the heart of West Germany, heading south through Hannover and stopping overnight at the Frankfurt Am Main Air Force Base. It was midafternoon the next day as they continued west, following the Main River, passing through the towns of Offenbach and Würzburg.

Alexandra sat on the edge of the backseat of the jeep, stretching her neck to see out of the opening in the canvas. Most of the drive had been very bumpy, and sometimes the potholes were so big that her daddy had to maneuver the car off the road to get around them. The few other vehicles they passed were mostly the same khaki color as their jeep. They came upon several carts pulled by horses and one pulled by two huge, lumbering animals that looked like giant hairy cows. Her daddy had called them oxen.

They maneuvered through the center of several more towns, and Alexandra noticed that most of the people they passed were dressed in shabby, ragged clothes. When she had asked about the people on the streets of New York who looked like that, the explanation had been that they were poor.

Leaning over the front seat, she spoke directly in her daddy's ear. "Why are all of these people so poor?" She glanced up into the rear-view mirror and saw his eyes looking back at her.

"Because there was a terrible war here," he said. "It lasted a long time, and most of the land that was used to grow food for people as well as for most of the cows, pigs and chickens was destroyed. Now everyone is trying to rebuild everything, but they don't have any money or tools, so it's very hard for them."

Sonia shifted in her seat next to Michael and stretched her arms. "I imagine that also means a lot of them are looking for work," she said through a yawn, "so we shouldn't have any trouble finding as many servants as we need…and that reminds me. There was a lot of talk on the ship about the black market. We should be able to find some real treasures."

Michael was about to respond when Alexandra asked another question. "Do they only sell black things in the black market, Daddy? Like frying pans and coal and witches' hats?"

Daddy's eyes smiled at her in the rearview mirror. "No, honey, not just black things. These German people are so poor that they have to trade their few valuable belongings for food because it is the only way they can get enough to feed their families. And some other people take advantage of that and trade things like cans of food and bags of flour for beautiful pieces of art or china or silver. Imagine what it would be like if the only way I could get enough food for you to eat is if I traded Grandma's beautiful crystal bowl or Mommy's blue china. The black market is really a very sad thing."

"Why can't they just go to the store and buy stuff?" asked Alexandra.

"Well, as I said, they don't have enough money, and there's not much food in the stores, so there are laws that only allow them to buy a little bit at a time. It's called rationing. But sometimes someone gets hold of a lot of one thing like butter or flour or milk. Then other people pay him a tremendous amount of money or trade important things for what they need."

"You know, Michael," Sonia said as she retied a silk scarf around her hair, "you make it sound like such an evil thing. Actually, if we gave these people coffee or sugar or flour or any of that sort of thing, we would be doing them a real service because they simply couldn't get it any other way. Not all of these transactions take place in dark alleys or shadowy corners of train stations."

"But nothing is *given* to them," Michael persisted. "That's why it's a miserable, degrading process that will continue as long as Germany struggles with shortages and rationing. Meanwhile they have to ransom the few tangible symbols of their heritage—heirlooms that have been in their families for generations—for something that they will smoke or brew or digest within hours."

Sonia reached over and patted her husband's cheek. "Dear Michael, my darling idealist. You want to be the prince of a perfect world."

Alexandra tuned out of the conversation at this point. It was never interesting when she couldn't figure out what they were talking about. Even Daddy's explanation about the black market was a little fuzzy. He never did tell her why it was called "black," but Mommy didn't like her to ask too many questions.

It was after dark when they arrived at the front gate of Herzo Base. They pulled up to a small hut, sort of like a playhouse, that was lit by giant bright lights that were attached to tall poles. An MP standing just outside the guardhouse came to rigid attention, saluting the jeep as the Kassovs drove through the gate. They pulled up to one of the dozens of Quonset huts that lined the narrow street. Two more MPs saluted.

Another man, dressed just like Alexandra's daddy, greeted them as well. Standing ramrod straight and saluting, he said, "Welcome back, sir. And welcome to Herzo Base, Mrs. Kassov."

Michael returned the salute. "Thanks, Mac." Then, after helping Sonia out of the front seat, he put his arm around her waist and said, "Sonia, this is Captain James McPherson, my exec, known as Mac."

"Hello, Mac," Sonia said with a wide smile. "I understand you're responsible for all of the arrangements that were made for our arrival. Thank you. I'm looking forward to settling in and assuming the responsibilities that come with being the CO's wife."

"Well, you are certainly most welcome, ma'am, and may I add that you are even prettier than your photos."

"Oh, Michael," Sonia said brightly, "this man is definitely senior officer material!"

Alexandra emerged from the backseat of the jeep. Michael took her hand. "And this is the princess. Alexandra, this is Captain McPherson."

"Hi," she said. "Do you have any kids?"

"Yeah, honey, I do, and they'll be here in a couple of weeks. My boy, Jimmy, is just about your age; you'll be in school together. Patricia is the baby; she'll be two in January."

"Are there any other children here, Daddy?" Alexandra asked.

"Not many, at least not American ones, sweetheart," he said. "But they'll be coming in from the States soon. I think we're expecting about a hundred and fifty altogether, right, Mac? Meanwhile you're gonna be pretty busy exploring the castle."

"Is it really a castle, Daddy?"

"You'll see for yourself the first thing in the morning. Right after breakfast, we'll drive out there."

For the time being, they would be living in the BOQ, the bachelor officers' quarters. As soon as the Kassovs were shown to their room, Alexandra began pulling out drawers, searching for anything interesting but encountering only emptiness.

Sonia removed her coat and sat down at a small writing desk, taking pen in hand. "There's so much on my mind," she said. "Will Mac be available later so I can go over some items with him? I'm not sure he'll understand exactly what I want just from my lists and notes."

"Slow down, Sonia," said Michael while he helped Alexandra off with her coat and hat. "Mac is *my* executive officer, not yours. He made some arrangements before you arrived, but he's not going to get any list and be at your beck and call." Sonia looked up sharply as Michael continued. "I'll be able to get some soldiers to help when we move in, but basically we're on our own. Besides, I doubt that the house will be ready much before the first of the year."

"The first of the year! That's weeks and weeks from now!"

Sonia stood up and began pulling clothes out of a suitcase. Alexandra sat down at the desk and started to draw a picture of Mommy and Daddy in their new castle. She knew Mommy didn't want help unpacking.

Michael stood behind Sonia and kissed the back of her neck. "I've spent a lot of time out there, trying to figure out the best and quickest way to get it ready for us. The owner, Herr Greiger, and his family moved out a few months ago, and the whole thing needed painting. Besides that, the roof needs repairing, the furnace has to be replaced, and there's probably twenty other things to fix." He bent over and nuzzled her neck again. "Living here in the BOQ for a couple of months is not SOP, but we'll be okay. And we'll be together for Christmas; that's what really counts. Meanwhile you can oversee some of the work that's being done at the house."

"SOP," Sonia repeated flatly. "Standard operating procedure. Well then, I'd like to start interviewing for servants right away. I assume they all speak English."

"To varying degrees," Michael said. "It might be a little too soon to hire them, though; they couldn't start until after Christmas."

"That might be true, but I want to be sure that I get the best candidates before the other officers' wives start hiring. And there are quite a few positions I need to fill. So we might have to pay some of them a little bonus, just to make sure we get the best ones."

"We're authorized to hire a staff of three."

"What about a nanny and a butler?"

"Any more than three servants, we'll have to pay for ourselves. But let's talk about that later."

"Okay," she said, already on to another topic. "When will I be introduced to the other wives? Are there many welcoming events planned?"

"There's a big effort to get most of the dependents here before the holidays, but a lot of it depends on the billeting situation. Finding housing for them all is a big job."

Well, is there any good news?" asked Sonia. "How about dinner tonight? Can we get a decent dinner?"

"I think you'll be very pleased with the chef here at the officers' club. I understand he owned one of the top restaurants in Berlin before the war, and he was trained in Paris."

"Lovely!" said Sonia, smiling for the first time. "Maybe he can find a cook for us."

After dinner, Sonia stayed in the officers' club dining room to speak with the chef while Michael took a sleepy Alexandra back to their room. She quickly drifted off, tucked into the cot at the foot of her parents' bed. Michael had removed his uniform and was lying on the double bed in his underwear, wondering if the bathroom door would muffle any sounds that he and Sonia might make while they shared a bath.

Sonia returned to the room, obviously pleased, and began to undress. "The chef said he knows a wonderful woman who used to work for one of the wealthy local families before the war. She's looking for live-in work. I assume there is room for servants to live at the house, right? I don't want to be dealing with all of them coming and going."

"Yes, darling, on the third floor, three bedrooms and a bathroom."

"And a separate stairwell to the kitchen?"

"Well, yes, but actually the kitchen is in the basement at the back of the house."

"In the basement?" Sonia repeated incredulously.

Michael explained how this arrangement was very common in these venerable old German manor houses.

Sonia shrugged. "I guess it doesn't matter," she said, walking into the bathroom. "I sure don't plan to spend much time there. Let's see," she continued without missing a beat, "the two maids can share one of the bedrooms, the cook and the butler can each have their own, and the nanny can have a room near Alexandra's." This last sentence drifted back to Michael from the bathroom as Sonia twisted bathtub faucets and adjusted the water flow to a steamy, bubbling cascade.

Michael looked down at his little girl. She lay on her tummy, head turned toward their bed. She was sound asleep. He stepped into the bathroom, quietly shutting the door.

"About the nanny," he said, gently running his fingers through Sonia's shiny black hair. "I was hoping that you'd decide we didn't need one. Alexandra will be in school pretty soon, which will give you some time without her, and I think the maids would be willing to baby-sit when we go out in the evening."

He reacted to her protest before she could verbalize it. "It's not that we can't afford it. The wages these people expect are pathetically low. It's just that I figured you'd want to have Alexandra with you most of the time."

Sonia said nothing and continued to take her clothes off, looking into Michael's eyes all the while. When she was completely undressed, she said, "Let's finish this discussion tomorrow." She knelt in front of him, pulling down his undershorts. "I've got the tub started, and now I'll get you started."

The following morning, Alexandra, Sonia and Michael drove into the village of Lebensdorf. The five streets that comprised its core were laid out like a game of tic-tac-toe, and, unlike many of the towns they had passed through yesterday, this one showed little trace of the devastation that pervaded most of Germany. The Allied bombs had spared Lebensdorf, instead finding their marks in Augsburg, Nuremberg and Munich, to the south.

The Kassovs drove on for several miles, the road winding its way through the thick forest, passing several large houses with wrought iron gates and tree-lined driveways. This land, Michael explained, had belonged to the local burgers who had owned the nearby businesses like the brewery and the sawmill. Now they'd moved in with other relatives and rented their estates to the US Army, who made them available to the command and staff.

Soon Michael pulled up to a massive wooden gate that opened in the middle, each half pivoting back to allow the breadth of two cars to pass through at one time.

The tires made a crunching sound on the loose stone driveway. No one spoke as they approached the house; each of them had a different set of expectations.

Sonia waited for the impact. From the very first glance, this house had to be imposing, hopefully more so than any of the other estates that they'd passed on their way.

Alexandra held her breath, eyes wide, ready to look upon the fairy tale castle that her daddy had promised.

Michael was anxiously anticipating both their reactions, hoping for signs that both of them were pleased.

A slight curve and dip in the driveway postponed an immediate view of the estate. As they made the turn, the turrets and gables came into view, and then the entire house appeared, preceded by another gate, this one embellished with a huge lion's head of wrought iron, which split in the middle when Michael got out of the car and pushed on the latch. A circular courtyard made of cobblestones sat like a small, bumpy pond that lapped at the foundations of the house.

"Why does it have three front doors?" were the first words from Sonia.

"Actually it's only one," explained Michael. "The three door frames are only ornamentation, and the middle one actually splits in half when the entire entry is open. Both sides have a separate lock, so I guess most of the time we'd just use one half of it."

"How very bizarre," said Sonia. "Why in the world would it have been designed like that?"

"No one seems to know for sure," replied Michael as he got back into the jeep and pulled up to the front door. "I asked Herr Greiger but he only shrugged his shoulders and made some reference to the imagination of his ancestors."

"Well, I would have preferred it if his antecedents had been a bit more conventional," replied Sonia as she took Michael's hand and stepped from the jeep.

Michael lifted Alexandra out of the backseat. "Well, princess, let's inspect your new domain." He put her down on the lowest of the three wide steps that led to the entry. Then, pulling a large brass key from his coat pocket, he unlocked one half of the door, standing back so that his wife and daughter could enter in front of him. They stepped into the frosty white marble vestibule and then entered the foyer.

Now Sonia took in a sharp breath, walking slowly into the middle of the vast hall, her gaze swinging from the marble floor to the damask-covered walls to the spectacular staircase. "They could have filmed *Gone with the Wind* here," she said in a husky whisper.

Alexandra spotted the balustrade and skipped ahead of her mother. "What are all those things holding up the banister?" she asked.

Michael walked over to the stairs and reached out to feel the first of the dozens of unique carvings that made up the balustrade. "I guess they're animals, princess," he said. "This one seems to be a giraffe, and that next one looks like a horse. I'm not sure at all what that third one is supposed to be."

Alexandra had climbed several steps, studying each baluster as she ascended. "Here's an elephant!" she exclaimed. "And a monkey and a squirrel!"

"Another example of ancient Teutonic imagination," said Sonia archly. "We might as well begin the tour upstairs since Alexandra is already on her way."

Alexandra bounded up the remaining stairs, stopped on the second landing, and looked down a long hall, the stairway marking its center. She promised herself that after the initial house inspection she would return to the banister to study all of the fascinating carvings.

"Which way should I go, Daddy?" Alexandra leaned over the rail as Sonia and Michael approached the top of the stairs.

"The master suite is to the left, and the other bedrooms and bathrooms are to the right."

"Let's save the master suite for last," said Sonia. "First we'll decide which room will be Alexandra's and which one will be for the nanny."

"My nanny?" asked Alexandra.

"Who else's?" replied Sonia. Michael let out a resigned sigh. Sonia smiled and gave him a quick kiss on the lips.

"Oh, this is perfect," proclaimed Sonia. "Both these rooms share one bathroom. Alexandra and the nanny can use these, and that leaves two other bedrooms on this side, each with their own bathrooms. We'll have two guest suites. Marvelous!"

They returned to the center of the hall, and as they passed the stairs, Alexandra noticed a small door set in the wall about four feet off the floor. "What is that funny little door for, Daddy?"

"That, my darling, is how the queen and princess have their breakfast in bed delivered. It's called a dumbwaiter. It's really a tiny elevator that starts in the kitchen and can stop at the dining room downstairs, here, and on the third floor as well."

Michael pulled on the knob, shaped like a bear's head, and the small door opened. He lifted Alexandra so that she could peer into a brick-lined well with several thick ropes that dangled from as far up to as far down as she could see. Michael supported Alexandra on his knee and reached in with his free hand to pull on one of the ropes. A combination of squealing hinges, groaning pulleys and thumping wood echoed up and down the well, and soon a wooden box appeared, a thick strand of rope looped through a steel ring in the top. The side of the box facing the opening was missing, and instead the bottom was edged with a three-inch wooden lip. Platters, bowls and trays of food could be placed inside.

"I could use this instead of the stairs," exclaimed Alexandra.

"Never!" said her father, putting her down and grasping her arms. "You are never to get into this thing. Do you understand?"

"Daddy! You're hurting my arms!"

"If the rope broke or if the box tipped, you could fall or be crushed. Promise me right now that you will never, ever get in there. Promise me!"

"I promise!"

Then, in a gentler voice, he said, "I'm sorry I squeezed so hard, princess." He pulled up her sleeves and massaged her arms then kissed the red spots caused by the pressure he had applied. "It's just that I have to make you understand how dangerous it could be."

"I understand, Daddy."

Sonia had gone ahead and was already standing in the center of the master bedroom. A canopied bed occupied most of the wall opposite the door. To the right was a massive stone fireplace, and to the left were two doorways leading to separate dressing rooms, each with a walk-in closet. A white marble bathroom extended from each dressing area, his containing a separate urinal in addition to the toilet, while hers featured a bidet.

Sonia, arms crossed, slowly circled the room. "It's a shame that the doorways, the fireplace and the bed take up all the wall space. It will be difficult to place a chaise lounge and a dressing table in here. But I'm sure I can figure something out."

Michael chuckled. "The chick never slept in a bedroom bigger than one of these dressing rooms, and now she can't figure out where to place the chaise lounge." He wrapped his arms around Sonia and nuzzled her neck. "But I have every confidence that my brilliant, beautiful wife will find the solution."

Another quick kiss from Sonia. "Show me downstairs," she commanded, walking back into the hallway.

"We haven't been up to the third floor," Michael said.

Sonia paused at the staircase. "There will be time for that later. It's just servants' quarters and storage. Am I not correct?"

"I suppose," he said.

Alexandra looked up the stairwell to the next landing, noting that the banister continued to be supported by more fascinating animal carvings. "Please, Mommy, let's go upstairs first. I want to see all these wooden animals, and also I want to find all those little towers that we saw on the roof."

"I like this dumbwaiter idea," Sonia said as she started down toward the grand foyer.

"Really," Michael said, "you ought to see the third floor."

"Eventually." The third floor was dismissed for now.

"Putting the kitchen in the basement is a fine idea," Sonia proclaimed as she glided down the stairs. "All the clanging kitchen noises, not to mention the steam and odors, are eliminated from the dining room."

Michael and Alexandra exchanged looks of resignation. Back on the ground floor, Sonia discovered the oval-shaped grand ballroom with bay windows of golden-brown leaded glass. More than two hundred guests could dance on the intricately designed parquet floor while four pink crystal chandeliers glittered above them.

Sonia's kiss lingered on Michael's mouth this time. "Oh, my darling, this is beyond even my wildest dreams. We can entertain the entire officers' corps!"

At the other end of the butler's pantry, where Alexandra found another little door in the wall, (yet another dumbwaiter portal) was a short hallway that led to a narrow stairwell.

"And finally," droned Michael, tour guide style, "we come to the true core of any home, the kitchen. Please follow behind me with caution," he continued in his best museum monotone. "These stairs are a bit steep and narrow."

"Are they safe?" asked Sonia, glancing down. "They surely need more light."

"Hold my hand," said Michael. "Alexandra, you hold on to the rail and stay behind me. These stairs are fine; they just take some getting used to."

Sonia stood on the bottom stair and surveyed the vast kitchen. "This place can't be managed by just one cook," she declared. "Of course the butler will help her, but she'll need at least one assistant as well."

"Butler!" Michael slapped his forehead in mock despair.

"Of course, darling, a butler, and at least two upstairs maids."

She glanced at the ovens, the eight-burner stove and the three titanic kitchen sinks. "I hope the cook will be capable of handling all this. I'd rather not come down here more often than is necessary."

"Aren't you ever going to fix us dinner, Mommy?" asked Alexandra as she peered into one of the three iceboxes.

"I don't plan to, and I hope I won't have to spend an inordinate amount of time training the cook. I'm sure that any candidate that is recommended by the chef at the officers' club will have sufficient skills, but I hope she's also flexible enough to adjust to our needs and my standards."

Sonia started back up the stairs. "So now, Michael, my darling," she said over her shoulder, "I've seen what I need to see in the house. Shall we inspect the grounds?"

As they passed through the foyer, Alexandra looked up the long, wonderful grand staircase.

"I'll be back soon," she whispered to the creatures holding up the banister. "Then we can all become friends."

She scurried out and followed her mother around the corner of the house. Michael caught up after locking the front door. The garden was closed in by a six-foot-high wall made from hundreds of loaf-shaped rocks, set randomly in thick globs of mortar, which had been left to dry without any amount of smoothing. It reminded Alexandra of icing squishing out from between layers of cake. Benches and low tables, fountains and birdbaths, all molded from mortar and plaster, were set in groups and bordered with flower beds, although nothing had been planted there in years. A narrow path covered with wood chips wound in and out of the various groupings. Apple and pecan trees formed canopies of shade. Beyond the wall were the remnants of a vegetable garden and a dilapidated stable that had been converted to a garage. The balance of the estate remained primeval pine forest.

Sonia had glanced around quickly. A gust of wind whipped through her hair, and she hurried back to the jeep.

"I need a martini," she announced. "Is the bar at the officers' club open at lunch?"

Michael lifted Alexandra and spoke softly into her ear. "You'll have lots of time to explore this whole place, my princess. Right now we'd better get your mother back to her royal comforts. After all, she is the queen."

Alexandra loved the days leading up to Christmas. Living in the BOQ was fun. Each morning, the first thing she did was to open another window in the Advent calendar, which depicted dozens of forest animals gathered around a huge spruce tree, decorated with berries and flowers. At the top of the tree was a sparkling star, its center painted with the numeral twenty-four. The first day, she'd opened windows one through seven, just to get caught up.

After breakfast in the officers' mess, her daddy went to his office, and she would return to their room, playing quietly until her mommy woke and got dressed. Sometimes Denise, a WAC who worked for Michael, came by and took Alexandra to the building that would become the Military Dependents' School when more children arrived. The playground equipment was already in place, and on sunny days Alexandra played in the sandbox or let Denise push her on the swings. They couldn't share the teeter-totter because Denise was as tall as Alexandra's mommy but probably weighed twice as much.

After lunch with her parents, Alexandra would climb into their bed and nap for a couple of hours. Late afternoons were spent in the lounge of the BOQ with various people from her daddy's office. There were many new board games to play, but they were hard to learn. Playing with a deck of cards was her favorite.

Best of all, she got to help trim the wonderful ten-foot spruce that had been brought in from the forest just outside the post. The tree reached all the way to the ceiling of the lobby in the officers' club. She was thrilled with all of the responsibility that she had been given. There were dozens of boxes of red, blue and gold ornaments. She was to choose which color would go on next and then to put the hook on it and hand it to one of the GIs, who often had to climb a ladder to place the balls high up. And it was Alexandra herself who applied all of the tinsel on the entire part of the tree that she could reach.

Every night when she was tucked into bed, her daddy read to her from her favorite book, and soon she'd memorized most of it, so that when the lights were out, she could repeat to herself,

"'Twas the night before Christmas

When all through the house

Not a creature was stirring

Not even a mouse.

Mama in her stocking

And I in my cap…"

She giggled at the thought of her mommy with a stocking on her head and her daddy in a nightcap, like the pictures in the book.

On Christmas Eve, she and her parents shared their table in the officers' mess with Captain McPherson and his wife and children, who had arrived just the week before. After dinner they joined several other families in front of the Christmas tree, and she cordially accepted the praise for decorating it. Everyone sang Christmas carols while one of the young lieutenants played the piano.

When she woke up on Christmas morning, she found a beautiful doll with golden-blond hair sitting in a miniature rocking chair. Next to it were three boxes, all different sizes, wrapped in red paper and green ribbon. Her mommy and daddy sat up in their bed and watched as she discovered the roller skates, the Mickey Mouse watch and the red velvet dress with white lace sash, white lace socks and a red velvet hair ribbon.

That afternoon, dressed in her new holiday finery, she and her parents joined the troops in the main mess hall for a traditional American turkey dinner. Several of the WACS and soldiers who'd spent time with Alexandra the last several weeks presented her with another Christmas present. She unwrapped the package then and there, discovering a porcelain figure of the traditional German Saint Nicholas.

On the second day of 1949, Michael, Sonia and Alexandra spent the morning in their new home while GIs unloaded the truck filled with all of the crates that had arrived from the States, as well as the furniture delivered from the army quartermaster. They would spend one more night at the BOQ, and then Princess Alexandra would come to live in her fairy tale castle.

As they drove toward the creaky lion's head gate to return to the BOQ, they passed a young woman riding a bicycle toward the house. When Michael saw who it was, he gripped the steering wheel tightly and accelerated.

Sonia had twisted around in her seat, peering out of the back of the jeep to get a better look. By then all she could see was long, shiny brown hair falling from under a knitted cap and cascading down a long, trim back to within inches of the bicycle seat.

"Who was that? I couldn't see her face," Sonia said. "I hope it wasn't one of the women who's supposed to work for us. I don't want her snooping through our stuff when I'm not there."

"I don't think it was," Michael replied as he looked into the rearview mirror.

"Then what do you suppose she's doing here?" Sonia asked with some suspicion.

"I have no idea, but the house is locked." Michael pulled up to the massive entry gate and got out of the jeep.

"Don't you think we should go back and find out who she is?" Sonia asked when Michael returned.

"She's probably at the wrong address or something," Michael said. "She'll figure it out. Meanwhile I know what both of us need as soon as possible."

"And what would that be?" Sonia asked.

"A dry martini prepared by Hobart, the bartender at the officers' club and, as you have ascertained by now, the best martini maker this side of the Statue of Liberty."

Later that afternoon, while Sonia and Alexandra took naps, Michael returned to his office, closed the door, picked up the phone and asked to be connected to a local number.

His call was answered on the second ring. He didn't identify himself. "Don't ever do that again," he said. "I told you to stay away. I meant it. Don't come to that house anymore." Without waiting for a reply, he hung up the phone.

Chapter 13

December 1998

The morning after the party, when Jeff had left for his health club, Georgia got out her suitcases and packed them. Whenever she planned a trip to Vegas, she followed a ritual that began with a call to the Mirage Hotel. Normally she would only speak with Stephanie Bellamy, but today she talked to Tracie, the receptionist, because Stephanie was out of the office, and within moments, Georgia had an open-ended reservation, beginning tonight. A three-minute phone session with a travel agent produced an eleven-forty-five pickup time for Super Shuttle and a confirmed seat on the one-forty Southwest flight from Burbank to Vegas.

The next phone call was to her office. Midge, one of her two assistants, answered, and Georgia told her that she was leaving town again. Midge Beck and Carey Paladin, the other "girl Friday," were to follow up on the few events that were on the books before Christmas. No one scheduled major fund-raisers too close to the holidays.

Then she spoke with Andrea, composing her words and thoughts simultaneously. "There's a good chance that I may not get back to the office for quite some time. I'm not sure how long I'm going to be away." Andrea said nothing, so Georgia continued. "I probably owe you more of an explanation than that, but this just isn't the time to go into it. Is there anything really important that you wanted to talk to me about?"

"No," Andrea said tentatively. "Nothing really important."

"Thank you for not asking any more questions. I really appreciate that right now. You know where to reach me if you need to."

Just as Georgia hung up, Sonnie walked by her office. She wore one of Jeff's discarded dress shirts, which reached below her knees, a ragged pair of gray sweat pants, and fuzzy pink slippers.

"Good morning, Merry Sunshine!" called Georgia.

Sonnie backed up a step and leaned on the door frame, combing her tousled hair with her fingers. "I couldn't sleep," she complained. "The cats kept walking on me."

"I'm sorry, honey," said Georgia. "They probably hid in your room during the party last night." Georgia stood up and hugged her daughter, sniffing in the wonderful Sonnie scent that was so distinct the first thing in the morning.

"I'm hungry," Sonnie said in her little girl voice. "Will you fix me pancakes?"

Georgia glanced at the clock. It wasn't nine yet. There was time.

Sonnie sat at the kitchen counter eating her breakfast. Georgia sat next to her, sipping a cup of coffee. "Sonnie, I'm going back to Vegas today."

"Today?" Sonnie repeated. "It's just a couple of weeks till Christmas. Don't you have a million things to do?"

"Actually my shopping is all done, everything is wrapped, and obviously there's nothing else to do to the house."

Sonnie had finished her pancakes and was draining a glass of milk, eyeing her mother over the rim of the glass. "When will you be back?" she asked, wiping her milk mustache with a napkin.

"I'm not sure," Georgia said quietly. "Do you need me for anything special?"

"Have you and Dad thought any more about letting me go with Billy's family to Hawaii?"

"I've thought about it a lot," Georgia said. "I really don't like the idea that we won't all be together for Christmas, but it seems like that might be the case one way or another. I also know how much you want to go. When do you have to tell them?"

Sonnie's voice was breathy, and she spoke between gulps of air. "Well…they've already counted me in the flight reservations…and Billy's dad has scads of frequent flyer miles…and they all really want me to come…they all said so."

Sonnie slid off her barstool and wrapped her arms around her mother's neck. "Oh, Mom, please, please help me convince Dad to let me go. It would be so great to start looking forward to it now!"

"You can go," said Georgia, kissing Sonnie on the temple.

"I can?" she shrieked. "Dad said it was all right?"

"I said it was all right," Georgia said emphatically then, in a softer tone, "So, aloha."

"This is going to be the best Christmas ever!" Then in the same breath, "No, not ever! I didn't mean *ever*," she said, giggling and apologetic. "We've had lots of best Christmases ever, but you know what I mean. I'm so excited! I have to call Billy right now!" Sonnie bussed her mother on the cheek and bolted out of the kitchen.

Georgia rinsed the dishes. So far it had been a successful morning, and she was feeling pretty good about everything she'd decided. Her business commitments were discharged, and with them went the accompanying stress, she'd made her daughter happy, and she was going back to Vegas. Not a bad start considering it was just 10:00 a.m.

She passed through the entry on her way back down the hallway to her office. Sonnie was tearing through the hostess gifts with extra fervor, her dark eyes shiny with happiness. *Perfect*, thought Georgia. At her desk, she wrote a note to Mike, explaining her departure, knowing he wouldn't get up until early afternoon and feeling no need to wake him. She assured him that it was fine for him to stay on in Idaho through Christmas.

Now it was time to put in a call to her own mother, who lived in a tiny but very posh Manhattan apartment on the Upper East Side, overlooking Central Park. It was half a city and worlds away from 115th Street and Riverside Drive, where Georgia's very first memories were rooted. Grandma Genya had lived there, and so had Georgia and her mother while they waited to join her father, Michael, who was stationed in Germany.

Thirty-five years later, when Georgia's father had died, her mother found a lovely little unit in a converted brownstone and furnished it with the treasures collected during her travels as an army wife. Now her days were filled with luncheons and the theater. In the summers, weekends were spent visiting friends on Fire Island or in the Hamptons. Several times a year, she flew to California and spent a week or two shopping in Beverly Hills, always in search of those "West Coast finds," which she loved to show off back in "The City."

The woman had a personality to match her self-esteem. She was beautiful and cultured, with the blood of Russian aristocracy in her veins. The Russian part had only become prominent in the last fifteen years or so, somewhat concurrent with the thawing of the cold war. Georgia thought it replaced the commanding officer's wife persona, which no longer carried any impact in her mother's present circle of friends and acquaintances.

The phone rang five times, as it always did. "Yes," Sonia declared in her cultivated, contralto voice. That was how she always answered the phone. The message to the caller was, "I'm not going to greet you until I know who you are, and then I'll decide if you are worthy."

She always seemed happy to hear from her daughter, even though it was usually "eons"—defined on a continuum of twenty-four hours—since they'd spoken. She had asked how the holiday open house had gone and, in the middle of Georgia's succinct report, had interrupted. "There's something important I must discuss with you, darling. I have an enormous decision to make, and I need your advice."

"Sure, Mother," Georgia said, actually relieved not to have to finish describing the party.

"I know that I told you that Dorothy Vandervere and Florence Galagher are leaving on a cruise to Europe."

"Yes, I remember."

"Dorothy called today to say that Florence has fallen and broken her hip and won't be able to go, and would I like to take her place on the cruise. Do you realize I have not been to sea since we returned from Germany when you were seven years old?"

"I know you like Dorothy very much, and I think she'd make a wonderful travel companion."

"Yes, yes, but that is not the quandary. Actually there are several problems. The first one concerns the holidays. It seems that this entire expedition has been planned around Christmas at sea. They sail on the twenty-second."

Georgia tried to keep the glee out of her voice. "I see your predicament. It would mean missing Christmas in California."

"Precisely. However, before I decline their offer, I thought I'd discuss this with you. After all, this is a rare opportunity. The tour includes almost two weeks in Russia. In all the travel your father and I did, I never got the chance to see my own homeland as an adult. I'm not sure that another opportunity like this will ever occur."

"I think you should go," Georgia said, sending up a silent prayer. "Our Christmas plans are a bit iffy anyway. Sonnie will be in Hawaii, and Mike is considering working and skiing in Idaho. So this might just be the right time for you to go."

"Really, you are allowing your children to spend Christmas away from home?" The judgmental tone of voice was right on cue, but then, as though the phonograph needle in her mind had skipped a few grooves, she continued, "Florence has cruise insurance, so she's willing to absorb the cost of her cabin upgrade. It's certainly an incredible bargain. And now that you inform me that there will be no family Christmas anyway, I'll have to think about it carefully. It would mean that I'd have less than a week to prepare."

"True. But you just said what a great opportunity this is. I think it would be worth the effort." Her mind was chanting like a cheerleader. *Come on, Mom! You can do it! You can do it!*

"I do have to let Dorothy know as soon as possible."

"Then you're going?"

"I suppose."

Now, before her mother's focus could swing back to Georgia, she needed to extricate herself from this phone call as adroitly as possible.

"Meanwhile," Georgia forged ahead, "I'll be leaving for Las Vegas today, so you can reach me at the Mirage."

"Don't you think you go there far too often?"

"I'll call you in the next few days to see how your travel plans are coming along."

Sonia's sigh efficiently conveyed its message, but she spoke the words anyway. "Georgia, darling, I really don't approve of all this gallivanting off to Las Vegas. You should really be a bit more conscientious about setting your priorities."

"Yes, Mother," Georgia replied and said good-bye.

There were two more phone calls to make. She left a message on Lena's answering machine, telling her housekeeper that she could be reached at the Mirage. Then she dialed a messenger service and requested that the courier come as soon as possible. She pulled out her "bills payable" folder, extracted several credit card statements that were in her name, and added several letters from the insurance company and the renewal notice for Jeff's favorite magazine. She put it all into a large manila envelope addressed to Jeff at his office. It would be hand delivered just about the time her flight departed for Vegas.

Sitting in the backseat of the limo headed for Burbank Airport, with her eyes closed, Georgia took in deep, calming breaths while her brain pulsed with confirming incantations: she had every right to do what she was doing. She was not a child. She did not have to answer to anyone but herself. She was right to stand up to Jeff. She no longer had to explain her every action to her mother. Her children, adequately financed and secure within their own egos, were mature enough to be on their own. Her business partner did not need her now. Her household duties had been dispatched.

Her self-imposed childhood had finally ended. The fairy tale years before she was six had been followed by nightmare decades. But remembering the happy, secure, loving days still brought her peace. Now it was time to make herself the first priority.

Alexandra
A novel by Georgia Kassov Cates

February 1950

Alexandra hopped off the khaki-colored, canvas-topped truck that served as a school bus for children of army personnel. She skipped up the tree-lined drive as an early summer breeze scuttled through the massive pines, rearranging the dappled carpet of sunlight beneath her feet. With all of her six-year-old strength, she pushed the giant lion's head that embellished the gate. Slowly, reluctantly, it split in the middle, and ancient metal hinges shrieked their complaint. Inside the circular cobblestone courtyard, an army jeep, its roof removed, was parked in front of the entrance. It was fun driving around in the bumpy, canvas-smelling jeep, especially with the top down, but she would have preferred a horse and carriage.

The princess in residence, as her father referred to her, was home, but she knew that this house was only on loan to her family and that it really belonged to somebody else, but how lucky she was to be able to live in it. She'd explored its gables and turrets, looking for any evidence of the centuries-old secrets of German lore that had been told to her by the servants. So far she'd found several pieces of heavy chain links, a sure sign that captives had once been imprisoned in those cold, dark and dank towers. And there were the odd scratch marks and scorch streaks on the stone walls—positive proof, as far as Alexandra was concerned, that dragons, as tall as the highest turret, had once attacked and had been repelled by a shining knight, dedicated to protecting whatever princess had been lodged there at the time.

Stone steps, rounded by weather and use, led up to the imposing doorway that swept up to just inches below the windows on the second floor. She was sure the triple-door entry had been designed to accommodate the many friendly giants who had roamed the countryside in fairy tale times. Looking through leaded glass, which must have been made from frozen ginger ale, bubbles and all, Alexandra could imagine silken-gowned princesses whirling around the ballroom in the arms of handsome prince charmings.

The massive entrance was like an ice cave. Every surface, from ceiling to floor, was covered in white marble, its sheen sustained by four hundred years of polishing. But this was only the vestibule. As she entered the grand foyer, the click of her shiny black Mary Janes bounced back to her ears as if they had gone ahead of the rest of her.

The floor was a gigantic marble checkerboard of black-and-white squares. The walls were covered in off-white silk damask and embellished with crystal sconces, each offering up a long white taper, as if in supplication.

The room was enormous, and she'd often wondered about its purpose. From the ceiling, three stories high, hung a massive crystal and brass chandelier, which had recently been electrified, although not too efficiently. Usually one or two of its dozens of flame-shaped bulbs were burnt out. Alexandra was always eager to report this news to Franz, the butler, after which she would congratulate herself, accepting his courteous words of thanks for bringing the problem to his attention, oblivious to his pinched and tight-lipped expression of annoyance.

She supposed that the entire foyer, this huge space in the middle of her palace, was necessary to anchor the massive spiraling staircase that swept upward for three flights. She had to reach above her head to put her hand on top of the banister. Counting the unusual balustrades time and again, she knew that there were twenty-three from the foyer to the second floor and twenty-one between the second and third landings.

Her favorites were Marvin Monkey (three up from the second landing) and Eloise Elephant (four down from the third landing). She always saved a moment for a few kind words to the balustrade creature who resided at the very top. He seemed lonely, and she was sure he had been placed there, out of the way, because he was so ugly. He was not like any animal she had ever seen in a book or at the zoo. She named him Franz because his huge ears and long nose reminded her of the butler.

Alexandra was the only one who spent any time here; everyone else just came and went. The exceptions were Franz, who occasionally teetered apprehensively on a ladder beneath the chandelier, and the maids, who were assigned to dusting and polishing. She often helped, caressing each mahogany creature with a soft cloth. She was their mother, bathing them, cooing and whispering, and promising each one that she would love them forever.

The busy little girl often stopped off in her room to look in on her dolls and toy animals. She would greet each one individually, spending a few moments rearranging them on shelves, bed and dresser. Raggedy Ann was repositioned so that she was a bit more comfortable, and the baby doll was tucked into her carriage and covered with Alexandra's very own baby blanket, thin as gauze and just a memory of pink. She would assure them all that they were safe and secure.

Recently a GI who worked for her daddy had spent several afternoons in her room, painting oversized figures of Walt Disney characters on the walls. Before the project had begun, Alexandra, chewing on a finger, eyes squinted, had circled her room again and again, deciding where each figure should be placed.

Mickey and Minnie greeted her from the wall opposite the doorway. Snow White and all Seven Dwarves danced above her bed. Donald Duck, Huey, Dewey and Louie surrounded her closet door, and Goofy seemed about to climb out of her window. The artist's signature and the date, "Bill Casten, January 25, 1950," were scrawled among the pebbles under Goofy's feet.

A few child steps down the hallway from her room, on the wall just outside her mother's bedroom, was that small door, set high up on the wall. In the mornings, her mother's tea and toast, steaming and fragrant, appeared here. When any member of the family was sick in bed, all meals were hoisted up to the second floor by the dumbwaiter. But best of all were the evenings, when the rattles, creaks and groans signaled the delivery of a cup of frothy hot cocoa and some freshly baked cookies.

She'd always wanted to climb into that child-sized elevator for a ride down to the kitchen. But dozens of warnings were etched in her mind, rotating with the faces of all those adults who had so severely cautioned her. Her father had been the first, but her mother, her nanny, the maids, even the butler had warned her repeatedly. It was very dangerous. Once, when a huge pork roast was being raised from the kitchen to the dining room, one of the ropes had broken. The tray tilted, and the meat became wedged against the wall, while tiny potatoes and carrots had cascaded down the shaft, showered with sprays of au jus.

Alexandra did have the choice of two staircases: the one that soared and spiraled out of the grand foyer and a narrow, dimly lit stairwell at the back of the house, which began in the attic and descended to the basement.

Here was where the enormous kitchen was located. A brick oven took up one whole wall, and in its center was an open hearth with hanging cast iron pots large enough for her to bathe in, although of course she never had. There was a modern gas stove, but heavy loaves of dark pumpernickel bread were baked, as they had been for centuries, in several wood-burning ovens surrounding the hearth. The remainder of the kitchen sparkled with the gleam of hundreds of square feet of white tile that covered the walls and floor.

An oak table, twenty feet in length, stood in the center. Alexandra would often arrive to find it cluttered with cooking and baking paraphernalia or laden with rows of silver trays filled with canapés or tarts, depending on whether those upstairs were expecting guests for cocktails or tea. At other times the table was set with napkins, plates and flatware. Alexandra would sit at her special place, gazing down the long expanse of aged wood, happily anticipating her meal.

But it was not the location nor the delicious aromas nor even the hearty food that most enticed the child to this warm, pulsing heart of the house. It was the cook, Frau Bruning. She had been hired before they moved into the house, and Alexandra couldn't imagine living there without her.

Frau Bruning looked like the grandmother in any German storybook. Her gray hair, with just a hint of its earlier lush auburn, had probably never been shorter than waist length. Now it was worn brushed back and caught up in a huge bun.

The seasons had no effect on Frau Bruning's wardrobe. She always had on a plain, long-sleeved, dark-colored dress with woolen stockings and worn leather lace-up shoes; the only accessory was a crisp white apron.

Her heavy legs and large stomach were balanced by broad shoulders and a full, soft bosom. Snuggling up against those soft cushions of warmth, six-year-old arms could not reach far enough around to complete a hug.

Frau Bruning—it never occurred to Alexandra that this woman had a first name—had characteristic northern European peasant features: a high forehead, deep-set brown eyes, and a large, broad nose. A ruddy complexion featured several moles, the most prominent one on the tip of her protruding chin. A smile exposed teeth in varying shades of brown and gold, interspersed with gaps of black. High cheekbones may have served her well in younger, slimmer days, but now they merely helped to support a vast amount of drooping flesh.

Sitting on that soft pillow of a lap, the little girl nuzzled into the fragrant refuge of generous breast. Caressed by husky hands, rough from years of hot water and harsh soaps and yet so amazingly gentle, Alexandra knew that she was where she belonged. Secure in the underground world of the age-old kitchen, she flourished on the boundless love of that wise old frau.

They communicated easily with a smile or a keen look. Sometimes they traded giggles; often they sat together quietly. Frau Bruning told her stories and softly crooned ancient German lullabies. The woman was a living compendium of Grimm's fairy tales. And although she always obliged the child by repeating her favorites, there was often time for a new one.

Alexandra always stayed in that gigantic house while her mother and father traveled throughout Europe. Although she wished her parents home many times each day, there were a few benefits to their absence. The entire household would relax. Some of the more stringent rules were conveniently forgotten, and Alexandra would delight in the freedom of expanded schedules, eating later, and, most pleasing of all, staying up past the official bedtime. Late evenings would be spent with Lotte (the nanny) or Franz (the butler), Frau Bruning or one of the maids who lived in the servants' quarters. She loved visiting their rooms, looking at their photographs of family and friends and listening to their conversations.

Once in a while, Frau Bruning would take Alexandra with her when she went to her own home. The child was always greeted with kindness and generosity and offered whatever German treats were available. They called her the American princess.

Chapter 14

December 1998

The American princess, a lifetime later, shoved her carry-on into the overhead bin and slid into her window seat. Soon the plane was on its way to Vegas.

Once again, this time much sooner than she had ever imagined, Georgia clambered out of that narrow, suffocating rut into which she seemed to stumble each time she returned to Creste Verde and flew away on the half-full 737 from Burbank to Vegas. The pilot kept apologizing for the bumpy flight. The attendants never unbuckled their seat belts; hence no drinks, no peanuts. Georgia felt her pulse beating in her forehead, her thighs, her toes, and she bit her tongue when the plane met the runway at McCarron about ten feet too soon. She joined in the applause when the flight attendant got on the intercom and asked everyone to thank "Captain Marvel" for the wonderful flight and exemplary landing.

The flight to Vegas through a terrifying succession of air pockets, climaxing with the bone-jarring landing, had challenged Georgia's entire nervous system, not to mention her digestive system. The taxi driver's penchant for popping starts and screeching stops had done nothing to soothe her. But now she breathed in and out deeply, relaxing tense muscles, willing her lower digestive tract to behave, as she stood behind a man who was pounding a fist on the check-in counter and usurping the attention of the entire "Mirage invited guests" staff. Georgia was grateful for the time to collect herself.

Finally, still sputtering about his million-dollar line of credit, the man was escorted into the VIP lounge and promised that his suite most certainly would be upgraded just as soon as the casino host approved it. The remaining clerk beamed a friendly greeting at Georgia.

Stepping up to the counter, Georgia said, "I don't know how you people stand that sort of crankiness all day."

"Hello, Mrs. Cates." The young woman grinned. "Nice to have you back with us." Then, leaning closer to Georgia, she confided, "Now that it's covered by the medical plan, it's much easier to deal with those kind once you've had the lobotomy."

As she entered her room, Georgia felt those tingles in her scalp again when she saw that the message button was flashing. This time voice mail produced her mother's plaintive words. "Oh, you're not in your room yet. Please call me as soon as possible." Once again Georgia had not been sitting on the side of the bed, waiting by the phone as Sonia seemed to expect.

Georgia unpacked, showered and put on a black silk and wool turtleneck sweater and gray tailored slacks, a silver belt and silver hoop earrings. After she dressed, she called her mother.

"Oh, Georgia, darling…thank goodness!" Sonia wailed. "I just hate waiting to hear from you. Oh, I know, I know, we just talked this morning, but then Jeff called me and I dreaded the thought that I wouldn't be able to reach you for the rest of the day."

"What is it, Mother?"

"You know, darling, I've always worried about you and Vegas. I realize that you don't really have a gambling *addiction*." Sonia pronounced the last word with too much emphasis. "But it has occurred to me that all this poker playing could be a sign of some deep-rooted problem that you should really be working out at home."

Georgia closed her eyes and asked softly, "What did Jeff say to you, Mother?"

"I was so frightened when I heard his voice. I was sure he must be calling because something happened to you. You know, dear, you are the only thing I have left in this entire world since your father died. If anything happened to you…"

"Mother, what did you and Jeff talk about?" Georgia asked not so patiently.

"He said that you seemed very high strung lately, not at all like yourself. He's very unhappy about this trip of yours to Vegas…really worried."

"He said he was worried?"

"Not exactly, but I know he is. He…"

"Mother, what did he say exactly?"

"Well, don't get upset with me, Georgia. I don't believe I deserve that impatient tone of yours." Then, after a pause that Georgia did not fill, "He wanted me to convince you to go home, and I think he's right." Again Sonia waited for Georgia to respond.

Silence.

"You know, dear," Sonia finally said, "I learned early on that I could get much more out of your father with a cube of sugar than a spoon of vinegar."

Several more seconds passed before Georgia said, "I've run out of sugar cubes."

"Well, go find some, dear. Your marriage could be threatened by this inexplicable attitude of yours. Georgia, dear, it's just not a good idea to let him get this aggravated with you. Sometimes a woman has to swallow her pride for the sake of a happy marriage. I did."

Georgia shuddered. She didn't want to hear this. Whatever her mother had to say about those early years in Germany (and she knew that was the time Sonia was referring to) could only threaten Georgia's carefully wrought equilibrium. She did not want to listen to her mother's interpretation of that time again. "Mother, I really don't need to hear about…"

"Oh, but you do, dear. You know what I went through—that horrid thing that happened just as we were leaving Germany. Even though we never thoroughly discussed it, you and I, it happened. The fact is, that woman, that Hannah, told Michael that she had a baby and he was the father. He had to tell me, and I never questioned his denial. He was not the father. I told him I believed him, and I did. I had to. And that was the end of it."

Georgia fought to keep herself in the here and now. How she dealt with what had happened thirty-five years ago could not be threatened.

"Georgia, are you still there? Hello?"

"Yes, I'm here," she said both to her mother and to herself.

"That woman…that Hannah, she was evil. I never should have let you be alone with her, but I didn't know then. Thank God nothing happened to you. The worst thing she did was to tell you those horrendous war stories like the one about the little girl and the chopped-off fingers. I can remember when you first recited that incredible tale to me. I just about died. But I never realized how horrid she truly was until your father and I confronted her together so she would know unequivocally that her blackmail was over.

"Do you know, darling, she threatened us even then? I'm not sure why, when you got older, we never told you that part. Your father ordered her to leave right away and that he would have her arrested if she ever came near us again. Thank God she didn't.

"But then when we got back from overseas, some very terrible letters arrived from her. Somehow she had gotten our address. Those letters came for years, even when we moved. But that was all, just letters, always postmarked from Germany. It did cause your father and me some amount of anxiety that she kept finding out where we lived. Then finally, years later, she gave up threatening us or maybe she died or something. But do you understand why I'm telling you this now? What happened between your father and me and how we overcame this challenge is the point I'm trying to make."

Georgia took in a deep breath. Closing her eyes, she forced herself to stay calm. She could only deal with the here and now. The *here* was the Mirage Hotel in Las Vegas, Nevada, and the *now* was this moment, this very moment.

"So let me get this straight," Georgia said. "Jeff asked you to call and tell me to go home?"

"He's your husband, dear," Sonia implored. "He's worried about you."

"If he calls again, Mother, tell him that I haven't decided when I'll be home and that I would prefer he didn't bother you with something that he should be discussing with me."

"Oh, I'm not going to tell him any such thing. Please, Georgia, don't get stubborn at this point in your life; you've always been such a placid individual. Except for that perplexing time when we returned from Europe and you insisted on being called Georgia instead of your given name, Alexandra. Other than that, you've never caused me a lick of trouble. I never could understand why you were so stubborn and obtuse about that one issue."

"I have to get off the phone now, Mother. I'll phone you in a day or two and see how your travel plans are coming."

"Call Jeff and work this out, dear. I don't want to have to worry about you while I'm away."

"You don't have to worry about me. I'm fine. Maybe better than I've been in a long time…maybe ever."

Georgia hung up the phone and sat staring down at her hands, fanning her fingers, looking for any scratches or chips in her long, tapered "Mainly Mauve" polished nails. With her left hand, she gently massaged the base of the fingers on her right hand.

Alexandra
A novel by Georgia Kassov Cates

January 1950

Very early on a crystal clear Bavarian morning, the sunlight glistened through Alexandra's bedroom window, reflecting off the thick forest that backed up to the ancient German mansion that was older than most of the trees. Alexandra floated on her own soft and foggy sea, with only the tip of her nose above the warm down comforter. When she opened her eyes, the Disney characters painted on the walls beckoned her to join them in a lively adventure. Often she would lie in her bed and her imagination would launch her into the world of Huey, Dewey, Louie, Mickey, Minnie, Donald and Pluto. But this morning her tummy kept reminding her about breakfast.

She had been living in the big house, her magic castle, for almost a year, and, until just a few weeks ago, Frau Bruning always had her hot cereal or sausage and eggs or pancakes ready for her, even on holidays. Now another woman was in charge in the kitchen.

Frau Bruning had tried to explain to Alexandra how her legs and feet had become permanently swollen and the nagging discomfort become constant pain. "Mein legs, they hurt always. No more can I stand in the kitchen all day."

Alexandra had hugged Frau Bruning's arm. "Then you just have to stay here and sit down most of the time," Alexandra decreed. "I'll tell Mommy that you have to stay. She'll let you, you'll see."

Sonia had been sympathetic, but the fact was that the loving and generous old cook could no longer perform her duties. A few days after her replacement arrived, Frau Bruning gathered Alexandra onto her lap, told the child how much she was loved, and promised to write to her and even to visit if she could. They had held each other tightly for several minutes then Frau Bruning had picked up her tattered old suitcase and wobbled out to the taxi that Sonia had paid for in advance with two packs of Lucky Strikes.

The new cook was very different in many ways. Her name was Hannah Kreiss, and she told Alexandra to call her Hannah. Just like Frau Bruning, she wore the typical drab brown and black wool clothes and heavy stockings, but Hannah's body curved in at the waist and out at the hips, and her breasts pushed against the fabric of her dress. She was much younger than Frau Bruning, probably about the same age as Alexandra's mommy. Hannah's dark brown hair was long and wavy, falling almost to her waist. She'd been quick to tell Sonia that she would always wear a hairnet when she worked in the kitchen.

Sonia had been impressed; in fact, she was delighted at how quickly this new woman caught on to the routine. Once again Herr Zucker, the chef at the officers' club, had found a good cook for the Kassovs. Actually he'd outdone himself. He'd told Sonia that Hannah had worked as his assistant until just before Sonia and Alexandra had arrived from the United States. He hadn't seen Hannah in about a year or so, but then, recently, she had come to him for a reference. She was a perfect replacement for Frau Bruning.

"She's so much better than Frau Bruning ever was," Sonia told Michael. "She asks questions. Something is going on between her ears. The old frau cooked well enough, but she was none too bright. This one is much more savvy about Americans and what they want. She has marvelous ideas, although she is a bit unrealistic about what ingredients are available in the commissary. But she's willing to try new things, and she has ten times the energy."

Several days passed before Michael had a chance to meet her. He and Sonia were sitting in the library, dressed for the evening, enjoying a cocktail before leaving for a dinner party. Hannah knocked at the open doorway, asking if she might have a word with Frau Kassov. Sonia invited her into the room, and when Michael saw her, all the color drained from his face.

"This is the new cook," Sonia said, never noticing the change in her husband's pallor nor the malice that sparked in Hannah's eyes.

Michael had stood up very quickly, assuming a rigid stance, as though greeting a superior officer.

"Well, that's hardly necessary," Sonia giggled. "You'd think I'd just introduced you to the Duchess of Windsor. Now, Hannah, what is it that you needed to speak to me about?"

Hannah kept her eyes on Michael a few more moments then turned to Sonia.

"I was reviewing the menus for this weekend, madam, and I see that among your guests are Colonel and Mrs. Clark from headquarters in Berlin. I worked for Mrs. Clark for a short time when they were stationed in Frankfurt, and she cannot eat fish. Perhaps we should make a pork roast instead of the trout."

"You are just completely too good to be true," chirped Sonia. "Michael, can you believe this? What a monstrous disaster it would have been to have learned too late that Noreen Clark cannot eat fish. Hannah, you are a guardian angel!"

"Danke, Frau Kassov," Hannah said, bowing modestly as she backed out of the room.

Michael sat down again and took a gulp of his scotch. Sonia studied him curiously. "She is very attractive, in a German peasant kind of way," Sonia remarked. "Don't you think so, darling?"

Michael finished off his drink and poured himself some more. "Why didn't you give me the chance to meet her before you hired her?"

"What on earth for?" Sonia replied, amused at her husband's discomfort. "What's wrong with her? Too pretty? Do I have something to worry about?" she teased. "Are you going to have a torrid affair with the cook? Don't I give you enough tasty tidbits to keep you satisfied? And mine aren't even fattening."

On a late summer afternoon, Alexandra sat on a plaster bench under the big oak tree, holding her head very still as Hannah caressed her hair, choosing one ringlet and then another, gently pulling each one, releasing and letting it snap back into the soft mass of curls.

"I will tell you the story of Katherina," Hannah said. "She was a little girl about your age who lived across the hall from me in Heidelberg. One day an SS officer and a soldier came to Katherina's apartment."

"Is an SS officer like my daddy, an army officer?" Alexandra turned to look up at Hannah.

"Yes, yes," the cook answered, "a German army officer like your daddy is an American army officer, but that was before the war. SS officers are all gone now, but let me tell you the story."

Hannah continued running her fingers through Alexandra's curls.

"'Guten tag, Frau Morgan,' said the SS officer to Katherina's mother. 'I am Captain Schneider. May we sit at the table? I have just a few simple questions to ask you.' Frau Morgan nodded, and when she sat down, she pulled Katherina onto her lap.

"'I need just a little information from you,' said the captain. 'Where is Herr Peter Gleiber and his family? We know Mrs. Gleiber is your sister, and we know Peter Gleiber is a Jew.'

"Katherina's mother did not speak, but her hands trembled and her eyes flew from one man's face to the other.

"'How beautiful this child is,' Captain Schneider said in a friendly voice. 'Come over here, my princess.'

"Katherina slid off her mama's lap and sat in the chair beside the captain. He reached over and patted her hand.

"'What a lovely little hand; it looks like a piece of Meissen,' he said. 'Now, Frau Morgan, you know that we have laws that must be obeyed. All of the Jews must report to one of the processing centers, but they will not be detained for long. They will be able to return after all of this terrible trouble is over.' He smiled at Katherina.

"Tears were sliding down the mama's face. The captain continued to pat Katherina's hand. His voice became louder. 'Where is your sister, Frau Morgan?'

"Katherina's mama shook her head. She opened her mouth, but no words came out. Captain Schneider took out his pocket watch.

"'I have another appointment in half an hour, Frau Morgan. I am a very busy man with many responsibilities, and I cannot spend all my time on these interrogations. Your kind of misplaced loyalty always slows down the process, but I have discovered a way to hasten the outcome with very satisfactory results.'

"With a quick look to the soldier, who was still standing, Captain Schneider put an arm around Katherina, pinning her hand to the table. The soldier pulled a small hunting knife from his pocket, and before she heard her mother's scream, Katherina felt the cold where her pinky had been. It lay a few inches apart from her hand, on the other side of a small pool of blood."

Hannah's voice had become quiet, the tone serene. She continued to caress Alexandra's hair, ignoring how rigid Alexandra had become and how shallow her breathing was.

"The captain held the child firmly. Her mama had fallen off her chair and fainted on the floor. The soldier lifted the woman back onto the chair and then slapped her face. As she began to scream again, the soldier reached over and sliced off Katherina's ring finger."

Alexandra sat up, covered her ears, and rocked back and forth on the bench. Hannah gently pulled the child's hands away from her head and massaged the little fingers as she finished the tale.

"'Do not faint again, Frau Morgan,' said the captain. "'If you do, another perfect little finger will be gone.'

"The mother screamed, 'Elmondorf Strasse! Number one-fifty-two! The attic, the attic!' Captain Schneider pulled a linen handkerchief from his pocket and wrapped it around Katherina's hand.

"'Take her to a doctor right away, Frau Morgan, and thank you kindly for the information. Auf wiedersehen.'"

Alexandra looked up at Hannah with wide eyes and in a whispery voice asked, "What happened to Katherina?"

"I don't know. I moved out of the apartment a few weeks later," Hannah said. "The last time I saw her, her whole hand was still bandaged."

Hannah lightly squeezed the base of Alexandra's pinky then her ring finger. "But enough of these terrible stories. Let's talk about America."

Chapter 15

December 1998

Still gazing at her fingers, Georgia walked toward the dresser then waved her hands in front of her face as though clearing away cobwebs. She chose a large, faceted topaz ring set in silver from her jewel case and put it on her right ring finger. Then she added several filigreed silver bands to the base of each of the other fingers. She went to the mirror to admire the effect of all that silver on one hand.

Five minutes later, Georgia was in the lobby. Beneath the buzz and bells of the casino, she could hear the little squeaky sound her leather slides made as she strode over the marble floor. At the cash center, she saw Marsha, intent on pushing the right icons on the screen of an ATM. The older woman went to the ATM a lot. Georgia doubted that she could afford to withdraw as often as she did. Thankfully Marsha never noticed her pass by.

As she entered the poker room, Georgia promised herself again, as she had many times before, that she would never get to that point. Georgia only played poker with money she could afford to lose. She had the discipline, but also she was fortunate to have the extra resources, the bankroll that poor Marsha could never even dream of.

The poker room had a distinct atmosphere during the day, although only a glimpse of daylight ever penetrated the depths of the casino where the poker room was located, and that was from the domed roof of the rain forest. More than once, Georgia had looked up after hours at the poker table to see the gleam of dawn slanting through the glass over the jungle waterfall and had felt that innate guilt that she was out too late. No matter that she was on her own, that no one expected or awaited her return; that no curfew was in place; that the good little girl could stay out all night if she wanted to. Then she'd have to remind herself that she was not breaking any rules, that she was not shirking any responsibility, that her children were safe and old enough to care for themselves, and she too was an adult, independent and free to choose whatever hours she wanted to sleep, eat, play poker, shop. Amazing, delicious freedom.

The games that had continued through the night consisted of some players who had been there since the day before and several who had just arrived after a good night's sleep, a shower and breakfast. Now, early in the afternoon, the room was quieter, more tranquil than it would be in the evening, when all the tables were filled and dozens more people wandered through, greeting each other and conducting business of all kinds, like a crowded marketplace in the heart of Marrakesh.

As she added her name to the waiting lists, a conservatively dressed man in a navy-blue Ralph Lauren polo shirt and khaki Dockers called her name. Georgia glanced in his direction, not recognizing him but realizing there was something familiar about the face, although it didn't seem to go with the thinning but neatly combed light brown hair. She smiled at him tentatively, and he grinned at her.

"Kruikshank," he said, "John Kruikshank," as though he couldn't fathom why she didn't recognize him.

"Kruikshank?" Georgia blurted before she could think. Then her mind caught up with her mouth. This clean-shaven, neatly dressed man with the steady hands and clear eyes of a neurosurgeon was the same person who had warned Milt and her about the pulsars and quasars emanating from the loudspeakers, not to mention the toxic gases that spewed from the air conditioning ducts.

"Don't you recognize me?"

"Of…of course!" Georgia stuttered.

Kruikshank patted the table in front of him. "Join me," he said. "I won't bite. And yes, I realize there are times when I seem somewhat unlike I do today, but I can explain."

Georgia smiled meekly. She pulled out the chair across from Kruikshank and sat.

Kruikshank leaned over the table toward her. "Old Doc who has been managing my medication has finally come up with a combo that keeps me tuned into local channels."

"Medication?" Unnerved as she was, Georgia tried for a chatty tone.

"Yeah, it was the pink pills that really blitzed me. I used to take twelve a day. Now I only take two and six robin's egg blue ones. They replace the bright yellow capsules, but enough about my personal pharmacology."

He smiled again and looked around the room. "You know," he said as if he were keenly aware that a change in topic would be best for both of them, "I spend a great deal of time perusing the patrons of this room. Have I ever shared my perceptions with you?"

Oh boy, Georgia thought, *here we go again*. "Actually," she said as casually as she could manage, "you have."

Maybe he hadn't heard her reply. "To the casual tourist, this is merely an extension of the casino, just one more place to gamble. But for some of them, the experience goes on for hours, even days, if their luck holds. Others get a quick, excruciating lesson in the difference between casino and kitchen table poker."

Georgia swallowed her surprise as best she could. Mr. Kruikshank was actually making sense. He continued to extol. "Lately a number of these vacationers arrive with more than a token amount of skill. That's because card rooms are popping up all over the country. But on the whole, even these less amateurish players tend to be looser than is prudent, playing odds that are not in their favor, and we 'locals' should welcome them enthusiastically."

"I agree," Georgia said, hoping her tone wasn't too patronizing, realizing at the same moment that Mr. Kruikshank probably was not capable of discerning the difference.

Kruikshank continued. "Then there are those locals who make their living from the game, like Milt Braverman. He usually arrives with a copy of the *Las Vegas Sun* tucked under his arm and orders coffee as soon as he walks into the room. To him, it's just another day at the office."

"The office," Georgia repeated, nonplussed beyond recovery.

Kruikshank was nodding his head like a professor verifying his own theory. "I notice that Milt stays as long as it takes to make his daily nut. Sometimes that's an hour, sometimes it's all day and all night, and even though he's probably one of the best players in the room, he has his good days and bad days, just like the rest of us."

"Georgia and Mr. K. for fifteen-thirty!" came the page over the loudspeaker.

As they both made their way to the table, Mr. Kruikshank pulled cash out of his pocket, dropping several crumpled hundred-dollar bills on the floor. Then, noticing it right away, he squatted to retrieve them.

"Oh, Georgia," he said as stood up again, "I am sure you have an abundant amount of common sense. Don't take it for granted."

Now what in the hell did that mean? Best to smile and keep quiet, Georgia thought, and she did.

During the day, many retired people frequented the poker room, most of whom had moved to Las Vegas to spend their days doing what they enjoyed most. Today, Jim Carruthers and his pal Bailey Markham sat at either end of a fifteen-thirty table. Jim and Bailey came in almost every weekday with their wives. Jane Carruthers and Claudia Markham played one-to-five stud with the same exhilaration and dedication that their husbands brought to the middle-limit games.

Before Georgia decided where she wanted to sit, she surveyed the players. At one of the tables, a woman with thinning yellow hair in a style that could only be achieved with pin curls was whining about the previous hand. Next to her sat a man who usually played much higher stakes, and across from them were two hotshot tournament players who added an element of frontier justice to games. This was not a lineup to Georgia's liking. She chose a seat at the other table while Mr. Kruikshank settled in next to the whining woman.

Mary Alice Clooney sat to Georgia's left. She was a retired history teacher who played poker like a rattlesnake. Her lace blouses under prim Chanel-cut suits gave no hint of the venom that could spurt from her chips and cards once she had set up her victims. Georgia gave her a great deal of respect in a game.

"Hello, Georgia, my dear," she said in her refined, finishing school inflection. "How lovely to see you again."

"Hello, Mary Alice," replied Georgia. "And how have you been?"

"Quite well," Mary Alice said, skillfully peeking at her two hole cards. She raised the opening bet to fifteen dollars. Two young men to her left both called, as did Bailey Markham and Jim Carruthers. Georgia folded. After the next card was dealt, the kid in the six seat bet fifteen dollars, Bailey folded, and Jim called. Mary Alice raised the bet to thirty dollars. Both young men called her, and Jim folded. At the showdown, Mary Alice won with an ace-high heart flush that beat an ace-high straight and aces up. All of the aces had come to play, but Mary Alice had controlled the action from the beginning.

"They should've put that big ol' fish tank from the lobby in here," drawled the kid who had lost with aces up. "This is where the real sharks are."

Mary Alice smiled like the Mona Lisa as she stacked up her winnings. On the very next hand, the same young man who had just lost to Mary Alice filled an inside nine-high straight and pulled in a hefty pot. "That's more like it," he said to his buddy then ordered two Coronas, no lime.

Georgia had been discarding one anemic set of three cards after another, and then, finally, her two red queens in the hole were joined by the open queen of spades. She was rolled up with queens. Mary Alice had the low card and put in her five dollars. Kid #1 raised with his jack of clubs. Kid #2 called with a ten up, and Bailey Markham raised again with the king of clubs. Georgia called the raises. She didn't want anyone to leave this pot. On the turn—the second card dealt up—Bailey Markham, with his king and six of clubs, bet; Georgia, who now had a queen and six of spades up, called; Mary Alice folded; and both kids called as well. On Fifth Street—everyone still in the hand had five cards now—Bailey, showing his king six and seven, bet again. The five of hearts had been added to Georgia's up cards, and now she raised. Everybody called. On the sixth card dealt—"Sixth Street" in poker lingo—Bailey's hand was still high, but he checked. Georgia bet; Kid #1, who showed a jack and three of clubs, four of diamonds and an ace of spades, called, as did Kid #2 with his three hearts and a diamond showing. Baily folded. On the river, Georgia's three queens were filled by a five of diamonds. She bet, Kid #1 raised, Kid #2 called, and Georgia raised back; the other two called, and Georgia presented her full house.

Bailey Markham nodded sagely. "You had to be rolled up," he said. "That's why you raised me."

Kid 1 sat staring at his aces up. Kid #2 was staring at his heart flush. Then they both looked at Georgia with stupefied, open-mouthed wonder. "You slow-played three queens," Kid #1 croaked. Bailey winked at Georgia as she pulled in the six-hundred-dollar pot.

The hours slid by as they always did when Georgia was playing poker. She checked her watch at five, and then it was seven thirty. At nine, the hunger pangs started, and by ten she was ready for a break. Again she was caressed by the amazing bliss of being on her own. She could eat when she wanted, sleep when she wanted, and play poker as much as she wanted. There was no one that she needed to please, or to compromise with, or even to consider but herself. No one but Georgia. Now she'd go to her room, order dinner, and then decide whether to go to bed or come back and play poker some more. She cashed her chips, luxuriating in the happy transactions at the cashier's cage that added several hundred-dollar bills to the wad that she'd begun the day with.

Georgia walked slowly toward the elevators, realizing how tired she really felt. The last thirty-six hours had caught up with her. The confrontation with Jeff, the impulsive decision to come back to Vegas, this realization that she was a woman with the ability and the resources to make independent choices; it was all so new to her. Yes, there was incredible joy in that; it's just that she hadn't had much practice, and it was exhausting.

Chapter 16

She had just passed the baccarat room when someone called out her name.

"Georgia," a woman's voice repeated, "over here!" Melanie Nallis stood next to a hundred-dollar minimum bet blackjack table, waving at Georgia. Her spectacular blond hair was piled on top of her head, held in place by a glittery clasp dotted with jet stones. Curly tendrils floated over her forehead and a few more fluttered down her back and shoulders. The black sheath—probably Donna Karan—fit her as if Donna had sewn it just for her. A black silk braided choker coiled around her long, elegant neck.

Both women reached out to hug the other. "I didn't expect to run into you so soon," Melanie said. "I thought you wouldn't get back here until after the holidays."

"Me too," Georgia said, "but the situation suddenly changed."

"I'm glad," Melanie said. "I was looking forward to seeing you again. How long are you going to be in town?"

"I'm not sure."

"We should get together," Melanie said then turned back to the blackjack table and put her hand on the shoulder of a man with several stacks of black one-hundred-dollar chips in front of him. "Jules," she said, "this is Georgia Cates. I was telling you about her, remember?"

He was tall and broad-shouldered, the Anthony Quinn type, including wavy dark hair and a Roman profile.

"Nice to meet you," he said. He had glanced at her for a moment before looking back at the cards that were being snapped out by the dealer.

"Nice to meet you too," Georgia replied, ready to shake hands, but his was not forthcoming.

Circling one of his arms with both of hers, Melanie said, "I told Jules about you, that you're a poker player too."

"'Poker player' is a relative term," Georgia said, smiling. "I've seen Jules in the poker room, and he plays in a very different neighborhood than I do."

Jules stood up, extricating his arm from Melanie's grasp. "Mel, take care of these," he said, indicating the stacks of chips in front of him. "Gotta get back to the poker room. Nice to meet you," he mumbled again as he walked away.

Melanie reached out and stacked the chips he had left on the table.

"Jules and I have been dating for a while. I met him through Jim Fields, and then we ran into each other a few times in the poker room. He used to be a pit boss at Caesar's, but then about fifteen years ago, he hit a big slots jackpot, something like half a million dollars. He told me that he invested almost all of it in dot-com stuff, his timing was good, and it really paid off."

She indicated to the dealer that she wanted the chips colored up, and as the dealer counted them out, she continued.

"He says the market is just another kind of gambling. Mutual funds may have better odds, but these days the action's in the dot-coms. Jules is also an investor in the Empyrean, and I think he's in cahoots with Jim Fields to bring me on board. Meanwhile I've enjoyed his quite charming company."

She reached out and scooped up the pink five-hundred-dollar chips that the dealer had put in front of her, leaving a green twenty-five-dollar chip for a tip. She slid the pinks into a round, crystal-encrusted Judith Leiber purse and began to walk away from the table. "Got time for a drink or a cup of coffee?"

Georgia wondered if Melanie was deliberately overlooking Jules's rather curt and close to arrogant manner or if she just didn't perceive it.

"Actually I was on my way to bed. How about tomorrow? Will you be around?"

"I'll meet you for breakfast. You pick any time after twelve p.m."

Georgia grinned. "Only in Vegas do people plan breakfast dates for after noon. How about twelve thirty?"

"Perfect," Melanie replied. "I'll meet you in the café. Sleep tight."

Georgia had slept for eight solid hours, never stirring until just a minute ago, when she awoke, hungry, eager to call room service—*no way can I wait until 12:30 for breakfast!*—and jump in the shower. The clock on the night stand glowed a red 7:55, and morning light seeped from the edges of the drawn drapes. She stood up and stretched blissfully. *No dream memories*, she thought. *I must have really slept well.*

While the hot water pulsed into her neck and back, Georgia allowed herself to consider how much she was looking forward to seeing both Phillip Vance and his daughter, Livy. Actually, that in itself was a bit strange. After her own kids had grown, she'd never had much interest in other children, but there was something very appealing about a little girl with Livy's combination of sweetness and poise.

As Georgia scrubbed herself with a loofa and an almond bath gel, she considered her initial reaction to Phillip Vance. Like daughter, like father? Not really. To be sure, Phillip was abundantly self-confident, and his charm was polished and practiced, maybe even a little too much so for her taste. And yet how pleased she'd been when he put her hand to his lips, and how strange that when he held it there for that extra few seconds, she had enjoyed it.

Enough! She'd better let this weird stream of consciousness pour down the drain with the cream rinse. Now it was time to dry off and get in her robe before breakfast was delivered.

By noon she was ready to leave her room. She wore three pieces of subdued mauve Egyptian cotton: slacks, tank and swing jacket and the same silver jewelry as yesterday, including the hammered silver hoop earrings. She said good morning to the housekeeping crew working in the room across the hall as she flipped the "Do Not Disturb" sign to "Service Please."

When she reached the lobby, Georgia melded into the hundreds of people coming and going from the casino, the pool, the arcade boutiques, the gift shop and the Caribe Café. Some of them pushed strollers or patiently guided grandmothers. Of course there were the scores of quixotic Easterners who believed that the desert sun was meant to be worshiped year round, even if the temperature never reached sixty-five. They clutched beach towels and suntan lotion.

Many people carried luggage, either arriving or checking out. Even if the direction in which they walked wasn't an indication of their destination, their body language made it obvious. Newcomers hurried along, bounding with optimism, eager to dump the suitcases in the room and start cashing traveler's checks. Those headed home moved with a less energetic gait.

A Chinese gentleman held a bright blue flag over his head while dozens of his countrymen—and women and children—herded around him. Over the loudspeaker came the announcement, first in Mandarin then in English: the Taiwanese Tourist Association buses were ready for boarding.

Georgia winced at the scores who stood in the interminable line for the coffee shop, knowing that those at the back would not sit down for close to an hour. Another little perk to be grateful for: the packet that she had been given by Stephanie included line passes. These little slips of paper authorized the holders to swoop by the queue to be seated by an accommodating hostess at the next available table.

A few minutes later, Georgia slid into a booth and ordered coffee. Just as the busboy returned with the steaming pot, Melanie appeared behind him. She wore a bright yellow silk shirt, which floated over a sea-green body stocking that covered her trunk and limbs to the neck, wrists, and ankles. All her accessories were clear acrylic, including high-heeled scuffs, three huge bangle bracelets and giant hoop earrings. Melanie ordered scrambled eggs and an English muffin; Georgia, still full from her room service breakfast, just had coffee.

"First of all," Melanie said as she handed the menu back to the waitress, "I was so surprised to see you last night that I forgot my manners. After I crashed your Christmas party I was going to send a thank-you note, which I obviously haven't done yet, and then when I see you, I don't even give you a verbal thank you."

"You're entirely welcome," Georgia said, "and please don't bother with a note."

Melanie nodded. "Okay then, let's get to know each other better. Tell me some more about yourself."

"Like what?"

"Like, for instance, how did you get into poker?"

"Poker," Georgia repeated. "How I got into poker. Well, I've always loved playing cards, any kind of cards. When I was a child, I lived in Germany. My dad was an army officer. Even back then, I can remember that playing cards was a big part of how they socialized, and I'd want to play too. I have one wonderful memory of sitting on my daddy's lap while he sorted his bridge hand. I loved the colors and pictures and the idea that some cards were worth more than others."

"How old were you when you lived in Germany?" Melanie asked the question as she signaled the busboy for more coffee.

"Uh, let's see," Georgia said. "I guess I was about four when we went over."

"That was what, about nineteen-fifty?"

"Yes, about."

"Do you remember what town?"

"It was called Erlangen, near Heidelberg. Why?"

"I just find this all so interesting. Do you remember a lot about what it was like then?"

"Not really. Why?" Georgia asked again.

"Just wondering," Melanie said, smiling and shrugging her shoulders.

"Well, I don't remember too much about it. In fact, that's the way most of my life has been. Nothing very exciting to remember or to tell about. I grew up on army bases all over the country; we never were assigned overseas again. I went to college, met Jeff, married him, had kids, did PTA, started a business. Pretty dull stuff."

Georgia picked up a teaspoon and idly stirred her coffee. "And I guess when I figured out that I could be paid for the services that I'd been providing gratis for all those fund-raising organizations, that was about as exciting as it got. That's when I started my consulting business." She stirred some more. "But it's really not about the dollars, and, besides, I've never taken a salary. All my end of the profits has gone back into the company."

Georgia spoke with a slightly apologetic tone. "It goes without saying that I married well, and I've always been able to afford just about anything I've wanted," she continued quickly. "But the fees I charge my clients are how I measure my skills and competence. You know how it works. In the business world, it's how you get respect and recognition, even the not-for-profit sector."

Unbelievable. Why am I spilling my guts to this woman? Did she spike my coffee with sodium pentothal?

"I think it's very interesting," Melanie said.

"Thanks, but that's about it." Georgia shrugged her shoulders, happy to have restrained her babbling. "Not much more to tell." Time to swing the spotlight in another direction. "What about you?"

"Oh, I've got volumes, but enough chatting for now," she said, reaching in her purse for her wallet. "So what's next on the immediate agenda? Maybe some seven-card stud?"

"Actually," Georgia said, deadpan, "I was thinking that I'd get my hair done; of course, my nails too…and a massage…and go to the mall…both malls…all the malls…and then sit out by the pool, and maybe play some keno. Oh yes, and take a tour of Hoover Dam and Boulder City…"

"Okay, okay," Melanie said, laughing. "I get it! But I hope you can take just a few breaks from the poker table. I'd love to talk to you some more. I have a feeling we have a lot in common."

"So do I," Georgia said, wondering why there was a tone of surprise in her own words.

Chapter 17

As the week went by, Georgia reminded herself time and again that whatever else in her life she'd have to deal with could wait. For now she'd concentrate only on the moment, like each deal of the cards. Georgia spent most of the time in the poker room, completely enmeshed in her own perfect world. The pattern gave her joy and contentment as her mind was alternately absorbed in the intricacies of poker and the banalities of the routine. The most momentous decisions that she had to make were at the poker table, and other than that her only concerns were when to sleep, what to wear, and what to eat. She relished every minute. The only variations in this schedule were the absorbing talk sessions with Melanie, a couple of quick meetings with Livy at the Habitat, and a VIP tour of Siegfried and Roy's Secret Garden—Livy's invitation, Phillip's arrangements.

Even these distractions seemed right. But most of the time Georgia was on her own, alone but not lonely, anonymous but not lost, free but not guilty.

Once in a while, she would be reminded that Christmas was fast approaching, and Georgia was definitely in the holiday spirit. But there were no meals to fix, no company to make comfortable, no lists to check, no command performances. Christmas was just for her, and the luscious, elaborate, sparkling decorations, the holiday melodies, the exaggerated energy of the season, all of it wafted over her spirit and, for the first time since her early childhood, carried with it no undertone of menace or anxiety. She was doing exactly what she wanted.

Really? Was she really doing exactly what she wanted to? Christmas without Sonnie and Mike? It would be the first, even the first without her own mother. And some vestigial fragment of her conscience mildly pulsed, reminding her that a mother was supposed to want to spend Christmas with her children and that a daughter should always welcome her mother. But they were all doing what they wanted, and more so, her freedom was intoxicating, and the natal instinct was numbed like a small ache after a glass of wine.

She had not spoken to Jeff since the night of their open house. How much longer before he called? No hurry. Both kids and her mother were off on their Christmas travels, and no business crisis had been reported from Andrea or anyone else. She'd talked to her mother twice more, and the conversations had focused on Sonia's plans. No more about Jeff or Vegas or, thankfully, the past. And now Sonia was on the open seas. Georgia had wished her a bon voyage, careful to keep the relief out of her voice. And the elation!

One early afternoon, just as Georgia was about to leave her room, Mike had called from Park City. "Hi, Mom. This is your son, Mike."

"Hi, son Mike."

"I thought you'd be home by now. When are you going back?"

"I'm not sure, dear, but it won't be until after Christmas."

"You're spending Christmas in Vegas? Cool! When's Dad coming?"

"He's not." Georgia waited for Mike to process her unexpected reply.

"He's not?"

"Your father will be spending the holidays in Oregon with Fran and Jim Fields."

"What's going on, Mom? Are you and Dad having problems?"

"Michael, you're twenty years old, and I'm not going to play 'for the sake of the kids' with you. Your father and I have had *problems* for most of our marriage. The only difference now is that I no longer see them as just *my* problems."

Once again Georgia gave her son time to absorb this information. Mike blew out a long breath. "Jesus! Are you splitting up?"

"I don't know. For now I'm just doing what I want to do, and that hardly ever coincides with what your father has in mind. I'm not too optimistic about a reconciliation either since I've done all the compromising I'm going to, and it's surely not your father's strong suit." Another long silence. "Mike, are you okay?"

"Okay with what? Learning that my parents are going to break up? I've had better pieces of news."

"I'm sorry to tell you this when you're so far away. But at this point it's really more about Dad and me than about you and Sonnie."

"Yeah, I guess so. But don't think this doesn't affect me."

"Of course I know it affects you, dear. I didn't mean to sound like that's not important. But you and Sonnie are old enough and independent enough to handle this, however it comes out. Now tell me what's going on where you are."

"Well, until this phone call, I was having a great time. I've got lots of hours on slope patrol, and I'll be making triple time on Christmas Eve and Christmas Day. I've also been at Krista's a lot. What are you doing on Christmas?"

"I'll be staying here at the Mirage. You know it doesn't shut down for the holidays." When there was no snappy retort, she said softly, "Michael, I'm happy here. I want to be here. Can you understand that?"

"I guess I'll have to. Have you told Sonnie about all this?"

"I haven't talked to her since she left for Hawaii. I called Maui yesterday, but she and Billy were out. Billy's mom says they're all having a marvelous time. I'll tell her when we're both back home."

Mother and son waited, hoping the other would fill in the silence. Finally Mike spoke. "Okay, Mom. This has been some phone call! I'm signing off now; I'll talk to you again on Christmas Day."

"Good-bye, sweetheart. Give my love and holiday wishes to Krista and all the Ferrarros. And keep on having a good time. You deserve it. And don't worry about your parents. They can each take care of themselves."

Georgia sat on the bed for a few minutes after she'd hung up. It had been a tough conversation, and yet she felt a sense of accomplishment, a culmination. She'd been very clear about her decision to stay in Vegas, and the words had come easily because she was discovering a power of conviction that she'd never perceived in herself before. Georgia was taking care of Georgia. How appropriate! How unusual! How incredibly overdue!

Mr. Kruikshank waved to her as she entered the poker room. She waved back, happy to see that he was still neatly dressed and clean-shaven. As she stood by the page desk waiting for the brush, Kruikshank walked over to her.

"Your friend is here too," he informed her, pointing to Melanie, who sat at a twenty-forty stud table. "She's been coming in every day. I heard she just started playing. And another thing…" He leaned toward Georgia, lowering his voice and barely moving his lips, "…have you noticed how she's dressing differently? That dazzling, over-the-top style of hers is modulating with more linen and cotton than spandex and more copper, pewter, quartz and coral, not so much acrylic and glitz anymore."

Now Georgia had to laugh out loud. "Mr. Kruikshank, you amaze me! I'd never have guessed that you are so tuned in to women's fashion."

"Oh, I'm tuned in to all sorts of things," Kruikshank replied. "All sorts of things." Again the man had been curiously on target. Yes, Georgia had noticed that Melanie's manner of dress was in transition and that she did play stud regularly—and at a limit that most beginners shy away from. But then it seemed that Melanie could afford to lose a thousand or fifteen hundred at a time, and it would never affect even the tiniest hundredth of a percentage of her bottom line.

Melanie looked up from her game and spotted Georgia. "Let me know when you're ready for a break," she mouthed.

Melanie always seemed ready for a break whenever Georgia was. Jules was not on the same schedule, and Georgia realized that she was relieved not to spend much time with him. She wasn't sure why, but he grated on her nerves, which was a shame because she was really beginning to like Melanie.

As the two women sat over cups and cups of coffee, Melanie began to ration out tiny bits of her history, and she reminded Georgia of a little girl feeding gulls at the beach, fearing that if she threw all of the food at one time, the birds would devour her as well.

"I'm not sure why I want to tell you all this," Melanie had said in the beginning.

Georgia wasn't sure either. But even though she didn't quite understand why Melanie had been so obviously available and attentive, she was happy for the connection in this new, unchartered territory that was Georgia on her own.

"Tell me what you want to, how you want to, and when you want to."

Melanie pursed her lips for a moment, making up her mind, then she cleared her throat as though it were the best preamble to prepare Georgia for what she had to tell.

"I had four younger brothers and three older sisters. My earliest memories are about sharing everything with a crowd. Our house had three bedrooms—one for my parents, one for the boys, and one for the girls—and the one and only bathroom was just part of the trouble. I was always waiting for my turn for everything. If it wasn't standing in line for the toilet, it was sitting at the dinner table, waiting to eat. No one was allowed to take a first bite until all ten or more plates were served up and prayers were said, first by my father then my mother and then every other person at the table, unless they were too young to talk. Anyone who didn't pay attention or fidgeted at the wrong moment had to kneel on the hardwood floor for the rest of the dinnertime while their knees went from dull ache to burning agony. I know because it happened to me more than once. And we spent countless hours in church, on our knees again, while the minister lashed out at unrepentant sinners and warned of the damnation awaiting them."

Melanie paused at this point and threw her arms in the air, proclaiming, "Hallelujah and praise the Lord!" Then she looked at Georgia and waited for a comment.

"A little different from the Russian Orthodox church I used to go to with my grandmother," Georgia said. "But some of the chanting and incense burning was a little weird too." When Melanie didn't say anything, Georgia went on. "Obviously you lost most of your religious fervor, if you ever had it, because you don't impress me as being particularly pious."

"You're batting a thousand," Melanie said approvingly. "But I'll bet that if I'd stayed around, I would have become a typical citizen of Cummings, Oklahoma, one-dimensional and dead inside."

"When did you leave?" Georgia asked.

"I was in high school." Melanie stared out over the casino for a moment then reached for her purse and said, in a radio announcer's cadence, "This concludes our program for today. Please check your local listings for dates and times of future broadcasts." Melanie was already sliding out of the booth.

As the days passed, Georgia allowed Melanie to gingerly serve up small pieces of her life story, like dollops of a delicate lemon soufflé. She always seemed so wary, hesitating to see how each tidbit would be received. Gently the tiny portions were accepted, as it became clear that Georgia was never greedy for more than Melanie could offer at any one time.

It was Saturday morning, and Georgia was both in a rush and on a rush. Earlier she had left the Mirage for a quick and efficient trip to the Fashion Show Mall. She had enjoyed the brisk walk down Las Vegas Boulevard in the clear, bright Nevada sunshine, and as she maneuvered through the crowds, she indulged herself with a gratifying tally of how much she'd won at the poker table lately. The last five sessions had each produced a profit.

When she cashed out last night, Montana Jones had paid her a compliment. "Nice win, sweetheart," he'd commented as she filled three five-hundred-dollar racks and counted out another seven hundred in cash.

"Thanks, Montana," she'd replied. "It was that great combination: a good game, lots of action, and my cards held up."

A pleasant gentleman in the two seat, a tourist who had lost several very large pots to Georgia, said sardonically, "Don't bother coming back on my account. I could manage for some time to come without running into a buzz saw like you again."

Now, on this sparkling preholiday morning, she was a couple of thousand dollars ahead. *Maybe I'm really learning how to play this game*, she thought.

When Melanie had learned that Georgia planned to stay in Vegas through Christmas, she had invited her to Christmas Day dinner at Jules Palentine's condo. Now, in less than two hours, Georgia chose and had wrapped all the gifts that she needed for Christmas in Vegas, several shopping bags worth. She got in a cab for the two-block drive back to the north entrance of the Mirage.

As the valet opened the door for Georgia, Marsha walked by on her way from the parking garage. The older woman slowed down to wait.

"You'd better go ahead," Georgia called to her from the driveway as the valet began to unload the packages from the taxi. "I have to make arrangements to have all this stuff sent up to my room."

"That's fine," Marsha replied. "I'm not in any hurry."

Georgia sent her purchases to her room with a ten-dollar tip to the bellman.

As the two women walked down the north entrance hall, Georgia said apologetically, "Actually I'm not going right to the poker room, Marsha. I have a lunch date."

"That's okay," Marsha replied with a sigh. She rubbed the bare spot on her right ring finger, and Georgia noticed that the lovely opal ring Marsha always wore was missing. "I have to make a stop anyway.

See you later." Marsha walked off in the direction of the ATM machines.

Georgia took a deep breath. *At least I've never hocked any jewelry.* And, she reminded herself, the money from the joint savings account she shared with her mother would never be missed. Besides, if Sonia needed the money for anything before taxes were due, Georgia would figure out how to replace it. She picked up her pace, quickly making her way to the Caribe Café. She promised herself that as soon as she could find the time, she'd take a cab to a Wells Fargo bank and make a deposit. Then she'd send checks to the credit card companies. Another couple of wins like the last few and she'd have those pesky balances paid off. But now she had no more time to think about Marsha or bank accounts.

As the hostess brought Georgia to the table in the coffee shop, she commented, "Your friend's hair looks just like yours. Same stylist?"

"No," Georgia replied, "I get mine done in LA."

"Well, it looks good on both of you, although it's a big change for her. Now you two could be sisters."

Melanie stood up, grinning at the perplexed expression on Georgia's face. "Yes, it's still me," she giggled. Melanie's hair had been cut to just below her chin, framing her face with graduated wisps and spikes that began from a soft part that was just slightly to the left of center. Subtle streaks like brushed gold were woven through lustrous brown hair. "I decided it was time for a change," Melanie tried to explain, still laughing at Georgia's astonishment. "Do you like it?"

"It looks great," Georgia said a little breathlessly, trying to absorb the incredible transformation in Melanie's appearance. Then Georgia noticed the hammered silver hoops, much like her own. Melanie wore an ice-blue wool sweater and slacks that subtly hugged her bust and hips, not nearly as spectacular as most of her outfits but very effective on her gorgeous six-foot frame. She'd never seen Melanie in anything this understated before.

They settled into the booth and ordered salads. Melanie spread both her hands on the table and studied her pale, frosty tan fingernails. "I've got a really weird question for you."

"Do I have to come up with a weird answer?"

Melanie acknowledged Georgia's wit with a brief smile, but it lasted only a moment.

"No, I…" Melanie hesitated as though still weighing the possible impact of what she was about to say. She clasped her hands together in an anxious kind of gesture then started the sentence again. "I know this is going to sound really strange, maybe even whacko, but can two women fall into friendship the way a man and woman can fall in love? Is there such a thing as trust at first sight? Like love at first sight?"

Georgia could barely absorb the concept, let alone come up with a response. The best she could do was to say, "You're right. That is a weird question."

Melanie ignored the quip. "My life seems to come in clumps of mild successes and avalanches of raging disasters. And there just hasn't been anybody who ever was interested in the whole thing. Maybe you'll be the lucky one I'll dump it all on."

"I could handle it," Georgia replied gently, at the same time wondering why she'd even said that. Why would she offer that kind of commitment to this person she hardly knew? She certainly couldn't reciprocate.

Melanie spoke a little faster. "If you believe in love at first sight, can there also be friendship at first sight? If the need is there. I mean that it might be possible to find someone to fill that void. Does this make any sense to you?"

"Yes, it does," Georgia answered softly and then with a final desperate effort to balance this solemn topic with a stab at humor, "Unfortunately, yes, it does."

Melanie pursed her lips then took a deep breath. "I've just made up my mind about something important. I've been wanting to tell you this, but I'm not sure how."

"Tell me what?" Georgia said gently.

Again Melanie was silent, and Georgia searched the woman's face for some hint of what she was thinking. "I'll have to do this slowly," Melanie finally said. "Will you be patient? Please?"

Georgia heard the urgent plea in Melanie's voice. "Patient," Georgia repeated softly.

"Then are you ready for another fourteen chapters of my life?" Melanie asked, suddenly sounding less like a desolate woman and more like a child who wanted to stay up past her bedtime. Georgia nodded.

With a sigh of relief, Melanie leaned back into the corner of the booth, her long, elegant arms wrapped around her waist. "I guess first I'll just give you more of my basic biography. I'll fill in the weirder stuff later." And another deep sigh. "The roller coaster ride that has been hurtling me through most of my life began its first uphill climb before I was two years old, but I'm going to fast-forward to twelve years later, okay?"

"You're in charge," Georgia said.

Melanie smiled gratefully. "My sister Ellen Louise was seventeen when she left Cummings. She just disappeared one day. I guess my parents knew more, but they never told the rest of us anything. For a while they prayed diligently, asking the Lord to send their oldest daughter home, but that seemed to be the only effort they made toward her return. Within a year, she had not only been deleted from the prayers but from any conversation that included either of my parents.

"Four years later, Ellen Louise reappeared, but she found no welcome from my parents. They let her stay in the house, although she slept on the couch in the living room. My parents made it very clear to the rest of us that Ellen Louise's return was no cause for celebration and that her visit was to be short.

"She told me that she had gone to junior college and learned wonderful things about the world, and that she was offering me a chance to escape, probably the only one I'd ever have. A day later, I packed what I could into a grocery bag and snuck out of the house in the middle of the night. Ellen Louise and I were on the five a.m. bus to Wichita Falls and then on to Fort Worth and finally Dallas. I was sixteen then.

"Ellen shared a tiny apartment with two other young women. All of them worked long, hard hours to make their living, but since the work ethic had been literally beaten into me, I couldn't imagine it any other way. I was instantly dazzled by their liberated lifestyle, and I prayed every night that my parents would not try to force me to go home. My prayers were answered; I never heard from them.

"I found a job as a cashier in a small grocery store and signed up for night school. My wages paid for my share of the food and rent with a little left over for one or two movie tickets each month. After I graduated from high school, I got a scholarship to the John Robert Powers Modeling School in Fort Worth, where I learned how to walk, sit and pose for the camera. I did pretty well because I was tall and thin but healthy-looking. I was told that my eyes were my best feature.

"I was doing a charity fashion show right before Christmas when I met Waite Harrington. I remember I was wearing a Bob Mackie gown. It was sapphire silk velvet with tiny sequins that were spaced so that when I moved, I gave off sparks of blue lightning.

"Waite was a tall and charming Texan from an aristocratic family who owned one of the largest cattle ranches in the state. He wasn't Paul Newman handsome, but his eyes were a soft, velvet gray, and he smelled like leather and lime and laundry soap, with a trace of whiskey that affected me more than if a pint of it had been injected directly into my veins. We spent the night together. I was a virgin, and he was gentle and patient. I discovered sensuality, intimacy and sanctuary, all at the same time."

Melanie was quiet for several moments then seemed to return from a very faraway place. "I was invited to the Harrington ranch… once. Waite really tried to show his parents how much he adored me, but they weren't impressed.

"In June, Waite canceled several dates, explaining that business problems were mounting and he had to spend more time in his office on the ranch as well as traveling to Houston and San Antonio.

In July, he told me that he had to accompany his father to New York and Boston and would probably have very little time to call, and he didn't know when he'd be back. That's when I started going to the public library, checking out several novels at a time. I chose only ones that were at least three inches thick. He called twice in the next two weeks, apologizing because he was always in a hurry and promising to call again as soon as he knew when he'd be back in Dallas.

"Then, on a Sunday afternoon at the end of July, Ellen Louise handed me a page from the society section of the *Dallas Morning News*. Under a fancy portrait of some sophisticated-looking young woman was the caption: 'Jennifer Worthington Summers Betrothed to Waite Tyler Harrington the Third.'"

Melanie paused for a moment, swallowed hard then said, "My sister Ellen Louise was so sweet to me. I know she was worried because I cried for days and didn't go to school or work. But then I dried my eyes, threw away all the junk like programs and dried flowers gathered in the months that I'd been with Waite, and told the other girls that I didn't want to talk about any of it again. Now, other than working or going to school, I read novels.

"And then it was my turn to worry about Ellen Louise. She had landed a job as a saleslady in the housewares department of Neiman Marcus, a colossal accomplishment for a young woman in Dallas without connections. She'd received a great first-year personnel review, and her hopes for promotion to one of the women's clothing departments were growing.

"Then she began to complain about being tired all the time, and she lost too much weight. The Neiman Marcus company doctor prescribed iron, said she was anemic. In August, she developed several large bruises, her gums bled, and her stamina completely vanished."

Melanie stopped to clear her throat again, unable to get rid of the raspiness. "When she collapsed in the employees' dining room and was rushed to the hospital, it took just twenty-four hours for the diagnosis to be made: acute lymphatic leukemia. At the same time, her lungs filled with fluid from pneumonia and she floated in and out of consciousness while I desperately tried to contact our parents. The family had never had a phone, so I sent a telegram to the auto repair shop where my father worked. No response. I read a novel on the bus coming home from Ellen Louise's funeral."

Georgia held her breath to cover her shock at how Melanie had just relayed this information.

Melanie continued without any verbal encouragement, "Then I got lucky again and was hired by a New York modeling agency and got all the bookings I could possibly handle. I did runway work as well as print. There was never any time for a social life. My days consisted of running from one appointment to another, and I was chronically late. Evenings were spent preparing for the next day, if I was so lucky, but often I had to be at night shoots or society benefit fashion shows. Still, I managed to read several novels each month, but most important and best of all, I never had any time to think about myself.

"On my twenty-first birthday, I met Marco. He was somebody else's date, but he called me the next day, and when I said I would never have time to go out with him, he began a single-minded campaign to prove me wrong. He managed to be almost every place that I worked. He always had flowers. He was consistent and persistent, soft-spoken, charming, handsome, and he always had a relevant comment about whatever novel I was reading. Finally I agreed to spend a free Sunday afternoon with him.

"He picked me up at noon, and I was hopelessly in love before six that evening. He had no family either—at least that's what he told me—but now we had each other. We were married a month later, and my career went on hold. He was a freelance writer, always pitching ideas to the big magazines like *Life* and *Look*. For six months we bummed all over the country while he gathered material to write about. We used up all my savings, but he kept assuring me that as soon as he sold a series of articles, we'd be back in the black. Unfortunately for him, and me, his ideas were the same as dozens of other writers', and somehow he always got aced out. Then he decided that we should go to Monte Carlo, and off we went."

Chapter 18

The waitress had been by their table several times in the past hour, but Georgia had been able to catch her eye and let her know with a quick look that she was not to interrupt Melanie. This time it was a waiter who ignored Georgia's signal and told them that he had just taken over Kitty's section if they needed anything. A firm "no thanks!" from Georgia sent him on his way, and Melanie gave Georgia a grateful look and continued.

"The plan was to stay several weeks while Marco interviewed players, dealers, cocktail waitresses, casino managers, and any celebrities who happened to be in town. His goal was to find a cross section and write stories about life and gambling on the Riviera then submit the serialized piece to the major magazines. After he had done his research, we would return to New York, where he would write, and I could return to the modeling agency. Weeks turned into a month; Christmas and New Year's came and went. Marco's project didn't seem to be progressing.

"Every night we dressed up and went to one of the casinos. Marco would settle in at a baccarat table, intent on getting an interview from the croupier or perhaps a fellow player. He insisted that I stay near, preferably standing behind him. When I questioned the amount of time he spent gambling, Marco would patiently explain to me that this was the only way he would ever make any contacts. Besides, he was on a winning streak, and his profits were giving us the chance to enjoy ourselves.

"Soon the main focus of the day for Marco was to get to the tables. And now I was not to stand or sit behind him. I was told to go away, to leave him alone, that I distracted him. The winning streak had ended. He had to concentrate, he told me, and if he played more, he'd win back what he'd lost. Somehow, no matter how much he lost, he'd always have more cash. When I asked where he got it, he would tell me not to worry about it. He said he knew what he was doing.

"I woke up one morning, alone in our bed for the very first time. I waited until late that evening for Marco to return then I set out to search the casinos. No one had seen him since the night before. Marco had vanished. I spent another twenty-four hours looking for him before I filed a missing persons report. The detective in the Monte Carlo police station just smiled at me with that Gallic shrug of the shoulders. I called him every day for weeks, but there was never a single clue as to what had happened to Marco. Contacting the American consulate didn't help either.

"I was alone in Monte Carlo, and I was pregnant. I had assumed that my modeling was merely on hold and that I could return to the agency whenever I wanted. I called, hoping they might even advance me the money for a ticket back to New York.

"My former agent put it into perspective. I still remember exactly what she said. 'In our league, pregnant models are as much in demand for photo shoots and fashion shows as nuns. The face may be pretty, but if you have to camouflage the body, what's the use? Call us again, sweetie, after the baby is born and then only when you're back in shape and in town.'

"I did what I had to do, and a sweet, gullible American GI paid my way back to the States. I wrote to him as soon as I arrived, thanking him and apologizing for misleading him. I promised to send him the money he had spent on me, but I never heard from him again, and my next letter was returned unopened.

"I got a job as a dresser for a modeling agency, and Ellen Louise was born in July. Then my life consisted of caring for my baby girl all day, grabbing naps when Ellie did, and then working in an after-hours night club, serving drinks on the graveyard shift. I would put Ellie to sleep in a basket and carry it across the hall when I left for work at eight. My neighbors, the Dimarcos, would keep her until six the next morning, when I could pick her up. It was really rough because I'd get home about five and have to stay awake until six when I could knock on their door."

Two men sat in a booth facing Melanie and Georgia. One of them kept looking at Melanie, not too subtly. Melanie never looked in his direction, but when he finally got up to leave, she gave a small sigh of relief.

"My looks were both a blessing and a curse," she said. "I know I made larger tips than the other waitresses, but I also lost time fending off men, customers and employees alike, who were constantly coming on to me. I had to learn how to smile away their offers without offending them.

"Then I met Bobby. He moonlighted as a security guard at the club where I worked. During the day, he was a bank teller. Bobby was about to turn forty. His wavy, sandy hair was a little thin on top, but his face was nice, and he had laugh wrinkles next to his eyes. Those eyes," she whispered, "those hazel eyes."

She swallowed a sip of coffee before she went on. "The first time he asked me out was to the circus, and he included Ellie in the invitation. I loved the idea, and we began to see each other on a regular basis, often including the baby in our plans. I hated to leave her with a sitter when I wasn't working. Bobby agreed wholeheartedly, and Ellie adored him. I filed for divorce from Marco on grounds of desertion. On December first, nineteen seventy-six, I became Mrs. Robert Nallis. I got back into modeling but on a much less intense level because I wasn't willing to travel or work crazy hours. Ellie began nursery school, and then, in nineteen seventy-eight, Robert Allen Nallis the Second was born."

Melanie closed her eyes as she continued. "Life was good for the Nallis family, and we moved to a three-bedroom house in Tarrytown. Then, when Robbie was four and Ellen Louise was eight, there was an attempted armored truck holdup at Bobby's bank. When the shootout was over, Bobby was dead."

Now Melanie opened her eyes again and looked across at Georgia, who had to hold her breath again to hide her shock. Melanie had narrated the events of her life in a monotone, as if she was reading a psychological profile or a police report. She did not prepare Georgia for the disasters.

Melanie said in a raspy whisper, "When Bobby died, a large part of my soul was amputated."

Georgia stifled the urge to fill the silent gap that followed with questions. Melanie was sitting so perfectly still that Georgia thought of a fawn in the woods, alerted to danger, who would dart away at the slightest movement. Georgia waited.

Finally Melanie spoke again. "The three of us lived in that little house in Tarrytown until Robbie graduated from high school. Ellie had gone to junior college and was working in Philadelphia. Robbie received a full scholarship to Michigan. His high school career as a running back had paid off.

"I moved to a small apartment in Manhattan, and I filled the two little rooms with framed photos that recorded all of the glorious, happy days with Bobby and the bittersweet years of raising Ellen Louise and Robbie on my own. That's when I began a systematic effort to read as much classic literature as possible. I spent a lot of time at the library learning about the writers themselves and what they wrote about. A few nice people gave me some direction as to what to read. I loved losing myself in history, politics and philosophy. Occasionally I dated. The few one-night stands were invariably mistakes, and one almost killed me and did change the rest of my life.

"He was very charming, almost shy, good-looking, impeccably groomed, soft spoken, and his smile seemed genuine. Oh yes, and he was about ten years younger than me. We went back to my apartment after a leisurely dinner and a good movie. He was a skillful lover, and I was just beginning to give in to the pleasure that he was very efficiently providing. What happened after that is so clear in my memory that sometimes I think I made it up. But I didn't."

Melanie looked down at her hands, took in a deep breath then, staring out beyond the coffee shop, exhaled slowly. When she started to talk again, the words came in wispy phrases.

"When those promising sensations that I had been focusing on began to fade, I opened my eyes to see why he had stopped. One of his hands still rested on my inner thigh, but he had lifted his head and was watching me. I remember I saw a small plastic envelope in his other hand. And then the orgasm that had begun just a minute before and dwindled was back working its way through my whole body. Almost simultaneously, the shivering began. I saw words coming from his mouth, but all I heard was a deafening roar from inside my head. Then this agonizing itch spread down my arms and legs, and the shaking got worse and I couldn't control my motions. The itch brought on an overpowering sensation of heat, and I tried to get up to find some sort of relief, but I couldn't. Then my body began to shudder, and I couldn't get enough air."

Melanie took in small gasps as if just talking about this experience took her breath away. She closed her eyes and went on. "Excruciating pain shot down my left arm, and I sucked in air through my nose, but the feeling of suffocation grew until it just all went black."

Melanie opened her eyes and blinked away the panic that was an echo of her memories. Another deep breath calmed her voice. "It turns out he knew exactly what to do. Maybe he was a med student or something, I don't even remember; I'm not sure I ever really knew. The doctors told me later it probably saved my life, but at the time I was in no shape to feel any gratitude. Anyway, what my young lover had done was pull my tongue flat and shove in wads of Kleenex.

"I woke up surrounded by tubes and machines. The doctor told me how lucky I had been to survive such a severe coronary. I knew what that man had done to me, and the doctor confirmed it. Only cocaine could put my body and mind into that torturous kind of chaos.

It had been absorbed through my vagina, and I had barely survived the overdose.

"I spent ten days in the hospital. The woman who lived in the apartment next to mine visited me in the hospital and told me that there had been a frantic knock on her door and that a man had yelled that someone in the next apartment needed help. The man was gone by the time she had stepped into the hall, but my door had been open. She found me convulsing on the bed and dialed nine-one-one."

One more deep breath in through her nose and out of her pursed lips, and Melanie kept talking.

"I was allowed to go back to work after twelve weeks, but my modeling days were over, and so was working as a dresser. I had to find something much less strenuous, so I took a job as a hostess in a coffee shop. That's where I met Jacob Lerner. He was seventy-two, lonely and rich. He paid for me to go to Hunter College. I got a degree in literary history. I would have married him if he asked me to, but he didn't. We spent five years living in New York and traveling all over the world. Then his lungs began to fail. He was a wily old guy, pragmatic and tough, but he showed me a sweetness that I think he'd never before had the chance to express to anyone. In those last couple of months, while he still could, he told me a lot about his life, which had been so financially successful and was ending with the fulfillment of his years with me. When he died, he left me millions. That was five years ago."

Melanie stopped talking and looked at Georgia a moment then lowered her head and blew out a long, wistful breath. "Since then, my life has been rather quiet. Of course I do just about anything I want, which is mostly traveling, and I've taken a lot of business and investment courses to learn how to deal with my money, even though there are plenty of people who want to help, if you know what I mean. The way I look at it, I can make a hell of a lot of mistakes and still not go broke. I came to Vegas because…" She paused and looked up at Georgia again. "Well, partly because I wanted to study the casino boom and decide if I should get into gaming finance.

"That's the facts, ma'am, just the facts," Melanie declared, playing a tattoo on the table with her fingernails. Half a minute passed and Melanie continued to tap on the table, but now with her fingertips instead of her nails, making no sound.

Georgia looked at her, nodding slightly. Eventually Melanie would go on talking. Melanie smiled at her with a that's-the-whole-story shrug of her shoulders. Georgia kept on gazing at her patiently, but Melanie now was looking at everything and anything but Georgia. A few more minutes passed as Melanie studied the keno board, watched a couple being seated in the next booth, and examined a tray of salads and sandwiches that were being served three tables away. Finally Melanie burst the bubble of silence that hung over only their table.

"I read somewhere that it takes two people to know the truth: one to speak it and one to hear."

"I'll listen as long as you want me to," Georgia said quietly. "You can speak your own truth and at your own pace."

Nodding gently, Melanie said, "Thank you. I know you realize how hard this is for me. I know I asked you to be patient, but that very patience scares the hell out of me. It's like I'm looking into the opening of a long, dark tunnel, and you won't stop me from going in. You're supposed to stand in front of that dark, scary tunnel and give me platitudes and clichés about how you can only imagine how tough I've had it and how impressed you are with what I've accomplished considering all the shit I've waded through. Then I can nod my head, tell you thanks for understanding, and pay for our coffee. Instead you just wait for all of the truth, and you won't even make it easy for me to put up my own roadblocks."

"I'm not sure what you mean," Georgia said. "Roadblocks to stop what? Bad memories? They're just minuscule electrical impulses in your brain. They can't hurt you if you don't let them."

Melanie's exquisite eyes filled with tears, and she whispered, "This package that I've wrapped everything in is loosening up, and I don't know what to do with the stuff inside. I'm scared to death. But I'm supposed to let it all out; that's the healthy thing, right?" She reached into her purse for a tissue and delicately blotted the corners of her eyes. "But I can't. At least not all of it, not yet." Melanie looked at her watch and, with a deliberate change of demeanor, said, "Wow! It's almost four o'clock! We've been sitting here for four hours."

"So?" Georgia said quietly.

Melanie whispered again, unable to sustain the bravado of a moment earlier, "I can't believe you let me talk all afternoon."

"I have all the time you need," Georgia whispered back.

Melanie was shaking her head in disbelief, grasping at a lighter tone as she slid out of the booth. "You didn't even ask to go to the bathroom! And we must have had three gallons of coffee. Amazing! Now the question is: can I get there in time?"

Georgia stood up too. "I'm right behind you."

Alexandra
A novel by Georgia Kassov Cates

February 1950

Alexandra sat eating breakfast at the long kitchen table. Her mommy would not be awake for hours, and her daddy was in his den with the door closed. She wished he had time to push her on the swing, but she knew better than to bother him when he was in his den with the door closed.

Franz, the butler, pattered down the stairs, entered the kitchen at a trot, and breathlessly informed Hannah that Herr Major Kassov wanted to talk to her in his office, immediately. Hannah, patiently and deliberately stirring a pot of oatmeal, smiled.

After a moment, Franz asked hesitantly, "Did you hear me? The major wants to see you in his office, and he said right away."

"Yes, Franz," Hannah said. "I heard you. I will go to him soon." She continued to stand over the stove, seeming to concentrate on the contents of the pot in front of her.

Franz fidgeted near the table where Alexandra was just finishing the last bite of apple pancake. "Would you like me to watch the cereal for you?" he asked, as though he were afraid of Hannah's reply.

"No," she said softly without turning around. "It is ready." Then she poured herself a cup of coffee and went to the table to sit next to

Alexandra. Franz was wringing his hands, seeming to be more and more agitated. He was about to say something to Lotte, who had just come down the stairs, but Hannah spoke first.

"Sit down, old man," she said in a voice that laughed and commanded at the same time. "And you, Lotte, get your hot cereal and join us."

Lotte and Franz looked at each other, and Alexandra wondered why they were both so nervous. This was great, she thought, to have all this company for breakfast. Too bad hers was finished, but she'd stay to enjoy the company. Lotte slid into a seat next to Franz.

Hannah sipped her coffee and seemed amused about something. "Tell me, Lotte, how did you come to find this job? Franz tells me he was hired by Frau Kassov. Did she hire you too?"

Franz was shaking his head nervously and spoke up again. "Hannah, this is not the time for idle conversation. You should go to see what the major wants."

"Soon, soon," Hannah repeated. "Tell me about yourself, Lotte."

Lotte's pale face and braided hair, almost the same shade as her sallow skin, produced a chameleon's effect; she blended into her surroundings, hardly visible and barely significant. She seldom spoke and then only in a timid murmur. Lotte too had survived the war, but the effect it had on her was somewhat different than Hannah's.

Lotte swallowed and spoke in a small, timid voice. "I was born in Munich," she said. Hannah continued to probe, patiently but firmly. Lotte's story came out in small bits, always prompted by another question from Hannah.

She'd lived in Munich with her family until 1943. Then, for more than two years, she had been hidden away in the basement of a cheese shop. Her younger brother and sister, Anna and Bram, the baby, Greta, and their mother spent their days and nights in one tiny room with a brick floor and walls and open supports overhead, where rods of light pierced the holes in the floor of the store above.

Often she had asked why her father was not with them, and the answer was always the same. "He's gone from us," her mother would say. "That's all we know. He's gone from us." Lotte could never learn more.

They only spoke in whispers, constantly fearing that a customer in the shop or a guard patrolling the street might hear them. The man and woman who owned the shop came down almost every day and brought food, candles and fresh water. Sand was used as a toilet, and they would change it often so that the smell did not become strong enough to be noticed in the shop, although the ripe aroma of the cheeses for sale was the perfect camouflage. In the second year, Greta became very ill, and it was finally decided that if she and her mother did not leave their hiding place, the baby would die.

Lotte, Anna and Bram stayed in the dark and damp room and did not step outside into sunlight until the American soldiers had driven through the streets assuring everyone that the Nazis were no longer in power. She never learned what had become of her mother or baby sister. Like her father, they had disappeared.

Hannah had pried all of this out of Lotte while Alexandra had listened with rapt, breathless attention. Finally, during a pause in the conversation, Alexandra asked, "Lotte, why did you have to hide away for so long?"

Before Lotte could speak, Hannah had answered the child's question with another question. "Wouldn't you hide if you knew that the Gestapo would take you away from your family, send you to a concentration camp where you would work like a slave, starving and pathetic, or maybe even be locked in a gas chamber and choke to death with thousands of other children?"

Alexandra nodded her head mutely. Yes, of course she would hide too.

"I learned a lesson early in life," Hannah told the nanny, the butler and a wide-eyed Alexandra. "Be very careful who you trust. Usually the less information anyone has about you, the more you are in control; and control is the most important thing. You only suffer when you lose control. Your secrets are your shields and weapons."

Hannah stood up and pleasantly told Franz to keep an eye on the coffeepot. She would return shortly. Lotte waited until she heard Hannah shut the door to the dining room above then she slipped out of her chair, quickly rinsed her breakfast dishes, and hurried up the stairs. Franz poured himself more coffee and murmured something that Alexandra couldn't understand. She didn't bother to ask him to repeat it. Franz had never been interested in conversations with her.

When she'd delivered her plate, fork and cup to the sink, Alexandra went out the kitchen door and up the steps to the backyard. The window to her daddy's office was raised just a bit, and Alexandra was about to call good morning to him when she saw Hannah walk into the room.

Michael shut his office door quietly. Hannah stood close to him, calm and self-assured. He walked around to the other side of his desk. With an amused expression, she sat down in the chair as she'd been ordered.

Still standing, he said, "I don't know how this happened or what you thought you'd get out of it, but it's already finished. You will tell Mrs. Kassov that you've had an unexpected family crisis and that you must leave this job immediately." His voice got louder. "Today!"

Hannah spoke to him in quiet, lilting phrases. "Michael, mein liebchen, there is nothing for you to worry about. You are safe and secure. No one will ever tell her of our love for each…"

"There wasn't any love!" Michael broke in. "You know that wasn't love. I told you from the start."

"Ah, but you showed me in so many exciting and creative ways! You didn't have to say the words. I knew. You must not be so worried. Nothing will disturb your happy life, or your daughter's, or your wife's."

Hannah stood up and leaned over Michael's desk. "Sonia will never know anything."

Alexandra stooped down below the ledge so that Hannah could not see her through the window. Then she duck-walked a few feet to the right so she could scurry around the corner of the house if she had to. But she stayed crouched in the hedge and peeked out enough to see back through the window.

Michael pivoted and strode to the other side of the room.

"Ja, ja," Hannah said. "We should not take any chances in this house. You are right. But, Michael, mein liebhaber, I waited so long for you to come to me. It has been over a year. You told me how very much you needed me. I know, I know," she went on quickly, cutting off his protest. "Your wife came. No more Hannah."

"So why are you doing this?" He couldn't keep a high pitch of anxiety out of his voice.

"Because this is a good job," Hannah said, soothing and placating as she walked toward him. "And because I wanted to be near you, and I hope that you might need me again." She came toward him, her words almost whispered. "I know I gave you pleasure. Maybe not more than your wife can, but different. You can still have that. We will be very careful. We are both clever. We can find a way." She put her hand on his face, and he slapped it away.

Michael's growl was menacing, like a cornered animal. "You've got to get out of here."

Alexandra ducked away again, instinctively knowing that she should not be witnessing this scene.

"But I can be so discreet. I would never tell anyone how you moan in that special way when you are inside of me or how I've kissed that purple mark on your groin. It looks like a perfect feather, you know. Has anyone else ever noticed?"

"You can't blackmail me," he said, his rage about to detonate.

Hannah's voice sounded dangerous. "Then you will tell Frau Kassov about what we did together? You'll tell her how I came out to this house for months before she and Alexandra arrived? How I slept with you in that big bed that squeaks like a cricket when we bounce in it, the one you share with her now? You will tell her all that?"

He stared at Hannah for a moment then turned and walked out of the room.

Hannah smoothed her apron then headed toward the dining room. Alexandra dashed back down into the kitchen so that Hannah would not see that she had been just outside the window in the garden.

Franz, still munching on his breakfast roll, looked up expectantly as Hannah came in, but she ignored him. Humming the tune to Tara's theme from *Gone with the Wind*, she resumed stirring the pot of cereal. Alexandra busied herself in the mud room, wrapping a long woolen scarf around her neck, then untwisting it and wrapping it around her neck again.

"Well, Fräulein Kreiss," Franz said, "what did Herr Major want from you?"

"How very curious you are!"

"I'm concerned that you may be in disfavor."

"Why should I be?"

"Was he not perturbed that it took you so long to get there? And why would the master of the house want to see the cook?"

"Don't worry about me, my dear Franz, I am not in trouble. In fact, everything is even better than I had hoped."

She opened the icebox and pulled out a pitcher of cream, dipping her finger in. "I think I will be here for a long time," she went on. She put the cream-coated finger in her mouth, holding it there a few moments, savoring the rich taste.

"Now, Franz, go to your duties. Frau Kassov wants the silver flatware polished. Bring it all down here and tell Erica and Mimi to make time to help us."

Franz pushed back his chair, stood, and shrugged his shoulders as he went up the stairway.

Then she spotted Alexandra, who was unwrapping the scarf for the third time.

"Ach, mein liebchen," Hannah said. "Are you coming in so soon? Maybe for a cup of café au lait?"

As the days passed, Alexandra was hopeful. Perhaps this energetic and agreeable woman, who paid a lot of attention to her, would be just like her beloved Frau Bruning. After all, Hannah certainly seemed willing to please, cooking Alexandra's favorite foods and offering even more sweets and treats than Frau Bruning had.

"We have a secret," Hannah said. "You drink Coca Cola and café au lait and eat chocolate, and we never tell your mama."

And there were more secrets to keep, like when Kurt, Hannah's young boyfriend, would come to the house, parking his motorcycle by the back door and teasing Alexandra about being an American princess. Then he let her sit behind him and hug his waist while he drove her up and down the driveway and once out onto the road, revving the engine and speeding for a mile or so down the bumpy road while Alexandra held on, unable to take in a breath because she was so frightened, and then begged to do it again and again.

Hannah often found time to push Alexandra on the swing in the yard or to sit with her in the garden. Unlike Frau Bruning, Hannah wasn't very keen on fairy tales and lullabies; rather, she enthralled the little girl with stories of the war, so recently ended. She described air raids and bombings, hidden refugees and encounters with sinister secret police, and how people she knew were tortured and taken away from their families.

What were the little blue numbers written on Hannah's arm? Alexandra had asked.

"Just some numbers," Hannah had answered. "Nothing important."

"Why don't you wash them off?"

"I can't," she said, and Alexandra knew not to ask any more.

Sonia held the silver-handled hairbrush in her right hand, tilting her head forward and to the left, studying the image of her own naked body in the mirror. Inky ripples of hair were loosened by the pull of the brush and drifted across her face, neck and shoulders. In the upper corner of the mirror, she spotted Michael's reflection. With only a towel wrapped around his middle, he was leaning against the closet door, watching her. Neither one of them spoke, but they focused on each other's images as though they were planning to soon unite inside the mirror. Sonia placed the hairbrush down on the dresser and turned to look directly at Michael, who was coming toward her as he dropped the towel to reveal his arousal.

"Mommy, Daddy, can I come in?" Alexandra's voice merged with the knock on the door.

Michael breathed out a resigned whoosh of air and reached for the towel. Sonia walked into the bathroom and slammed the door behind her.

"Come on in," Michael called.

Alexandra opened the door carefully and peeked around the jamb. She was ready for bed, her curly, bunny-brown hair still damp from the tub. She wore dark red flannel pajamas and white terry cloth slippers. "I didn't get to say good-night to you or Mommy yesterday or the day before." The words had an apologetic lilt.

Michael had put his silk robe on, wrapping it tightly around himself and tying the sash, leaving the towel that covered him firmly in place underneath. "Well then, come here." He sat down in a boudoir chair, and Alexandra climbed up on his lap.

"Lotte says you and Mommy are going to a ball tonight. Will it be like Cinderella's ball?"

"Not quite," Michael answered with a soft smile. "More like General Eisenhower's ball."

"Who's General Eisenhower, Daddy?"

Sonia came out of the bathroom wearing a robe of the same black silk jacquard as Michael's.

"He's your father's boss," she said as she sat down at the dressing table again. "So please, Alexandra, don't make us late." She began to powder her face. "Come now...quick kisses for Daddy and me and then off to bed."

"Daddy, I want to tell you about the story that Hannah told me about a little girl named Katherina."

"Another time," Sonia said, and Alexandra hugged her daddy one more time then slid off his lap and went to her mommy, who pecked her once on each cheek, keeping her at arm's distance.

"Not too close," she cautioned her daughter. "I don't want to catch your sniffles." With a gentle shove toward the door, she said, "Off you go now. Sleep well, my little bunny." Then more loudly, "Lotte! Alexandra is ready for bed."

The nanny had obviously been waiting just outside the room because she appeared instantaneously. "Jawohl, madam."

"Now, Lotte." Sonia spoke to the image in her mirror as she sketched in her thin, arched brows with a kohl pencil. "Make sure you understand the schedule that I gave you for the week. I will be extremely busy, and I don't want to worry about Alexandra."

"Ich verstehe, Frau Kassov."

"And speak in English please," Sonia said.

"I understand," Lotte said.

Michael remained seated in the boudoir chair. "I'll hear the story about Katherine another time, princess."

"Katherina," Alexandra corrected. "Good-night, Mommy and Daddy." She turned and followed Lotte down the hall.

"So you have a busy week," Michael said with a touch of sarcasm. He untied his robe and let the towel drop to the floor again.

Sonia stood up from her dressing table and went to sit on the side of the bed. Pulling black sheer stockings up her legs, securing them to a lace garter belt, she said, "Yes, Michael, I have an extremely busy and quite stressful week." She twisted around to check that the seams on the back of her stockings were straight. "Do you deny that? Isn't it true that an army officer and his wife share his military career? Aren't we both committed to these eternal rounds of social affairs; in fact, aren't most of them defined as command performances?"

Michael rummaged in his dresser drawer for socks and underwear. "Oh yeah," he said. "You have most quickly and admirably adapted to this lifestyle, my darling wife—directing the household staff as though you'd been born and raised on an estate in the Hamptons instead of a three-room apartment in the west end of Manhattan."

Sonia narrowed her eyes then immediately softened her expression as she pulled a black faille evening gown from her closet.

"Do you think Ike will approve of this number?" She held the gown up to her bodice; it was strapless. "Or is it too revealing to wear to a reception for the Republican candidate for president of the United States?"

Michael shook his head in resignation. He stepped into his crisp white uniform trousers. "You're going to wear whatever you decide anyway, and whatever it is will look like a million bucks."

No more was said while Michael finished dressing. He tucked his dress hat under his arm and reached for a pair of white kid gloves. "I'll go down to see if our driver is here."

As the commanding officer of a military base, tiny as it was by army standards, Major Michael Kassov was afforded many benefits and luxuries. Besides the magnificent home and servants, a car and driver were always available for evening affairs as well as for any other needs. After Michael was driven to his office each day, the driver would return to the large house, park in the circular courtyard, and wait to take Sonia wherever she wanted to go.

Sonia's daily schedule was determined by the dozens of responsibilities that befell the wife of the commandant. Even if she roused herself early enough—and that was never easy because she rarely got to bed before midnight—there was hardly enough time for the constant, urgent demands of running a home of that proportion. Servants had to be given directions, and the entire house needed constant inspection.

Her social calendar was the paradox in her life. It was friend and foe, pleasure and frustration, combined to keep her constantly fussing and fretting. Sonia loved being the center of the social microcosm of that small military outpost. She reminded herself that she had a duty to fulfill, in spite of harassing schedules and tiring back-to-back social events.

The number of occasions requiring her presence was many. Absolutely no one in that compact and limited social hierarchy would consider inviting more than three guests without including the commandant's wife. Coffees, luncheons, teas, cocktail parties, receptions, dinners and dances could keep Sonia dashing in and out of the house, literally all day and evening, and her obligations did not end there.

Although Herzo Base was small, it was a link in the complex network of military facilities that had proliferated throughout western Germany. Officers and their wives participated in a constant round of socializing and interaction. Although every army officer was given free housing, Michael and Sonia did pay a price to live in that lavish home, but it was not exacted in dollars and cents or even Deutsche marks and pfennigs.

The Kassovs were expected to host parties, both formal and informal, as well as grand receptions. Undoubtedly there was a generous stipend—these were the days of unlimited military expenditure—and there was always plenty in the budget for entertaining. It was the commandant's wife who planned the functions, hired the extra help, devised the menus and saw to the myriad of details from invitations to flowers, not to mention the dreaded, thankless task of determining seating arrangements.

To add to her burden, poor Sonia had yet another overwhelming distraction in her life; she had become addicted to playing bridge. Dozens of obligations were strewn in her path each day, and the one temptation that could lead her astray was the opportunity to join three other women at a small, square table with two decks of cards. In addition to the local games, she often traveled to Heidelberg or Frankfurt to play party bridge or duplicate at the officers' clubs on these larger army bases. She also indulged herself in continual bridge lessons, always wanting to learn more about the intricate game.

If Sonia had any concern about spending so little time with her daughter, she would remind herself that the child was very well cared for. Besides, Alexandra never complained about anything; in fact, she often expressed great enthusiasm for all of the activities in her young life. Sonia's peace of mind was further reinforced by all the positive reports from the nanny, the cook and other household staff. This was a happy, healthy and contented child who needed little of her mother's time or attention.

But all this was merely the blancmange atop a very sumptuous torte. There were even more lavish riches to be claimed, and Sonia was prepared to procure her share. The black market had become a tacitly accepted, though officially illicit, source of treasures for many Americans. Sonia quickly became an expert in identifying items that would form the basis of a priceless collection to bring back to the United States.

The cupboards in the butler's pantry were kept stocked with dozens of cartons of cigarettes, ten-pound sacks of sugar and flour, boxes of candy bars and tins of coffee. In exchange for these items, German artisans would offer their wares and services, enabling Sonia to have cabinets customized with individual velvet-lined niches to place each of the 450 pieces of sterling flatware that made up the service for twenty-four, luncheon and dinner, as well as serving pieces for every conceivable culinary concoction.

Murals had been painted in the drawing room and master bedroom, and a formal English garden planted beyond the courtyard. She also acquired Capo di Monte vases, Waterford bowls and many pieces of Meissen, Dresden and Lowestoft.

Sonia dismissed the frowns, even the scowls, which Michael would display when he learned that one of these transactions had taken place. Sonia calmly explained that she was doing a very kind thing for these people, that they needed the flour and sugar and other staples more than their silverware or china and that this was the way that the craftsmen made their living. And besides, she was the most generous in her payments of anyone she knew.

For all of this wonderful good fortune that had befallen the young major and his wife, there was yet more. It was the jackpot, the supreme reward, the almost orgasmic pleasure that was derived from the ultimate of bonuses: the chance to travel. Michael and Sonia were able to see and experience, to live the adventure of all of free Europe. From the Swiss Alps to the Italian Riviera, from Holland during the Tulip Festival to Spain when the bulls were running, Michael and Sonia craved these adventures and always seemed able to organize their lives around train schedules and hotel reservations.

Major Kassov could leave his deputy in charge, particularly when he planned in advance to clear any and all commitments for a certain time span. Mrs. Kassov also was able to manage her affairs with travel as the priority. All social events were scheduled so that vacation time would never be infringed upon. Even bridge lessons could not pre-empt a trip.

Parental responsibilities had hardly to be considered when the chance to travel arose. Since Alexandra was so capably cared for each and every day, there was hardly a ripple of change in her daily routine when her parents left. Furthermore, if the nanny was not available, the other members of the household staff seemed more than willing to step in if necessary.

Sonia and Michael could leave without an iota of remorse, kissing Alexandra good-bye, promising presents and souvenirs. Any tears or protest from the little girl were dismissed, and Alexandra was firmly informed that she was safe and well cared for and that her good behavior would be rewarded when her parents returned.

And so Alexandra and Hannah were often together because it seemed that the nanny, Lotte, was more than happy to abdicate her duties to the much more enthusiastic cook. Although Alexandra spent a great deal of her time with Hannah, it was the nanny who was officially responsible for the child's care. As soon as Hannah had moved into the servants' quarters, she began dropping in while Lotte helped Alexandra dress, prepare for bed or take a bath. Lotte was not yet eighteen and seemed very pleased that a woman as worldly and compelling as Hannah was interested in being her friend.

Lotte's brother and sister, Anna and Bram, lived in an orphanage just a few miles from Alexandra's house. Occasionally they were brought to visit their sister. Alexandra was excited whenever they came, but when she suggested that they join her on the swings or come up to her room to see her toys and games, they simply shook their heads and whispered secrets to each other.

Anna gazed at Alexandra's shoes, the shiny patent leather Mary Janes. Then she looked down at her own drab, worn-out sandals and, taking her brother's hand, scurried away.

Alexandra asked Lotte why the children would not play with her. After all, she could talk to them in German, so why did they always run away from her? Lotte had merely shrugged her shoulders, so Alexandra went to Hannah for an explanation.

The cook had chuckled, tousling Alexandra's hair. "Those two are very shy, not used to playing with other children. But why should a little American girl with beautiful dresses and shiny shoes want to play with poor German *kinder* whose clothes are old and ragged? And you have all your toys piled high in the closet in your room!"

Alexandra had protested. "But my toys are much more fun to play with when other children are there. And now that Grace moved away, I need a new friend."

Grace Jacoby, the daughter of another army officer, had come often to play with Alexandra. She did not have a nanny, and her mother was always happy to accept Sonia's offer to have Lotte or Hannah keep an eye on the child while the mothers played bridge. But Grace's daddy had been transferred to Berlin.

Hannah took Alexandra's face in both her hands, pinching in the child's cheeks until her lips puffed out fishlike. "Never mind Grace or Anna or anyone else," Hannah said. "Hannah will be your friend."

For all of her past trauma, Lotte managed to take adequate care of Alexandra, overseeing bathing and dressing, playtime and nap schedules, or waiting for the army truck that picked up the child for school in the morning and returned her in the afternoon. But whenever she could, the young woman would bury her mind in a book, looking up to answer Alexandra's questions in mumbled monosyllables. It was no wonder that Alexandra much preferred the company of those who were more friendly and outgoing, and the cook was certainly at the top of that list.

Hannah often stayed on after her own work was done, offering Lotte some time off. The nanny was always more than willing to abdicate her duties to the cook.

Alexandra loved evenings alone with Hannah. Besides the harrowing stories that Hannah told about the war, the cook often inserted a chapter from her own younger years. And everything about Hannah's past was exciting to the little girl who fervently believed in fairy tales. When Sonia was away, the best part was the make-believe games they played together in her mother's bedroom. They dressed up in her clothes and jewelry and used her makeup. Hannah would fill the tub with bubbles and wonderful-smelling oils, and both of them would get in, giggling. Hannah always did something silly like wringing a wet washcloth over Alexandra's head or reaching under the water to tickle her in silly places. They'd squeal with laughter, holding hands over mouths, trying not to make too much noise.

They always cleaned up very carefully, putting everything back exactly as they had found it. Hannah even wiped off the wet spots inside the tub. Alexandra had to promise not to tell her mother. That was fine with her because she knew that if Mommy found out that they were playing in her room, she would forbid it.

Alexandra cuddled under the covers of her bed. "I love the way I smell," she sighed as she sniffed her own arm, inhaling the scent of her mommy's bath salts, a combination of vanilla and roses. "I love taking a bath with Mommy's stuff. Now we both smell like her."

Hannah had curled up under the covers next to Alexandra and began gently pulling on the damp ringlets of the child's hair.

"Yes, mein liebchen," Hannah murmured, "we have many wonderful secrets to share. All the Coca Colas, the café au laits and candy, and rides on Kurt's motorcycle, and the bath in your mommy's room. Such fun we have together. And no one knows about it but us."

She began to run her fingers ever so lightly across Alexandra's face. "Good friends should always have secrets to share. That makes them important to each other. We both keep secrets well. That is why we are such good friends."

Alexandra's eyes were closed as she enjoyed the lovely way Hannah was making her face and neck feel. The soft, almost teasing caresses were sending her off to her soft and foggy sea, but she did not want Hannah to think she had fallen asleep; then Hannah would leave.

"Can you tell me some more secrets?"

"More secrets? What kind of secrets should I tell you?"

Alexandra opened her eyes. "I don't care," she said in a pleading tone. Hannah's eyes were closed as she continued to run her fingers lightly over the child's skin. Alexandra's own lids were getting heavy; her whole body seemed to be drifting off on a soft, sleepy wave.

Hannah shifted her position so that she lay on her back, resting her head on her arms and hands. "I have not told you the most important secrets. I have told no one because I do not want people to feel sorry for all the terrible things that happened to me. If I tell you, you must promise more than you ever have before that you never give my secrets to anyone else."

"I promise," Alexandra said, her eyes wide open now.

Hannah began to speak, but her eyes were still closed. "I was born a princess. Well, not a princess who lives in a castle like you, but my papa always told me that our family had once been nobility, that my great-great-granduncle had been Frederick the First, the king of Prussia. How sad my papa was that royalty was no longer important in Germany. But it was important to him; he told me all the time. His name was Reinhold, and my mama, his wife, was also his cousin, not a close cousin, but a member of the same royal bloodline. He was a professor of mathematics at the University of Basel."

Hannah pulled one hand from behind her head and began to lightly caress her own face. "My mama died the day my sister was born. She was named Maria after my mother. I did not want her to have that name. It was her fault my mama had died. She should not have her name, I thought. But she did. I was the same age as you are now, almost six years old. My papa would cry at night. I could hear him from my bedroom.

Sometimes he would howl like a sad, sad dog. He had a friend, an older man, who came to see him. The man's name was Friedrich Nietzsche. He was also a professor at the university. Sometimes other men would come too, and they would talk until morning.

"My papa would tell me that I must be prepared to take my place in the new generation that would become the power of Germany and then the world. I would be one of the elite in the new age. He told me that I would inherit the power of the new order that his friend Nietzsche predicted. My sister was too young to be molded at this time, and she was just another female anyway. I was older. He did not have a son to bring into the fold of the ruling class of *übermensch*… how you say in English, superhumans. So his older daughter would be prepared to take her place in the succession of the new order. He would discipline her. He would make her brave and loyal. She would become poised, capable of controlling any passionate outbreaks, self-contained and aloof, just as Nietzsche had defined a member of the master race. There was not a son, so it would be me who was instructed and disciplined. There was simply no other option."

Hannah did not speak again for some time, and Alexandra thought she might have fallen asleep. Then Hannah took in a deep breath and blew it out through pursed lips.

"My papa tried to explain to me what his reason was for torturing me. He would say that the masters of humanity would become powerful because of a stern discipline, which must be taught in early childhood. According to Nietzsche, these leaders would be able to keep control because they had been taught an exacting self-discipline."

"What is 'exacting self-discipline'?"

"It is not important that you understand all of this. The truth is simple, and you will learn it if you are patient and listen."

Alexandra turned onto her side, bringing her knees up to her chin. She believed Hannah, so she blinked back her lack of comprehension and tried her best to interpret, in her own six years of experience, this convoluted tale of Hannah's childhood.

Hannah's voice was gentle and subdued, as though she was telling a fairy tale. "My training began when my mama died. Pain and fear, my papa preached, were to be conquered by practice. He would spank me then lock me in an empty room and not let me out until I stopped crying. Soon I learned that if I did not cry at all, I would not be put in the room. When I got older, the spanking became whipping. The longer I could stand the pain, the more my papa praised me. Self-discipline, he kept telling me, would make me strong. When the pain would get so bad that I would want to cry out, in my mind I would become the princess who was being tortured by the evil wizard. And I promised myself that one day I would get revenge. I would conquer the wizard and destroy him."

Hannah was quiet. Alexandra waited. After another deep sigh, Hannah spoke again. "My younger sister, Maria, who had been spared any attention from Papa, would learn these crazy lessons as I did. But I taught them to her. I tortured her. I was old enough by then to take care of her by myself, and so we were alone together often. One day I forced her into the oven, which had not cooled down completely. Maria went into convulsions and bit her tongue very badly. No one ever found out about the oven, but the tongue became so infected that it had to be surgically removed. Maria would never speak again."

"Because she had no tongue?" Alexandra's words were breathless. She tried to imagine what it would be like to not be able to speak.

"I did not torture her anymore after that. My father became sick, and he did not torture me either. He died from tuberculosis when I was sixteen, and I went to live on my own. I do not know what happened to my sister.

"Now I had to take care of myself, find a place to live, food to eat, and I soon learned that selling my body was the best way to make money."

"How can you sell your body?" Alexandra inquired. "Who would you sell it to, and why would anybody want to buy someone else's body?"

Hannah's chest heaved as a chuckle erupted from her throat. "Ach, mein liebchen, many men would pay for a woman's body, believe me. I had no trouble finding men who would pay for mine." Abruptly she stopped laughing. "Let me finish my story," she said.

Alexandra still didn't understand, but she also knew not to ask any more questions.

Hannah began to run her fingers over her own face again. "When I met Peter, I thought my whole life would change. He loved me, he said. He was a violinist, a student from Munich, and we planned to marry. Peter was killed by the SS for hiding a fellow student who was Jewish. I was alone again, but now I did not want to sell my body, so I found work as a kitchen helper for the family of a wealthy SS officer. He had a son, Clause, who was twelve years old. Clause and I became friends. I would go to his room late at night and slip into his bed. We shared secrets too, just like you and me.

"When the war ended, I immediately applied for a job with the Americans. I learned to speak English, and now I work for your parents, and you and I are friends, and we keep secrets about each other."

Chapter 19

Christmas was just two days away, and early on that Friday afternoon, in the vast glassed-in gallery of the huge Mirage cabana suite, Livy Vance counted the packages that were lying under the ten-foot tree that glittered with crystal ornaments while tiny lights seemed to hover and float an inch or so away from the branches. Livy had just returned from Caesar's Forum, where, under the ever-vigilant eye of Wilbur, she had finished her Christmas shopping.

She and her daddy had been living here at the Mirage since before Halloween and would stay until the plans for the Empyrean Hotel and Casino were complete. Her daddy had helped Steve Wynn when he was planning Bellagio, which was being built right up the street, and now Steve was helping Daddy with the Empyrean. Soon, her daddy had promised, they would move to where a house was being built just for them. She would be able to have pets—a dog for sure and maybe even a pony. Meanwhile she pretended that the tigers that lived in the Habitat and in Siegfried and Roy's Secret Garden were her pets. She'd met both Siegfried and Roy the first time that she had seen their show. She and Daddy had been invited backstage. She'd been to the show again and again and loved the spectacular magic each and every time. Wilbur had taken her twice, and so had Zivah, and one night she went with some of Daddy's British friends and their son, Albert.

And Christmas would be fun here too. On Christmas Eve, lots of her daddy's business friends would be here, along with some of their pals from the poker room and the casino. Maybe they could invite her new friend, Georgia.

Both Wilbur and Daddy had assured her that Santa would make his Christmas present delivery, even with all the security in the hotel. Livy thought she should probably confess that she knew that Santa was not real, but it was still fun to pretend. And besides, Siegfried had told her that he still believed in Santa Claus, and if he had all that powerful magic, maybe, just maybe, Santa was real too.

Livy spoke to Wilbur in her most plaintive, beguiling tone of voice. "Oh, Wilberry, please, please, could we go to the casino?"

"Mr. Vance is still in a meeting," Wilbur mumbled from behind the newspaper.

"Oh, Wilberry, pretty, pretty please, with cherries and whipped cream on top!"

"Mr. Vance does not allow you to loiter around the casino when he is not present."

"We won't *loiter*, whatever that means. I promise. I just want to find Georgia. Maybe she's in the poker room. We can page Daddy and tell him to meet us there. Oh, Wilberry, come on," Livy cajoled. "Please, please, please?"

Georgia and Melanie came out of the ladies' room and strolled along the edge of the rain forest. The casino was as packed as ever. The fact that Christmas would come and go in the next seventy-two hours seemed to be of no consequence to any of these people.

"Good afternoon, Georgia," said a man behind her. It could have been Jeremy Irons or Ronald Coleman. It was Phillip Vance. "What astounding good fortune is mine to have found you again so soon. I've been looking forward to our next encounter."

Before Georgia even had a chance to reply, Livy skipped up, pulling a less-than-ebullient Wilbur behind her. Phillip bent down and kissed the top of his daughter's head. "You have made quite an impression on my Olivia," he said to Georgia.

"Daddy, doesn't Georgia remind you of a beautiful queen, like the one in *Sleeping Beauty* or *The Princess in Disguise*?"

Georgia took in a quick breath. "Those are both Grimm's fairy tales."

"That they are," replied Phillip. "You too are a devotee of the brothers Grimm."

"My daddy is like the King of the Golden Mountain." Livy was bobbing up and down, but her feet never left the floor. "He's wise and old and kind."

"Actually 'wise and kind' is quite acceptable," Phillip said with a patronizing smile, "but I'd prefer not to be depicted as too elderly."

Livy shrugged her shoulders. "Can Georgia have dinner with us tonight?" she asked.

Georgia wondered what was making her spine tingle. Embarrassment? Trepidation? Exhilaration?

Phillip's face lit up. "That would be absolutely delightful—that is, if you are not otherwise engaged," he said to Georgia. "We'll dine at Melange; the time is flexible."

"Please!" Livy pleaded, executing a few more of her distinctive, quirky little curtsies.

"And Melanie," Phillip added quickly, "we'd be pleased if you would join us as well."

"How kind of you," Melanie replied. "But I already have plans."

"Do you have plans?" Livy looked up at Georgia pleadingly.

"No, and I'd love to have dinner with you," Georgia answered, not sure why she really meant it.

"Marvelous!" Phillip replied. "What time do you prefer?"

"About seven?" Georgia suggested.

"Perfect!" Livy exclaimed.

"Gotta go," Melanie said. "I could be late for my own funeral but not for my nail appointment." She waved at everybody and hurried off.

When Georgia walked into the poker room, Tommy, the brush, was standing at the cashier counter, concentrating on the hundred-dollar bills that were being fanned across the counter, ten at a time, then another ten on top, and another, and another.

"...forty-eight, forty-nine, five thousand," droned the poker room cashier. Tommy's eyes were fixed on the bills as he counted along silently then he scooped up the cash and turned, almost bumping into Georgia. "Oh, hi, pretty lady," he said. "I put you on the ten-twenty and fifteen-thirty, but I've got page-long lists. It's gonna be a while."

"How about twenty-forty?" Georgia asked.

"No such animal," Tommy said. "You wanna try forty-eighty? I've got a seat right now."

Georgia was about to say no then reconsidered. "Can you lock it up for me? I'll have to get some more cash."

"Sure thing," Tommy said, taking the twenty-dollar bill that Georgia handed him.

Walking out of the poker room toward the casino cashier counter, Georgia felt the same curl of excitement that had preceded her very first casino poker game. At forty-eighty, the minimum buy-in was eight hundred dollars, but Georgia knew that sitting down with less than two thousand was silly; one pot could easily cost her three or four hundred. If she had a slow start, she'd be finished in less time than it took to buy the chips. She wrote out a check for two thousand dollars then pulled out her Mirage player's card that was needed to access her line of credit.

When the cashier punched up her file on his computer screen, he said, "Your line is three hundred thousand dollars, Mrs. Cates. This check will reduce it to two hundred and ninety-eight thousand until it clears." He counted out the twenty one-hundred-dollar bills, making just two fanned layers on the counter.

"Thank you," Georgia said as she put away the money, making sure she zipped her purse before she walked back into the poker room. That was all she would cash against the line of credit. That was enough. Anymore and it would noticeably affect the balance in the checking account, and then Jeff would get involved, and that was the last thing she needed.

She pulled out the empty chair at the forty-eighty table, removing the post-it note that had been affixed to the twenty dollars that reserved her seat for twenty minutes. She caught the eye of a chip runner and signaled that she needed to buy chips.

"I'll sell you some, pretty lady," said Montana Jones, who was sitting to her right. He had at least ten shafts of reddish-orange ten-dollar chips in front of him, each neatly stacked twenty high. He pushed a thousand dollars' worth in her direction, and she placed ten one-hundred-dollar bills in front of him, which he expertly slid under the stacks. By then the chip runner had arrived, and Georgia gave her the remaining thousand.

"A thousand behind," announced the chip runner to everyone else at the table.

Several of the other players acknowledged Georgia with a smile or a nod, and the dealer welcomed her officially. "Ready for a hand?" he asked in her direction, and she slid the ten-dollar ante out in front of her.

"Haven't seen you play much at this level," said Montana as one up and two down cards were dealt to each player. His was the low card up, and he made a thumbs-up gesture as he plunked four ten-dollar chips right next to the pile of antes. He was bringing it in for a full bet instead of the minimum required for low card. Before Georgia could reply to Montana's comment, the player on the other side of Montana said, "Reraise." He tossed out eight chips. Everyone looked at Georgia, even though there were still five other players to act before it would be her turn again.

"You've never seen me play at these *limits*," Georgia corrected, concentrating on her tone of voice. "This is the first time, but I've been playing on your *level* for a while."

"Touché," Montana replied with a wry grin.

She fought the impulse to swallow hard and swept her smile around the table from left to right. Everyone's eyes went back to the pot, which was steadily growing as several of the remaining players called the raises. Georgia was being initiated into the bumping and shoving club. The friendly demeanor in these games often hid an icy subsurface where the pots, often a thousand dollars or more, were the current that pulled the participants out into the deep water where the barracudas played.

She added her own chips, concentrating on her poker face. She reminded herself of the basic tenets of good poker play, repeating them to herself like a mantra: *Betting is good, raising is better, calling should be kept to a minimum. Just play the nuts. Don't count on the river card. If you need that river card to make your hand, you're usually playing catch-up.*

The ace of spades sat open in front of her. She had the ten and seven of spades in the hole. Often she'd fold these three cards with two raises in front of her, but she knew she had to play loose just to counteract some of the bullying that was going on. Her next card was the king of spades. Playing loose was always easier if you were lucky. After two checks to her left, she bet forty dollars. Montana raised it to eighty, and two other players called.

Georgia's tongue was glued to the dry roof of her mouth, her heart was pounding, and she was having trouble controlling her breathing. She raised another forty and only got called by Montana, who was showing two eights. On Fifth Street, she got the queen of spades, and Montana flung his cards at the dealer, muttering an obscenity under his breath. The first pot was hers, but more than that, she had withstood the rough play and gained a modicum of respect from the other players. Certainly, she didn't have their skill and experience, but pushing her around was not going to keep her out of the game.

And oh the glory of not having to wait for the river card. For the next couple of hours, she consistently got cards, and whether or not she had to wait for the river to make her hand, it almost always won out in the end. There were times, she decided, when that last card, the river card, had a life of its own. It seemed to glow as it made a good two pair into a whopping full house or turned an ace-high flush draw into a winner. That was not playing catch-up; that was playing poker. She was the queen of the river, at least for this afternoon.

Another promising hand started the same way: the ace and king of hearts in the hole and a heart seven up. Montana raised with the ten of hearts, and Georgia called; so did two other players. On the fourth card—*the turn*—Georgia got the nine of hearts, and she raised. Everyone called, and then came the six of clubs and the nine of diamonds. Blank, blank.

Come on, river card, don't let me down now, she cajoled silently as the dealer sent her seventh card. She peeked at it and was immediately disappointed to see the black color. It didn't matter what it was; it hadn't made her hand, but then no one else seemed to have been too satisfied with their river cards because everyone had checked. *Okay, Poker-Face Cates*, she said to herself, *no flush this time, not even a pair*. Obviously there were big pairs in several other hands. There was only one way she could win this pot. She flipped out her eighty dollars. Everyone folded, and the dealer pulled all their cards into the muck. She tossed her down cards toward him, and as he gathered the chips together to push in her direction, those very secret hole cards of hers bounced off his sleeve and flipped up for everyone to see.

"Son of a bitch," said Montana Jones. "She bluffed us all out." He raised his glass of bourbon to her. "Most little ladies don't bluff like that."

Georgia gave a moment's thought to letting the condescending remark pass, but the temptation was too strong. "Why not?" she said. "If *little ladies* can fake orgasms, why can't they bluff at the poker table? It usually accomplishes the same thing."

Had she really said that? Yes, she had, and everyone laughed, and a couple of the players even applauded her. Montana Jones just lifted his glass to her again in silent deference.

At five in the afternoon, she cashed out for a profit of $2,845.

Now I'm a forty-eighty player, she told herself.

Normally she stayed in the same outfit all day and evening and occasionally until the next morning, if she got involved in a poker marathon. But the cable knit sweater she'd had on all day felt heavy and itchy. She'd bathe and dress for dinner with the Vances.

Chapter 20

At a little after six, she was ready to leave her room again, having showered and changed into a black crepe jumpsuit with a brass-studded belt and shoes to match. As she reached for her purse, simultaneously there was a knock on her door as the lock whirred open. Georgia assumed it was the maid service, checking to see if she had left for the evening so that her bed could be turned down. She was wrong. Sliding back the security bar and opening the door, she said, "I was just about to…"

"You were just about to what?" Jeff stepped around her and walked into the room. "Surprise," he said, the smile only on his lips.

"Surprise is right," Georgia said as she struggled to keep a startled expression off her face. "How did you get a key?"

"It seems that the Mirage security procedures allow for a bit of flexibility when a guest's husband arrives and says he wants to surprise his wife for their anniversary."

Jeff took off his trench coat, threw it on the bed, and immediately began to loosen his tie.

"The clerk said he had to get approval, but when I reminded him of the substantial line of credit I hold here, both he and the supervisor were touched to hear that I had rescheduled a very important business trip because I wanted to romance my wife."

He sat down in a chair and propped his feet up on the edge of the dresser.

"Our anniversary is five months away." Georgia remained standing by the door.

"I decided not to call," Jeff said, ignoring Georgia's statement. "You needed to get this tantrum out of your system. Now it's time for you to come home. We're flying into Klamath Falls tomorrow. From there, we'll caravan with Fran and Jim and their son and daughter-in-law. Jim rented a Range Rover..."

"I'm not going back to Creste Verde or to Oregon. I'm spending Christmas here."

Jeff eyed her acrimoniously, the pulse in his cheek shifting into overdrive. He stood up, walked over to the far end of the room, and picked up the luggage that was stored behind the armoire.

"We're booked on a ten-ten to Burbank. That's plenty of time to pack and get a bite before we have to go to the airport."

"I'm not going with you." She said the words quietly. "I have an appointment at seven, and I want you to leave now."

"You know," he said, walking up to stand just inches from her, "I've always been so proud of how astutely and congenially you come to reason. I've never had to waste time and energy persuading you. Now you're forcing me to insist that you comply."

One of his hands grasped the back of her neck and he put his face an inch from hers. She could smell gin and lime. When he started to speak, the words came out between clenched teeth, his wet lips grazing her cheek.

"You will come home with me tonight because you understand that this is the rational thing to do and that acting like a spoiled child will not advance your well-being or my negotiations with Communicorp."

"Are you threatening me now?" She stood perfectly still, careful not to twist or in any other way struggle against the grip that Jeff had on her neck. She held his dark, angry gaze until he released her neck. Georgia wondered why she didn't feel the usual panic that Jeff could normally evoke in her. What made her different this time? She'd have to analyze that later. Now she stepped past him and picked up the phone receiver by the bed. It felt heavy and hard and cold in her hand, like a weapon. She pushed zero, and an operator answered instantly.

"Good evening, Mrs. Cates."

Looking directly at Jeff, she spoke into the phone. "This is an emergency. My estranged husband was allowed to come to my room contrary to my instructions, and he is harassing me. Send security up immediately, inform the front desk that I wish to speak with the supervisor, and please stay on the line until I'm safe."

Then, in a firm voice, she said to Jeff, "If you leave now, I will tell security that the situation has resolved itself and no further action is necessary."

Jeff's pale blue eyes were steel barricades, blocking any trace of emotion. Without a word, he picked up his trench coat, went to the door, pulled it open and walked out. The door swung shut of its own volition, and the force of it made Georgia shudder.

"Thank you," she said to the operator. "I'm okay now."

"Security is on the way," the operator said.

"Good," Georgia replied. "And please tell the supervisor that I'll call down later."

She hung up and went into the bathroom, poured herself a glass of water and gulped it down. Then, looking into the mirror, she assessed the damage. Makeup, hair, clothes: all clear. Pulse rate: elevated. State of mind: only mild trauma.

After assuring the security guards that she no longer needed their aid, she allowed them to escort her to the elevator. She was fine now, she informed them.

Little Georgia was all grown up and on her own. Finally!

The maître d' at Melange guided her to a table in the far corner. Phillip stood and took her hand, again just barely caressing it with his lips but holding on that extra moment while his eyes looked into hers. Livy had not stood, but she was bobbing up and down in her chair.

"Hi," she said. "You look beautiful!"

"I concur," Phillip added as he guided Georgia's chair closer to the table.

"I'm sorry I'm a little late," Georgia said. "I had a slight security problem, but it's been taken care of."

Phillip's brows expressed his concern. "Are you quite sure? Perhaps I can ameliorate any dilemma you might have."

"Thank you. It was only a minor incident, and everyone was quite competent in dealing with it. Now I'm starved and in dire need of that wonderful-looking cracker bread."

"I love it too," Livy squealed with excitement. "We have so much in common! We like all the same things."

"I've ordered a special entrée for us," Phillip said. "I hope you enjoy lamb; if you don't, I'll fetch the menu post haste."

"I love lamb."

"I knew it! I knew it!" Livy was bouncing again. "We like all the same things!"

"Oh, how I hope that affinity blossoms and thrives," said Phillip.

Livy was still bouncing. "How about Siegfried and Roy? Do you like Siegfried and Roy? Have you seen their show? I've seen it five times."

Georgia remembered Sonnie at this same age and how it took so much stamina to deal with all that enthusiasm.

"Yes, I've seen it," Georgia replied, "and it was wonderful."

"Would you like to see it again with me?" Livy was wound up like a top, and something had sent her spinning. "My daddy took me once, but he's always busy now. You know, my daddy is just like Puss in Boots. Only instead of working for the Marquis of Carabas and tricking the king and the giant, he gets lots of people to give him lots of money by telling them how wonderful the Empyrean is going to be. He's crafty, cunning and clever, just like Puss."

"Olivia!" Phillip chided with a jittery laugh. "What a ghastly way to describe your father! You make me out a rogue and a scoundrel!"

"Was Puss in Boots a rogue and a scoundrel?" Livy asked as if to make her point.

"I suppose it depends on one's perspective," Phillip replied, and in the same breath, "Georgia, I hope you enjoy Merlot. I've ordered a bottle of my favorite."

"Lovely," Georgia replied a bit too emphatically while she tried to decipher Livy's curious comparison.

The rack of lamb was superb, and the elegant ambience of the restaurant, the subtle but skilled service, and the pleasant conversation with Phillip and Livy drew Georgia deep into the moment. She was having a wonderful time. Georgia and Phillip had coffee, and both sampled the chocolate soufflé that had been served to Livy.

"Are you going to be here for Christmas?" Livy asked.

"Yes, I am."

"You are?" Livy was bouncing again. "What are you going to do? Is anyone else coming to spend Christmas with you?"

"Not that I know of," Georgia replied as the recent scene with Jeff flickered through her mind.

"Then are you going to be all alone?"

"Olivia, my darling," Phillip said, his British inflection a bit more pronounced. "Don't be so inquisitive. You are intruding on Mrs. Cates's privacy." The last word was pronounced with the British inflection.

"You are sweet to think about me, Livy," Georgia assured the child. "Actually I haven't firmed up my plans yet."

"Then spend it with us! Please!"

Georgia looked down at her coffee cup, finally nonplussed by the child's candor. *Poor Phillip. What is he going to do now?*

He was shaking his head, his expression a mix of resignation, amusement and chagrin. "Georgia, I beg you to forgive my daughter's impetuousness. But she does have a genius for slicing through irrelevant proprieties and affirming the profound. The truth is we'd both be extremely pleased if you'd join us on Christmas Eve. Melanie Nallis and Jules Palentine will be there, as well as several others. I'm hosting an authentic British Christmas repast, prepared by a chef whom I've imported from London to help me plan the restaurants at the Empyrean."

"Please! Please!" Livy's familiar refrain.

"Melanie?" Georgia asked. *I'm stalling,* she thought to herself.

"Why, yes," Phillip replied. "A delightful coincidence. I've known Jules for years. We both spend a significant part of our lives playing poker around the world, and Melanie has recently displayed a keen interest in both the game and the Empyrean project."

Georgia could only think to say, "Thank you both for the invitation. I'd love it."

"Splendid." Phillip was grinning now. "The festivities will begin at eight." Then his expression sobered. "Oh dear, it's traditionally a formal affair. I hope you don't mind. Actually I'm sure any of your elegant ensembles would be appropriate."

"You've never seen me in anything but slacks and jeans," Georgia confirmed with a grin. "But don't worry. I'm very resourceful."

"We open some of our presents then too!" Livy was implacable. "Not all of them, but the ones from the people who are there."

Phillip put his head in his hands. Georgia laughed. Livy giggled and almost vaulted herself out of the chair.

Georgia walked into the poker room after her dinner with Phillip and Livy. Stephanie Bellamy came out of her office, grabbed Georgia's arm, and propelled her back out into the casino, speaking with her jaw locked and lips barely moving.

"What the hell is going on? All shit breaks loose, and you disappear!"

"What are you talking about?" Georgia asked, rubbing the skin on her arm where Stephanie's nails had left a series of little red arcs.

"I've been totally frantic!" Stephanie shot back as she yanked Georgia into a quiet corner by the express cash machines.

"About what?" Georgia asked nervously. "What's going on?" This was all so out of character for the unflappable Stephanie Bellamy.

"Well, let's see," Stephanie began sarcastically. "Where should I start? So your husband comes up to me in the poker room and tells me that you called security and had him removed from your room. It's obviously bullshit, but he's calm and cool…and really spooky. Then he goes into this thing about how I don't know the whole story and that I shouldn't get involved with something I don't know enough about, and I don't have a clue as to what he's talking about. Do you?"

"I'm not sure," Georgia said quietly.

Stephanie obviously didn't care about the answer. "You want more?" she asked then didn't wait for a reply. "I called your room but nada. I checked the coffee shop, the Pizza Kitchen, the snack bar, the ladies' room, and I had you paged about twenty times. Then I decide to go back to my office, and I see your husband again. This time he's talking to the receptionist, demanding that the remaining days of your hotel reservation are to be canceled. The little office girl says she doesn't have the authority to do that, and he tells her to get the poker room manager. When Patrone says he can't force you to leave the Mirage, Jeff orders him to call the hotel shift manager. By now, several people have gathered outside the office door, and I can kind of lurk back behind them and hear what's going on. Patrone's trying to get someone with authority on the phone. Lucky for you, he might as well have been trying to page the pope. Anyway, finally Jeff just stalks out of the poker room." Then in the same breath, "Where the hell were you?"

"I was having dinner with Phillip Vance and his daughter."

Stephanie was dumbfounded. She began shaking her head, looking up toward the ceiling. "Before or after you called security?"

"After."

Now Stephanie sat down on a stool by a slot machine, her tongue making a bulge in her right cheek. She stared up at Georgia.

"Look," Georgia said, "this is not such a big deal. Jeff came up to my room and ordered me to go home with him. I had to convince him quickly that I had no such intention, and calling security seemed like the most efficient way. It worked; he left. When security got there, I explained to them that I was very displeased, that I had specifically requested that my estranged husband not be given a key to my room."

"You requested that?"

"No, not exactly. But if they ask, I'll just say I don't have the slightest recollection of whom I spoke to on the phone when I made the request. Anyway, the security guard tells me he'll follow up with the front desk, and I am to call if I have any more problems or concerns, and he apologizes for the error."

"Then you blithely pop off to a dinner date?"

"Stephanie, I know it sounds strange." She put her hands on the younger woman's shoulders. "I'm really sorry that you had to deal with Jeff, and you are sweet to be so concerned. But it's all okay, really."

"Are you sure?"

"I'm sure."

Stephanie was still shaking her head but sighed and said, "I guess I'm sticking my nose in where it's none of my business."

"I really appreciate your concern." Georgia immediately wished that hadn't sounded so stilted.

"All right, I get the picture. You want me to bug out." Stephanie stood, and they started back to the poker room.

Georgia let Stephanie lead the way and was much relieved when a high-limit player caught up and asked about comps. Georgia kept walking, although now her pace slowed as she mulled through all the commotion that Jeff's sudden appearance at the Mirage had caused. Thoughts and emotions were rolling around inside her head like keno balls.

She walked past the poker room entrance and out to the Habitat, where two sleepy tigers ignored her as well as everyone else. Soon she was on the moving sidewalk leading to Las Vegas Boulevard. She stood to the right and let her contemplations unroll at the same slow pace as the passing landscape.

She'd never really stood up to Jeff before. He was astounded and very angry. And it was very unlike him to rant and rave as he had in the poker room. But eventually he was going to have to figure out that the little girl he married and lived with all these years is gone. Forever.

He's better off anyway. He'd have no idea how to deal with me, nor the patience, nor the temperament, and he couldn't stand not having his way.

When she reached the end of the moving platform, Georgia pivoted right back onto the return walkway and began to pick up her stride as she walk-floated her way back to the entrance. When she stepped off the sidewalk, she increased her pace even more. Walking fast for a few minutes would help to relieve the tension that had been caught up inside of her for hours now.

As Georgia passed the roulette table, positioned right outside the poker room, Melanie Nallis slid off one of the stools and called her name.

"I already have a seat in twenty-forty," Melanie explained as she cashed her roulette chips with the dealer. "I was just taking a little break. That little old lady, your friend, you know the one from Europe somewhere, what's her name: Zelda? Zena?"

"Zivah?" Georgia said. Another dose of bewildering non sequitur.

"Yeah, Zivah. I keep catching her looking at me. It kind of gives me the creeps."

"That's just her way," said Georgia, trying to convince herself more than Melanie. "She used to do it to me too. I think she does it absent-mindedly."

"Well, besides that, I lost three hands with straights and decided it was time to clear my head. I guess I haven't got that whole concept of when to stay with straight and flush draws."

"It took me a while to get that too," Georgia said. "Even now I know I don't do it right all the time."

They had strolled into the poker room as they spoke, and Georgia added her own name to the appropriate waiting lists, including the forty-eighty game. Melanie sat down at her table, and Georgia found a chair against the rail. *It shouldn't be too long*, she thought. There were four tables playing her range of limits.

Normally she never minded the wait, enjoying the chance to be distracted just by people watching. But it had been a very complicated evening, and she couldn't shake a sense of waiting for another shoe to drop.

Enough! She'd done all the deep contemplating and soul-searching she could for now. She just wanted to get into a game as soon as possible. Concentrating on the cards would alleviate some of this obsessive need to connect all the dots on the crazy grid that was boomeranging around in her brain.

Georgia looked around and spotted a woman who stood a few feet from her, talking on one of the house phones. The longest, thinnest cigarette Georgia had ever seen hung from her lips. Her platinum hair was no more than an inch long and spiked like a punk hedgehog. She had chosen a size eight silver Lurex jumpsuit to wear on her size fourteen body, and she spoke Brooklynese in a deep whiskey-smoke voice.

The phone conversation seemed to be about where and when to have dinner. There was an obvious difference of opinion, which the woman resolved by calmly suggesting that the caller stick his own dick up his own ass. There didn't seem to be much more to say after that, so she hung up and, stubbing out her cigarette, yelled to someone several tables away.

"Audrey! Let's go eat!" Georgia couldn't be sure who Audrey was because everyone turned their heads at once. Just then a man reached for the house phone.

"Hi, Milt," Georgia said as he waited for his call to be answered.

He looked down at her and grinned. "Well, look who's here," he said, replacing the phone on its cradle. "I saw you come in a while ago with that other gorgeous lady, but I never had a chance to say hello. I figured you two were friends because she's asked about you a couple of times, even before you got back in town."

Melanie was asking Milt about me?

A page came over the loudspeaker. "Milt Braverman, you have a call on line one."

His face expressed apology and annoyance at the same time. He picked up the phone again and pushed a button. "Braverman," he said. A pause. "Yeah, I'll come over and talk to him."

He hung up. "Old Hank Beuhler is stuck again and driving the dealers and floor men nuts. Jim Chandler, the shift supervisor, wants me to try to calm him down. For some reason Jim thinks Hank will listen to me."

"About Melanie..." Georgia began, but Milt was still tuned in to another wavelength.

"About a month ago, Hank was on a major league rush; then he was Mr. Conviviality. You wonder why he didn't take those winnings and go on a vacation." Milt shrugged his shoulders, answering his own question. "You hang around here long enough and you see every big winner give it all back. That's what most poker players do. It's like they can't stand the thought of putting the money anywhere except back into the game."

He turned away to answer another page. Georgia wanted to ask more about Melanie.

A moment later the dealer at a fifteen-thirty game yelled, "Seat open!" The brush signaled her from across the room. She mouthed a "thanks" and walked over to the table. She'd make up her mind about the forty-eighty game when a seat opened up. For now she plucked five one-hundred-dollar bills from her wallet and tucked her purse in front of her. When her chips were delivered, she pulled them toward her and began unconsciously riffling them as she threw in her ante.

"Hey, Georgia," said the dealer. "Are you gonna return to Planet Earth any time soon?"

Georgia realized that the two people to her right had already folded. She slid her cards toward the dealer.

Marsha, who sat to her left this evening, also folded. "Georgia, dear, you threw away your cards without looking at them! Are you okay?"

"I guess I've got a lot on my mind." A moment's pause. "It's funny," Georgia said. "Normally when I come to Vegas, the poker table is like a vacuum cleaner, sucking everything out of my brain but card playing. The vacuum seems to be unplugged tonight."

Marsha shrugged as she peered down at her own hole cards.

Then it was time for another ante, and the dealer had to remind Georgia to put in her two dollars. Three more hands were dealt, and after the ante, Georgia had no part in any of them. It had been almost eleven when Georgia had finally sat down to play, but her rush of the last several days was over.

A half hour went by in a flash.

Play tight or don't play. She'd thought the same thing for the third time in as many hands. Each time she'd been counting on the river card, and each time it hadn't come. She bought a second rack of redbirds—another five hundred dollars' worth—and moved to a twenty-forty game. An hour later, she bet the last of the one-hundred-dollar bills that she had taken out of her purse when the second rack had been sucked into pots that were never hers. After losing eighteen hundred dollars, furious at how poorly she was playing, she forced herself to give up on trying to get *unstuck* and went to her room.

Chapter 21

A basket of fruit from the front desk manager had been delivered with a note of apology for the security mishap. She had five voice messages, four from Stephanie, all prior to their last conversation, and one from Livy to say how much she'd enjoyed dinner and how excited she was that Georgia was coming to the Christmas Eve party. Georgia was amused that a nine-year-old would have the aplomb to make such a phone call.

Georgia looked into the mirror above the dressing table and said to her reflection, "Well, if it isn't Cinderella, home before midnight again."

She turned toward the window, and, sure enough, the volcano, thirty floors below, was just beginning to spew its smoke and fire, as though it had been waiting just for her. She stood, staring down at the amazing display as it built to its powerful climax and then, spent and satiated, sputtered for a moment before it returned to its half hour of dormancy.

After washing up and changing into her nightgown, she switched on the TV and tried to concentrate on the news, but fragments of all that had happened recently kept reeling through her mind, bumping up against knots of anxiety.

What exactly was she worried about? Jeff? She pondered that for a few minutes, and all she could accomplish was to tick off in her mind, over and over again, how well she had handled that situation. No, Jeff was not the primary problem; in fact, thinking about how she had sent him away brought on a definite sense of glory.

So what was causing the stress? Was it the money she had lost at poker tonight? She'd make that back on another rush.

Then what about the invitation for Christmas Eve at the Vances? She probed at that for a while, but there were no qualms there.

Melanie's traumatic life story. That seemed to cause a little twinge of something. *What about Melanie?* Was it because Milt said she had been asking about her? Or was it because Melanie had complained about Zivah watching her? Something else? A connection? A connection with what?

Maybe the truth was that Vegas was such a vastly different world from Creste Verde that it was impossible to see everything here in a logical perspective, like a science fiction novel where reality is suspended by placing the action in some unrecognizable dimension.

If only she were tired enough to curl up and float off to her soft and foggy sea. She took a sleeping pill and heard the distant rumble of the final volcano eruption of the evening before she dozed off.

Several hours later, Georgia was startled awake by that intensely disturbing kind of dream she had once in a while. She never remembered the details even though the dream scene was still etched in her mind, like that white image that appears after staring into bright light and then looking away. Remembering the dream was not important. Controlling the terror was. Lying very still, with shallow breaths, she whispered to herself that she was safe and in control.

She must have drifted off to sleep again, because this time when she opened her eyes, a halo of full morning light surrounded the closed drapes. An hour later, dressed in a white suede jacket, a red turtleneck, and forest green wool slacks, Georgia was determined to get in the holiday spirit and hoped that she didn't look too much like the Italian flag. She reminded herself again that, for the first time since childhood, she didn't have to think about anyone else's needs, much less their opinions. No meals to fix, no messes to clean up, no lists to check. Christmas was just for her.

Weaving her way among the rows of slots, Georgia darted through the casino like a broken field runner, changing directions instantly to gain the most yardage in the least amount of time. She usually tried to stride through casinos as fast as possible in an attempt to compensate for the many hours of sitting at the card tables.

Now she needed to get a seat at the poker table; then she could focus on the cards, and any shreds of fear or depression or anxiety or whatever would be efficiently swept away.

As Georgia came into the poker room, she noticed Marsha sitting alone at an empty table. Her rounded shoulders were more stooped than usual, and the ornate Christmas sweater clung to her back, revealing deep crevices where her bra cut into the soft flesh. She waved sadly at Georgia then hung her head low again, staring at the felt. When Georgia approached her, Marsha straightened up a bit and forced a smile.

`"Waiting for a seat?" Georgia asked.

"Sort of," Marsha replied, looking around the room. "Actually, since it's Christmas Eve, I decided to come in here early to wish everyone happy holidays. Then I find out there is something wrong with my ATM card, so I'm waiting for Mary Alice to come in. She said she'd cash a check for me." Marsha smiled innocently but did not look at Georgia.

"I'll loan you a couple of hundred," Georgia said softly, immediately wishing it had come out more matter of fact, not so pitying.

"Okay," Marsha quietly said without hesitation.

Georgia pretended not to notice the deep sigh of relief from Marsha as the older woman went to add her name to the waiting list.

Now Georgia gauged the holiday mood that was woven in among the usual gaming atmosphere, much like the plastic holly that surrounded the cashier counter: well-meaning but a bit artificial. Christmas greetings, packages, cards and kisses proliferated, as did cracks about pots being Christmas presents, tight players being Scrooge and losers being Santa Claus. Dealers and floor men received more than the average tips, and even the crabbiest old cranks were forced to allow some small vestige of yuletide cheer to escape from behind their well-perfected poker face masks.

And then there was Mr. Kruikshank, this time dressed in full Santa regalia, including boots, beard and tummy pillow. His "ho-ho-hos" were greeted with varying degrees of enthusiasm. Georgia wondered if the rainbow pills he took were still doing what they were supposed to.

"Merry Christmas, little girl," he said to Georgia and handed her a candy cane. "Fröhliche Weihnachten, liebling."

German? Why would he wish her merry Christmas in German, of all languages? Was Kruikshank a German name?

But other than Kruikshank's candy cane, there were no treats for Georgia that afternoon. She had gone through three thousand dollars in just a few hours, and then another five hundred dollars disappeared in three hands, two of which she'd made full houses on the river, only to be beaten by bigger full houses.

I shouldn't have been in either one of those pots. I was playing trash. My two small pair never had a chance against the kings up, and when my third eight came along, so did the other guy's third king. Serves me right. I'm pressing my play. I know better. What's the matter with me?

She noticed that Marsha had also received some more cash from Mary Alice Clooney, but that it was already invested in more chips and not earmarked to repay Georgia. And now Georgia needed more cash too. So she stood in line at the cash center. And then her worst fears were realized as the insidiously mute messages appeared on the ATM screen, over and over. Her credit cards were maxed out. She stood there for a few minutes, trying to catch her breath, struggling against the dizziness, holding on to the ledge of the ATM machine.

Large gulps of air helped to clear her head. There was only one thing left to do. She pivoted toward the front entrance and marched out of the casino. By the time she got out of the cab in the parking lot of the Wells Fargo bank on Flamingo, Georgia had run the full drill of rationalizing. It was going to be okay because she was staying in control.

Georgia told the driver to wait for her. Getting a taxi out here in *normal land* was never easy. It was worth paying the time. She walked into the bank, wrote out a check, and stood in line to get it cashed. She wished there were not so many people in front of her, but after all, she reminded herself, it was Christmas Eve.

It's okay; this is just another financial situation, she reassured herself as she took the few steps that kept her place in line. Cashing a check on the account she shared with her mother was just that: cashing a check. If her mother ever needed the money for anything, Georgia would take care of it. Meanwhile her mother was out of the country, had plenty of traveler's checks, and would never have to know about the withdrawal. Anyway, the bank statements were sent to Georgia because Sonia didn't know how to reconcile her account and didn't want to learn. Managing this account was Georgia's responsibility.

Georgia was back in her room by four and convinced that part of her problem had been that she never had enough cash. Pulling out small amounts of money at a time just didn't work. She would play better, and her luck would hold better, if she had a big wad with her. She counted the seven thousand dollars in bills that she had been given at the bank. The wad took up more than half the space in her evening bag, and there it would stay while she concentrated for the next several hours on bathing and primping before she went off to Christmas Eve hosted by Phillip and Livy Vance.

The hotel voice mail held two messages for her: the first was from a Gerald Ellsworth, who identified himself as the Mirage assistant security supervisor. He was following up on the incident of December twenty-second.

Then there was Livy's nine-year-old voice with the thirty-something diction and syntax.

"Oh, Georgia, I'm so sorry to have missed you. I was calling to tell you how happy I am that you are going to be at our party. Because of you, this will be a wonderful Christmas Eve for me. Au revoir!"

As Georgia shampooed her hair in the etched-glass shower stall, she thought about the message from Livy. *How does a child learn to speak with so much poise? By emulating her erudite father? And are father and daughter in cahoots? Cahoots about what? Seducing me? Seducing me to do what?* She twisted a towel around her head and climbed into the Jacuzzi tub, which had been foaming and filling. She tried leaning back to relax but kept slipping then flailing in the water to regain her balance. The bubbles made her itch. She really wasn't a bath person.

Wrapped in her terry robe, Georgia organized clothes and accessories for the evening. She'd found a deep-green taffeta skirt at Saks yesterday. Yards of gathered fabric fell from the three-inch-wide waistband to just above her ankles. She'd also found a simple black file evening bag at Neiman's to go with her open toe Jimmy Choos with the three-inch heels. Jewelry wasn't a problem; emerald earrings and the red-and-green dinner ring were plenty. She would wear her white silk high-necked blouse and the black velvet matador's bolero that she'd purchased in Mexico several years ago.

By six o'clock Georgia had given herself a facial, styled her hair, and put a fresh coat of "Rubies in the Snow" on her nails. Now she lay back against the pillows on her bed, tuned the radio to an all-Christmas-music station, and closed her eyes.

Less than three minutes was all she could tolerate. She hated when this happened. If she didn't immediately drift off to her soft and foggy sea, her thoughts would skulk off into dark corners of her mind, and that was not acceptable.

She sat up and reached for the TV remote, but channel surfing produced not one possibility for tucking her consciousness into some comfy, mundane distraction. She glanced at the clock. It was not yet six fifteen, still almost two hours before the evening festivities began. Another few minutes of trying to concentrate on a *Card Player* magazine, and she knew she was in trouble. There was only one alternative left. She'd have to get dressed right now and go down to the casino to wait out the time. Hopefully twenty dollars in a video poker machine would do the trick.

She was transferring the necessities from her purse to the evening bag, fitting everything around the wad of cash, when the phone rang, and along with fuzzy static came Sonnie's far-off voice.

"Merry Christmas, Mom, and aloha!"

"Sonnie! I'm so glad to hear from you, but I barely can. This is not a good connection."

"Sorry," Sonnie replied with just a trace of annoyance. "I'm on a cell phone. We're at the beach."

"How wonderful! Are you having a good time?"

Another smidgeon of irritation crackled along with the static. "Of course I'm having a good time. I'm in Hawaii, aren't I?"

Georgia forged ahead; this Christmas Eve conversation would remain positive and pleasant. "What are your plans for the rest of the holiday?"

"We're having dinner at a ranch near Kona tonight, and tomorrow we're going to the Mauna Kea. What about you?"

"I'm leaving for a dinner party in just a little while, and tomorrow I've been invited to another friend's."

"I talked to Dad today," Sonnie said, and Georgia could not miss the accusation in her daughter's voice. "How come you left him alone for Christmas? Wasn't that a bit extreme?"

"Is that what he said? That I left him alone? Actually, Sonnie, I simply chose not to go to Oregon with him.. Did he mention that he'd made those plans without ever asking my opinion?"

"Never mind," Sonnie said. "I'm just not going to let Daddy's and your problems ruin this great trip."

"As it should be," Georgia agreed. "When are you coming home?"

"The second."

"Then I'll look forward to meeting up with you on the second. Meanwhile give my regards to Billy and his sister and parents, and a special merry Christmas to you, my baby girl. I do adore you."

"I love you too, Mom. Bye."

Georgia put the phone back on the cradle and checked the time. It was not quite seven. She fit a tiny gold-foil-wrapped package into her evening bag and walked to the elevator bank, inspecting herself in the wall of mirrors. She was content with what she saw.

Chapter 22

What was so different about Christmas Eve in the casino? True, it wasn't swarming with the throngs of players and hangers-on that gathered three and four deep at every table and clogged the aisles and exits on the Saturday night of any three-day weekend, but there were still plenty of people around. Most seemed as intent on their particular gaming chore as ever, and the dealers and pit bosses were definitely operating in a business-as-usual mode.

Maybe only Georgia felt the difference. The piped-in music was the same, nothing seasonal that could have been distracting for the players. But tonight it seemed as if a subliminal theme echoed just beyond the generic musical garble with a Brazil beat. The nebulous message reminded her that essentially she was on her own, and for the first time, her lifelong holiday rituals had been deferred, indefinitely.

She watched as a twenty-dollar bill was silently sucked into the slot machine. Perched on a stool, evening bag tucked in front of her, she began to push buttons. A half hour later, she had tripled her money. She pushed the *cash out* button. If she could win even at the preposterous odds offered by this perfidious and voracious video poker machine, maybe it was time for another rush and her luck would follow her back into the poker room. Now she had sixty silver one-dollar coins to excavate and load into a plastic bucket. After she had exchanged the bucket's worth for cash, she went to wash the metallic residue off her hands and check her makeup.

Ten minutes later, Wilbur, the bodyguard/butler, answered the door to the Vance's cabana suite. He was dressed like a Wall Street Christmas card: three-piece charcoal suit, red silk tie, a heavily starched snow-white dress shirt with holly leaves embossed on the starched wing collar and a red carnation with a bit of bright green fern pinned to his lapel.

"Good evening, Mrs. Cates." He greeted Georgia as a subaltern should, bowing slightly, never making eye contact.

Phillip, dressed in classic Armani formal wear, was at her side instantly, taking her hand again as he had in the casino.

"At last," he said, "our most anticipated guest." The words and the way he spoke them reminded Georgia of an old Ronald Coleman movie. Was he for real or was he just trying for humor at his own expense? He brought her hand to his lips, kissing it gently, keeping it there.

Melanie joined them in the entry hall, looking amused. Georgia immediately noticed that her new friend had suspended her recently acquired moderate fashion image for the evening. She was dressed in black again, probably another Donna Karan. This time it was a silk crepe gown that clung to her body from just below her chin all the way to her black satin evening sandals. An oval opening plunged down from the base of her neck and beyond her considerable cleavage. Lying against the exposed skin, from her windpipe to just between her breasts, was a solid chain of three-carat diamonds, probably close to two dozen in all.

Her hair was pulled off her face on one side and caught by a diamond clasp. Diamond studs the size of thumbtacks adorned her ears, and Georgia noticed that a second pair of pierced holes was empty.

"Georgia, meet Nick Loggin." Melanie reached for the long, lanky arm of a man who also wore a tuxedo, though not at all well fitted. This one came with a red and green silk cummerbund offered by rental services for that seasonal touch.

Somewhat sheepishly, Nick said, "Hi," as he shifted his weight back and forth from one foot to the other, calling attention to his scuffed black wing tips.

Phillip was still holding Georgia's hand; she gently pulled it out of his grasp. "Hello," she said in Nick's direction.

"Actually I guess you've met before but not formally." Melanie seemed to be enjoying herself. "I understand all three of you put on quite a scene in the poker room."

"Oh, this lovely lady was merely a hapless spectator," said Phillip, putting his hand on the small of Georgia's back. Georgia took one subtle step forward, but the pressure of Phillip's hand remained constant.

"Where're you from, Georgia?" Nick asked her, obviously desperate to shift the focus.

Phillip intoned, "Georgia Kassov Cates is from Creste Verde, California, the daughter of a military officer who, as a child, lived in Europe as well as several locales within the United States."

Before Georgia could react, Melanie said quickly, "He didn't get all that from me."

"Actually I should say it was Zivah who told me," Phillip said. "Come now, everyone, let us move on from the entry." He ushered his guests into the living room just as Jules Palentine, who had been standing nearby, introduced Brady Cranston.

Georgia remembered that Stephanie Bellamy had shown her the file card that noted Cranston's unique hotel room requirements. Why did he insist on a Nordic Skier when it was abundantly apparent that this man rarely, if ever, exercised? Although he was very tall, he was also very wide, like a life-sized balloon from the Macy's Thanksgiving parade. Maybe years ago his jaws had been visible, but now his jowls folded into his neck when he lowered his chin, and his red-veined nose seemed to melt into his cheeks. His thinning hair was very white, long and curly in a Mark Twain fashion and matched the full mustache with the twisted ends.

Tonight he sported what Georgia supposed was the riverboat captain version of a formal outfit: a white jacket with tails over a red silk vest, white shirt and green silk ascot. He greeted Georgia with a slight bend at the waist. "My pleasure, madam," he said with a low drawl.

Jules said, "Cranston and I are expecting big things out of this Empyrean project. We've both bet big bucks on Phillip and his creative and pioneering plans."

Phillip smiled, but his eyes were unreadable. "Now, now, Jules, you accord me much too much credit. I truly have no new ideas. I'm simply proposing that we combine some successful concepts in a new manner."

"Sure thing," said Brady Cranston, rocking back on the silver-plated heels of his boots. "Like he says, he's gonna use the original approach to hustling the gambler, like they did back in the forties and fifties when this place got going. You know," he said as though he were the first person ever to have the guts to point this out, "the mob knew how to run Vegas. Ya think this whole Vegas thing would have ever took off if some corporations had come out here in the forties? No damn way. Back then the most important thing in a casino was the player. Bugsy Siegel knew that; so did Benny Binion and all those guys. The player was the one who walked in with the money, and he was the one who had to enjoy losing it."

"I've heard this spiel a few times now," said Melanie, rolling her eyes in mock impatience. "Now comes the part about how the mobsters knew the best way to handle the clientele. The old 'the customer is always right' policy."

"So very true," said Phillip, speaking directly to Georgia as if her impression were the only one that mattered. His hand had been gently reapplied to her back. "The corporate bottom line has blotted out the basic premise of 'keep 'em happy,' as you Yanks say it. I just plan to combine a little 'I never met a man I didn't like' with 'you can fool all of the people some of the time.'"

Melanie spoke as she slipped her right arm into Jules's left, while still holding on to Nick Loggin with the other.

"PT Barnum meets Will Rogers and forms a syndicate with Batman and Robin to create a new Gotham City in the far reaches of the Nevada desert."

Georgia was about to ask for a clarification on the Batman and Robin reference, hoping to use the opportunity to move closer to Melanie and out of Phillip's grasp, but to her relief—and that was a surprise unto itself—he stepped away to greet the next guests to arrive.

Ishiro Zenri, another familiar face from the poker room, was as polished and refined as Brady Cranston was lumpy and gaudy. Zenri wore an impeccably tailored dinner jacket, black tie and a pleated formal shirt with jade studs. He was the tallest Japanese man Georgia had ever seen. Zenri's hair was a shining black helmet, and his Japanese features were even and appealing, his jawline as definitive as Cranston's was nonexistent.

His companion was Mindy Cameron, the all-American girl cocktail waitress, who was dressed like Tokyo Rose for this occasion. The red silk mandarin sheath hugged every voluptuous inch of her that it covered. Her blond hair was gelled to the max, brushed back from her face, tucked behind tiny ears, and then tapered forward under her chin.

Mindy was coming to this party on the arm of one admirer when yet another was sure to be there. Was this such a great idea for this Generation X vamp? Did Mindy care? Georgia doubted it.

Wilbur, who had returned to the front door, now ceremoniously herded a new trio into the circle of guests.

"It is my utmost pleasure to present the Buckinghams," Phillip announced. "This is Niles, his wife, Gladys, and their son, Albert."

The Buckinghams belonged in a Charles Dickens novel. Niles was short and squat, having passed portly about thirty pounds ago. He wore an Edwardian dinner jacket, too tight. His dull brown toupee was overstyled.

Gladys was also more than plump and, like her husband, had drab gray-brown hair, which was pulled back from her too-high forehead in a profusion of split ends and then trapped in a tight bun at the nape of her neck. Her pasty face, devoid of any attempt to add some eye or cheek color, was shining with perspiration. The burgundy velvet evening gown looked like she'd draped herself in worn-out drawing room curtains, and the strands of gold filigree chains around her puffy neck were crooked and twisted.

Fifteen-year-old Albert wore a navy-blue suit about two sizes too big. He'd probably gotten a Beatles-style haircut months ago, but now the dishwater-blond hair hung over his eyes, which were grossly over-magnified by thick, horn-rimmed glasses. He seemed intent on studying everyone's shoe style.

After the introductions, Phillip made a smooth transition back to the crucial topic.

"The Empyrean is gaining an exalted patronage," Phillip explained to Georgia. His hand touched her back again, just a centimeter lower than previously. "Along with our Japanese colleague, Mr. Zenri, Niles Buckingham has joined our merry band of investors."

Now he dipped his chin and raised a hand with a flourish. "How truly fortunate we are to have convinced such farsighted global entrepreneurs that their funds will be extremely well invested in the ultimate of luxurious resorts, a self-contained island in the ancient antediluvian seas of the Nevada desert."

"That was for my benefit," Melanie quipped. "Phillip is hoping that I too will join the pack or, as he puts it, his 'merry band of investors.'"

As Phillip was about to reply, the door chimed again, and a moment later all eyes were fixed on an amazing sight. The latest guest didn't bother to wait to be announced, pushing past the decorous Wilbur, bustling right up to Phillip, and planting a big, wet kiss on his mouth.

Layers and layers of bright red tulle surrounded a massive female body. Long, bright-yellow hair cascaded, a la Ginger Rogers, down flaccid, bare shoulders, and a strand of graduated pearls dug into the place where chins met chest. The profuse makeup was a three-dimensional oil painting on an aging face. False eyelashes and heavy black liner encased truly beautiful cornflower-blue eyes, whose impact was greatly reduced by all the cosmetics. Nevertheless, they sparkled with friendly, self-deprecating good humor as Roxanne Roiballe was introduced by a slightly disconcerted Phillip. She greeted everyone with genuine warmth.

Phillip spoke again as he accepted a tissue from Wilbur to blot the bright red lipstick from his face. "Roxanne as well has honored me by investing in the Empyrean. She is indubitably a most perspicacious businesswoman, and I consider it a major accomplishment to have enticed her into our little venture."

Roxanne swung a beefy arm and pounded Phillip on the shoulder.

"I do declare," she said breathlessly, and completely incongruently to the breadth and depth of her bosom, "you do go on, Mr. Vance." Then, in a more robust voice, she added, "Truth is, my business smarts developed as I became the most successful madam New Orleans has seen in modern times. Then I saved my pennies, took some sage advice from a few helpful johns, and dipped my tiny toes into the stock market. The rest is history."

Jules Palentine put a proprietary hand on the nape of Melanie's neck. "Roxanne is an astute businesswoman. She immediately understood and recognized the merits of Phillip's basic casino philosophy."

"What's so hard to understand?" Roxanne chortled. "My original profession uses the same principles. There are basically two ways to sell the product, be it the business of gaming or the business of sex. Every service has a price list, and the range of those prices is determined by the package available. The hooker in the short red leather mini, bare midriff, fishnet stockings and *fuck-me* pumps can charge anywhere from twenty bucks to a hundred and twenty. But the selective prostitute, the elegant call girl who dresses in Christian Lacroix and Fendi, can offer a menu with prices beginning in the four figures. The same is true for a honky-tonk saloon versus a high-toned pricey establishment like the Empyrean is going to be."

Niles Buckingham genteelly cleared his throat, eyeing his wife, who had literally put her hands over her son's ears as the boy squirmed.

"Madam Roiballe states the truth, albeit in a bit more ribald manner than I would. I will add, however, that what impressed me the most about Phillip's vision is that he will market the Empyrean as an establishment that is not concerned with the rules as such as is the more common casino owner. Instead, the paranoia about cheating will be replaced with the elegant hospitality of a baron who enjoys pleasing his guests. The Empyrean will not be merely the game holder; it will be obvious that they enjoy owning the playing field and will profit from those who also enjoy a good match."

Phillip had been looking down at the floor with what Georgia assumed was his version of diffidence. Now he spoke to Georgia again as if no one else were present.

"Confident hospitality is what I will offer." Georgia smiled and nodded, although all she wanted to impart was polite attention, nothing more.

Oh God! First I was the "hapless spectator"; now I think I'm the hapless victim of a double entendre.

"Merry Christmas!" Livy cried, loud enough to get everyone's attention as she appeared from the hall to the bedroom wing. Georgia guessed the child, who was dressed in an elaborate costume, had deliberately waited to make her dramatic entrance. She was Sleeping Beauty, or maybe Cinderella, in a floor-length pink satin gown, which ballooned out from her tiny waist to cover a billowing hoop skirt. A small crystal tiara held in place the mass of curls that had been pulled up, a bit hit or miss, onto the top of her head.

"Do you like my costume?" Livy asked.

Several people answered her in unison. "Wonderful," Melanie said. "Bravo!" came from Niles Buckingham. Mindy Cameron added, "Too cute!"

Georgia noticed that Nick Loggin had retreated to the marble bar at the back of the room and leaned against it, displaying the ultimate poker face, which was belied by his overly casual body language.

Livy was looking only at Georgia. "What about you, Georgia? Do I remind you of your favorite fairy tales? Like we talked about before?"

"You make a beautiful princess," Georgia replied.

"Most assuredly," added Phillip.

"Well, you can be the queen," Livy said to Georgia. "You can be my mother, the queen. Okay? You know," she went on before Georgia could respond, "I'd never give you anything to be unhappy about. I promise." The last words came out in a beseeching whisper.

Georgia glanced around, relieved to see that everyone within listening distance had been distracted when Roxanne Roiballe backed into the Christmas tree, causing it to teeter precariously.

Georgia took Livy's hand and led her over to a quiet corner. Then she knelt down so that her eyes were level with the child's. She spoke softly and gently.

"Livy, I have a daughter, and she's already grown up. I can't be your mommy, but I do believe that you and I were meant to be great friends."

"But you could marry my daddy," Livy continued in a pleading tone, every shred of precociousness and sophistication stripped away to reveal a desperately lonely little girl.

Alexandra…Alexandra had been this lonely.

Phillip stood over them. "May I interrupt this intimate tête-à-tête to escort the two most captivating ladies in the room to dinner?"

He didn't seem aware of the intensity of the conversation he had just interrupted—or maybe, Georgia thought, simply chose not to notice.

Everyone was seated at a massive dining table set with gleaming black enamel chargers and crystal goblets. The centerpiece was a Steuben Glass sculpture of a spectacular iceberg with a polar bear posing on its pinnacle. Black silk jacquard napkins were tied with deep-red wired ribbon that perfectly matched the roses that were arranged in a dozen diminutive crystal vases, one at each place setting.

Phillip sat at one end, Livy on his right and Georgia on his left. Albert Buckingham was seated on the other side of Livy, but neither young person engaged in any chitchat. Albert concentrated on his food, and Livy looked over at Georgia.

The dinner conversation was lively and appropriate to the occasion. Toasts were made by many to the success of the Empyrean, to the host, to the season, to the wonderful evening. Georgia joined in the refrains of "Hear, hear! Salud! Kanpai! Merry Christmas!"

She took several sips of wine, quickly realizing that the payload in her goblet was never allowed to diminish more than a half inch before it was refilled. She couldn't ignore the soulful gazes of the little fairy princess who sat directly across from her. Livy's eyes were speaking—no, that was not right; they were shrieking.

See me, Georgia! See me! See the real me! Not the adorable, blithe and sunny little girl who seems to think that every moment of life is perfect. Don't just look at the outside of me. See my need, the desperate yearning to be loved by you. Give me the chance to be loved like that. Please! Please!

Maybe that wasn't the message at all. Maybe Livy really didn't feel the desolation, the isolation, the starvation that Georgia was interpreting. Maybe it was only Alexandra who had felt that way. Once she had become Georgia, and Alexandra had been banished, she had been loved and cared for, nurtured and protected at all times. That was why she had survived, healthy and intact; because Georgia was strong and complete.

Was Georgia the only one who sensed the child's anguish? Was she supposed to save Livy from annihilation? No one had saved Alexandra. Georgia had been forced to save herself by restricting the damaged Alexandra to a hidden cloister deep in a remote niche of her being.

Georgia managed to sequester these thoughts in a corner of her mind while responding to the spirited interchange when it was necessary and appropriate, grateful that several major egos were present to usurp generous chunks of attention.

Between mouthfuls of food and gulps of wine, Roxanne Roiballe gave a not-so-brief summary of her life: from Kentucky farm girl to top-dollar call girl, from successful madam to prosperous investor to attaining a seat on the New York Stock Exchange.

A first course of crab bisque was followed by pheasant under glass. By then the spotlight had been taken over by Jules, who opined on the concern voiced in the media about the national trend toward the proliferation of gambling establishments and what it was doing to the economy as well as to the moral fiber of the country. His view, which was definitely in favor of more casinos, was shared by almost everyone else at the table. By the time the prime rib and Yorkshire pudding were served, the conversation had drifted from gaming to politics with brief detours to New Year's Day football games, religion, sociology and Japanese rock stars.

Melanie, seated at the far end of the table between Ishiro Zenri and Niles Buckingham, had been a lively participant, but when she wasn't quipping or bantering, her gaze invariably migrated toward Georgia.

Was Melanie aware of how hard Georgia was fighting to stay tuned in? Why else would she keep looking at her so often?

The magnificent meal was crowned off with a choice of raspberry trifle or flaming figgy pudding. Then fifty-year-old port was served in the living room. There was rum-free eggnog for Livy and Albert as well as teetotaler Gladys Buckingham.

Livy, who had regained some of her bubbling and bouncing demeanor, opened presents. She thanked everyone properly, but when she unwrapped a strand of miniature garnets that Georgia had found in an arcade boutique, she handed the necklace to Georgia without a word then leaned over so that it could be fastened behind her neck.

Livy whispered into Georgia's ear, "Thank you. I love you."

Georgia hugged the child and gently murmured, "You are welcome, my little friend."

Livy nodded as though she had expected this reply. Then she went back to the sparkling Christmas tree to help her father distribute gifts to each of the guests. Georgia received a gold Cartier key chain with her name on it.

Amazing, she thought, to have been invited to this dinner only the day before, and Phillip had been able to get this last-minute gift engraved on Christmas Eve day. Now here was the ultimate proof of status and power.

For a while, everyone was involved with opening packages and sipping port or eggnog. Then Roxanne Roiballe commandeered all the attention.

"Enough of this Christmas crap," she announced. "Let's remember that this is Vegas and we are at the Mirage, and the poker room is still open. I, for one, have only two more days to indulge myself before going back to the East Coast. I believe I'd like to spend the remainder of this 'oh holy night' playing poker. Anyone care to join me?"

"I took the liberty of anticipating the desires of some of my Christmas Eve guests," Phillip said. "I've already made the arrangements. We have a table reserved on the top section awaiting our pleasure."

Niles Buckingham was patting his corpulent belly and nodding in approval. "Excellent," he said.

Gladys turned to her son, who had never uttered more than the monosyllabic responses that were required of him.

"Come along, Albert, we can place our telephone calls to your aunt Julia and grandmother Wellscroft. They should be preparing to attend Christmas morning services shortly. I do believe there is an eight-hour time difference."

Albert was already waiting at the front door by the time Gladys had finished speaking.

"I am very honored and most pleased to be invited to join in such a distinguished poker game," said Ishiro Zenri, bowing elegantly. He took the arm of his companion, Mindy, whose smile was a bit cool. Apparently she was less enthused at the prospect.

Phillip spoke to Georgia again as though they were alone.

"And you, my dear, what are your intentions for the rest of this evening? Could I possibly entice you to join our congenial game of stud?"

His arm had found its way around her waist again, and he was gently preventing her from leaving his side as he accepted thanks and more Christmas salutations from his guests.

Georgia laughed nervously. "Sure. I'll be the sugarplum fairy or maybe Georgia Claus. I could fill all your Christmas stockings with my chips."

"Or maybe you could deck your own halls with hundred-dollar bills," Melanie chimed in. "I bet you can give everyone here a run for their money." She had hooked her arm into Jules's again. "Right, darling? Don't you agree with me?"

"I never saw her play," Jules mumbled.

"Then again," added Melanie, "I imagine your husband, Jeff, would hardly approve of his wife playing in this kind of high-limit game. Isn't that true, Georgia?"

Georgia forced a laugh. "Are you trying to goad me into this, Melanie? What's in it for you?"

"Why, how could you even ask such a thing?" Melanie was well into the banter now. "I just think that if you wanted to take some money and buy black and pink chips to play with on Christmas Eve, you're entitled. It can be your present to yourself. And if you get lucky, you could have one of those holiday rushes that every poker player dreams about. You could even buy yourself something. And if you lose, you'll still have done what you wanted to when you wanted. Isn't that a treat in itself?"

"I'll think about it," Georgia said, wondering why Melanie was baiting her. "I'd like to spend a little more time with Livy, and then I think I'll change into something a bit more comfortable. I assume if there is still a seat, I can join the game any time."

"You are so right," Roxanne Roiballe answered. "You just make up your own mind, honey. Don't let all these hustlers talk you into anything. And now I'm on my way. See ya in the poker room!"

After Roxanne's departure, Melanie stood up, walked over to Phillip, and kissed him lightly on the cheek.

"This was an absolutely wonderful evening, Phillip. Obviously I will not be joining you at the poker table, so let me express my thanks and Christmas Eve cheer and how much I look forward to you and Livy joining us tomorrow. It will be quite a simple affair compared to this fabulous evening, but hopefully we will all enjoy some more Christmas cheer."

When all the other guests were gone, Georgia sat by the tree with Livy while Phillip checked his messages, both telephone and e-mail.

No one would be conducting business on Christmas Eve, Georgia thought. But she was mistaken, because he stayed in his office, probably putting replies on answering machines and into e-mail boxes around the world.

She and Livy had a few minutes together alone. Georgia was torn between the temptation to take the little girl onto her lap to cuddle and coo the kind of Christmas magic that she had murmured to her Mikey and Sonnie when they were little. But that was hardly fair to Livy, who already harbored unrealistic fantasies about how Georgia should fit into her life. So instead they spoke of how Livy had decorated the tree with Wilbur's help.

Then she said good-night to Livy, told her she was looking forward to seeing her again the next day, and gave her a light peck on the cheek. Phillip was still in his office, and Georgia was just as happy not to have to go through the "wonderful evening" drill again.

Livy looked up at Georgia with pleading eyes but simply whispered, "Good-night."

When Georgia reached the end of the walk, she looked back to see Livy still standing in the doorway of the suite. She waved at the child one more time, but the little princess in the pink satin gown, her sparkling tiara now slightly off center, did not wave back.

Chapter 23

On the way to her room to change, Georgia thought about playing in a poker game where the minimum bet was five hundred dollars and it could cost a thousand dollars or more to see another card. No, that was not the way to think about it. Was she ready to sit down with hundreds of thousands of dollars and be willing to lose it all? That was the question. Winning wasn't the problem; losing was. Getting the cash was easy. Three minutes at the main cashier counter would be about the time that chore would take. And there'd be plenty of time before the bill arrived to pay off the marker. And then all she would have to do is write a check. What about Jeff's reaction to what a withdrawal like that would do to the balance in the checking account? But that wouldn't be for weeks and weeks.

Then again, she could simply sit down at a twenty-forty or even a forty-eighty game. Thanks to her quick afternoon trip to Wells Fargo bank, she had more than plenty in her purse to buy chips for those games. Well, she'd decide for sure when she got down to the casino.

She changed quickly, replacing silk and taffeta with a pearl-gray cashmere sweater and slacks to match. She left the small emerald studs set in hammered gold circles on her ears. *Christmasy enough.* She pulled the wad of bills out of her evening bag and stuffed it into her large black microfiber handbag.

The poker room was surprisingly busy for Christmas Eve, but most of the action was up in the top section. There, every table was in use. Roxanne Roiballe was holding court at table number one, billows of red tulle puffing up from under the table like red suds from an over-soaped washing machine. Jules Palentine, Brady Cranston, Phillip Vance, Miles Buckingham and Ishiro Zenri were seated at the table, as well as a couple of local high-limit players who had been waiting for this bigger game. Mindy Cameron stood behind Zenri, massaging his neck and shoulders.

Henry, the brush, had one ragged ten-twenty game with just six players to offer Georgia. There was an even less populated fifteen-thirty and two full twenty-forty games on his stud list. She would be sixth in line for one of those seats.

"Want to try forty-eighty again?" Henry asked.

Georgia could feel the bulge of money inside her purse. "Sure," she said out loud. "Why not? Maybe the poker gods will offer me some Christmas spirit."

As she reached into her purse for money to buy chips, she noticed Zivah at the ten-twenty table. She walked over and said, "Merry Christmas Eve, Zivah."

"Ah yes, merry Christmas," said the older woman. "How was the fancy party?"

"Very fancy," Georgia replied and then glanced up to the platform. "Looks like it's still going on up there."

Zivah nodded. "And where is that pretty new friend of yours?" she asked as she casually reached for four red chips.

"Probably getting ready for tomorrow."

"Ah yes, tomorrow," Zivah said, as though it had just occurred to her that this was Christmas Eve. She was tapping her fingers on a pile of chips.

The hand continued, and Georgia could politely move away, so she stepped up on the platform where one of the forty-eighty games had seats available. Henry put a rack of ten-dollar chips in front of her, and she looked down at the five stacks of chips that added up to a thousand dollars.

Her first two down cards were both queens, and the up card was as well. She had rolled up queens! Six hundred and fifty dollars later, she lost with her three queens to fives full. The back of her throat burned as she breathed in as slowly as she could.

It's just one hand, she reminded herself. *A bad beat...shake it off.* She reached for the bills in her purse, peeled off another thousand dollars, and put the money under her less-than-half-filled rack.

Three hours later, the last of the seven thousand dollars was lost when she couldn't fill aces up, which she'd had from Fourth Street. With each thousand dollars that she had removed from her purse, Georgia had convinced herself anew that this was what she needed to win back what she had already lost. People made big comebacks all the time, and she could do the same. All seven thousand dollars proved her wrong, hundred-dollar bill by hundred-dollar bill.

She stumbled as she stepped off the platform on her way out of the poker room but caught herself before anyone noticed. Her legs ached terribly but in a strange way, as though they were pumped full of adrenaline.

No thoughts right now, Georgia warned herself. *Just walk out of here. Put one foot in front of the other; look straight ahead; don't catch anybody's eye. Just walk out.*

Milt Braverman had once given her some advice when she'd gotten a bad beat.

"Keep that poker face in place," he'd said, "even if you lose the hand. Don't let them see you suffer."

At least this was one thing she was very good at; no one would know what she was feeling. It was one of her specialties.

Chapter 24

The percussion of the ringing phone hit Georgia's ears like a buzz saw cutting through steel. She reached over to answer it, squinting to read the time on the clock. Ten thirty.

At the sound of Georgia's groggy hello, Melanie asked incredulously, "You're not up yet?"

"I assume that is a rhetorical question," Georgia said as she stretched her tight, aching back and leg muscles. The sleeping pill had worked, but she must have slept in a bad position.

"Did you stay at the poker table all through 'silent night, holy night'?"

"Actually I got stuck again and went to bed about three."

"Stuck?" said Melanie then quickly, "Oh yeah, that means you lost."

"Anyway, I'm up now. Merry Christmas."

"And the same to you. I just wanted to make sure about this afternoon. It'll be very casual as compared to last evening, so dress comfy and come along."

"Tell me what you're serving so I can get some wine."

"Again, in contrast to last night, we're keeping it light and simple. Shrimp cocktail, chicken crepes, fruit, and Christmas cookies."

"You're making chicken crepes and Christmas cookies?" Now Georgia was incredulous.

"Is that so hard to believe? Yeah, I guess it is. Okay, actually everything is being delivered by Waiters on Wheels."

"That's more like it," Georgia said. "I guess either a Chardonnay or a Riesling would go, or, better yet, both."

"Sure, and come over early if you want. I might need you to show me how to turn on the oven."

Georgia stayed in bed until room service arrived with her breakfast. She signed the room charge ticket and then tipped the waiter an extra ten dollars in cash. It was Christmas, after all. She tuned the radio to an all-Christmas-music station and sipped coffee and munched rolls. For once, she was in no hurry.

She felt as if she had been physically beaten, kicked and bruised at the poker table last night. She wouldn't even think about poker until she had returned from the Christmas festivities. Instead, she leisurely perused her wardrobe, pulling out combinations of slacks, shirts and sweaters, finally choosing a creamy-white cashmere cardigan with slacks and a silk blouse exactly the same shade. An emerald-and-crimson-print chiffon scarf would flow around her shoulders.

She asked the taxi driver to stop at a liquor store on the way to Jules's townhouse, which was in Spanish Trail, about six miles west of the Strip. She bought a half dozen bottles of wine.

Jules was at the door to greet her when the cab pulled up and wet-kissed her full on the lips before offering to take the several wrapped gifts and bags of wine bottles from her. She tried her best to furtively wipe his saliva from her mouth before she greeted Melanie, but she knew the effort had not been completely successful, and Melanie got a secondhand dose of Jules's mouth juices.

After the bustle of relieving her of her packages, most of which were placed with others on the fireplace hearth, Georgia was seated in a comfortable leather swivel chair and served a glass of wine. She took a sip, then a deep breath, then a good look at her surroundings.

The twenty-foot-high ceiling in the living room could have showcased a spectacular Christmas tree, but the only indication of the season was the dinner table, which was decorated with evergreen boughs and gold ribbon. Bright red linen added a slightly pink glow to the whitewashed walls.

The Buckinghams arrived at three thirty, immediately followed by Phillip and Livy, and dinner was served at four. Melanie had followed the heating instructions carefully, and the crepes, along with everything else, were great. Georgia was pleased to see that Livy ate with a good appetite and was touched as the child tried valiantly to start a conversation with Albert Buckingham. Her efforts were hardly productive. Once again Albert, calibrated into a completely separate adolescent reality, chose only to utter monosyllables.

Jules played host, pouring the wine with a generous hand, and, toward the end of the meal, when bottle number five was empty, he pulled several more from a steel-and-oak wine rack that took up one whole wall of his den. Georgia noticed that as he poured wine for everyone else, his own glass was refilled from a bottle of blended scotch.

More presents were exchanged. Melanie loved the leather backpack that Georgia had picked out for her. Livy handed Georgia a package, giggling and bouncing as Georgia unwrapped an electric-blue-and-fuchsia-print silk scarf.

She graciously accepted Georgia's thanks and then added, "My daddy was going to give it to one of his secretaries, but I wanted to give you a present just from me, so he said he'd get her something else tomorrow." Everyone laughed, including Livy, although she seemed a bit unsure of why her statement was so funny.

Melanie handed Georgia a red foil gift sack. Inside, wrapped in tissue paper, was a sepia-toned photograph set in a three-by-five-inch brushed gold frame.

"I hope it's okay with you," Melanie said as Georgia sat mute and flabbergasted, staring at the picture of a little girl with Shirley Temple curls, dressed in jodhpurs, looking up at a decorated Christmas tree.

Georgia had to clear her throat before she could say anything, and even then her voice was shaky. "Where did you find this?"

"The picture or the frame? Actually I found the frame at a little antique store in Boulder City."

"Thank you," was all Georgia could manage.

"Who is it?" Livy asked, peering over Georgia's shoulder at the photograph. "And why is she dressed in those funny pants?"

"Those are called jodhpurs," Georgia said, her voice steadier now but still breathy, as though she were speaking to herself. "They're worn for horseback riding, but they were all the rage for little girls when I was young."

"Is that you?"

"Yes, it's Georgia," Melanie answered quickly. "I didn't mean for the picture to be such a big deal. The frame is really the present." She looked back at Georgia, and Georgia understood she would have to defer her need to question this and that they would talk about it again later.

Then, reaching into the remaining pile of unopened packages, Melanie said, "What's next? Oh, here's one for Albert."

By eight thirty, Jules's magnanimous host persona had subsided. He had become very quiet, even sullen, as most of the bottle of scotch was emptied into his glass. He hardly acknowledged the Buckinghams as they made their farewells. He did manage to plant another sloppy, wet kiss on Georgia's lips as she thanked him for his hospitality. Georgia joined Philip and Livy in the Mirage limo. When they got to the poker room entrance, Wilbur was waiting.

"I thought Wilbur had the day off," Livy said.

"He did, my darling," Phillip answered her, "but Zivah was not available, so he agreed to stay with you this late evening."

"Where is Zivah?" Livy asked. "I haven't given her a Christmas present yet."

"Indisposed, my sweet."

"Does 'indisposed' mean she's sick or just had something different to do?"

Phillip bent over and kissed Livy on the top of her head. "Neither in this case, my darling. I'm sure she's quite well. I'll explain it all tomorrow. Now off you go."

The child reached up to hug Georgia and said, "I'm really glad you spent Christmas with us. I wish we could spend every Christmas together."

Georgia searched the child's face for some indication of how she was dealing with the emotions that had been so apparent just last evening. Livy had been cheerful today, if a bit subdued. Now her clear, guileless eyes were begging again.

"I'm glad I spent Christmas with you too," Georgia replied, hating herself for not responding to the child's plea but very sure that this was kinder than raising false hope.

"Good-night, my golden little princess," Phillip said. "Off you go with Wilbur now. Pleasant sugarplum dreams."

Livy silently reached up and took Wilbur's beefy hand. No bobbing, cheerful good-night curtsies this time. Little girl and big bodyguard turned and walked away and merged into the early evening crowd of hundreds of people who had returned to the tables after whatever their own version of Christmas celebration had preceded earlier in the day. Of course there was some portion of gamers who had never left the casino at all. Georgia knew that Christmas was always a slow time for casinos, but the Mirage was as crowded as ever. Right now Georgia wished she too could slip away into the multitude of players, watchers and passersby.

"I must repeat what my Olivia expressed so endearingly," Phillip said. "I too am elated that you were able to share so much of this holiday with us."

He took Georgia's hand and held it to his lips. After a moment, Georgia tried to pull away, but he held on firmly, opening his mouth ever so slightly, so that his breath warmed the spot that his lips touched. Seconds passed before he released her hand. He was about to say something else when Zivah walked out of the poker room, just a few feet from where Georgia and Phillip were standing.

"There's Zivah now," Georgia said, a bit puzzled because Phillip had just indicated that Zivah was not available.

"Merry Christmas!" Georgia called, realizing how relieved she was at this chance to extricate herself from Phillip's grasp. Zivah had obviously spotted the two of them but did not acknowledge Georgia's greeting. Georgia wondered if the older woman had not heard her. But she had certainly seen her.

Phillip too watched Zivah walk away. "Oh, by the by," he said, offhandedly, "I've informed Zivah that I will no longer be requiring her services. I've been less than pleased with some of the ideas that old woman has put into my Livy's head. The child is so inordinately bright, but she must be encouraged to acquire information with the proper balance of facts and perceptions. Zivah, it seems, is quite fanatical about the Holocaust, and Olivia was beginning to focus much too much on that horrible chapter in our world history. It seems Zivah has told her some extremely harrowing tales about the horrors of life in Germany during the war, and as you can well imagine, I'm most concerned that they could have a traumatic effect on my daughter. I gave Zivah a very generous recompense because I am aware that she had been relying on her income from me, but I will not be employing her services in the future. Olivia's well-being is my top priority."

Before Georgia could completely process this surprising announcement, Phillip bowed curtly. "And now, my dear, my presence is required on the platform. Perhaps we could meet later for a nightcap? Say around midnight?"

"I'm not sure I'll be up that late," Georgia replied. "But thank you anyway."

"But if you are, my darling, if you are…"

He reached for her hand, but Georgia swung it behind her back. He raised one eyebrow then bowed again and walked into the poker room.

Georgia stayed by the entrance. She looked around, focusing on one and then another of the dozens of people who were sitting at nearby blackjack tables. She made a silent assessment of the impact of the last few minutes. Neither Phillip nor Livy Vance was meant to occupy a significant place in her future, of that she was suddenly very sure. Phillip was Jeff with charm. *Not again*, Georgia promised herself. *Not ever again*. And Livy was needy and oh so vulnerable, but Georgia could offer neither the maternal sustenance nor the spiritual commitment.

Been there, done that, Georgia thought, *both for my own children as well as for the Alexandra I used to be.* Livy would hopefully find someone else or perhaps, as Georgia knew was sometimes necessary, learn to provide for herself.

And then there was Zivah's situation. Phillip's dismissing her seemed so unfair and extremely poorly timed. And yet, at the same time that she felt concern for the old woman, she wondered about those disturbing tales about war and the Holocaust that Phillip had mentioned. Were those stories like the ones that Georgia remembered? And did they affect Livy as much as they had burdened her? Deep inside her carefully constructed and reinforced fortress of denial, an alarm began to vibrate.

Not now, not now.

Georgia turned around and walked past the railbirds. *Time to get back to poker*, she thought. *Lord knows I need the distraction.* But then she remembered the red foil gift sack that was hanging from her arm, which held the photograph that she wanted so much to quiz Melanie about. Why had Melanie chosen this particular picture? And when? Was it during that Christmas open house just a few weeks ago? It must have been. She couldn't have just wandered down the long hallway that led to the bedroom wing where the office was located. Was she deliberately searching through the house?

Georgia decided she'd figure out how to ask these very questions when she saw Melanie. They had plans to meet the next afternoon. She took the package to her room, intending on leaving it, refreshing her makeup, and returning to the poker room. Instead, she undressed, took two sleeping pills, and quickly fell sound asleep.

Alexandra
A novel by Georgia Kassov Cates

October 1950

Alexandra had been waiting all day. Finally, in the middle of the afternoon, she heard the sound of crunching gravel on the driveway of the ancient German manor house. The mail! She dashed down the circular stairs, ran across the checkerboard foyer, and swung upon the massive front door. Her daddy had told her that the packages from America would be delivered today. And now they were here!

Three boxes were unloaded from the back of the military mail truck. Franz, the butler, carried them up the steps. One of them was addressed to her. She tore it open right there in the vestibule.

"Oh my," she breathed, pulling the soft yellow gown from the wrapping paper. She had seen a sketch of the Little Bo Peep costume in the catalogue, but it was much more beautiful now that she held it in her hands. Digging back into the box, she found the petticoats, the pantaloons, the bonnet and the ballet slippers. Franz was walking off with the other packages.

"Isn't this the best Halloween costume in all the world?"

Franz bowed appropriately, saying, "Ach, wunderbar!" but he really didn't seem excited at all.

She dashed back to her room, wriggled into the pantaloons and petticoat, pulled the dress over her head, and became Little Bo Peep.

Even though she couldn't button all the buttons or tie the sash on the bonnet, she twirled before a mirror, loving the swishing sound of yellow taffeta sliding over itself, giddy with the ultimate pleasure of spinning around so that the full skirt was lifted into the air, exposing layers and layers of petticoats and, ultimately, the lacy pantaloons.

She scurried through the house, looking for anyone and everyone to share her excitement. Lotte, the nanny, looked up from the book she was reading.

"Schön," she mumbled as she tied the sash and finished buttoning the dress, but Alexandra wasn't sure if Lotte had even taken her eyes off the page in her book.

Alexandra put her hands on her hips. "That's all you can say?" she asked in exasperation. Lotte looked up momentarily. "Schön," she repeated then went back to reading.

Alexandra's parents, Michael and Sonia, had left for Switzerland earlier in the day, and by now most of the servants were on their way home to enjoy the weekend off. But Hannah was still here! Alexandra hurried down to the basement kitchen.

"Look, look!" Alexandra shouted as she scampered down the last few stairs. "Look at my costume!"

Hannah sat at the huge kitchen table. Her long hair had been released from the heavy black hairnet that she was supposed to wear whenever she was in the kitchen. In front of her was a bottle of schnapps and a small juice glass more than half filled with the clear, syrupy liquid. As Alexandra approached, Hannah lifted the glass to her mouth and gulped down all of it.

"Isn't it beautiful?" Alexandra twirled in front of Hannah, who said nothing as she lifted the bottle and filled the juice glass again. "Isn't it?" Alexandra repeated. "Isn't it beautiful?"

Hannah's eyes were red around the rims, her lips were wet, and a small stream of saliva dribbled off her chin. "Beau...ti...ful," she said, pausing between each syllable.

"It's my costume for the officers' club Halloween party, and it will be my Fasching costume too."

The servants had told her all about the masquerade celebration that began one special night sometime after Christmas. She had loved hearing about the costumed merrymakers who danced in the streets, while those nearby threw candy from their windows. It was the German version of Halloween, and this year Alexandra would be part of the merriment. Her parents would be away on another trip then, but she would go with Lotte.

"Go to your room and put the costume in the closet," Hannah pronounced through shiny red lips that seemed to be having trouble forming words clearly. She stood up, swaying a little as she pulled down the sleeve of her dark brown wool dress to cover the blue numbers that had been inked on her arm. Alexandra had asked her once why those numbers never washed off. Hannah had not replied, and the child was reluctant to ask again.

"You go now," she said quietly, perniciously.

Alexandra tried to find a friendly glint in the cook's eyes, but none was there.

"Okay," she said, trying to keep her voice neutral, even though she was greatly disappointed at Hannah's—as well as everyone else's—lack of enthusiasm about her costume.

Back in her room, wearing only her undershirt and panties, Alexandra hung up the gown and placed the ballet slippers side by side underneath it. She was trying to fold the petticoats and pantaloons when Hannah appeared in the doorway.

"Come with me," Hannah said, the words slurring from her wet lips.

"Should I get dressed first?"

"Nein. It is just you and me in the house now. Lotte has left, and there is no one else to see you. Come quickly."

Alexandra wondered why Hannah's face looked so strange, as if she was happy and angry at the same time. Meekly she followed the woman out into the hallway. Hannah picked up a chair that stood nearby and placed it directly below the small square door to the dumbwaiter.

"Rauf mit dir, bitte." The words were a polite request to step up on the chair, but the tone of voice threatened icily, murderously. Alexandra clambered up while Hannah tugged at her arms until she was standing on the seat. Hannah opened the dumbwaiter door, reached in, and pulled on the ropes until the old box had creaked and squeaked up to their level.

"Get in," Hannah said.

Alexandra was amazed at this order. "I'm not allowed to get in there," she said. "My daddy says I can get hurt in there."

"Get in," Hannah repeated in the same menacing monotone. Her fingers wrapped around the base of Alexandra's thumb and pinched hard.

"But even you told me I must never get in there." Alexandra's voice was thready and high-pitched as she tried to pull her hand away from Hannah's grasp.

"Get in," Hannah said again, this time grabbing Alexandra's arms and pushing her toward the small doorway.

"You're hurting me!" Alexandra cried.

"Get in." Hannah's teeth were clenched tight as she dug her fingernails into the skin of Alexandra's arms. Alexandra scrambled through the opening. She had just placed one knee into the rocking wooden box when her head hit the frame on the opposite side then her other leg was being pushed under her, and she was slammed up against the wooden slats. The box bumped against the bricks that formed the dumbwaiter shaft. Before Alexandra could cry out, the door in the wall slammed shut. She was trapped in the darkness, stuck tight in a wooden crate, suspended inside a black well that would swallow her up forever.

Chapter 25

December 1998

Georgia awoke at five in the morning from a nightmare that was interrupted by her own real scream. She instinctively launched into her lifelong drill of assuring herself that she was safely awake now and not at the mercy of her dream demons. After several minutes her breathing slowed to normal, and she got out of bed, wrapped herself in a terry robe, and sat by the window watching the sun rise over the mountains to the east.

She tried to remember what the terrible dream had been about. This was not a familiar exercise for Georgia, who had always instinctively submerged any memory of her nightmares as soon as she awoke. But now she was sure that there was a message to be retrieved from some subterranean part of her mind, and she needed to excavate it. She had to, even if it was dangerous, even if it threatened her existence.

She stood up and begun to pace. How to quarry through the layers and layers of defensive strata that she had so diligently deposited each and every day of her life? How to get below the bedrock? That was the problem. And why was it so important to mine this treacherous chasm in her memory? She only knew that she had to. She needed to plant a soul-wrenching explosive then detonate it to find out how much courage she really had, and if she had enough, then she could face anything.

What could she use for TNT?

Then the answer came to her with that brilliant sheen of certainty that glows from defining a fundamental truth. Playing high-limit poker; that would be the TNT!

Hours later, having spent the rest of the dawn sleepless and agitated, Georgia stood at the window, watching the heavy waves of rain wash across Las Vegas Boulevard. Not much leisurely strolling and typical gawking were going on outside this morning. Umbrellas bobbed at intersections as people waited for the lights to change. Most of them were probably muttering complaints about how the weather had been so great until *they* started their vacations.

Besides their rotten luck with the barometer, did they all feel the usual letdown that Georgia always did the day after Christmas?

Well, it's different for me this time. Everything is different, and Christmas and its recent passing has no significance.

As she showered and dried her hair, she concentrated on the decision she had made when the night had still been dark and desolate. Now that the murky light of a rainy day filled her room, she reassessed the logic.

Playing poker for high stakes was a way out, no matter the outcome of the game. If she won, she'd use the money to buy herself out of her marriage. If she lost, what better way to prove she was independent? She'd take the chance of a lifetime. She would weigh the consequences and then decide on her own to take the risk. And when she won—oh yes, and she would win!—her financial resources would be her own, and her spirit would be tried and true and deserving of the kind of freedom she craved. If she lost—*if* she lost—it would only be money she lost. What she would win either way was the opportunity to deal with Jeff. What was the worst thing he could do to her?

Until now, the worst thing, what she had feared all of her years with him, was that he would abandon her, set her adrift, and now that very possibility had become the beacon that she glimpsed on the far horizon, the reason to keep swimming.

She did not turn on the TV, even when her breakfast was delivered. Slowly she ate her oatmeal and grapefruit, concentrating on the taste of each mouthful. Everything she did today had to be accomplished precisely, calmly and deliberately. The rain had increased, and sheets of dark wetness fell on the street below, layer after layer.

Something bright…I need color today. She put on a royal-blue silk knit turtleneck sweater tucked into black wool slacks. A thin gold belt went around her waist. Her earrings were five-dollar gold pieces set in blue onyx bezels. She could have added the silk Hermès scarf, the Christmas present from Livy, but she did not.

When she was ready to leave the room, she put in a call to Melanie's apartment. Melanie's words on the answering machine were cryptic. "Leave a message."

"It's me," Georgia said into the phone. "I'm on my way down to the poker room. I've decided to play up. That means play at higher stakes than I usually do. I could use a little moral support. Page me. Bye."

Georgia walked slowly through the lobby. The holiday crowd had multiplied in the last twenty-four hours. Christmas Day was over, it was midmorning on the twenty-sixth, and now tens of thousands would descend on Vegas, gathering until the thirty-first to celebrate New Year's Eve, like a nation of raincoated and umbrella-wielding shaman convening to worship their gaming gods at the vernal equinox.

She had to wait in line at the VIP cashier counter while two Chinese gentlemen were informed by an interpreter that their Taiwan bank had yet to respond to the Mirage's request for confirmation of funds. The two short men, both with protruding bellies and balding heads, reminded Georgia of Tweedledee and Tweedledum. They seemed to be having difficulty understanding the casino's reluctance to give them each a million-dollar line of credit solely based on the fact that they enjoyed such amenities in casinos all over the world. The two men kept bobbing their heads and speaking at the same time as the interpreter repeatedly apologized to the casino host for not being able to clearly translate what the two were saying. There didn't seem to be a quick solution to this dilemma, and another young man, whose identification pin read "Kent Marshall," was called over to assist Georgia.

She placed her Mirage player's card on the counter as she said, "I'd like to cash a check for one hundred and fifty thousand dollars against my line of credit."

Just like asking for the time of day, right? Then she tried to swallow, but her mouth and throat were utterly devoid of moisture.

"Of course, Mrs. Cates," the solicitous casino executive said. He smiled at her with dazzling white teeth, probably about ten thousand dollars' worth of caps. His long, thin, perfectly manicured fingers poked at the computer keyboard while he studied the monitor to his right. His thin eyebrows, which Georgia guessed were kept in shape with waxing or at least tweezers, began to furrow.

Kent Marshall played some more tunes on his computer keyboard, eyes glued to the monitor, which was turned away from Georgia. He drummed his right fingers on the counter as he waited out the requisite pauses that the computer demanded before it would display new data.

Finally he looked up at Georgia with the automaton gaze of a cyborg and mumbled, "Excuse me. I'll be right back."

Georgia's lips were sticking to her teeth and gums as she tried a smile to indicate her indulgence of this little delay. She had just accessed the line of credit a few days ago and had been told all was in order and she had $298,000 at her disposal. Nothing should have changed since then.

A minute later Kent returned accompanied by a woman who was dressed in an exquisitely tailored dark blue pinstripe skirt and jacket with a feminine version of a white dress shirt. The heels on her navy pumps had to be at least four inches high. She smiled warmly, reaching her hand across the counter to shake Georgia's as she introduced herself.

"Mrs. Cates," she said, her tone quiet and intimate, "I'm Sybil Anderson, assistant casino manager. Would you mind stepping into my office for a moment?"

Georgia took a deep breath. She knew better than to stand her ground in front of the cashier counter and demand to know what was going on. The invitation to Sybil Anderson's office had been made to offer Georgia the opportunity to deal with whatever was amiss in private. She appreciated that. When they were seated in two low club chairs that faced a sleek black desk, Sybil Anderson opened a file folder that she had been holding to her chest.

"Mrs. Cates," she began in a gentle but professional tone, "your husband was here on December twenty-second and filled out the forms to remove you from this account. Because all of the funds that back the account are in his name, with you being only a secondary party, he can legally do this. I'm sorry, but the only thing I can offer you is an application for your own line of credit, which would have to be based on assets or income that does not include those of your husband."

Georgia took in a ragged breath, closed her eyes a moment then managed to reply calmly.

"The truth is that I'm not completely surprised. However, I am extremely disturbed that I was not informed of this change of status in my personal line of credit. Wouldn't that have been proper?"

Sybil Anderson's eyes were kind and said something different from what came from her mouth. "Normally that is the procedure, Mrs. Cates. But it is noted here that your husband insisted that he tell you himself, and we were not to notify you until he informed us to do so."

Georgia was sitting up very straight, concentrating on her body language, intent on seeming completely in control. "And obviously no such notice has ever arrived."

"That's correct."

Georgia sensed that the woman wanted to say more but was caught in her position as a top female casino executive who had better not ever display any distaff ideology that might be counter to Mirage corporate policy.

Cool and dispassionate, Georgia said to herself. *Me too. I am cool and dispassionate as well.* She rose from the deep cushions of the club chair, grateful that her knees didn't wobble; they felt like overcooked linguine.

"I won't take any more of your time," Georgia said with a friendly smile.

Sybil Anderson was standing too. "Would you like an application? I'd be happy to process it for you as quickly as possible."

"Thank you, Sybil," Georgia said, deliberately using her first name. "That won't be necessary. But I do appreciate your kindness and patience."

"And thank you, Mrs. Cates. You are a very admirable woman."

Not really.

Georgia left the office, which was located behind the cashier's cage. It was getting more and more difficult to move through the casino. Dozens of groups of people were gathered as barriers against hundreds of individuals who were trying to traverse some small portion of the floor with minimal success.

She made her way into the poker room and found Edward Patrone. The largest limit that was being spread right now was 75-150, she was informed. The bigger games would probably start in the late afternoon or early evening. Georgia gave the man a twenty-dollar bill and told him to lock up a seat for her in the main game of the day, whatever that would be. He looked at her doubtfully, probably thinking that she had no idea what she was requesting.

"That could be a five hundred-to-one thousand," he said. "You sure that's what you want?"

"Actually I would prefer an even higher limit."

Half a smile stalled on Patrone's face, and Georgia knew he was desperately trying to interpret her response. Was she serious or pulling his sleeve? He opted for the professional approach.

"Of course, Georgia, if you're sure that's what you want."

"I'm sure," she replied and walked away.

Minutes later, Georgia approached her room, relieved to see that the sign requesting quick housekeeping services had been removed. Thank God this was one of the best-managed hotels she had ever stayed in.

As soon as she was inside, she reached for the phone. First she tried Melanie's number and got the answering machine again. Maybe she was on her way to the Mirage. She left a terse message.

"It's me again," was all she needed to say.

Next she pulled out the Yellow Pages and called the Wells Fargo bank that she had visited just a few days ago, asking to speak to the manager. Three minutes later, arrangements had been made for her to come in to get a cashier's check for $500,000.

She was back down in the casino in less than fifteen minutes, speaking with the manager of the main cashier. She hoped Sybil would not be offended that she had gone over her head, but she had learned long ago to always insist on dealing with managers, not their assistants; it saved time and aggravation. She was assured that she could establish her own line with a certified check but would need the poker room supervisor to authorize the line as well.

This was all so very easy. It must be the right thing to do. Not that she'd ever use all that money, but playing serious poker required a bank roll, and she was getting hers in place, just that.

Patrone assured Georgia that he would accompany her to the main cashier just as soon as she returned with the check. He also offered to order a Mirage limo for her trip to the bank.

Oh, how big bucks did bring out the unctuous charm in the poker room manager.

This time on her way out of the poker room she stopped at the page desk to leave another message for Melanie. Then she made her way to the main entrance of the casino, where the limo was already waiting.

Her carefully formulated plans for this day needed a bit of adjustment. But she could do that. She took deep breaths, inhaling the moist tang of the mid-December day.

A half hour later, Georgia emerged from the bank. In her wallet was a cashier's check in the amount of $500,000. The balance on her business operating account was now less than three hundred dollars. Most of the money belonged to the Caroline Foster Foundation and was needed to fund the Winter Ball, which was to be held in the middle of February at the Beverly Wilshire Hotel. The invitations and patron solicitations would be put in the mail by her staff on this very day, and even though the reservation fees and donations would start coming in right after the first, she'd need $200,000 to reserve the hotel facilities. She'd have to replace the money before the deposit was due for the hotel, the food and flower suppliers, as well as the orchestra.

She told the limo driver to take her back to the Mirage. As they headed toward the Strip, crawling along in the dense traffic that had clogged all the rain-soaked streets, Georgia gave herself another personal pep talk.

So you were looking for TNT. Well, you have it right here in your purse, and you're about to light the fuse. This must be the right thing to do; otherwise it wouldn't be so easy.

As she paid the cabby and slid out of the taxi, she realized that she felt lightheaded and squeamish. *Physical? Emotional? Both?* Maybe if she had some soup and hot tea, she'd feel better.

Georgia was sidestepping her way through the entrance by the north valet when she spotted Milt Braverman coming off the escalator from the self-park garage. He saw her at the same time and waited for her to catch up to him.

He was wearing jeans and a pale blue striped dress shirt. A leather jacket was hooked over his thumb.

What a wonderful neck he has, and his hair is soft and curly with a few raindrops still glistening in it.

"Been *malling* again?" he asked as she joined him.

Georgia had to clear her throat before she spoke. No, the truth was her throat was fine; it was her mind that needed clearing.

"Actually I've been taking care of a business matter," Georgia replied. "Had to go to the bank."

"And now you're heading back to your office?" He grinned at her. "Me too—back to the daily grind."

"Actually I'm not going to play right now," Georgia said. "After I check in to see if I have any messages, I was going to the coffee shop for a bowl of soup."

"Want company?"

"Sure," Georgia answered, surprised at how very pleasant that prospect seemed to her, even at one of the queasiest moments of her life.

They made a quick stop in the poker room for a line pass and to learn that Melanie had not been in nor called to get the message Georgia had left for her.

In the Caribe Café, Milt ordered a club sandwich and iced tea, and while they waited to be served, he chatted about how the poker action in Vegas was different at holiday time.

Georgia was grateful for the company, and yet she was struggling to pay attention to what he was saying. She was a bit distracted by the fact that she had a half million dollars in her purse, so she focused on his smooth, tanned complexion and the tiny laugh lines by his eyes. She liked his eyes, and she wondered why looking into them made her feel so safe.

And suddenly she wanted to know more about him, but she was going to embarrass both of them if she let him talk on without a clue as to what he was saying while she floated off on her soft and foggy sea.

There was only one way to remedy this. She had to get him to talk about what interested her, and right now that was him. Finally she took a chance that interrupting him wouldn't seem too rude or, worse yet, too weird.

"I'm trying to figure out where that twang of yours comes from. I haven't been able to place it. It's definitely not East Coast or West Coast."

"I'm a transplanted cheesehead," he told her. "Grew up in Wisconsin."

"And?" she prompted as she placed her elbows on the table, cradling her chin in her hands.

"Life story?" Milt hesitated a moment then said, "Pretty dull."

"*Readers Digest* version?" she prompted.

"More like *Mad* magazine version."

Georgia tried the silent technique, and sure enough, Milt finally smiled and began to talk. She loved his smile, she loved his voice, she loved the way his Adam's apple bobbed up and down.

"I grew up in a little town called Wauwatosa, a suburb of Milwaukee. My dad was a postman, and my mom taught fourth grade. There's just my sister, Julie, she's eight years younger than me. I did pretty good as a quarterback in high school, got a scholarship to play ball at Wisconsin then I was drafted by the Cincinnati Bengals, probably the best day in my life so far."

"I don't know a lot about pro football," Georgia said apologetically, "but my son will be impressed."

Milt shook his head, and his smile was sad at the corners of his mouth.

"He never heard of me," he said with certainty. "My pro career ended during the first preseason. I ruptured three discs in the first game. After a whole season of rehab, and even though I could walk without a limp, the docs couldn't give any positive prognosis for my playing again, so I was released from my contract."

Georgia thought she should say she was really sorry, but Milt continued talking, and she was relieved.

"After I literally cried in my beer for a couple of months, I figured out that I wanted more out of life than what my BA in poli sci would probably get me, so I went to law school in Chicago."

"You're a lawyer?" Georgia asked, unhappy that the question came out in such an incredulous tone.

Milt's smile was crooked again, but his eyes sparkled with amusement.

"Pretty hard to believe, huh? Actually I didn't ever practice law. I did some legal investigation, like tracking down missing witnesses, that sort of thing. I was pretty good at it and actually liked it better than going into an office and staying put all day. So I got a job with a private investigation firm; they liked my legal background. I was really good at working my way through court documents for pertinent information."

"Was that still in Chicago?"

"Yeah, for a while. But then one of my cases brought me to Vegas, and basically I've been here ever since."

"How long?"

"Fifteen years in June. Jesus," he sighed, "that's a long time. Well, anyway, it was probably the right move. I've liked it here and never had the urge to try anywhere else, even after I got divorced. I married a poker dealer; that's how I got into the game. But she had problems, and luckily there were no kids yet when she left me for a high roller who promised her the moon. Haven't heard from her in years. I don't think she's even in Nevada anymore."

For yet a third time, he didn't allow her to comment. "So I've been a bachelor for a long time and do my best not to get fixed up by too many well-meaning friends."

"Didn't you want a family?" The question popped out before Georgia could stop herself.

"Oh, I've got a great family," he said. "My kid sister and her husband moved out here about twelve years ago, and I was there to see both my nieces and my nephew within minutes of their births. Then, about three years ago, my brother-in-law decides that forty is a good age to jettison the wife and kids, marry a twenty-year-old bimbo, and start all over again…in Tahiti. So I spend a lot of time with my sister, Julie, and the kids. I'm really enjoying getting into Little League with Matt. He's the eleven-year-old."

What an absolutely perfect answer, Georgia thought, or did she say it out loud?

Oh my God! I did!

"A perfect answer to what?" Milt asked.

"Oh," she said, stuttering, "I, uh, I meant that if a woman has to be abandoned by her husband, how great to have a loving, caring big brother around to help with the kids. That's what I meant."

She took a gulp of ice water and then busied herself with wiping the condensation off the outside of the glass.

Milt watched her, that crooked grin on his face. Finally he said, "You seem kind of nervous today. Is everything all right?"

A nanosecond before, Georgia had not even remotely considered telling Milt about the money.

"I just withdrew half a million dollars from my business account, and I've locked up a seat in the main game."

The crooked grin was gone. "Why do you want to play for those stakes?" he asked gently.

He just wants to understand. So did she.

She was amazed that their eye contact had not been interrupted. No judgment, no accusation, no cynicism.

"It's complicated," she murmured.

"I should hope so," he said with just a hint of a smile. "I'd hate to think that you were doing this on some dumb whim."

"I don't think I can explain it all to you because I have yet to accomplish that for myself, and besides, it would be a waste of time unless you knew more about me, and I'm not going to inflict that on you, but thank you for not getting on my case right away. I appreciate your patience."

He looked at her for a long moment then said, "So you've decided for sure?"

"Yes." Now she looked away from him. She needed to be on her own again.

"Want some tips?"

"Okay," she said, not really sure that anything Milt would tell her could make any difference.

"They play a different game up there. It's more about chips than cards, so tip number one: play your usual game; don't try to play theirs. Tip number two: use your common sense. And tip number three: keep your cool."

The crooked grin again. He reached over to take her hand. She thought he was going impart more advice, maybe something a bit more specific, but he didn't. After several moments he said, "Good luck."

Georgia and Milt walked back to the poker room without any more conversation, concentrating instead on picking their way through the masses of tourists who had coalesced into a nearly solid entity. When she entered the poker room, Georgia noticed Mindy Cameron seated behind Ishiro Zenri up on the platform, leaning against him in a very intimate way while his right hand massaged her inner thigh. Mindy looked up in time to make eye contact with Georgia and then pointedly looked in the direction of the manager's office. Standing there was Edward Patrone, scowling back at Mindy, whose lime-green spandex minidress could easily be mistaken for a bathing suit.

Georgia guessed that Patrone was less than pleased that one of the poker room cocktail waitresses was having her thigh fondled by one of the high rollers, even if she was off duty. That just couldn't be a good career move. Obviously Mindy was either too dumb—or maybe too libidinous—to know better, or simply didn't care, or all of the above.

When Georgia looked back to Patrone, his expression had morphed into a solicitous smile, and it was aimed at her. He came toward her, hands held out in greeting.

"Hi, Georgia," he gushed. "I put your name on the list for the main game. Are you ready to do that little errand we spoke of earlier?"

Of course, Georgia thought. *I suddenly have taken on some significance! I'm being welcomed into the high roller club.*

Patrone was still babbling. "Since you didn't leave a preference for which seat you preferred, I checked with some of the dealers. I locked up the two seat for you, but the three and six are still available if you prefer."

Oh brother!

Georgia smiled pleasantly and thanked him. "The two seat is just fine," she said.

The card room manager was at her beck and call.

"At your convenience, we're off to the main cashier."

"Thank you. I'd appreciate that," Georgia replied as she noticed that Milt had already taken a seat in a ten-twenty game.

In less than twenty minutes, Patrone and his own personal security guard were back in the poker room with Georgia's $500,000 in cash and chips. Unhurriedly she stepped up into the top section, Patrone right behind her. He pulled the chair out from the table like the maître d' at Melange. She sat down and waited while he bent over and placed the pile of cash and chips in front of her.

Then, quietly, he said into Georgia's ear, "I'd be happy to arrange for a safe deposit box if you like."

"Perhaps after I play," she replied. "We'll see."

Georgia was enjoying this, even though she was scared beyond any sense of monetary peril. What if, after this ridiculous poker session she was about to engage in, there were no cash or chips left to consider stashing in her own safety deposit box?

Besides Ishiro Zenri, only Niles Buckingham was seated at the table. Lance, the dealer, took his place in the box while the poker room manager unlocked the chip rack cover. Several of the other players were soon in the process of settling in.

It really wasn't about winning money; playing seven-card stud was what she wanted to do. Georgia had been telling herself that since the first time she had sat down at a casino poker table. Now it was time to admit that she needed to win the money. She had to—her survival depended on it. She casually riffled a stack of white five-thousand-dollar chips. She hoped it looked as if she had everything in control. She had perfected her poker face, and no one could guess that the elegant, perfectly composed exterior was a façade. Inside was jelly.

Playing cards was supposed to be for fun, recreation, relaxation and distraction from the stresses in life; that had always been Georgia's philosophy. Suddenly poker had become the ultimate stress. How had she ended up playing in a game with these stakes? She was gambling with her career, her marriage, her scruples and her future.

Stop it, you twerp! You're here, the money's here, the game is on, and you're in it.

Now that a dealer was seated at the table, Georgia could leave, knowing her chips and cash would be safeguarded. Although she continually congratulated herself on how well she was masking the bilious terror that was increasing by the minute, her bladder was not cooperating. A trip to the ladies' room was mandatory.

When Georgia sat down at the mirrored dressing tables, Mindy Cameron, who had been waiting for her while she washed her hands, asked, "Are you nervous?"

"About what?" Georgia pulled her makeup kit from her purse.

"About playing five-hundred stud!"

"I guess," Georgia answered, trying very hard to keep her hand steady as she applied lip liner.

"Well, I'd be nervous," Mindy stated. "Geez, I'm nervous just sitting and watching those games. One bet is more than I make in a week."

Georgia just smiled as she blended more gray shadow into the creases in her eyelids. What could she say? *You're right, bimbo, this is light-years out of your league, and I don't even belong in the same galaxy.*

"Ishiro promised that if he won tonight, he'd take me to Cabo tomorrow. Nothing personal, but needless to say, I'll be rooting for him. I've never been to Cabo."

"Of course, nothing personal," Georgia said.

"Now don't get me wrong. It's not just that I want to see Cabo. I also want to be with Ishiro. He's a fascinating man. Really deep. He was telling me about his family and how he made all of his money. You know, his grandparents lived near Nagasaki when they dropped the atom bomb. How's that for intense? He was born over here and ended up spending a couple of years in Manzanar. You know the Japanese internment camp in Arizona?"

"Yes, I know," Georgia replied.

"Well, anyway, he grew up in Long Beach and went to Stanford. He got into electronics and took some ideas back to Japan. I guess he made gazillions."

"How nice for him." Georgia immediately regretted the acerbic retort but then realized it had been completely lost on Mindy.

"Yeah, I know," she replied, practically swooning. "Now my big problem is how to deal with Nick, and…"

"Hey, Georgia," Roxanne Roiballe called as she bustled toward the stalls. "I just heard you're gonna play five hundred," she yelled as she slammed and locked a stall door. Now everybody in the entire thirty-stall ladies' room had been informed; maybe a few out in the casino heard it too.

"She sure is!" Mindy confirmed loud enough for Roxanne to hear. "You ladies have a lot of guts."

"It doesn't take guts, sweetie," Roxanne yelled back. "Just money!"

Georgia began to shove everything back into her purse. She had to get out of here.

A moment later Roxanne came around the corner and went to the sink. She wore a bright green scoop-necked silk blouse over gigantic palazzo pants made from yards and yards of gold Lurex knit, a gold rope bracelet on one thick wrist and a man's Rolex watch on the other. Huge green metallic disks hung from her ears, pulling her lobes into long, rubbery pendulums.

Mindy was about to add more commentary, but before she said any more, Georgia spoke up. "Excuse me, ladies, but I want to get settled at the table. See you there."

It was nearly four in the afternoon, and there was still no word from Melanie. Georgia went to a house phone just inside the poker room and called her friend's apartment again. The phone rang twice, and the answering machine came on. Just as Georgia was beginning to leave another message, Melanie picked up the receiver.

"Hi, Georgia." Melanie's voice was soft and raspy. "I've been screening my calls. Are you having a good day at the tables?"

"I haven't played yet. Did you get my other messages?"

There was a long pause. Georgia wondered if they'd been disconnected. "Melanie?"

Melanie tried to clear her throat. "I just needed a little down time. I was going to get in touch with you later."

"What's going on? You don't sound right." Georgia waited for an answer. Silence. Then Georgia asked, "Are you sick?"

"No, I'm not sick," said Melanie with a deep sigh.

"Then what?" More silence. "Look," Georgia continued, "I don't want to stick my nose in where it doesn't belong, but I'm willing to listen. You know that."

"I had a little accident, and I need a few days to get over the soreness."

"What the hell kind of 'little accident,' and why do I have to twist this information out of you?"

No response.

"Okay, now you can't get rid of me."

Silence again.

"I know you're politely telling me to mind my own business, but it's too late. You think you're sore now! Wait till you add the pain in your rear that I'll become unless you give me some information. I'm not going away, so stop wasting our time. What happened?"

So much for the subtle approach.

Another deep sigh from Melanie, this one with a catch of breath in the middle.

"I can't talk about it now, Georgia. Maybe we can get together in a few days."

"Are you alone?" Georgia asked.

"Yes."

"Then I'm on my way, and I'm hanging up before you can tell me not to come. It wouldn't matter anyway."

Georgia replaced the receiver and went to Edward Patrone's office. Within ten minutes, she had signed for a safe deposit box and placed the $500,000 in chips and cash inside. When it was locked into the wall, she pulled an address book from her purse and made her way to the main entrance.

Melanie's twenty-story apartment complex was just a few blocks east of the Strip, but it took the cab a good twenty minutes to maneuver through the rainy late afternoon. The doorman greeted Georgia cordially, helping her out of the cab. This was a high-security building, and the receptionist looked as if she and the doorman could be partners in tag-team wrestling.

Melanie answered the page, and Georgia was allowed to join another member of WrestleMania who operated the elevator.

Melanie was waiting in her doorway. She was dressed in a white terry robe and slippers to match. Her hair, still damp from the shower, fell across her forehead in strands. Although they were very close to the same age, Georgia had always thought that Melanie looked at least ten years younger, but those years had been there, under expertly applied makeup. Even so, her eyes were the same, their impact astonishing.

Melanie held her right arm to her chest, supporting it under the elbow with her left hand. She stepped aside, and Georgia entered the small hallway.

"I'm afraid I'm just about useless," Melanie said. "If you're hungry or thirsty, the kitchen is to your left. I have to put a sling on for my arm. Give me a few minutes. Getting dressed takes me a little time."

Georgia was about to swoop down on her friend, demanding details. But Melanie's faint voice, the slow way she moved, and the sad light that came from those remarkable eyes warned Georgia to proceed slowly.

"I don't need anything. I'll wait in the living room."

Melanie walked gingerly toward the doorway to the left, and Georgia went to the right. A sofa, love seat and an extra wide easy chair, all plump with oversized soft blue cushions, faced a slate hearth, which took up the entire far wall. An irregular slab of gray granite had been chiseled flat on top to hold a pane of beveled glass, which served as the coffee table. Several spiky houseplants were set in corners. There was no other furniture.

One entire length of the room consisted of glass, and the wall opposite held an immense quilted artwork done in varying shades and textures of blue and black and gray. All of the lighting was recessed, its glow merely bringing the room out of darkness, but not in any way calling attention to itself. Several small pieces of cobalt crystal dotted the coffee table.

The most dramatic furnishing in Melanie's living room was the view, a vivid pulsing mural of the Las Vegas Strip. Georgia looked out at the vista of lights from south of Tropicana Boulevard to north of Sahara Road. In between were located most of the larger casinos in Las Vegas, vying to out-neon each other. The Mirage, with its golden glow and volcano, very efficiently usurped much of the spectacle on the entire street.

People called Vegas crass and trashy, dangerous and sinful. Georgia knew better. She dimmed the lights and looked out through the glass wall of Melanie's living room.

How strange to be standing in this apartment, nineteen floors up and several blocks from the Strip. Vegas had a life-force like no other city, while at the same time offering a retreat from the soul-numbing, conventional existence that was her life back in Creste Verde.

Getting in trouble in Vegas only happened to gamblers whose sole intent was to beat the odds, be it at gaming or anything else. But for those who sought a haven of anonymity, nowhere in the world was safer.

She shuddered. She was about to step over the line.

Melanie came into the room.

"Let's sit down," she said as she cautiously lowered herself onto the sofa. "You sit in the easy chair. You get the full view from there." She had changed into a velour warm-up suit that matched the cobalt on the table.

Georgia curled up right next to Melanie.

"I want a full view of you. Are you ready to talk to me?"

The vivid color of her outfit made Melanie seem very pale, and the glittering specks of silver and gold in her eyes were refracted by tears. She shook her head as though she were trying to clear it, to wake herself from a bad dream.

"Sure," Melanie said with a deep sigh. "Sure, fine, I'll tell you all about it. Here we go, you lucky girl. Sit back, relax, and let me give you an update on the latest wreckage and rubble that I'm stumbling over in my life."

Melanie was trying for bravado, and Georgia wanted to tell her not to waste her energy, but she kept quiet.

"After everyone left last night, I had some trouble with Jules."

Melanie shifted gingerly, trying to find a comfortable position for her arm.

"I had just finished cleaning up the kitchen. Jules was sitting on the sofa, finishing off the scotch. He was pretty drunk, and I remember thinking that this was probably not going to be a very romantic Christmas night, but that was fine. I was tired in a happy way; it had been a nice day. I'd just listen to some music and maybe have one more glass of wine myself.

"But as I came over to sit by him, Jules looked up at me and said, 'Take all your clothes off.' I started to laugh. I didn't think he was serious, but then he screamed at me, 'I said take off your clothes, cunt!'

"I still wasn't sure if he was kidding, but I didn't like the game if he was, and I told him so."

Melanie painfully repositioned herself, continuing to cradle her arm.

"In the months that we've been together, there have been a few times—always when he's had too much to drink—that he's proposed some kinky stuff that didn't much appeal to me, but he never pushed it, so when he stood up and put his arms around me, I thought he was going to apologize, but instead he grabbed my hair, yanked my head back, and started to slobber on my neck. I pushed away, and for a moment he stood there like an ape, his arms swinging at his sides and drool coming out of his mouth. I was too furious to speak, and I turned to walk away. All I could think of was calling a cab and going home, but he grabbed my wrists, dragged me into the bedroom, and then picked me up and threw me against the headboard."

Melanie gently rubbed her shoulder.

"My shoulder made contact first, and the pain shot down my arm and into my hand. Then he leaned over me and spit on my face. And he said, 'Not so cool and confident now, huh, cunt?' I tried to pull away from him, but the pain in my shoulder paralyzed me."

Melanie took in several quick, gasping breaths.

"It was like the time I had the heart attack." More quick breaths. "He ripped open my blouse and with one yank tore off my bra. I tried to push him away with my other hand, and he punched me in the stomach."

Melanie slowly stood up and walked to the window.

"It's been more than ten years since my heart attack, but I can still remember the panic. This was the same. I couldn't get a breath, and the room was closing in on me. I knew I had to fight the dizziness; I couldn't pass out. I was sure this time I'd die if I lost consciousness."

She stared out into the night, taking slow, deep breaths.

"I was fighting to get air in my lungs. He pinned my arms above my head and began to suck on my nipples, groaning and drooling and mumbling about how he was going to fuck me his way. I concentrated on regulating my breath. My life depended on getting air into my lungs. I must have made some terrible kind of noise because he pulled his head up, wiped his mouth with the back of his hand, and glared at me. I remember thinking, *Somehow I've made him understand that he can't get away with this.*"

Tears welled up again in Melanie's eyes. Her voice became raspy.

"Wrong! I was so wrong! I can't take care of myself. Look at all the shit that happens to me, over and over, and I've never had control over any of it. I didn't yesterday either."

Now she began to sob, and Georgia stood up and gently put her arms around her. A few minutes passed. When Melanie stopped crying, Georgia said softly, "Come and sit down again and tell me what happened after that."

"Could you go into the bathroom and bring me some Kleenex?" Melanie sounded six years old.

When Melanie had blotted the tears from her face and chin and blown her nose, she said, "I still was having a lot of trouble breathing, and I probably looked like hell. He let go of my arms and just sat there watching me, I don't know for how long. But finally I could feel my heartbeat slow down a little, and I tried to roll over and get off the bed on the other side. The pain in my shoulder and side was unbelievable, and I must have gasped in some awful way, because all of a sudden Jules scooped me up, wrapped the bed cover around me, and carried me into the garage. He put me in the passenger seat of his Corvette. I couldn't catch my breath again; I was sure the pain was going to destroy me. I sat as still as I could, trying to concentrate on breathing. He drove out of Spanish Trail and up Rainbow to the emergency room at Spring Valley Hospital.

"The pain had let up a little, and then I realized that I was naked to the waist and held on to the bed cover for dear life. He got out of the car, came around to my side, and opened the door. Finally I could say, 'I'll be okay. Take me home.'

"An EMT came out of the building, and when he saw Jules supposedly trying to help me out of the car, he yelled back to someone.

"Jules says to the EMT, 'My lady and I were having our own Christmas celebration, and I'm afraid we got a little carried away. She really scared me there.' Then he said, 'She was breathing very strangely, and I think she might have also injured her shoulder. I guess it was some kind of seizure.' By now two more medics have come with a gurney, and I'm being lifted out of the car.

"I say again that I'm okay, but they strap me down and wheel me inside. Thank God for the bed cover."

Melanie gently rubbed her shoulder again.

"They took X-rays, and of course I had to tell them about my previous heart attack. I was still in tremendous pain, although the X-ray showed no breaks. Anyway, after six hours in the ER, they let me go home. My heart rate was still a little elevated, but no one seemed too concerned. I guess the electrocardiogram was normal, although no one actually said anything about the results. They did tell me I have a severely strained shoulder and bruised ribs.

"Solicitous Jules, the unnerved and worried lover, had been at my side or waiting nearby every minute, and by then I was too exhausted to object, so he drove me home. On the way, he tells me he's sorry, that he got carried away, had too much to drink, and it won't ever happen again. I never said a word. It was about five this morning when we pulled up in front of my apartment. I was wearing a hospital gown over my slacks and boots. Freddy, the night doorman, came over, and I told him to help me get out. He knows better than to ask too many questions, and as soon as I was out of the car, Jules drove off. I guess he knew I wouldn't have let him come in anyway.

"So Freddy helps me into my apartment. I took a pain-killer, but it was after eight before I finally fell asleep. Jules has called a couple of times, but I don't pick up. I don't know what he thinks is going to come of this. I'm not going to press charges or anything; I don't need to deal with that kind of crap, but once is all it takes. I'm through with him."

Both women were quiet for a few moments then Melanie stood up again, rubbing her shoulder and smiling gently.

"I have to pee."

When Melanie left the room, Georgia checked her watch. It was nearly seven in the evening, and the main game was probably in full gear.

While Melanie was in the bathroom, Georgia went into the kitchen, found a can of chicken noodle soup and heated it in two mugs in the microwave. She toasted slices of rye bread and boiled water for tea. She and Melanie sat down at the kitchen table and ate in silence.

Georgia rinsed the dishes while Melanie sat, sipping her tea.

"What about you?" Melanie asked suddenly. "What's going on with you?"

Georgia kept her eyes on the kitchen faucet.

"Something's up with you, besides my crap," Melanie said.

Georgia sat down at the table again but said nothing.

"You know, Georgia, you think you have this poker face thing perfected. And you're probably right most of the time. But not now, not with me."

Georgia tried to keep her gaze steady, but after only moments she looked away and said, "I took a half million dollars out of my business account."

"Half a million," Melanie repeated vaguely, as though they were talking about shades of nail polish instead of stealing $500,000.

"I got a cashier's check from Wells Fargo and deposited it at the Mirage. They gave me the cash, and it's locked up in the poker room cashier's cage."

As Georgia was about to try to explain more of this, Melanie slumped in the chair, grimacing in pain.

"I'm staying here tonight," Georgia said.

"Oh no, you're not!" Melanie sat up straighter. Then her voice softened. "I'm okay, honest. Tell me about the money. Why did you take it? Are you in some kind of trouble or…?"

The rest of her sentence was cut off as she closed her eyes and gasped, obviously in pain.

Georgia reached across the table and put her hand over Melanie's. "What can I do for you?" she asked.

"Nothing," Melanie said hoarsely. "I need to take some pain pills."

"Sure," Georgia said. "And you also have to get in bed and rest and sleep."

"What are you going to do with all that money?" Melanie closed her eyes again, and the pain registered on her pale face.

"I'm okay," Georgia replied. "I'll be careful. You don't have to worry about me right now. You just have to rest."

Melanie's eyes were still closed. "I think you'd better go now. I've got to make a quick phone call, and I'm really exhausted and I hurt. Honest, I'll be better off if I'm not dealing with you staying here too."

"Okay, I'll stop bugging you and get out of here, but if you need me, you'd call my room or page me, right?"

Georgia stood up, then asked, "The call you said you have to make, is it something I can do for you? The pharmacy or something?"

"No, not the pharmacy," Melanie said, her eyes open now but just barely. "I can take care of it." They walked to the front door.

As she reached for the knob, Georgia hesitated then gently put her arms around Melanie, who leaned against her.

"You are going to be just fine, I know, and so am I. Call me when you wake up tomorrow."

They stood that way for a while, Georgia aware of how comforting it was to be this close to someone she cared so much about. Finally Melanie took in a deep breath, flinching in pain.

"You have to go to bed," Georgia said, gently kissed her friend on the cheek, and walked to the elevator. When she turned to wave goodbye, Melanie had already shut her door.

Chapter 26

As Georgia stepped off the elevator in the lobby of Melanie's apartment building, the receptionist looked up from her desk. "Do you need a cab, ma'am?"

The rain had stopped for the moment. Georgia shook her head. "It's early. I think I'll walk, but thank you."

Her normal pattern would have been to catch a cab and challenge the driver to make it to the entrance of the Mirage in less than five minutes. Now the zeal to sprint back to the poker table had vaporized. *Why?*

As she walked toward the Strip, she tried some self-analysis.

What had happened to her friend last night was horrifying. And although she knew that Melanie had the ability, gained from a lifetime of dealing with adversity, to withstand the emotional trauma of last night's assault, there had obviously been some substantial physical damage as well.

Should she have insisted on staying? But she also had to respect her friend's autonomy, and Melanie had made it clear that she didn't want Georgia as a houseguest, certainly under these circumstances. She had been adamant that she didn't want to be burdened by Georgia's presence. She wanted to go to bed and be alone. So leaving had been the only option, and she'd just have to check on her friend as often and as best she could.

So what else? Melanie obviously was beginning to trust in her. She wouldn't have been able to tell her so much about herself otherwise. But it was also clear that, for some reason, she still kept in place a margin of safety, sort of like the fifteen-second transmission delay on talk shows. Georgia's safety zone was much broader. No need for a fifteen-second delay when you never broadcast the program in the first place. Nevertheless, she wished that she had been able to ask Melanie about the photo, the one in the frame that Melanie had given her last night. Now it would have to wait.

She continued walking, forcing her thoughts back to her own terrifying decisions of late, which included grand theft. Georgia increased her pace.

By withdrawing that money from her business account, she was actually breaking the law! The real law! Not her parents' rules or her husband's edicts but statutes laid down by the government whose offenses were punishable by a prison sentence!

Now she was passing everyone on foot, charging down Las Vegas Boulevard. She had to get that money back into the bank account right away.

Shit!

Georgia stopped suddenly, and several people behind her had to make emergency maneuvers not to plow into her.

The bank is closed!

Georgia began to walk again, slowly. She had reached the block in front of the Mirage, now allowing the frantic first-timers to bustle by her. Normally she would have kept pace with them, annoyed if anyone impeded her progress. But her usual single-minded charge toward the casino had been deferred.

Stepping onto the Mirage moving sidewalk was a momentary triumph as torrents of rain splashed just outside the covered walkway. She stood to the left, allowing those who chose not to experience the slow, leisurely approach to pass on the right. Usually she led the way.

Why did I ever withdraw that money in the first place? Why was it so important that I play in a poker game that costs hundreds of thousands of dollars? Why am I still tempted to do it? Because it would be so easy? Because everything is already in place? All I have to do is walk back into the poker room and merely look at Edward Patrone, and all that money will be placed in front of me. And then it would be up to me and no one else to decide when to hold 'em and when to fold 'em.

But why? For the thrills? For the sense of liberation? To get even with Jeff? With Mother? Or just because I can?

Questions, questions and more questions without answers.

Georgia continued on into the casino, but without her usual gridiron dash. Instead, she plodded along, keeping her place within the interminable glacier of sightseers until she was at the far end of the casino by the elevator bank.

Back in her room, she found five messages on her voice mail. The first was from Mike, apologizing for not calling on Christmas Day—something about an emergency on the slopes.

Next came Jeff's tense and cryptic words. "We have important matters to discuss concerning your very inappropriate behavior. Please contact me as soon as possible." No good-bye.

No need for good-byes.

Then there was Phillip's voice, but the normal savior faire was missing, replaced by a yelping panic.

"Georgia, Olivia is missing! For more than an hour! Can you think of anything? Anywhere she may have gone? Please, please think of something! Help me!"

The next two messages were also from Phillip, each one a few notches up the frenzy scale.

She dialed Phillip's villa, and when he answered, she knew instantly: Livy had not been found. Georgia did not bother to identify herself.

"Phillip, have you tried Zivah?"

"Of course! I've been calling there constantly. No one answers, and there's no message machine."

"And the police?"

Phillip's voice was octaves above its normal range.

"Of course I called the bloody police! And Mirage security and anyone else I could think of!"

Georgia took a deep breath and tried to sound calm. "Phillip, there has to be a simple explanation."

"I have to know where she is right now. I can't stand this! Oh my God!" He began to sob.

"I'm on my way," Georgia said and hung up.

The rain had returned with a vengeance, and Georgia hurried through the dark, blustery deluge to the entry of Phillip's villa suite. Before she could ring the bell, Wilbur opened the door for her, just as he had on Christmas Eve. But this time his face was pasty white with red blotches on his chin and throat. The big man's eyes were red-rimmed, dark and tormented. He'd been crying, his nose was running, and his hands were shaking. He didn't speak, just stepped back and let her in.

Phillip was pacing back and forth in front of the Christmas tree, a cell phone in one hand and a cordless in the other. His hair, usually brushed back and gleaming, was now hanging in greasy strands, revealing a bald spot at the crown.

When he saw Georgia, he yelled into the cordless, "Hold on! Hold on!" Then to Georgia, "Have you thought of anything? Anything?"

Georgia shook her head. "No, but then I don't really know what's going on. Tell me what happened."

Phillip spoke into the phone again.

"Loggin, listen to me. Get Loquasto and Bennett and…everybody, anybody you can think of! I want the hotel searched again. Tell Dan Considine that I have to see every videotape from the entire surveillance system. Tell him I want every room in the hotel searched." Pause. "Yes, he can!" Phillip screamed. "He must, and he will!"

He pushed the disconnect button then flung the phone across the room. It knocked over a Lladro statue of a girl with her hair and gown blowing in a fantasy wind. Silently Wilbur began to pick up the shattered fragments of statue from the marble floor. Georgia could see his hands trembling.

She sat down on the sofa. "Phillip, can you try to tell me what happened?"

Phillip drew in a horrible-sounding breath, like someone having a severe asthma attack. He was spiraling toward hysteria. Georgia reached for his arm and pulled him down next to her on the sofa.

Phillip sat with his head bent over for a moment, gasping like someone who had just run a hundred-meter sprint. When he began to talk, his words were directed at the carpet between his shoes.

"Olivia seemed just fine last night," he gasped. More quick breaths. "I left about nine this morning to talk with the architects then more meetings all afternoon."

Wilbur continued when Phillip began to cough. "She did express some sadness this morning when I told her that Zivah would no longer be caring for her. Livy stayed in her room most of the day. About three, she asked me to take her to the Habitat. On our way there, she went into a ladies' room by the sports book. I waited several minutes then became concerned and asked a lady to call out her name in there. She came out to say no one had answered."

Now Wilbur's voice was edged with panic. "I rushed into the ladies' room, but Livy wasn't there. I ran to the Habitat then scanned the sports book area, the California Pizza Kitchen and most of the casino. Then I called Mr. Vance. I had already notified security, and I got Nick Loggin from the poker room, and…"

"Enough!" Phillip had caught his breath by now. He waved an impatient dismissal at Wilbur, who nodded dutifully and, holding the shards of Lladro, silently backed out of the room.

Phillip coughed again then roughly cleared his throat.

"As I said, I immediately notified Mirage security, and they insisted that the police be called. Then I tried reaching everyone who Livy knows here. Of course I started with you because she has become so fond of you, but then I called everyone I could think of. Only the Buckinghams have not responded.

"Oh yes, and I rang up Zivah's flat right away," he said. "Nothing, no bloody answer! I told the police that I suspect that Zivah is involved."

"You think Zivah could harm Livy?"

"Why not?" Phillip screamed, vaulting to his feet. "There are crazy people everywhere! Zivah could be one of them. Look at her background. Anyone who went through what she did in Germany could be crazy. She could be taking it all out on Livy!"

Georgia's heart was racing. "You mean because she has a concentration camp number? Actually she told me she was never…"

"Yes! Yes! Oh my God, yes!" he wailed. He pulled at his scraggly, gel-stiffened hair. "The woman is completely psychotic. She could be torturing my Olivia right now! Or worse!"

Hazy waves floated in the perimeter of Georgia's vision.

"But, but," she stammered, "Zivah told me she had not been in a death camp, that she had the numbers tattooed on her arm in the memory of her family."

"What difference does that make?" Phillip shrieked. "Anyone who would deliberately have a death camp serial number permanently branded into their skin must be insane!"

Zivah is who I think she is—no one else. This is Phillip's hysteria, not mine.

Georgia looked up at Phillip, who was sobbing now, rubbing at his eyes with the heels of his fists. She had to keep asking questions, desperately searching for logical answers—answers that would cut short a horrifying slither of fear and suspicion that was coiling in the pit of her stomach.

"Phillip, listen to me. What do you know about Zivah, about her background?"

Phillip stopped pacing. His jaw was slack, and his mouth was wet and quivering.

"I…I…" He cleared his throat and started again. "I had just received a report from my investigators on Christmas Eve. They have not completed the inquiry yet, but there are some very suspicious facts. It seems that Zivah herself has been surreptitiously stalking someone. It seems that she has hired a private search firm and that she has had a great deal of snooping done in county records offices and has made inquiries of governmental agencies."

That chilling, paralyzing mist was billowing again, and she fought the urge to close her eyes and let the haze envelope her. Georgia had to concentrate on each word, and still she slurred them.

"Do they have any idea who she was looking for?"

"No. Do you think that's important?" Phillip sat down in a chair opposite Georgia.

"I don't know." Her voice was getting scratchier, and it hurt her throat to take in a breath. "I need a glass of water," she managed and stood up.

With his hands gripping the arms and his head tilted back, Phillip yelled, "Wilbur!"

The wretched bodyguard hurried into the room, a mixture of panic and hope on his pale, sweaty face.

"Yes, sir?"

"Mrs. Cates needs a glass of water, and I want another Courvoisier." He gestured toward an empty brandy snifter on the side table.

"Yes, sir," Wilbur repeated as he picked up the crystal snifter.

Neither Georgia nor Phillip said anything until Wilbur returned with their drinks. Georgia took a gulp of water and began to sputter and cough as some of the liquid found its way down her windpipe instead of her esophagus.

"Are you all right?" Wilbur asked in alarm. Phillip didn't seem to notice. Georgia forced herself to take air into her lungs and then expelled it in more wracking coughs. After several attempts, she was finally able to stop choking, but her voice was still deactivated. Wilbur saw that Georgia was recovering, and he left the room again.

When Georgia felt able to test her voice, she asked, "What do the police say? Are they looking for Zivah as well as Livy?"

Phillip still sat with his head thrown back. His eyes blinked sporadically. Softly he said, "This may be about ransom."

"Zivah would kidnap Livy for ransom?" Georgia was shaking her head. "That's just impossible."

But even as she uttered the words, her thoughts were contradicting them.

Was all the familiarity, the sense of connection that she had felt for Zivah misconceived? Instead of reminding her of Grandma Genya, could it be that her memory had short-circuited in some subconscious attempt to protect herself? How old would Hannah be now? What would she look like? Could the monster of Georgia's childhood have morphed into a clever, charming old lady?

"Maybe it's not Zivah," Phillip said.

Georgia jerked her head in his direction. *How could he know what I was thinking?*

"There are a lot of people who hate me enough to do something awful to me. I've made enemies."

Georgia struggled with the segue. Phillip was talking about his own dilemma; it had nothing to do with her demons.

"What kind of enemies?" She fought to catch up with his reality.

"All sorts." He stood up and walked toward the large window that overlooked the dolphin pool. With his back to her, he tipped the brandy snifter to his mouth and emptied it, wincing as the liquid went down.

"How to explain?" he murmured. "How to account for the ruthlessness?"

He still had his back to her, and Georgia noticed how narrow his shoulders were. This was the first time she had seen him in just a shirt, and she realized now how much his tailored suits enhanced his physique.

"I grew up in London," he said. "My father was a grocer, and we lived in a flat over the store in Chelsea and often went to Dover to visit my grandmother. My sister, Livy…"

His voiced cracked, and he cleared his throat. "My sister, Olivia, was four years older than me. In nineteen forty-two, during the Blitz, when London was being attacked by the Luftwaffe, I was sent to live with my grandmother in Dover while my parents and sister remained in London. All three were killed when bombs destroyed an entire block of buildings."

Now he turned to look at her, and Georgia could only present her poker face. She had no notion of how else to react. After a moment, Phillip went on.

"My grandmother had a stroke soon after and died. I was shuffled around for the remaining years of the war. I spent some time with an uncle in Cheshire, but he had seven of his own, and his wife had died of influenza. By the time I was eight, I had lived with a half dozen different families, some to whom I was barely related. Another uncle paid my tuition to boarding school. I lived there, including most holidays, until I was accepted at Cambridge. I graduated in three years and then signed on to a merchant fleet and worked my way around the world on various freight vessels. I was a bursar, an accountant, even a galley worker once. And I played cards."

Phillip looked at Georgia a moment then sat down and leaned back, directing his words to the ceiling again.

"I never returned to Dover or Lancaster or any of the other places I had lived as an orphan. And I traveled the world with a desperate urgency, although in those days I hardly had the self-realization to define my need. I would acquire a great deal of money; that was the goal. I would establish a dynasty, I told myself. I fell in love with every healthy, beautiful and intelligent girl who came my way, and there were plenty. But it seems my karma was flawed, and, for varying circumstances, none of my first three marriages were successful nor produced any progeny."

Phillip reached for a crystal-framed portrait that stood on a marble side table. He gazed at it but said no more.

"Is that Livy's mother?" Georgia asked finally.

"Yes," he said. "By the time I met her, I had accomplished a portion of my goal; I was wealthy. That part had come easily; I had to apply such an infinitesimal effort. It seemed that all my projects were successful, and the horrendous backstabbing and double-crossing were just a part of the entrepreneurial poker game, just as my card playing was sanctified by the gods of good fortune. Lying and stealing are condoned in poker, and all successful enterprise is merely another form of the same game."

Phillip placed the portrait back on the table and stared at it.

"Olivia was actually conceived before our wedding, and I had found eternal happiness. The Vance dynasty had been established and would thrive and prosper."

A small sob escaped from Phillip's throat, and his voice faded from hoarseness to whisper to whimper.

"Disastrously, Sharon had listened to my ranting about this dynasty obsession of mine, and she had absorbed it into her own heart. When she learned that her kidneys were malfunctioning because of a tumor and that terminating the pregnancy was her best chance to survive, she unequivocally refused to consider the option. This was the only child she could give me, and she would not sacrifice it."

He turned around to face Georgia again, his cheeks shiny wet, tears dripping from his chin.

"When Sharon died, I was catapulted into hell. Of course I saw to it that Olivia had the best of care, but I myself had very little to do with her. I was a monster in mortal pain, powerful and arrogant. I wallowed in my grief, utilizing my wealth to remain isolated from everyone but specifically my beautiful, perfect, innocent baby daughter. And as the years have passed, I've gone through the drill of playing the father, but until now, I had not an iota of a notion of the true precious worth of that child."

He sobbed for a few moments then pulled his fingers across his eyes to clear the tears.

Phillip looked up at Georgia, waiting for a response. She knew he was seeking refuge, but she had none to offer. She returned the gaze as honestly as she knew how. He shook his head and began to pace again.

"I am much like a tragic figure of mythology, doomed to repeating my hubris over and over again, except now I know that Olivia has become the only thing in my life that I cannot afford to lose."

His face contorted. "I can't stand this!" Phillip howled. "I have to find her!" He began to sob again.

Wilbur rushed into the room, alarmed at the horrible sounds that Phillip was making. Without a word to either man, Georgia left the villa. She hurried through the dark rain, trying to get her bearings, stumbling through the deep, wet shadows, suddenly blinded by the bright reflections of glaring spotlights. It was like maneuvering in a storm-swept house of mirrors. Then, finally, she saw the entrance to the casino.

She was back in the lobby of the Mirage Hotel. She'd passed through this exact location hundreds of times, but now everything was out of synch. She tried to use the compass in her mind to balance her world, to keep from falling off. Right now that compass was failing her. Each way she turned, the scene seemed skewed, out of proportion, foreign and hostile. She was surrounded by hundreds of people who smiled and chatted with each other, high-fived at the craps tables, applauded a dealer busting at the blackjack table…every one of them safe and secure in their own reality while she doubted that she would ever find the real world—her rational version of it—ever again.

She seemed to be drifting toward the edge of the earth, and if she fell off, never would she be able to return. Her only hope was to locate a landmark—something real and reassuring—that would enable her to dig in and hold on.

Georgia had to figure out how to tether her own fragile spirit to reality. First of all, she had to believe that Livy was safe, and there would be a simple, expedient explanation for her disappearance. And Georgia would find Zivah, sitting at the 10-20 table, her old purse in her lap, her whole being focused on the cards, like always. She would look up at Georgia and smile, and Zivah would be only the sweet old lady who played a lot of poker, no one else. She could not be anyone or anything else.

In the poker room, Georgia found no Zivah and no solace.

Mr. Kruikshank had seemed particularly worried when Georgia asked if he had seen the old woman.

"Not good," he said, ominously shaking his head. "Not good at all."

Milt Braverman was playing a hand at the 10-20 table. Georgia waited anxiously while he finished and pulled in the chips from the pot he had just won, adding three more one-hundred-dollar stacks to the six that were already in front of him. Then she tapped him on the shoulder, and he glanced up at her, grinning.

"My rush continues," he said. "First the pot and then the attentions of a pretty lady."

"Can you spare a minute? I need to talk to you."

Milt's grin vanished as he reacted to her shaky voice. He got up from the table and followed Georgia over to an empty part of the room.

"Livy Vance is missing," she said, finding no other way to begin. "I've just come from Phillip Vance's suite."

Georgia quickly summarized what Phillip had told her about Livy's disappearance.

"And there's more, but I can hardly understand it myself, so I can't possibly try to explain it to you. But right now it seems there are several of us who could use your help."

Milt looked down into her eyes for a minute, and Georgia wished that she could read his mind.

"I'd have to talk to Vance," Milt said. No other questions.

Georgia went over to a house phone, called Phillip, and returned to where Milt was waiting for her.

"Let's go," she said.

Milt asked the floor man to cash out his chips for him and hold on to the money.

After a few minutes with Phillip and Wilbur, Milt left for Zivah's apartment. Georgia sat again in the plush main salon of the villa suite, watching Phillip orbit the room, mumbling to himself.

"May I use a phone?" she asked. "I'd like to check in on Melanie Nallis."

Phillip handed Georgia the cordless that he had been gripping in his left hand, asking urgently, "Do you think she could know something?"

"About Livy? I doubt it."

Once again Melanie picked up the phone as Georgia was speaking into the message machine.

"You sound a little groggy," Georgia said. "Did I wake you up?"

"I'm really hurting," Melanie said in a weak, breathy voice.

"Have you called your doctor?"

"What doctor? The one in the emergency room?"

Melanie's words were strained, and she was panting, as if she was talking while working out on a stair master. "Someone…from there called a while ago to…follow up from yesterday…and when I told them I was in a lot of pain, they told me to call my own doctor, but…" Another pause and several fast breaths.

"Then we have to find you a doctor," Georgia said. "Do you want me to make some calls?" Georgia waited a few moments for a reply.

"Melanie?"

She could here Melanie's gasps for air.

"Melanie! Talk to me!"

More harsh breaths, and then Georgia heard a weak moan.

Yanking her address book out of her purse with her free hand, she yelled at Phillip, "Give me the cell phone!"

She grabbed it from him and dialed 911. After Georgia gave Melanie's address to the emergency operator, she spoke back into the cordless.

"Melanie! Talk to me! Melanie!"

No response but weak gasps. On the cell phone again, Georgia dialed information, requested the front desk at The Regency, and told the receptionist that Melanie needed help and that the paramedics were on the way.

While she had been making these calls, Phillip had been standing over her.

"What is bloody going on?" he demanded.

Georgia jumped up from the sofa. "I think Melanie may be having another heart attack!"

"*Another* heart attack? What are you talking about?"

Georgia was already out of the living room on her way to the entry.

"Milt will call here." She tossed the words behind her. "And I'll check in too."

"Please, Georgia," Phillip called out, "wait! We'll find out where Melanie is being taken and call. But I need you here!"

"I can't help you any more at this point," Georgia said gently, making eye contact with Wilbur, who had come out of the kitchen. Wilbur nodded and stepped over to open the door. Georgia was not sure exactly why she was in such a desperate rush. She couldn't leave the hotel until she knew where to go, where Melanie would be taken, but it was definite that she had to get away from Phillip.

Desert Springs Hospital looked more like an upscale shopping mall than a medical center. Well-manicured grounds surrounded the parking lot, which was almost empty. Georgia ran through another deluge as once again the black sky released its payload.

Thankfully it was not long before she was allowed into the cardiac intensive care unit. Melanie looked up as Georgia came into the cubicle that consisted of a bed, a night stand, and monitoring equipment. A screen above the bed and to the right displayed several sets of numbers as well as the readout from a cardio monitor.

"Can you sit with me for a while?" Melanie asked, her astounding eyes searching Georgia's face for reassurance.

Reaching for the rail to Melanie's bed, Georgia said softly, "I'll have to stand. I guess they don't encourage visitors to stay for long."

"Am I still ticking?" Melanie asked as Georgia took in the bewildering display of data.

"It seems that way," Georgia said.

"Well, it's not ticking the way it's supposed to," Melanie said, gripping at the sheet, which was pulled up to just below her chin.

Georgia took Melanie's hand, careful not to disturb the tube that ran into a catheter in her wrist.

"It's going to be okay, and so are you."

"I'm really scared, Georgia. I think they're going to put in a pacemaker."

Melanie was whispering as though it would be dangerous if anyone heard what she was saying.

"Has anyone called your children?"

"Ellen Louise is visiting a friend in Chicago. Even if I could remember the friend's name, I know she has an unlisted number. I wrote it on the margin of my desk calendar."

"Would you like me to get it for you?"

Melanie nodded her head. "Yes, and Robbie's number is in my address book."

"Do you want me to call them?"

Melanie closed her eyes for a moment then sighed. "I guess, but please…I don't want them coming to Vegas, understand? Promise me."

Melanie looked back at the monitor that was silently recording her heart rate. "But I guess they should know I'm in the hospital…just in case something happens to me."

Georgia brushed a wisp of hair off of Melanie's forehead. "I'll go to your apartment."

Melanie's hand, the one that Georgia was holding, had been resting at her side. Now she clutched at Georgia's fingers.

"But there's something much more important than even that," she whispered. "I have to tell you something."

Her grip on Georgia's hand got tighter.

"I've lied to you. Right from the first time at your Christmas open house. It was not just a coincidence that I was there. I knew Jim Fields did business with Jeff, and it seemed like a good way to make a connection with you."

As Georgia tried to say something, Melanie's weak voice was strained with effort.

"Just listen to me. See, the truth is that I've been looking for your family for a long time. I paid a lot of investigating firms a lot of money and finally learned about you and your life in Creste Verde, as well as all the time you spend in Vegas. And I started coming into the poker room when I found out how much you played. At first I just wanted to see you, see what you looked like, and then I wanted to watch you, and then I knew I needed to meet you, and then I did. I had to link you to me, one way or another."

Georgia started to say something again, but Melanie closed her eyes, weakly shook her head, and said, "You have to let me tell you this my way. Let me try to explain. Please be patient. I'm doing the best that I can, and I have to do this now."

Georgia squeezed Melanie's hand. "Okay," she whispered.

Melanie opened her eyes again. "I really don't like poker much, but it was a way to connect with you, and that was the most important thing. I always knew that all the lies I told you would have to be explained sooner or later. Now I might not get another chance, so I have to tell you everything, but it's hard right now to sort through all of it and give it to you in some kind of order that will make any sense."

The door to the room whooshed open, and the nurse stepped in.

"It's time for your friend to leave," she said to Melanie as she noted some of the readings from the monitor on the chart. "Your heart rate is up, and your respiration has increased. You have to stop talking now."

Melanie tried to lift her head, but the nurse kept a firm hand on her shoulder. "You have to relax, Melanie," she said as she gestured to Georgia to leave the room.

Melanie's voice was a raspy, panicky whisper. "Promise me that you'll come back here just as soon as you can."

"I promise. You rest now," Georgia said. Melanie's hand relaxed, and her eyes closed, and Georgia could see tears caught in her lashes.

As soon as Georgia left Melanie's room, she found a pay phone and called Phillip.

"Nothing!" Phillip cried into the phone. "Nothing! Not a shred of information…nothing. And I have not heard from Milt. What could he be doing? Why the bloody hell hasn't he called?"

"I know this is torment for you, Phillip, but going off the deep end now is not going to help Livy. Milt will contact you when he knows something. Just hold on."

No response and then came the serene yet eerie recorded message: "If you want to make a call, hang up and try again." Had Phillip hung up on her? She redialed.

"Yes? Yes?" Phillip's frantic greeting.

"We were disconnected," Georgia replied.

"What the bloody hell are you doing?" Phillip screamed. "Stop calling unless you know something!" And once again the line went dead.

Chapter 27

The security guard at The Regency unlocked Melanie's apartment then waited in the entry while Georgia went into the bedroom in search of Melanie's desk calendar and address book. The unmade bed was a twisted profusion of blue-and-white delft print sheets, comforter and pillows framed by a massive whitewashed oak headboard that matched the night stands, dresser and desk. The white walls were bare, but dozens of framed portraits and snapshots were arranged on the night stands, the bureau, the desk and the broad base of the headboard.

As Georgia reached for the address book on the desk, a small photograph caught her eye. A young woman with long, shiny hair, holding one dark rose, stood beside an army jeep.

A throbbing began just inside Georgia's temples and grew quickly until it echoed in her ears to the rhythm of her heartbeat. The long brown hair, the strong, big hands, the clothes, the jeep, the trees in the background all fit into a delicate and tender slot in her carefully guarded memory. She remembered the smell of Hannah, the warm breath and sweaty skin, but the image in her mind had a blank face.

Georgia steadied herself against the dresser, staring at her own reflection in the mirror.

You are who you are: Georgia Kassov Cates. Alexandra Georgia Kassov survived and became me. And I am safe.

Georgia picked up the address book and tucked the brass-framed picture into her purse.

When Georgia returned to the hospital, she was denied entrance to the CICU. Melanie had been taken to surgery, where, based on a catheterization, the decision would be made to either implant a pacemaker, do an angioplasty, or maybe both. Under the best of circumstances, she would not be allowed visitors any time soon.

Georgia put in a call to Ellen Louise, apologizing for waking her up. By the end of the conversation, Ellen Louise agreed to wait for further updates before making any arrangements to fly to Las Vegas and would contact her brother, Robbie.

In the taxi on the way back to the Mirage, Georgia pulled out the small picture frame that she had taken from Melanie's desk.

It's okay. I can stare all I want at this, and I'll still be okay.

She tucked it back into a compartment in her purse and reached for her wallet to pay the taxi driver.

As soon as Georgia stepped into the lobby of the Mirage, she went to a house phone and was connected with the Vance villa. When Wilbur answered, Georgia could hear the stress in his voice, followed by disappointment when he realized she had no news of Livy.

"Mr. Vance is on another line," he said. "He's trying to talk the chief of Mirage security into letting him personally review all the surveillance videotapes. Nothing new from the police and nothing from Mr. Braverman. Everyone else has called or come by except the Buckinghams."

"I've been out of the hotel on another emergency, and I'm not sure when I'll have to leave again. I'll keep checking in with you. If I don't answer in my room, you can page me in…"

"She has to be okay!"

"Yes, Wilbur," Georgia said. "She has to be okay." The words, spoken quietly, were a prayer.

She put the phone back on the hook but did not let go of the receiver.

What should she do now? Go to her room? To Phillip's villa? Certainly not to the poker room.

Then she remembered that along with Phillip's frantic messages, one from Jeff had also been on her voice mail. That had been hours ago. He had instructed her to call him as soon as possible so that they could discuss her "very inappropriate behavior."

Well, this was still not as soon as possible.

The thought of sitting in her room was horrible, but not as horrible as the thought of sitting with Phillip.

She skirted the rain forest again and went out the north entrance, following the driveway to the Strip. Walking as fast as she could, she found herself several blocks past the Fashion Show Mall, short on breath and unable to clear any of the confusion that was surging through her mind.

She retraced her steps, and as she entered the casino, called the Vance suite.

She's okay!" Wilbur shouted hoarsely. "Livy's okay!"

Georgia closed her eyes for a quick, silent litany of thanks. "Where is she?"

"Milt Braverman just called a few minutes ago. He found her!"

"Where?"

"I don't know. He..."

Phillip's voice replaced Wilbur's.

"Georgia, Livy is safe. Yes! Yes! Livy is safe! There was never a kidnaping. She was on a romp with Albert Buckingham. I have few other details. Both children were located driving around in a Mirage limo. Young Albert had somehow concocted this adventure, and Livy was duped into joining him. That is all I know at this time. The limo is returning to the Mirage as we speak."

"Thank God," was all Georgia could say or think.

Phillip's speech was returning to the Ronald Coleman school of diction.

"Mr. Braverman said he'd explain it all when they arrive." And then in the same breath, "Georgia, please come to the villa. I want you here when Livy returns. It will be good for her to see us together. We can both talk to her and sort out what happened. I know that would mean a great deal to her—that is, to have you here with me."

"No." Georgia was surprised by how unequivocal she sounded. "It would not be in Livy's best interest if I were there when she returned."

"Ah, but my darling, of course it would be. We can present a united front."

"Phillip, you and I are *not* a united front."

"Perhaps not officially. But we can discuss that as well."

Georgia tried to say something, but Phillip went on quickly.

"I believe you are well aware that Livy and I would both be pleased if you assumed a more significant role in our lives."

My God! How quickly he's recovered from the worst crisis of his life.
"That cannot be."

"Of course it can. I know you adore Livy. And I am also aware that you are less than content with your marriage. I talked to Considine, the Mirage security chief. He told me about the incident in your room, that your 'little security problem,' as you termed it, was in reality a rather intense confrontation with your estranged husband. Georgia, allow me the opportunity to prove to you that I can make you happy, and that you and Livy and…"

"Phillip, stop."

Georgia could feel the moisture from the sweat that was collecting between her ear and the receiver. She also was aware of a peculiar tension.

"I do not intend to play a significant role in your life, and I am less than pleased that the chief of Mirage security has so little professionalism as to discuss confidential matters with you. And your presumptions based on that information are extremely inaccurate."

Was this anger? If it was then she would have to overcome it, remain rational, deal with this situation in a sensible fashion. *But is this what it's like to feel genuinely and righteously pissed?*

She took in a quick breath and continued, spurred on by an extraordinary rush of certitude.

"I am very happy…no, I am profoundly relieved and thankful that Livy is safe. And now I am going to end this conversation. Goodbye, Phillip."

Georgia hung up the phone and closed her eyes again to thank God properly for Livy's return. *The end of one crisis. And what about all the other crises? Which one will preempt which?*

She shut her eyes tightly and shook her head. With a strange sense of salvation—as though she had found a new path out of a dense and dangerous jungle—she realized that she had to focus on reality, on what was happening to Melanie now, and subdue the growing anarchy of her memories.

She stepped over to a pay phone and dialed the hospital. Melanie was out of surgery but would be in recovery indefinitely.

Too many questions again. Too much to process. Be careful of overloads, power surges, short circuits. Keep busy; stay in the here and now. Start by putting one foot in front of the other and walking away from this phone. There's always the ladies' room.

After she had washed her hands and touched up her makeup, Georgia pulled out her wallet and counted the cash: $1,536. Plus the $500,000 in the safe deposit box. She looked up into the image of her own wide eyes.

Melanie's fate rested in the hands of the medical profession. And whoever Zivah really was, the only way to cope with that worst-case scenario was for Georgia to prove to herself that she would not be coerced by any fear from the past. Georgia Kassov Cates was able to make the right choices. As long as she wasn't trapped, begging to be freed, and she would never let that happen again.

Alexandra
A novel by Georgia Kassov Cates

October 1950

Alexandra's breath came in small gasps because she was doubled over in the tight prison of the dumbwaiter box, stuffed in and unable to move. She heard the echoes of her own cries; she sniffed in the residue of cooking odors, dust and mold that had traveled up and down this ancient brick shaft for hundreds of years then she tasted the sour bile as it erupted from her stomach and stung her throat. She felt the rough wood planks under her knees, but when she tried to adjust her position, the whole contraption swung and bumped against one side of the brick well and then the other.

All she could see was a sliver of light, just a straight, thin line on the brick wall not more than an inch from the box that imprisoned her like an animal caught in a trap.

Then she heard Hannah's muffled voice coming from just outside the small door that had closed behind her. The cook called out in a singsong voice, "Can you hear me? Oh little American princess, can you hear me?"

"Yes," Alexandra replied. "Please let me out of here!"

Please let me out of here!

It sounded like another little girl who was trapped below her, but Alexandra knew it was her own echo.

Hannah, giggling and hiccupping, mimicked the same pitiful plea. "Please let me out of here!"

"Please!" Alexandra begged. "I'm scared!"

"Then why did you get in there in the first place? You know how angry your papa will be when he finds out. You are a very bad girl."

Alexandra tried again to shift her weight to take the pressure off one of her knees. Maybe then she could turn around so that she could talk to Hannah straight ahead instead of over her shoulder. Maybe if she was facing the right way, this would all make more sense.

How could Hannah think she had climbed into this terrifying place on her own? Hannah had forced her!

But try as she would, Alexandra could not budge. Her feet were wedged between the slats behind her, and the crown of her head pressed up against the wood in front of her. There was not a fraction of an inch in which to maneuver. Any attempt to flex or relax muscles just caused excruciating pain in some other part of her body. She was clamped in place, paralyzed, as though she'd been trussed up like a piece of meat ready to be roasted. Tears flowed out of her eyes and dripped on her arms and hands, but when she tried to pull in a deep breath so that she could let out a sob, the musty air could barely get past the constriction in her tortuously twisted neck and diaphragm. She coughed, causing spasms of pain to surge through her body.

"Please," she gasped. "Please let me out of here!" More coughing.

"Of course, mein liebchen," came Hannah's muffled voice. "But first you must promise never to climb in there again. Do you promise?"

"I promise!" Alexandra hoped she'd said it loud enough for Hannah to hear. It was getting harder and harder to breathe. Finally the thin line of light began to widen, and then Alexandra felt the fresh air as Hannah opened the little door.

"Ach du lieber!" cried the woman. "How did a big girl like you get into such a small place?"

She began to maneuver Alexandra's feet, loosening them from between the slats and giving the child a small amount of leeway to adjust her position. Then Hannah lifted Alexandra's legs over the edge of the doorframe and pulled her into her arms.

Finally Alexandra could take a full breath, and when she let it out, sobs of terror and relief came with it. Hannah carried her back through her bedroom and into the bathroom, sitting the child on the edge of the tub. Alexandra was still sobbing. Hannah wet a washcloth and pressed it to Alexandra's face, wiping away some of the grime and tearstains.

"Alexandra," cooed Hannah, her breath still minty from the schnapps but not enough to offset the odor of cigarettes and tooth decay. "I know you will never do that again. So we will not tell your mama and papa. They would be so angry with you."

"But I didn't want to get in there! You made me!"

"I made you?" Hannah repeated with an incredulous laugh. "Why would I ever do such a thing?"

She pulled Alexandra to her feet and guided her back into the bedroom, reaching again for the small child fingers, caressing them.

"I know you are very scared, and you know what you did was bad. But mein liebchen, do not say I put you in there. That is so unfair! We will both be quiet about this, and no one else will ever know."

She pulled back the covers on Alexandra's bed. "Now you lie down here and rest while I put water in the bathtub for you. A nice warm bath will make you feel better, and then we will go down to the kitchen and I will make you macaroni und butter. Okay, mein liebchen?"

Alexandra climbed up on her bed, wincing when her sore, chafed knees touched the sheets.

"Okay."

She lay back and took in deep, ragged breaths. She would never be bad again, she promised herself. She was lucky; at least Hannah was not too angry with her.

Chapter 28

December 1998

Georgia was still looking at herself in the Mirage ladies' room mirror when she realized that two other women were both eyeing her curiously. She busied herself pulling out her make-up again as the two women left.

She had to make a plan. She had to decide exactly what she was going to do next. Step by step. Maybe she should get the cash out of the safety deposit and hightail it back to the bank.

She watched the sardonic expression appear on her own face.

Well, for one thing, she couldn't make a deposit until the bank opened tomorrow morning. But then, after she did, she could go back to Creste Verde, tell Jeff that their marriage was over and that she knew she was doing the right thing because she had withdrawn $500,000 from her business account that was not hers. So what did that prove? That she had the guts, the gumption, the fortitude—whatever—to steal money for twelve hours and then put it all back where it belonged? So what?

Her eyes narrowed, her mouth tightened. She was in control. If she lost all the money at the poker table, Jeff would have to cash in some securities. That's all. They had the money. They had plenty of money. She could take a million dollars, and they would have the means to replace it. *It is only stealing if you can't replace* it. But if she won...If she won, it would be her money! Georgia would control it.

Several more women had come in, washed up, primped, and left. Now she saw Mindy Cameron hurry by. A moment later, a metal door banged once then again and again. Georgia came around the corner to see Mindy stumbling out of a stall.

"The fucking door won't shut!" Mindy dashed into another stall, sat down on the toilet seat, put her head in her hands, and began to sob. When Georgia stepped into the doorway, Mindy grabbed her arm and yanked her into the stall then reached around her to shove the door again. This time Georgia managed to get the lock to slide before Mindy resumed her hysterical door slamming.

"Patrone fired me!" Mindy blubbered and slumped back on the toilet seat. "Just now! He told me to leave the poker room. Just like that!"

"Why? Can he let you go without any notice? Why would he let you go at all?"

Mindy said something that was lost in the sobbing.

"You have to calm down," Georgia said. "I can't understand what you're saying."

"He goes, 'I'm not going to let anyone in the poker room think I'm your pimp.'"

Mindy let out another howling wail. Georgia could hear women gathering outside the stall.

Someone called, "Is everything all right in there? Do you need some help?"

"Thanks," Georgia said loudly enough to be heard over Mindy's sobs. "She'll be okay. Thanks anyway."

Then another voice said, "I can call security if you need me to. I'm the attendant."

"We're fine," Georgia replied as she gestured to Mindy to quiet down. Mindy grabbed some toilet paper to muffle her sobs and gulped in big gasps of air.

Georgia turned around and unlocked the door. "I'll wait for you out there."

A few minutes later the two women left the ladies' room and made their way to the Baccarat Bar. When they had settled at a small table, Georgia signaled for a waitress. Mindy was still taking in pitiful little gasps of air, valiantly trying to control her emotions.

"A Perrier," Georgia told the waitress.

"Stoli on the rocks, a double," Mindy sputtered.

When their drinks arrived, both women took long pulls, Georgia wondering how Mindy could down the vodka with the same ease as she did the Perrier. Mindy sucked in another long, deep breath of air, held it for a moment, and then released it.

"That's better," she said. She took another swig then reached into her purse for a compact and began to dab a powder puff just below her eyes.

"Patrone has been so coming on to me ever since he hired me. I just always shined him on but never turned him off, if you know what I mean, and that seemed to work just fine. But then, when I started dating players, he got, like, really stressed and told me that it wasn't professional. I told Nick and Ishiro both not to let on that we were dating, that it could so cost me my job. You know, killing three birds with one stone. I figured that was a way to keep each of them from finding out I was dating the other one, and also, as long as I didn't fool around when Patrone was in the room, like... you know."

She pulled out a lip pencil and started to outline her mouth in prune purple.

"Also..." She paused to skillfully slide the pencil from one corner of her bottom lip to the other, "...it was such a rush when Ishiro and Nick were there at the same time, especially when they were at the same table. It wasn't easy to keep them both happy, but I seem to have a real knack for that kind of thing, at least I thought I did."

She snapped her compact shut and shoved everything back in her purse.

"But I guess I wasn't careful enough. When Ishiro and I come into the Vances' Christmas Eve dinner and I see Nick, I go 'uh-oh.' Anyway, today all the shit hits the fan in one big, crappy lump. First Patrone stays way past the time he usually does and sees Ishiro and me on the platform, and then Nick comes in and goes over to Patrone and tells him that I've been soliciting the players, that I'm a hooker, and that Patrone better get rid of me or he'll be out of a job too. Why can't everyone just mind their own friggin' business? Fuck!"

Georgia sipped her drink, concentrating on keeping a neutral expression. All of Mindy's shock and grief over losing her job had passed in minutes and had been replaced with righteous indignation. Thankfully, because Georgia couldn't think of something to say that was not too sanctimonious.

Mindy finished off the remains of her drink and stood up.

"I'm going back to the ladies' room to finish fixing my face then I'll page Ishiro and tell him I want to fuck. That should pry him out of the game."

She started to walk away then turned back and said, "Thanks for listening." She flashed a quick smile and paraded out of the bar.

Georgia put money on the table for the drinks and a tip. She looked at her watch.

Well, hadn't this been a delightful little diversion?

And now maybe there was some news about Melanie. But a call to the hospital produced no new information.

Go play poker. Prove you're a winner. Prove you have the control. Test yourself, Georgia, test yourself to the max.

Georgia walked back into the poker room, making her way among the tables, carefully focusing way ahead so as not to make eye contact with anyone until she stepped up on the platform. Her heart thumped, and her head throbbed to the beat.

As she steadied herself, leaning on a table for help with her equilibrium, Jules walked over to her.

"How is she?"

Georgia did not respond immediately. Instead, she turned to Patrone, who was hovering nearby, and nodded.

"All of it?" said Patrone.

Georgia nodded again, and he literally snapped his heels together then briskly walked off toward the cage, ordering the chip runner to follow him. Georgia moved away from the poker table, out of earshot of the other players. She knew Jules was right behind her; his cologne, sweet and piercing, was irritatingly familiar.

"How is she?" he repeated. "I found out she was taken to the hospital, but they won't give me any information."

"She's out of surgery but still in recovery," Georgia replied.

"Have you talked to her since yesterday?"

"Yes. And she told me what happened last night." Georgia was careful to keep her voice neutral.

"What happened where?" Jules's bewildered expression was not convincing.

"At your townhouse."

Roxanne Roiballe, sitting just to the left of the dealer at table number one, called over. "Hey, you two! Either one of you coming into this game?"

"*I* am," said Georgia and walked over to slip into the two seat. She looked back at Jules and saw that his baffled expression had been replaced with a scowl. Hers was the consummate poker face. He turned and walked off the platform and out of the room.

The chip runner returned, carrying three racks of pink five-hundred-dollar chips and a stack of orange five-thousand-dollar chips. Patrone was right behind her, pushing a cart that held paper money in five-thousand-dollar bricks, which he counted out, then presented her with a safe deposit form to sign.

"Glad to see you brought bullets," Roxanne chortled. "And of course you know," she went on, "in this game there is no limit to the number of raises. You understand that, don't you?"

Georgia nodded because her heartbeat was overtaxing her lungs and any capacity to use her vocal cords.

"May we proceed?" Niles Buckingham was drumming impatient fingers on the table. His toupee seemed a bit off center. This had not been a good day for him. His son had caused a huge amount of trouble and his wife had been beyond hysterical when she learned of the whole debacle. It had taken hours of patient comforting and several Xanax tablets to calm her down. Now he sat in the three seat, and only a few hundred dollars in chips lay on top of his pile of currency. Obviously this was not how he had started the game.

Ishiro Zenri sat down at the table, having just returned from taking a phone call. Whatever the message had been or the conversation had been about, it did not seem to impact his intentions of playing in the game about to begin.

"Most assuredly we can give Georgia a moment to collect herself," said Zenri. He looked placid and composed as his long, elegant fingers slid up and down a foot-high column of chips. He had ten stacks in front of him, arranged in a perfect triangle, on top of a bunker of five-thousand-dollar bricks.

Georgia was grateful for his courtesy.

The man in the seven seat had close-cropped curly black hair and was resting his stubble-studded chin on a hand that sported hundreds of carats' worth of gold and diamonds, one ring on each stubby finger, including his thumb. This was Hassam Agrevi, the S and M fan.

A girl—she couldn't be much older than eighteen, although she must have had ID that showed she was twenty-one—sat in a chair a little behind him and to the left. She had sleepy blue eyes lined with a thick black pencil, and her lips hung open as if she was drugged. Long wisps of dead-white bleached hair fell over her face, and one large strand ended inside her mouth. She caressed her own breasts, which were ample and barely covered by a sliver of metallic-pink tee-shirt that hugged her midriff high above her belly button.

Brady Cranston sat in the eight seat, watching her manipulations, making absolutely no effort to conceal his pleasure. Agrevi didn't seem to notice.

Nick Loggin had turned his chair around and was straddling it, resting his chin on the back. His wraparound reflective sunglasses made it impossible to interpret the smile he sent in Georgia's direction. Georgia wondered whose money had paid for the chips in front of Nick. It was clear that he didn't have this kind of bankroll. Someone had put him into this game. Could it have been Phillip?

Between Loggin and Agrevi sat Montana Jones with his cowboy hat tipped low over his face. Lance, her pal, the biker dealer, was in the box. He winked at her.

I wonder what he thinks of all this. He knows I'm way, way out of my league. Does he think I'm crazy? Am I?

Georgia added her one-hundred-dollar ante to the pot, and Lance snapped off the cards. Zenri was low and had to bring it in for five hundred dollars. Nick Loggin raised it to a thousand, and everyone else folded. Georgia felt her stomach make a leisurely roll, flip-flopping over on itself. *Great, just what I need. Now I have to worry about vomiting right here at the table.*

She put out another hundred-dollar ante.

How am I going to react if I ever have to call? Or raise? Right, like I could really ever raise at these stakes.

She reached for her new cards and peeked at them, pressing her fingers into the table to keep them from trembling.

Oh shit! Pocket aces!

A minute later she pulled in a twenty-five-thousand-dollar pot, which she had won with two pair.

She sipped on a glass of Perrier that had been delivered during the hand, sure that those nearby had heard the gulp as the liquid was forced down her tense and dehydrated throat. She tried to stack the chips that she'd won, but her fingers wouldn't make a team effort. Finally she swept them all close in front of her and tried to handle the next three cards, which had already been dealt. This time she had split kings, one up and one down, with a queen kicker.

Not again!

Grabbing from the pile of chips in front of her—the ones she hadn't had a chance to stack yet—she raised, and this time Nick Loggin, who was showing an ace, raised her back. Georgia silently thanked Loggin as she folded her hand. Sure, he could be bluffing, but she didn't care. And mercifully, she got nothing on the next deal. As the hand continued without her participation, Georgia finished stacking the remainder of the loose chips.

Look, dork! Either settle down and play or get the hell out of the game!

Forty-five minutes passed—the longest forty-five minutes Georgia had ever spent at a poker table. It had become menacingly clear that pleasant social intercourse was a part of the feigned nonchalance and did not in the least mitigate the killer instinct of high-stakes card players.

Ishiro Zenri had three fours and a king out in front of him as he made the bet two thousand dollars. The last down card, the river card, had not been dealt yet. Nick Loggin winged his cards at Lance, and the dealer deftly blocked them before they slid off the table. Montana Jones muttered a cowboy expletive then folded too. Hassam Agrevi, showing two tens, a six and an ace, raised.

Brady Cranston gave a philosophical shrug and slid his cards toward the dealer.

"As Catfish Hunter used to say," he drawled, "'the sun don't shine on the same dog's ass every afternoon.'"

Lance was the only one who smiled.

Roxanne Roiballe, chewing on her fuchsia-lined lips, reached inside her bright-green blouse and adjusted a bra strap as she contemplated everything on the table. Finally she flung four thousand dollars into the pot.

Now it was up to Georgia. In the last forty-five minutes, she had lost with every conceivable type of hand: a flush and two full houses had been three of the most catastrophic. Now, just before the *Good Ship Disaster* sank to the bottom of the sea, the Seven-Stud Navy had arrived with four unbeatable eights. It was her turn.

She peeked at her hole cards again. Yes, she had four eights; she'd been rolled up with two eights down and one up from the beginning, and now she'd caught the fourth one on Sixth Street. She wasn't worried about Zenri. The most he could have was four fours, but he probably was raising on a full house. She also had seen an ace and a ten, so Agrevi too could have nothing better than a full house. Roxanne had the five, six, seven and jack of hearts in front of her. But Georgia knew she couldn't get a straight flush because the three of hearts had been folded earlier and all the eights were miraculously accounted for. She was holding the unbeatable hand, "The Nuts."

Many raises and reraises later, she threw in her last six thousand dollars and said, "All in."

"All in," repeated Lance for everyone else's edification. "Any new bets will be on the side."

As if they hadn't noticed.

Everyone called the pot. They had to; it was just too big not to. This concept of pot odds was the ultimate ice cream sundae topper: "The Nuts." This time they belonged to Georgia.

Everything that had happened in the last twenty-four hours, the last week…month…decade…her entire lifetime, dissolved in a wave of serenity. She simply could not sustain the delirium, the euphoria, or even the sense of salvation. The excruciating panic of losing all that money that was not hers to lose was replaced by calm.

This must be some sort of metaphysical trance.

She had been floundering, adrift in her soft and foggy sea, trying to keep her cards and chips from washing overboard. Now, suddenly, she was back on deck and in command. And the river card didn't matter.

Lance dealt a last card down to each of them. A small crowd had gathered as the pot had grown to titanic proportions. Niles Buckingham was shaking his head. Two players who had come over from another table on the platform stood behind him. Ishiro Zenri sat rigidly, his dark eyes focused on the pot, while he tossed in another thousand dollars, making sure it didn't splash the main pot.

Nick Loggin slouched over the back of his chair, scowling. Montana Jones sat back, arms folded, as he surveyed the scene. He too was now merely a spectator. Hassam Agrevi sucked on the last half inch of a Turkish cigarette. His young companion was still off in Quaalude land, her eyes half closed, chewing on the strand of hair in her mouth and continuing with her breast massage.

Agrevi called, winging his chips hard enough that Lance had to block them with his hand. Brady Cranston was shaking his head and mumbling under his breath, while Roxanne Roiballe, still fiddling with her bra strap, tossed in her chips with her other hand.

"Call," Lance said, adding the chips to Zenri's and Agrevi's for the puny little side pot as he glanced up at the bubble in the ceiling that held the video camera. Then, as though he knew this moment might be a clip on the morning news, he intoned, "First, let's see the two hands for the side pot."

Zenri's four fours got him the thirty-thousand-dollar side pot. As Lance pushed the chips toward Zenri, Georgia glanced out across the casino at the huge tropical rain forest dome, dark now that night and rain surrounded it.

Out in the employees' parking lot, two women in housekeeping uniforms sprinted through the rain just as an eighteen-wheeler turned into the driveway. The driver saw the women just in time to wrench the wheel to the left, missing the two but plowing into a utility pole, which crumpled at its base and fell on top of the cab. Sparks flew, crackling and popping, while dark smoke curled into the murky night.

Georgia peeked at her hole cards again.

Maybe this was all one awful hallucination. Maybe those were really not two eights. Maybe she wasn't even really sitting at the poker table. Or maybe she was about to float away again, into some parallel poker universe where four eights was not the best hand. No! She was here, and this was as real as it could get.

She flipped up her three hole cards. And then everything evaporated into absolute, mind-blotting darkness.

Someone yelled, "Cover your racks!"

For several seconds, the Mirage poker room as well as the entire casino and hotel was black as deepest, darkest purgatory. Then the auxiliary lights burst on, and everything was enveloped in an unearthly yellow radiance. Some people were looking around in mute astonishment, others murmuring to each other, some laughing nervously. All of the dealers were leaning over the racks of chips in front of them. Some of the players held the same position over their own funds. Lance had pulled the enormous pile that lay in the middle of the table into his rack, making a huge muck of loose chips and cash, plus several of the up cards from Georgia's as well as other players' hands.

The loudspeakers shrieked with the repetitious and ominous whine of the alarm system. Somehow, amid all the chaos, it was Mr. Kruikshank's face that caught Georgia's attention. He sat at a ten-twenty table, arms calmly folded, lips pursed, nodding sagely.

Then came a woman's recorded voice, like a sound bite from some "alien Amazons invade the earth" movie.

"Attention! Attention! The cause for the previous alarm has been eliminated. The alert is over."

A three-second pause and then again, "Attention! Attention! The cause for the previous alarm has been eliminated. The alert is over." As the standard lights blazed on, replacing the yellow pall with the normal brightness of the card room, the enormity of the situation hit Georgia like an icy tidal wave. Her pot, not to mention two of the eights that comprised her winning hand, had been scooped up and tossed into the dealer's rack like so much debris after a cyclone at sea. The noise level started to rise as her realization was being duplicated all over the room and other players beheld what three seconds of darkness had done to decimate the previous hands. Some of them voiced their apprehension while others were chortling their relief and elation that the hand they were about to lose had just been snatched back by the poker gods.

Edward Patrone's voice boomed over the microphone. "Your attention, please, ladies and gentlemen. Our momentary blackout has caused some concern among the players. It is the policy of the Mirage poker room to decide each table dispute on an individual basis. We ask you to be patient as we go through this process as quickly as possible. Thank you for your cooperation."

Predictably, Patrone made his way to the platform first, where even Lance, the imperturbable, the most professional dealer in the room, was showing signs of strain. His face was red and shiny with sweat as he sat, stoic, arms outstretched to encompass the clutter in front of him. He was doing his best not to react to the antics that had begun at the table.

Brady Cranston, Montana Jones, and Nick Loggin were out of their chairs and milling among the scores of people who had gathered around the main game.

Hassam Agrevi was shouting, "Misdeal! Misdeal! Misdeal!" over and over like a forty-five record with the needle stuck. His teenaged companion had stopped caressing herself and tugged anxiously at her stringy hair. Ishiro Zenri was sputtering in Japanese to another countryman who had dashed up on the platform to witness the excitement. Roxanne Roiballe was fanning herself with a *Card Player* magazine as though she might momentarily swoon, but at the same time she was vocalizing a duet with Agrevi, adding her own chorus of "Dead hand! Dead hand!" to Agrevi's "Misdeal!"

Only Georgia sat silently, rigidly. The serenity of a few moments ago sucked up into a vortex of poker room chaos. The tremendous effort to keep herself anchored to the rational world had just been obliterated by the unthinkable. And now, even though all the lights were back on, the room was closing in on her, getting dark again. Her mind was trying to bail out of this spiraling death dive that had begun when she sat down with $500,000 in stolen money, all of which was now either stacked in front of other players or was part of the chaotic heap that lay in front of Lance. She took deep breaths, willing herself to stay conscious.

Edward Patrone was talking, and Georgia forced herself to focus on what he was saying.

"...so the dealer is now going to make a tray count, which will then give us the precise amount that was out in the middle of the table. Then he is going to count down the pot, and all players' chips from the last hand will be returned to them."

Everyone spoke at once.

Georgia had to get Patrone's attention, but when she tried to stand up, her knees did not support her, and her words were lost in the clamor as she fell back in her chair. This was like the nightmare when no one could hear her calls for help. But Lance had seen her attempts, and he nudged Patrone, pointing in her direction.

"I have a question," she heard herself saying. "Why is it a misdeal?"

Patrone's words were slow and measured, as though he were repeating the same phrase for the tenth time. "Because we cannot determine the origin of the up cards—that is, whose hand consisted of what cards."

"What about the video camera?" Lance was looking at Georgia as he posed this possibility. Georgia knew he was stepping way out of bounds to do this for her.

Patrone's jaw locked, and he spoke through his teeth. "That is not the normal procedure in this case."

Now Georgia, surprised but grateful that her vocal cords remained functional, spoke up. "Well, this is far from a *normal* situation."

She gulped air then blurted, "I officially request that all the money in the pot be held by the house…" Another gulp of air. "…until this matter can be dealt with under calmer circumstances."

All that air she'd just swallowed! Now she had to burp and did so as unobtrusively as she could. "Excuse me," she murmured.

"Of course you're excused." Mr. Kruikshank was standing next to her.

"Pardon me," said someone else. Georgia looked up to see Phillip, hair combed back into its former perfection. "Edward," he said, putting a fraternal arm around Patrone's shoulders, "this is becoming an extremely delicate matter."

Delicate matter? My burp? No, that can't be. Georgia, get a grip!

Phillip was still speaking. "I would assume that those who have a corporate and vested interest in the Mirage Hotel and Casino, not to mention the Nevada Gaming Commission, will be most concerned about the entire consequence of this evening's power failure. Best you do not add to the calamity by mishandling this particular incident."

"Of course, Mr. Vance," Patrone said in a low, less-than-fervent tone.

Georgia looked at Mr. Kruikshank and was reminded of his bizarre description of the poker room. Somehow it seemed particularly accurate right now. She did feel as if she'd just arrived from another galaxy.

Not everyone involved agreed with Phillip's position on delaying the decision, but after several minutes, despite Zenri's, Agrevi's, and Roiballe's protests, the ruling became official. It was apparent to everyone that the entire casino blackout was going to indefinitely delay getting the surveillance tapes, so forms and plastic bags that could be sealed and annotated to store the chips were retrieved from the office.

Lance went about counting down the pot as those who still had a vested interest in the process looked on. He was very proficient, and there were no more disputes. The chips and cash were sealed in the plastic bags, annotated, and signed by each of the participating players. Everyone at the table racked their own stacks except for Georgia, whose entire bankroll (not to mention her life and future) was part of the pile that Lance had pulled into the rack. For now, the main game was over.

Georgia tried standing again, and this time her knees worked better, although she felt inordinately stiff all over. She made her way toward Phillip, who excused himself from a large cluster of people.

"Thank you," Georgia said.

"Of course," Phillip replied. The timbre of his voice was deep again, and Georgia realized that when he was calm and in control, Phillip consciously lowered it.

"My Olivia is safe and sound in her bed, and I am most gratified that I arrived here in the poker room when I did."

"And Zivah and Milt?" Georgia asked.

Phillip clutched Georgia's arm. "Won't you please come back to my suite? We can talk so much more comfortably there, away from all this muddle."

Georgia ignored Phillip's attempt to usher her off the platform and said, "I want to check on Melanie."

"By all means," Phillip said, bowing slightly as Georgia reached for a house phone.

While Georgia was waiting to be connected with the ICCU, she looked out over the poker room and spotted Milt. He was watching her, and he made a discreet wave, barely wiggling his fingers. She kept eye contact with him as she was told that Melanie's condition was listed as critical but stable after the surgery. Under no circumstances would Ms. Nallis be allowed any visitors before 8:00 a.m., and then only after the doctor had given permission.

Georgia hung up the phone and turned to find Phillip hovering nearby, and she realized that he and Jules used the same cologne.

"What news is there of Melanie?" His intonation seemed overly solicitous, or was it merely his exaggerated British enunciation? Georgia told him what she had heard from the ICCU receptionist. "Then won't you accompany me to my suite? I can't imagine that you would be able to sleep after all this, and perhaps, now that this immediate crisis is deferred, I can nullify some of the negative effect prompted by our last phone conversation."

Phillip reached for her arm again and tucked it into his own.

"I'm afraid I wouldn't be very companionable," Georgia said as she gently extricated herself from Phillip's grasp. She stepped off the platform and walked over to where Milt had been watching.

He turned toward the entrance and headed for the Sports Bar a few feet away.

Georgia followed, never letting even her peripheral vision stray back toward the high-level platform, where she knew Phillip was watching her.

"Let's get away from here," she said.

They sat on stools at the bar outside Kokomo's on the other side of the casino. Milt ordered a draft beer and Georgia got a Perrier.

"Okay," he said after both of them had gulped down half their drinks. "When I got to Zivah's, she was just coming in with groceries. She almost dropped the bag when she saw me, but she pulled herself together pretty quick, and we went into her apartment. She denied knowing anything about where Livy could be then let me look all over her apartment. No sign of anything to do with Livy. Zivah says that maybe Livy went in search of Siegfried and Roy. Livy had told her several times that she believed that they had real magical powers. Then I got an idea and called a friend at Metro who has an in with the limo companies that provide cars for the Mirage, and we hit the jackpot on the second call he made. A limo had taken a fare from the Mirage out to Siegfried and Roy's ranch, about fifteen miles out of town. But then the driver called in to say that his passengers were still with him because they had not been admitted at the guard gate to the ranch. He was now driving them to Boulder City.

"The driver was told to go back to the Mirage and wait for us at the north entrance. We got there just about the same time as the limo, and guess who else is in the car besides Livy: this kid named Albert Buckingham. I had called Phillip, and he and Wilbur were waiting there too. Wilbur cried like a baby.

"This Albert's parents didn't even know he was missing. They thought he had gone to visit a friend or something, and they had spent the day at some seminar at UNLV. Somehow the kid had gotten the hotel to provide the limo."

She closed her eyes and shuddered. "Thank God," she said.

"There's more, though," Milt said. "Zivah told me more."

"About Albert Buckingham?"

"No, not about that."

"Not about that? I'm not sure I'm ready to deal with anything else."

"Well, I don't think you're going to be able to ignore this, even for a while. It's about Zivah and Melanie."

Georgia was having another out-of-body moment. "Zivah and Melanie," she repeated incredulously and started to shiver.

"Hey, easy," Milt said, gently pulling her out of her chair and wrapping his arms around her shoulders. "There must be even more to this than I thought if you're this shook. Let's go," he said, guiding her out of the bar. "I'll explain the part I know about on the way over. I promised that I would bring you to the hospital. Zivah is there waiting for updates on Melanie's condition."

"Melanie's condition? Zivah is waiting to hear about Melanie? What does Zivah have to do with Melanie?" Georgia felt herself being boomeranged back to some distant galaxy.

Chapter 29

Three small sofas filled most of the space in the ICCU waiting room. Zivah sat in the corner of one, hands clasping her ancient leather purse. Her white hair was pulled up into a bun as usual, and she had applied a brilliant pink lipstick to her thin, old lips. She kept pursing them together, as if she was very conscious of the inappropriate brightness on her pale face.

"Georgia, I have a story I must tell to you," Zivah said as she patted the sofa cushion next to her. "Sit by me."

Georgia ignored the offer and took a seat on the opposite sofa, willing herself to look directly at Zivah, steeling herself for whatever the old woman was about to reveal, knowing that whatever she was about to learn, she would have to face it alone. Even though Milt sat just a few feet away, he would not be able to protect her.

Zivah rearranged her skirt primly over her knees and then clutched her purse to her chest. "I will begin many, many years ago so that I can make you understand everything."

Moments passed, and she said no more. Finally her eyes opened but were focused beyond some internal horizon.

"Right after the war, I found work as a kitchen helper for the family of a wealthy SS officer. He had a son, Clause, who was fourteen years old. Late at night I went to his room and slipped into his bed. He told his father, and then I had to hide, and I lived in barns and basements until after the war, and then I spent more years in DP camps."

Now she looked up for a moment, glancing at Georgia.

"Do you know about these DP camps? 'DP' is for displaced persons. There were many of us who had no home, no family, no community. Our towns and cities were destroyed, our government was a void, and the Allied forces tried to cope with the thousands of us. The camps were not like the concentration camps, no one died from being shot or gassed, but we still suffered.

"Sleeping with men was the only way I could survive. That was how I got food, or shoes or medicine if I was sick. Then I had a baby. I was very weak and frightened after the birth, and a woman came to me in the hospital and said that she could help me to sell my baby daughter to an American army officer. In just a few days, she made all of the arrangements. They gave me five thousand dollars in American money."

Zivah twisted the strap to her purse around one finger while she took in a deep breath. Words came out with the exhale. "I did not know how it would be so painful for me when the baby was taken far away. I had spent the first days of her life feeding her from my breasts and sleeping with her, holding her to me, finding *glücklichkeit*...ah, happiness, that I had never known before. By the time they came for her, I had grown to love her as only a mother can love a child. Then she was ripped away."

Zivah went on twisting and untwisting the purse strap, but her eyes sought out Georgia's, as though she were calibrating the shock and fear in them.

"That was when I had the number tattooed on my arm. I would use this symbol to take advantage. I would be pitied, and I would use that pity. My life went on. I worked for many years for many families, and eventually I married a good man. Twenty years later, when my husband was killed in a train accident, I used the insurance money and the legal settlement money...so much because the accident had been so bad, and the train company had been at fault...to come to America to search for my lost daughter. I never had another child."

Georgia's voice was faint. "Did you find her?"

"When I came to America, I hired a company to look for her. Through adoption records, they found the man who had paid me for my daughter. He lived in Oklahoma. He did not know where the girl had gone. He said she ran away from home when she was fifteen. Finally I found out that my daughter lived in New York City. I went there, and I found her. Ach! She was so beautiful and so lovely to watch, but I stayed away. I would not let her know me until I was ready, and I would not be ready until I knew more about her. But then she disappeared again. She had gone to Europe, I found out, and then I lost her again, but I never gave up.

"A couple of years after that, I found her back in New York, and now she had her own daughter, my granddaughter. I was ready to tell them who I was, but I became a coward. It was easier for me to follow her from the shadows than have her hate me. When she left New York and came to Las Vegas, I did the same. I am very good now at following my beautiful daughter without her knowing it."

Zivah stopped speaking and looked in Milt's direction for the first time. Until now, her eyes had been fixed on Georgia. "I would make a good private detective, yes, Milt?"

Milt said, "I'll go check on Melanie," and left the waiting room.

Zivah closed her eyes and said, "Today, when Milt told me that Livy was lost, I realized that in my life, I have lost everyone, every single person that I have loved. Finding Livy was easy, but now I know that I could no longer keep my secret. Yes, I found my own baby again, only now she is a beautiful woman and she does not know who I am. And then Milt tells me that maybe she will die. I cannot lose any more. I must take the chance, even if she will hate me. That is not the worst thing. The worst thing would be if she never knows I am her mother." She let go of the strap and brought the purse to her chest. "I hope it is not too late."

"I hope so too," Georgia said quietly. "I hope so too."

Milt came back to the doorway. "Melanie is stable, but no visitors indefinitely."

Zivah was weeping softly, still clutching her purse. Georgia said quietly, "Zivah, can I ask you a question?"

"Of course." Zivah sat up straighter and dabbed her eyes with a hanky she had pulled from her pocket.

"Who was the father of your baby?"

"I am not sure."

"All the research you did, and the investigation firms you hired, they were only to find Melanie? No one else?"

"Who else?" Zivah asked. "The father? That would be a waste of time after all these years, and I don't need to know that."

"And there is no one else you are looking for?"

"Who else could there be?"

"Alexandra."

"I do not know Alexandra. Who is she?"

Georgia willed herself to look deep into the old woman's eyes, wishing she had the power to see into Zivah's heart. "She doesn't exist anymore," Georgia said quietly, "and I hope to God that you are telling the truth."

"Ach, the truth," Zivah said. "What is the truth? I tell you what you need to know about me. Nothing more, nothing less. That is enough for now. The rest I save for my Melanie. The rest of the truth is for her."

Milt turned off Spring Mountain Road and into the driveway that led to the Mirage. The traffic had been light, and it had only taken a few minutes to work their way across town. Neither of them had spoken since they had left Zivah in the ICCU waiting room, and Georgia was grateful. Not that she had been able to process much of what the old woman had told her. Was there more to Zivah's story that entwined with her own? Zivah had hedged so much about what was the truth. *What if she was Hannah? Then what? So what?* She had no answer to that.

When Milt stopped the car, Georgia gestured to the valet that she was not ready for him to open the door to Milt's black Jeep Cherokee. She turned in her seat and put her hand on Milt's arm.

"Would you come in and talk to me for a while?"

When Milt turned off the engine, Georgia heard the lovely, squeaky sound his leather jacket made as he moved around to face her. "Are you sure you're not too stressed or too tired?"

"I'm not too tired." She opened her door and stepped out into the brisk predawn air. "Actually," she said as Milt signaled the valet that he was leaving the car, "I wouldn't mind walking for a while."

Milt pointed toward the Strip in mock astonishment. "Outside?"

"Outside."

When they reached Las Vegas Boulevard, they turned right and strolled past the lagoon that surrounds the Mirage volcano, which was becoming a legendary landmark. At this time of the day, the mist from the immense, cascading waterfall glowed with the first glimmers of light that appeared over the buildings to the east. Even now, at the crack of dawn, a tourist was focusing his camera on the scene. He wore a black tee-shirt that proclaimed "Lordy, Lordy, Bob Is Forty" in neon-yellow lettering.

Georgia and Milt smiled at each other.

"Oh boy," Milt observed. "I can remember when I would have been embarrassed by that tee-shirt; now I only wish I could wear it without grossly under exaggerating."

"Me too," Georgia said as they walked on in companionable silence. Crossing Flamingo Boulevard took them from the Roman extravagance of Caesar's Palace to the opulent banks of a northern Italian lake, which reflected the breathtaking vista of the Bellagio Hotel and Casino. They walked past the ornate white marble wall that surrounded the water, gazing at the intricate architecture of the vast resort. It would not be open for some months yet, but Steve Wynn had outdone himself. The Mirage was fabulous, but Bellagio was going to be the hallmark of elegance and lavish ambience that would be nearly impossible to surpass.

Georgia looked up to see that Milt was looking at her instead of the scenery.

"Thank you for finding Livy," she said. "Oh, I know she would have been back with Phillip sooner or later." Georgia had cut off whatever it was that Milt was going to say. "But it could have been hours more before those kids were found."

Milt nodded, and Georgia went on. "And you came back to the Mirage and waited for me while all that insanity was going on up on the platform, and then you took me back the hospital. You got yourself involved in all this, and you didn't have to. And that's not all."

"I'm all ears," Milt said with a warm, lopsided smile. "I accept thanks for anything and everything that I can possibly take credit for."

Georgia slipped her hand around his arm, catching the scent of his leather jacket. "Okay," she said, happy to feel him tuck her arm in his. "Thank you for being my poker pal, for giving me all those tips and answering all my dumb questions. No, no, let me talk," she said, squelching his response again. "You've always been patient with me, and I want you to know I'm grateful. Like yesterday, when I told you about the money I'd withdrawn from my business account. No judgments from you, no reprimands or warnings. You just listened, and you knew that what I needed was someone to tell, nothing more."

"Nothing more?" he asked. He had stopped walking and turned to face her. Softly he asked again, "Are you sure there's nothing more?"

Georgia looked up at him and answered quickly. "There's more, lots more." Then they both turned around without letting go of each other and, with a deliberate pace, walked back toward the Mirage. No more strolling, and Georgia kept talking, although her words were spaced with quick, deep breaths. From the exertion? Partly.

"For example," she said, "what I find quite wonderful about you is that you let me tell you what I need to without getting in my way."

"I'm a quick study," he said. "You don't have to shut me up too many times before I get the idea that you want to tell me what you want to tell me when you want to tell me. So tell me."

"The amazing thing is that I'm not nervous." Several short breaths. "No, that's not true. I am nervous but in a funny, kind of giddy way, like I know that what I'm going to say is right, and that I should, and that you want me to."

"So say it!"

"In my room," she said and reached for his hand. Milt held the heavy glass door of the Mirage main entrance open for Georgia, who ducked in under his arm. They walked through the rain forest, and Georgia realized that she had not entered the casino this way in years. When the elevator door opened at Georgia's floor, she could feel the dampness that had gathered between their two hands, which were still engaged.

She let go, smiled, and said, "Sweaty palms."

He grinned back at her. "Isn't it supposed to be fluttering heart, not sweaty palms?"

"That too," she said and led him down the hall and put the key in the lock. They stood very still, looking at each other but not making contact.

Finally Georgia spoke. "This is when you're supposed to take me in your arms and kiss me tenderly but passionately."

Did that sound as dumb to him as it did to me?

Milt did not move. "Is that what you want me to do?"

Georgia crossed the room to the window. Milt still stood by the door.

"You can come in," she said softly. He stepped farther into the room, removed his jacket, and laid it over a chair.

Georgia put her purse on the table and went back to the door to slide the security lock. "I guess I'll stay for a while too," she said, but the light little laugh she was trying for came out more like a nervous guffaw.

They both went back to the window. Now the entire Strip was visible as the sun rose into full early morning, without a trace of yesterday's storm clouds. She leaned toward him, and he allowed her to rest her weight against him.

After a moment she said, "Are you ever going to make a move or is it all up to me?"

"I'm being patient," he said with a mischievous smile.

"Enough with the 'patient.'"

He turned his head and gently laid his mouth on her temple. Their arms went around each other, and he bent his head to softly kiss her lips, pulled back to look into her eyes then kissed her again.

This is so easy...so easy.

She opened her mouth and found his tongue. He tasted and smelled wonderful. They dissolved into each other. Clothing was gently removed, he helping her, she helping him. No fumbling, no grabbing, every movement willing and deliberate.

Now Milt took the lead. Gently he laid her down on the bed and brushed his mouth slowly over her face and neck then her breasts and belly. She lay back, aware of every individual caress until a need to return the touches overwhelmed her, and her mouth found his delicious, smooth, firm skin, and her nose absorbed his unbelievably erotic smell. She could feel a throbbing ache building in her and knew that only filling herself with him would relieve it. And she wanted him in every part of her.

"Please," she whispered. "Please, now!"

And then he was pulling away from her, standing up and going toward the window, where all their clothes lay.

What had she done wrong? Had she told him to stop? She hadn't meant to, but she had done that so often with Jeff because that's what Jeff had wanted to hear; it had been her husband's signal to propel himself into her. Had she groaned some sort of protest from habit? She didn't want Milt to stop.

She was naked and alone in a big bed, aching beyond anything that was comprehensible. Everything that had happened in the last day roiled up inside her head like a montage from a thousand nightmares. She had lost her grasp again; she was going to fall off the earth. She turned onto her side, pulled her legs up to her chest, and her vocal cords released the terror.

He was shaking her, his hands gripping her shoulders, his words finally penetrating her sobs.

"Hey! Hey!" He grasped her to him, and she threw her arms around his neck. If she held on tight enough, she would not fall away. Finally her breathing slowed. Milt's arms were still wrapped around her, and she felt herself being rocked back and forth. She pulled her head away and looked at his face.

"What the hell was that?" His tone of voice softened the words. "What happened?"

Suddenly Georgia became aware of her nakedness. She let go of Milt's neck and reached for a pillow, which she held up to her chest. Milt got up from the bed. The blanket and sheets had been folded back by housekeeping the evening before. Milt pulled them up over Georgia then sat next to her on the edge of the bed, whispering soothingly, "It's okay, Georgia. It's okay."

Minutes passed as he sat quietly, gently stroking her hair. She lay still, her eyes closed, willing herself to calm down.

"What happened?" he asked again.

Georgia took in a deep breath and held it a moment. Then she said, "I'm not sure." The words came out unevenly, and she cleared her throat. "When you pulled away from me, I kind of freaked out."

"Kind of," he said. "I was going over to my stuff to get a condom. You know that's what I was doing, right?"

She shook her head. "No, I didn't know that's what you were doing. I never even thought about a condom."

Milt held his hand out, and Georgia pulled hers from under the covers and took it. He moved closer to her.

"Oh God," he breathed. He pulled her hand to his mouth and kissed it gently. "You thought I was bailing out?"

Georgia couldn't answer him. The only thing she could think to say was yes, and that was just too incredibly stupid. She looked into his eyes and found a haven. She didn't have to answer him in words. She reached up, putting her arms around his neck, pulling him toward her, at the same time kicking off the covers then wrapping herself around him.

His whisper was a warm, lush current washing her skin wherever his mouth traveled. "Tell me what to do," he murmured. "You tell me what you want."

But she didn't need any words. She opened herself up and he found her, first with his gentle hands, and then he was part of her. He moved carefully then more firmly, and the sensation began to throb in her and build as he adjusted himself over her, moving instinctually to find just the angle that worked for her.

"Oh my God!" she heard herself scream.

This was the antithesis of pain, and for the first time in her life, she understood the difference.

Georgia pulled the rumpled covers over herself and snuggled into the pillow that had absorbed some of his sharp, powerful scent. She could hear the water running in the sink and then the flush of the toilet. She hugged the pillow, rocking back and forth. Now all she heard was the faraway drone of a vacuum cleaner as housekeeping began its rounds.

A minute later, Milt came out of the bathroom. He was dressed, and his hair was wet and combed back. "I borrowed your hairbrush," he said and sat down on the edge of the bed. They looked at each other for a few moments and then very softly, as though he were speaking to a frightened little girl, he said, "Do you want to talk to me?"

Georgia nodded but said nothing. He waited another minute. "I'm going to go down to the coffee shop," he said quietly. "You take whatever time you need then page me and we'll decide what to do next." He stood up, kissed the top of her head, picked up his jacket from the chair, and left the room.

As soon as Milt closed the door, Georgia got out of bed, flipped the security lock, and went into the bathroom. She was careful not to look at her reflection in the mirror. When she came out, wrapped in her terry robe, she called the hospital. It was a little before seven in the morning. Melanie's condition had been upgraded; she had been transferred from recovery back to the ICCU, but it would be some time yet before the doctor would approve any visitors.

Half an hour later, dressed in jeans and a Mirage sweatshirt, she dialed Milt's pager number. While she waited for the phone to ring, she studied herself in the wardrobe mirror. She had dried her hair to its natural curly softness, not too sophisticated, but that didn't matter right now. She'd applied her makeup with a light touch, and she'd put on the hammered silver hoop earrings.

"I guess I don't look like too much of a fool," she said out loud.

When the elevator doors opened at the lobby, Milt was waiting. They walked back to the Caribe Café and sat down at the table where Milt had waited for her. The busboy hurried over, placed a glass of ice water in front of Georgia, poured coffee into a cup for her, and refilled Milt's.

"Are you okay now?" Milt asked.

"Yes, I'm okay now," Georgia replied quietly, amazed again at how easy this was. Milt made things so easy. She gave him the update on Melanie.

When their breakfast arrived, they said very little while they ate. Each of them polished off a plate of eggs, sausage, hash browns and several pieces of raisin toast.

When the dishes had been cleared, Georgia said, "I need to tell you some more."

"Tell," he said, putting his hand over hers.

Sitting there with him in a booth in the coffee shop of the Mirage Hotel in Las Vegas, Nevada, cocooned from the rest of the world, she let go again—not as she had upstairs a while ago but also not as she had ever before in her life.

She began with her "Alexandra" years, the memories of living with Hannah, the harsh and insidious German cook, and then escaping Germany and becoming Georgia.

Milt sat quietly, squeezing her hand in response but saying nothing.

Just a few days ago, she had sat in a booth very near to where they were right now, listening to Melanie. Now Georgia was finally able to be the one who spoke the truth to the one who would listen.

"Now for the really weird part," she said, trying for a light tone but failing. "No, I don't really mean *weird*, but I don't have another word for it right now. You see, I think Zivah may be Hannah." Georgia waited for a reaction from Milt. He nodded as though he had already known.

"Okay," he said finally. "Let's get this out of the way. I've been wanting to tell you something for a while, but with all that's been going on, I just kept shelving it because you had enough to deal with, and this was pretty vague. But now, based on what you've just told me, it seems too coincidental to ignore, so here goes.

"I think I mentioned way back before all hell broke loose that Melanie had asked about you a few times. Well, I had also heard through the poker room grapevine that Zivah had been asking a lot of questions about you too. At the time it seemed a little strange to me because I knew you two were sort of buddies and that Zivah could probably get any info she wanted directly from you. I didn't put much importance on it because I wasn't sure how accurate the scuttlebutt was in the first place. But it seems Zivah has a very full and complicated agenda, and playing poker is far from the top of her priority list."

He shrugged his shoulders. "That's it." He waited a moment for Georgia's response. "So now what?" he said softly.

"I don't know."

"Then we'll have to wait until you figure it out."

Georgia nodded. "I think I should go to the poker room and see Edward Patrone."

"Okay, but let's take another minute to think about that. You know that Patrone is going to stay with his ruling that the hand is dead and all the money should be returned to each player. But there is always the chance of taking it to the gaming commission, and you've got a shot because there were eyewitnesses to the hand who were not in the pot."

"Do you really think Roxanne or Zenri or Agrevi would really say they saw my two eights?"

"Not a chance. But the dealer, he saw the cards too. Not putting Lance in that position would be a good thing for him. He'd pay a big price for screwing the other players, maybe even lose his job. But the biggest problem I see is the publicity that comes with one of those hearings. Especially when it involves Roiballe, Zenri and Agrevi. Do you want it in all the papers that Georgia Cates, who handles hundreds of thousands of dollars in philanthropic funds, was playing in a Vegas high-stakes poker game?"

Georgia inhaled calmly. There was no easy way out of this. But no more panic. Panic took energy, and she didn't have enough left.

They held hands walking through the casino. As they passed by the Rain Forest Snack Bar, they spotted Wilbur and Livy sitting at a table. Wilbur stood as they approached; Livy sat, looking down at her feet.

"Mr. Vance just left a minute ago. He had a very important meeting," Wilbur explained a bit too earnestly, Georgia thought.

"Good morning, Livy," Georgia said gently. "I'm very happy to see you."

The little girl looked up at her but said nothing. Georgia knelt down. "How is your hot chocolate?"

"Okay," mumbled Livy, her gaze fixed on the floor again.

"What are your plans for the day? Anything special?" The child shook her head.

"Then could you meet me at the Habitat at about five o'clock?"

"Okay," Livy said again.

Georgia straightened up and patted Wilbur on the arm. "I'm glad you are *all* okay," she said.

"Me too," said Wilbur and sat down. "Thank you, both of you."

Georgia and Milt walked out of the snack bar. It was after ten in the morning, and she had not slept in over twenty-four hours, and there was no residual of any of the adrenaline that had coursed through her system lately, on the average of every several hours.

Still so much to deal with. An itchy fuzziness had settled in her eyes, and she felt a loss of equilibrium as her system, now sated with a good breakfast, tried to go into suspended mode.

The poker room was as quiet as it would ever be. Most of the all-nighters had left, and the day shift players were just beginning to trickle in. The receptionist told them that Edward Patrone had left word that he would be in about the middle of the afternoon. Georgia and Milt strolled back into the casino.

"I'd like to suggest a plan of action," Milt said, pulling Georgia's hand to his lips again. "We both could use some sleep. No, let me rephrase that. We both will *collapse* if we don't get some sleep. Why don't you go up to your room, and I'll go back to my place, and I'll come back here about three thirty this afternoon?"

Georgia nodded then reached up on tiptoe and kissed his cheek.

Back in her room, she undressed, pulled the heavy drapes closed, and climbed into bed. She still heard the vacuum cleaner out in the hall as she drifted away on a soft and foggy sea, and then, what seemed like just a moment later, a shrill blare came through the mist, then turned into the ring of the telephone. Georgia opened her eyes and glanced at the clock as she reached for the phone. It was two fifteen, and this was the automatic wake-up call she had requested right before she got in bed. She lay still for a minute, trying to catalogue the events of the past thirty hours.

"Never mind," she said out loud, climbing out of bed. "No time."

By three o'clock she had styled her hair with the blow-dryer, reapplied her makeup, and replaced the sweat shirt with a yellow silk blouse. Once again she sat down on the side of her bed, picked up the phone, and dialed. Half an hour and three phone calls later, just as she put down the receiver, the phone rang again.

"Been chatting?" Milt's voice was deep, like a smile.

"I'm sorry," Georgia said. "Have you been trying to get through? I was taking care of some business."

"Oh? Anything you want to share with me?"

"Yes, everything, but not right now. Are you in the casino?"

"Uh-huh."

"I'll meet you in the poker room."

"Aye, aye, Captain, but I think you should know that Vance paged me and we've been talking for a while. He really does want to help you. He said he got Patrone to show him the videotape and he thinks you can prove your hand by it, but Patrone disagrees."

"I'm on my way," Georgia said and hung up the phone.

Chapter 30

Edward Patrone leaned against the door to his office, staring out into the poker room. On his desk was the voucher for $480,000 and change, now referred to by everyone in the poker room as the "blackout pot." Next to it was the videotape that he had just played for Georgia Cates. Phillip Vance had watched it again too.

Patrone was well aware of the speculation that had been fast and loose as to how this situation would be resolved. He knew some money had been wagered on the outcome among several locals. Roxanne Roiballe, Hassam Agrevi and Ishiro Zenri, however, had a much larger stake in the decision. They had each contributed many thousands of dollars to that dubious pot and were not the least bit interested in the side wagering. They each wanted their money back. They were a coalition of three who knew that the best possible outcome for them would be to have that hand declared a misdeal and all money returned. They had been lobbying intensely all day to achieve their goal, calling him at home and in his car.

Georgia Cates, on the other hand, obviously held a different point of view, and at this moment she was seated at an empty poker table surrounded by her advocates. Patrone watched the conference that was taking place right here in his poker room and clenched his teeth.

Phillip Vance was talking while Milt Braverman sat by quietly, and the Cates woman, dressed in her expensive silk shirt and designer jeans, alternately shook her head and then nodded then shook her head again.

The videotape had shown without a doubt exactly how the hand had proceeded. Every up card was clearly visible, and every bet, raise and call had been accounted for to the dollar. Even Patrone had smiled at the moment on the tape when Lance Bennett, the dealer, had glanced up into the video camera.

The puzzler, the ever-growing cramp in Patrone's ass, came at the end of that segment of tape when supposedly Cates had flipped over the spade eight and the heart eight at the precise moment that the electricity had failed. The videotape had been blurred for that last tenth of a second, and the image was not clear enough to unequivocally verify that she showed four eights. He had made a decision at the time of the incident, without the benefit of the videotape, and he knew that the best possible outcome for him was to have that ruling validated. Zenri, Agrevi and Roiballe, all three of them who put hundreds of thousands of dollars onto Mirage poker tables, and even more out in the pit, were in his corner. That didn't hurt his cause either.

Nick Loggin had joined Braverman, Vance and the Cates woman at the table. Loggin was a hotshot loudmouth and a cheap son-of-a-bitch. He was just Phillip Vance's toad and had probably already hit the peak of his poker playing career—not much chance he would ever be a high-limit player, or tipper. Loggin had never toked him so much as a five-dollar redbird. But the skinny creep was in with the big boys, and that made him a dangerous thug. And now he was out to get even for that time when Loggin had gone apeshit about that crazy Kruikshank. Then there was the thing about Mindy. Loggin was threatening to tell everyone that Patrone was pimping for her. *Motherfucker.*

But compared to Phillip Vance, Loggin was a mosquito. Sure, Vance gave Patrone a black chip every so often—big deal. He'd like to tell the fucker to take those blackbirds and shove them up his ass, but that would never happen because the limey was at the top of the food chain.

Patrone would have to be very careful how he handled all of this or be out on the Strip, trudging from one human resources office to the next, trying to find a job, and when that didn't get him anywhere because the good old boys would make sure the word got out that Edward Patrone was not a team player, he'd have to try the East: Tunica, Mississippi, Atlantic City, or Foxwoods in Connecticut. No way. He wasn't moving back East. He liked his life here in Vegas, his four-thousand-square-foot house, and all the juice that trickled his way as the manager of the Mirage poker room.

Patrone shook his arms out at his sides like a swimmer about to dive into a hundred-meter sprint. Then he walked over to the table and sat down across from Georgia Cates.

"Georgia," Patrone said, smiling with his teeth, "I realize that this has been a difficult situation for you, but I hope you can see that I am also burdened with doing the right thing here. And I am…"

"The right thing here," Phillip Vance interrupted, "is to award Mrs. Cates the pot that she won fairly and squarely, as you Yanks say, a circumstance that has been corroborated by videotape."

Out of the corner of his eye, Patrone saw Ishiro Zenri, who had just walked into the poker room and was making his way toward them. Mindy Cameron, in what looked like a black bra and white pants that had been shrink-wrapped onto her, was right behind him. As they approached the table, Mindy's body language said it all. She could dress any way she liked now that she was no longer a Mirage employee.

Zenri bowed formally and then sat down at the table. "I have just paged Mr. Agrevi and Ms. Roiballe," he said. "They are coming."

Mindy stood behind Zenri and began to massage his neck.

Patrone glanced at his watch and said, "I'd like to suggest that we adjourn to somewhere more private. I've reserved one of the executive conference rooms. Can we meet there in, say, a half hour? That would be four thirty."

"I don't think that will be necessary," said Georgia. "I believe we can resolve this issue right here and now."

"Georgia, my dear." Phillip's tone was mild and placating. "Perhaps you and I should discuss this a bit further. Most significant at this point is the option of taking this dilemma to the gaming commission. You can subpoena the dealer and the other players who witnessed you exposing your hole cards before the blackout. More than likely the other participants in the pot will have developed a form of fiduciary amnesia in this case, but the dealer should be impartial. He can testify on your behalf. Indubitably, Georgia, you have that right."

"Thank you, Phillip, but none of that will be necessary," Georgia said, looking at Milt, who smiled back at her with his eyes. "It would be best to end this whole situation as quickly as possible."

Ishiro Zenri was standing now. Mindy kept one hand on his neck. "Mrs. Cates, you must wait until the other principals involved are present."

"No," Georgia said softly. "No need to wait." She turned to speak directly to Patrone. "I agree with you that the last moments of the videotape are inconclusive, and I cannot prove that I had four eights. I also know that if this were taken to the gaming commission, they would uphold your ruling because the tape does not clearly indicate that my two hole cards were eights. Everyone, including those who had already folded, should get their money back."

Patrone had to struggle to keep the immense relief from turning into a giggle.

"Georgia, Georgia, you sweet, naïve child," Phillip intoned. "That money is indisputably yours."

"No, it's not," Georgia answered almost in a whisper. Then, looking back at Milt, she said in a stronger voice, "But that is my problem to deal with, no one else's."

Chapter 31

Two white tigers rested on the upper shelf in the far right corner of the Habitat, curled up like huge kitties. Neither one of them seemed the least bit concerned that some three dozen or so sets of eyes stared at them, willing them to make the slightest movement. The big cats slept on in feline oblivion. Livy stood against the rail, Wilbur very close by. Georgia came up behind her and gently patted her shoulder. Livy did not turn around.

"Hi," Georgia said gently. "Want to go get a soda?" Without a word, Livy turned toward the casino. Georgia looked at Wilbur and said, "I'll bring her back here in a little while."

Livy and Georgia walked toward the snack bar, pausing every so often to allow pods of gaping tourists to pass by. When they had their drinks, Livy hiked herself up onto one of the tall bar chairs that surrounded the snack tables.

The child took a few sips from her straw then, finally looking into Georgia's eyes, asked, "Are you gonna make me tell you why I ran away?"

"No," Georgia replied. "I would never *make* you do anything."

"Well, I want to tell you," Livy said then bit at her upper lip. "But it's hard. Daddy didn't really understand. He said he was just so happy that I was safe that as long as I promised never to do anything like that again, I wouldn't get into any trouble."

A minute passed, and Livy sat stirring her soda with the straw. Georgia sensed that the child needed more reassurance. "You can tell me anything you want, and you don't have to tell me anything you don't want."

Livy stared into her soda, fidgeting with the straw. "I thought that if I ran away, just for a little while, that everyone would be so worried about me, that when they found me they would be so happy that…" Livy looked up, waiting for Georgia to complete the sentence.

Georgia prompted, "That they would be so happy that…" The child needed to complete the thought in her own mind, no suggestions from Georgia.

"I called up Albert Buckingham," Livy said, obviously not ready to verbalize the rest of the previous thought. "Even though he wasn't very friendly, I told him that I wanted to find Siegfried and Roy's ranch. I told him that if he took me, I'd give him one hundred dollars. Daddy always left money on his dresser, and I didn't think he'd miss a hundred-dollar bill.

"I knew Wilbur would never let me go, and besides, Albert said he would do it but that I couldn't tell anyone because if I was gone, even for a little while, then everyone would think something bad happened to me, and Albert didn't want to get blamed.

"So Albert and I made a plan. Getting away from Wilbur was the hard part, but Albert told me what to do. I stuffed one of Daddy's undershirts into my backpack and a new scarf that I knew Wilbur hadn't seen yet. Then when Wilbur and I were on our way to the Habitat, I went into the bathroom and pulled the undershirt over my clothes and put the scarf over my head. Then I waited until a whole bunch of women and a couple of little girls were walking out at the same time. I hurried along right in the middle of them. I kept my head down, and Wilbur didn't notice me. Albert was waiting for me at the valet, and we got into one of the big Mirage cars. Then when we got all the way out to where Siegfried and Roy live, the guard wouldn't let us in the gate. Albert told the driver that we wanted to go to Boulder Dam instead, and we were driving out there, and then the driver gets a call on his radio, and he says he has to take us back to the Mirage."

Livy's eyes filled up, and her mouth twisted. "I didn't mean to get Wilbur in trouble," she said, her voice cracking, "but I just thought if everyone was really happy when they found me that you and Daddy would..." She took in a ragged breath. "I wanted so much for you to be my mommy." The tears rolled down her cheeks.

Georgia stood up, wrapping her arms around the little girl, and whispered into the mop of curly hair, "We'll be very special friends, I promise. We can love each other that way, like special friends."

The child slid off her stool, nodding her head solemnly. Her words were whispered, but the intensity was thunderous. "If you make a promise like that, you can never, ever break it."

"Oh, Livy," Georgia finally managed. "Never, ever." They held on to each other, standing there in the snack bar until someone asked them if they were still using the table.

Holding hands, Georgia and Livy walked back toward the Habitat, where Wilbur was waiting. He hurried over to them, calling out, "Mrs. Cates, you have an urgent message! Ms. Nallis is asking for you."

"Three minutes," the doctor said. "Three minutes is all you get. She wrote your name on the tablet and won't even let us take it out of her hands. She just keeps waving it, over and over. I hope seeing you will calm her down."

Melanie lay still on the bed, the lower half of her face covered with tape that held the mouthpiece to the respirator in place, her right hand clutching a pad of paper. As soon as Georgia had come into her line of vision, Melanie's eyes locked onto her; those amazing, glorious eyes still gave out their own energy.

Georgia gently patted Melanie's arm. "I can't stay long, but I'm here right now. I'm here because you want me to be. Now you have to relax and concentrate on getting better."

Melanie's eyes widened then she blinked several times.

"I know you want to talk to me," Georgia said softly, "and I need to talk to you, but we're both going to have to be patient. We'll have plenty of time. Meanwhile nothing is going to change. While you rest, and you know that's what you have to do to get out of here and back home, you have to rest and let the medication and the procedures make you strong again. And while you do that, I have to go back to Creste Verde for a few days, but as soon as you can, we'll talk on the phone. And I promise I'll hurry back here as fast as I can. I promise."

Many promises made today.

Melanie's eyes closed again, and Georgia could see some of the tension in her face ease away. The doctor, who had been standing nearby, indicated it was time to leave. Georgia carefully removed the tablet from Melanie's hand, laid it on the night stand, and tiptoed out of the room.

Georgia and Milt sat next to each other at the end of a row of chairs at Southwest gate 34.

"I'll be back as soon as I can," she said.

Milt reached for Georgia's hand, held it to his mouth, and kissed it gently. "I know," he whispered. "You've made a lot of promises lately, and I'm just glad I made the cut."

"I just have to figure out how to get rid of some of the kinks and knots in my life. Actually the kinks are easy. Actually most of it is easy now that I've laid the groundwork over the phone. I told my business partner, Andrea Gleason, about the money that came from the business account and that I've already replaced it. As soon as I can, I will sign over my share of Cates, Gleason et Cie to her. She has agreed to keep this quiet, and hopefully our clients will never know that the Cates of Cates, Gleason was a rookie embezzler. The business will keep its integrity, and Andrea will be well-compensated for my unbelievably stupid and close to completely disastrous stunt. I'm giving, not selling, my share of the business to her, including all the capital investments I've made. And Jeff can't do anything about it."

The announcement came over the PA system. "Southwest Airlines flight eleven-oh-four to Burbank is now ready for departure. Anyone with small children or the need for assistance with boarding the plane can step forward now." Everyone around them began to gather their belongings in anticipation of joining the masses that soon would be herded onto the plane.

Georgia stood up and pulled Milt to his feet. She reached up on tiptoes and pecked him on the cheek. Milt put his arms around her and whispered into her ear, "I love you. Can Jeff do anything about that?"

"No, only I can, and I plan to. Jeff will give me a hard time about a divorce settlement, but one way or another, I'll end up okay because the only thing he has any power to manipulate is money, and there's plenty of that. I'll get enough."

Georgia caught the eye of the young man waiting to take her boarding pass. He spoke into the microphone. "This is the final boarding call for flight eleven-oh-four. All passengers should be on board the plane. Let's go, lovebirds. Whichever one of you is flying south better get over here."

Chapter 32

December 30, 1998

It was the day before New Year's Eve, and Georgia finished another of the dozens of calls that had punctuated the hours since she had returned to Creste Verde. Melanie was slowly improving. The respirator had been removed, and she had been allowed to talk to Georgia on the phone. But Melanie's throat had been too sore to do more than croak a feeble greeting. Georgia had promised again to get back to Vegas as fast as she could. Meanwhile Milt was checking in at the hospital. The nurses told him that the old woman with the German accent was in the waiting room most of the time.

In the past three days, Georgia had accomplished a lifetime's worth of resolution. Sonnie had returned from Hawaii, and mother and daughter had spent hours together thoroughly discussing how this amazing change in Sonnie's heretofore stolid and reliable mother would affect the young woman's life. By the time Sonnie left with Billy for a New Year's house party in Big Bear, Georgia was very certain that her daughter would be able to accept, to the best of her nineteen-year-old capability, and eventually come to understand why her mother was "bailing out of such a cushy life," as Sonnie had phrased it.

An hour on the phone with Mike, who was still in Utah, had accomplished the same thing. Her son had also questioned why she was ending what he had described as "a marriage set in concrete." Actually, she told him, it was only she who had been set in concrete, not the marriage.

Sonia had called from Oslo a couple of days ago, and the conversation had centered on the marvelous trip that she was having. Georgia would save the bombshells for another time. Informing her mother about the divorce, giving up the consulting business, and moving to Las Vegas could be done much more efficiently—and inexpensively—when they were not communicating by international long distance. *Oh yes, it could definitely wait.*

Everything had been settled with Andrea Gleason. All the money was now back in the business account, transferred from a Cates, Gleason et Cie money market account. Andrea had become more than a business partner to Georgia; they were dear friends. Georgia had wanted to explain why she'd stolen the money, but Andrea had cut her off.

"It doesn't matter to me why you did it," she said gently. "I'm not going to judge, and besides, absolutely no one else would gain from knowing the details, certainly not me."

Now the business would be known simply as Gleason et Cie. On Georgia's suggestion, the new company would be structured to include profit sharing for employees. Andrea Gleason would get all the support she needed from her staff, and the business would thrive.

But Georgia had not been prepared for the tremendous sense of loss she experienced as the ex-partners had signed the final papers. This business was a measure of her worth. She had once explained to Melanie that the money she made in the business was a way to calculate the value of her efforts and services. And now she realized that modest sum was much more than that. It was the symbol of the beginning of her emancipation, and she could finally admit to herself that the financial success she had achieved with Cates, Gleason et Cie had been the on-ramp to that convoluted freeway that she was careening along as she continued on the trip that was taking her from the life she had passively accepted for so long to wherever she was going to end up.

It had never occurred to her to simply leave Jeff, to divorce him. *Oh no, Georgia Cates could never do that.* Her business was like the button on an emergency escape valve. And then, just as the need for escape became critical, the valve had malfunctioned, and she'd had to try to rescue herself by pushing other, more dangerous buttons. *She was such a slow learner!*

Georgia heard the car door slam in the driveway followed by a short, shrill whoop as Jeff engaged the alarm system on his 1963 Jaguar XKE. The front door lock clicked open, and footsteps sounded in the entry. She turned in the swivel chair and made a quick assessment of her appearance in the glass panels of the bookcase. Her white fisherman's sweater hung to her knees. It was comfortable, and she loved wearing it with jeans and a turtleneck. She combed her fingers through spiky strands of hair and checked to see if lipstick had smudged her teeth. *Old habits*, she thought as she took in deep, controlled breaths, as if she was preparing to jump into very cold, very deep water.

"I'm in here," she called out as casually as she could. *Damn! Squeaky voice again.*

Then he was standing in the doorway of her office, his tall frame blocking the entire opening. His salt-and-pepper hair was windblown and yet so well cut that it fell into a perfect pattern of casual layers. He wore impeccably tailored gray slacks and a blue cashmere sweater. Georgia had never seen this outfit before. *Christmas presents maybe. No, Jeff had picked these out himself. Jeff Cates always found time to shop for clothes.*

Georgia waited for a greeting, but none was forthcoming. He stared at her with his version of a poker face. He was a lousy poker player, partly because of that throbbing muscle in his right cheek. It was his tell, always had been. He could certainly never hide his agitation from her; it pulsated on the side of his face, announcing that Jeff Cates was nervous, angry, excited, whatever. Just fill in the blank.

"Won't you come in and sit down?" Georgia offered. Jeff didn't move. He continued to fill up the doorway, posing like Mr. Clean, legs spread apart, arms folded across his chest.

She tried again. "Would you prefer to sit in the den?"

Georgia followed Jeff down the hall, stepping around storage boxes that held the Christmas decorations. Everything was packed away but the porcelain Santa, still standing on lonely vigil in the center of the living room mantel. Georgia planned to take him with her when she flew back to Vegas, which was about three hours from now.

Georgia hurried past the suitcases that she had placed in the entry, hoping against hope that she was about to grab hold of the last loose end that would untangle the snarl that kept her bound to an unhappy existence. She came into the comfortable, intimately furnished den, where Jeff had already settled on the deep-green distressed-leather sofa.

"Would you like a drink?" Georgia asked as she walked toward the wet bar.

"No." Jeff glared at the far wall.

She pulled a Perrier from the refrigerator below the counter and twisted off the cap then hiked herself up on a barstool.

"Then let's get down to business," she said.

No response from Jeff, who sat more rigidly now, scowling at the empty fireplace as though he were trying to conjure up the power to produce spontaneous combustion. Georgia sipped her Perrier for a few moments and then spoke.

"I'm willing to try to explain my decisions to you, if you're interested. But if not then we should probably discuss a few practical matters and leave the rest to the attorneys."

"Why did you want to talk to me alone?" He was still looking into the fireplace.

"I'd like to tell you why I've made this decision, and it's really no one else's business."

Jeff turned his head to focus on Georgia. A fierceness flared in his eyes, and it occurred to her that rarely had she seen so much emotion in them.

"Cut the crap!" Jeff spat the words at her. "I don't give a shit about your motivations, or how hard you tried before you gave up on your marriage, or how much you've sacrificed of the real you, or any of that psychobabble bullshit."

For a moment Georgia fought to keep her voice from broadcasting the fury that was pounding inside her, afraid the words would emerge with the squeal of a small, injured bird.

Old habits again. Fuck it.

"My marriage. You refer to it as *my marriage*. It was *our* marriage. That in itself says a lot about why it's ending." Not much of a squeal, actually quiet calm and forceful.

"Yeah, and it's *our* bank account that you just wrote the three-and-a-half-hundred-thousand dollar check on!"

"Of course the money is more important to you than the rest of this."

"This is all bullshit!" He kicked the hassock that his legs had been resting on, and it skittered across the pegged and grooved planks in the floor. Then immediately he stood up, repositioned the hassock at the foot of the chair, sat back down, and morphed into the insidiously calm, reasoned Jeff, who had always been able to overwhelm her with his dogmatic rationale.

"If you think I'm going to listen to you explain in boring detail why you're filing for a divorce, you're mistaken. I don't care that much. You served your purpose in my life."

He gestured toward a framed picture that sat on a side table. It was a photograph of Georgia, Sonnie and Mike taken about five years ago.

"You had my kids and took care of them; you ran the house and did a competent job of providing the lifestyle to impress my clients. Now I don't need you any more than you think you don't need me." He placed the photo facedown on the table.

Georgia tried to assess the effect of Jeff's words and his actions. Of course he meant them to be intimidating, and certainly hurtful, but they'd missed that mark by miles. Her concerns as to how Jeff would respond to any or all of her decisions had just been summarily dismissed. Emergency escape valve no longer required. He was releasing her, not deliberately, not consciously, but nevertheless whatever remained of the thin, decaying tendrils of devotion and sentiment she'd retained for this man had just been snipped clean.

She smiled at him sadly. "You know, this scene isn't going the way it often does in the movies or in novels where the wife finally stands up for herself and then the contrite and beseeching husband tells her that he's seen the error of his ways, that he's realized how awful all the years must have been for her, and would she find it in her heart to give him another chance because now he knows his life would be empty without her."

Jeff stood up and walked behind the counter of the bar. He reached for a bottle of Glenlivet and poured several inches into an old-fashioned glass then carried it back to the sofa and sat down again. He took a pull on the scotch, closing his eyes as he swallowed. When he opened them again, they seemed to have lost some of their intensity.

His voice was lower. "I know that you've always deferred to my ambitions, my goals, my whims. And I never expected any different. You were the perfect mate for me; you never rocked the boat, and I did appreciate that. And I showed it in every way I could. You could have whatever you wanted—plenty of money for clothes, the house, the kids, entertaining, vacations, cars—and then there was the financing for your business, not to mention a substantial investment in jewels. I don't know what else I could have given you."

"And there you've scored the bull's-eye, a direct hit at the core of the problem. You had no idea what else you could have given me."

"Okay, so you want more from me..." His voice trailed off as he gulped some more scotch. He waited a moment to assess Georgia's reaction, but all he saw was a blank face and unreadable eyes.

He shifted gears. "You know," he said as though the idea had just that moment occurred to him, "maybe we can work this all out. Maybe both of us can prevail—you know, a win-win situation."

Another pause. Nothing from Georgia. He drained his glass and went to the bar again.

"Here's the proposal," he said, pouring more scotch. "We stay married, no hassle with divorces and settlements, etcetera. You go back to what you do best, being Mrs. Jeffrey Cates, but you spend more time in Vegas."

Finally a spark flashed in Georgia's eyes. Jeff saw it and continued quickly. "Look, this is about figuring out how to live our lives on our own terms. Right? Obviously you never really wanted what I thought you did. Or if you ever were happy raising our kids and spending my money, that seems to be in the past. So once we've straightened out this financial mess you've gotten us both into, you can still play poker, because that seems to have taken priority over your family, while I can still have the seemingly ordered home life that I would like to be perceived as living."

She stepped down from the barstool, walked over to the end table, and carefully and deliberately set the photograph back in its original position. Then she returned to sit at the bar.

Another length of silence.

Jeff put the glass down on the table. "I am trying to be as reasonable as I can, considering these circumstances. I don't know what else to offer you, so this is it."

When Georgia didn't reply, the pulse in Jeff's cheek beat in double tempo. Finally he said, "I really don't want this to turn into some kind of melodramatic scene where all is revealed and perceived. Neither one of us has to experience an epiphany at this point. You probably think you already have, and I don't need one. I let bygones be bygones, forget about the fact that my wife is an embezzler."

Georgia marveled at the truth of his statement. There was no question that she was doing the right thing for everyone involved, including Jeff, who wanted and needed nothing more than his "ordered life."

"I don't regret our marriage," she said. "It was supposed to be. Sonnie and Mike are the positive proof of that. More so, I am who I am right now because my life has been what it's been." Jeff nodded, but Georgia wasn't sure what he was affirming, or if he was simply morphing from contentious to patronizing. "So I guess we'd better get on to the practical matters at hand. The divorce."

That concept again: divorce. Maybe it was so easy because it was so right. She waited for his reaction. It was silent and malevolent.

For once her voice did not betray her, but maybe that was because, finally, she really believed in herself.

"I'll tell you my immediate plans," she said.

He stood up again, drained the remaining inch or so of Glenlivet, and put the empty glass on the counter. "I really don't need to know about your plans," he said as he went to the doorway and stood there, blocking the light that came from the entry, just as he had in her office.

"I'll call a real estate agent about the house. Gerald Gould told me that you had retained him to represent you in the divorce proceedings. You're wise to choose the best in town. I'll call John Kendall about the divorce. He's been my legal anchor for a long time, and I have no doubt that he'll take care of this as efficiently as anything else. Oh, by the way, he also mentioned something to me about the Caroline Foster Foundation."

No reaction from Georgia.

"You've gotten really good at this poker face thing," he mumbled. "Well anyway, Kendall heard that the foundation board chairman was starting an investigation. Somehow they got word that you'd made a five-hundred-thousand-dollar withdrawal. How much of that money belonged to them?"

Jeff didn't give her a chance to respond. "Well anyway, they want to know where it went and why. Kendall thinks maybe you should consider hiring a criminal attorney. I think you may have a problem."

He gazed at her for a moment. She stared back at him, inhaling and exhaling cautiously, yet afraid that she was about to suffocate.

"I'll be staying at the California Club until I find something to buy," he said. "Probably on the west side."

A minute later Georgia heard the little whoop of his alarm system again, then the noise of the engine as he drove away. The cuckoo clock that hung over the bar ticked away the minutes. The far-off wail of a siren and the drone of a lawn mower from somewhere down the street were the only other sounds. Georgia was all alone again, still battling to catch her breath.

A flock of words and terms dipped and soared in her brain: Caroline Foster Foundation, investigation, criminal lawyer, embezzler! *I can deal with this, I will. I'll find the help I need.*

Just one last thing. Even though she herself might be facing a criminal investigation, even an indictment and trial, her question about Zivah, no matter how much she wanted to ignore it, to deprioritize its significance, remained and pestered her like a loose hair caught under her tongue.

She pulled several small storage boxes from below a built-in shelf filled with dozens of thin leather photo albums. She carried the boxes over to the coffee table, set them down, and then poured herself a shot of brandy. *I hope this helps.* She took one huge gulp, squeezing her eyes shut as the liquid burned down into her stomach.

Her mother had never had the time or the inclination to sort through more than forty years of snapshots, and they had gathered in drawers, to be packed away in boxes each time they moved. When Sonia had settled into the little apartment in Manhattan, she had insisted that her daughter take all of them. Georgia had purchased designer storage boxes, filled them with the snapshots, and stacked them on the bottom shelf of the bookcases in the den. They had been sitting there for years.

Georgia had scrupulously catalogued the photos that had accumulated over the length of her own marriage. Every year she would fill a new album, beginning with snapshots from New Year's Eve, followed by ski vacations, graduations, Fourth of July picnics, Thanksgiving dinners, birthday parties, etc. The last page of each album held the latest Cates family Christmas photo.

She'd never been able to cull through all those other old snapshots, the ones from her childhood and before her marriage. Now she had to.

It took close to an hour and another shot of brandy before she found the group of pictures from that time in Germany when they lived in the huge house with the dumbwaiter. There she was, six years old, posing in front of the Christmas tree, sitting on a sled on a snow-covered driveway, swinging from an ancient metal gate. Her thirty-something mother and father stood with her among the tulips in Holland, and sat with her on the beach at Nice, and smiled indulgently as she opened birthday presents.

And then she was staring at an image of herself and the beautiful house servant who had been her tormentor. There in the tiny black-and-white photo with pinking shear edges, Hannah stood next to little Alexandra, who was dressed in the yellow satin gown and huge-brimmed bonnet of a Little Bo Peep costume. Hannah's arm was stretched toward Alexandra like a circus barker introducing a new act.

Georgia picked up the photo, holding the corners by her fingertips, as though the surface was caustic. Reaching for a magnifying glass, she focused on the tiny numbers that snaked up Hannah's arm. The first one, just above the wrist, could be a four. Georgia closed her eyes, visualizing the numbers on Zivah's arm: 42348. She remembered how they floated up haphazardly from just above the old woman's wrist.

Georgia peered back again through the magnifying glass. But squinting and moving the lens up and down, over and over, could not bring any of the other numbers into focus. And the best she could ascertain was that perhaps the numbers seemed more uniformly placed than the ones on Zivah's arm.

She pulled a small envelope from a drawer in the desk, placed the photo inside, sealed it, and carried it back to the entry where she tucked it into a zippered compartment in her wallet. When she got back to Vegas, she would have it enlarged, and she'd have another piece of truth. Then what?

Chapter 33

Georgia peered out of the window as the plane banked toward McCarron Airport. Off to her left, the Strip radiated its impartial greeting to all who approached from the sky. She spotted the golden glow of the Mirage and longed for the familiar sense of security that the sight of that building had always provided for her, even from a thousand feet above it. Not tonight.

Minutes later she emerged from the walkway that connected the Southwest jet with the terminal. Milt was the first person she saw. He was leaning against a post, wearing a soft green wool plaid shirt and blue jeans. With arms crossed in front of him, head tilted at an angle, his body language conveyed an intimate welcome.

The sanctuary she had missed as she had gazed from a thousand feet above the Mirage now enveloped her. Here again was that recognition of safety, only now it was emanating from this man. He embodied the shelter she was craving, not necessarily as a rescuer, but certainly as a haven in which to gather strength and prepare for whatever battles lay ahead. She decided in that moment to delay telling him about the foundation inquiry. Nothing could be done about it now, tonight, and she wanted his full focus to be on her, not her problems.

"Hi, jet-setter," he said as he wrapped his arms around her. "Nice of you to drop in for the evening."

"Hi, yourself." She buried her face in the collar of his soft, woolen shirt and breathed in the smell of him. She'd missed it.

"We have to go to baggage pickup. I brought a ton."

"A ton of what? Furniture, hardware, dried goods, cash?"

"Clothes and a few other things." She gave him a loving punch in the ribs as he took her carry-on and swung it over his shoulder.

"Clothes!" he mimicked. "Clothes for what?"

"Clothes to live in for some time to come. I'm staying for a while…a long while."

"And of course you need at least three changes a day."

As they walked toward the tram, he pulled her to him and kissed her temple. "Are you going to change your clothes again this year? You have about an hour left."

"I hadn't planned to. Actually I like that we're both wearing flannel shirts and jeans. It means our karmas are in synch, or something like that."

"'Karmas in synch is cool, but I'm glad your shirt is yellow and not green or we'd look like 'Ma and Pa Kettle come to Vegas.'"

"God forbid!" She grinned at him. *Amazing! I'm facing the possibility of jail time, and I've never been this happy before in my whole life.*

When the three pieces of luggage had been stowed in the back and they were both in the Jeep, Milt gathered her in his arms and kissed her. She wrapped her fingers around the back of his head, loving the feel of the prickly soft hairs at the base of his neck. His mouth left hers, but the kisses didn't stop, not from either one of them.

"Hold it, hold it," Milt said after a few minutes. "I'm getting a muscle spasm in my back. Only adolescents have the muscular and skeletal pliancy to make love in the front seat of a Jeep. And my guess is that you would prefer better accommodations and ambience than the backseat, even though we are parked in romantic and exotic level C of the short-term parking building."

"Then take me away from all this," she said, reaching up for her seat belt.

While they spiraled their way toward the exit, Milt asked, "Where to?"

"How about the hospital? I know it's almost New Year's, but I really want to see Melanie. Would you mind ringing in the New Year in the ICCU?"

"We might as well," he said. "We're not going to be able to get near the Strip anyway. The cops have it blocked off by now." He turned onto Paradise Road and headed toward the hospital.

As they entered the lobby, there was less than a half hour left in 1997. The main waiting room was completely empty, and a doctor was being paged in the standard drone of the hospital PA system. When Georgia and Milt reached the ICCU desk, the only sound they heard was the beep of the computer monitors. Two nurses sat working on charts. Both were wearing paper party hats. One of them looked up at Milt and Georgia and said, "Welcome to Times Square."

Georgia smiled. "Would it be possible for us to see Melanie Nallis for just a few minutes?"

"Oh, so you're the party of two," quipped the other nurse. "We've been holding your reservation. Actually your friend has been upgraded to better accommodations. She's got her own room now, just on the other side of the waiting room. You can see her, but for just a couple of minutes, okay?"

The nurse stood up and came around the counter. "I was just going in to check on her, so follow me. Oh yeah, and that elderly lady is still in the waiting room."

As they passed the waiting room, the nurse pointed to Zivah. The old woman sat rigid in a straight-backed chair, staring up at the TV, which soundlessly displayed a view of the Strip as New Year's Eve revelers filled every inch of open space. Georgia felt a twinge of an ancient writhing, curling fear in the pit of her stomach.

As Milt began to step into the waiting room to greet Zivah, Georgia grabbed his arm, shook her head, and pulled him along with her toward Melanie's room. Milt looked at her quizzically but followed.

The nurse knocked on the door of a corner room, pushed it open, leaned in and announced, "Guests for the Nallis party have arrived."

Melanie turned her head slowly toward them, and a smile spread across her lovely but ghostly pale face.

"Happy New Year," she said, reaching out with a hand that was tethered to several different tubes.

Georgia crossed the room quickly, leaned over, and kissed her on the forehead.

"Happy New Year."

"I've been waiting for you to come back," Melanie said then tried unsuccessfully to clear her throat.

"I'll be out there," Milt said, indicating the waiting room.

The nurse scanned the readout on the monitor behind Melanie's bed, checked her IV lead, made a quick note on the chart, and left.

"Bring the chair up here closer," Melanie said as she pushed the button that raised the top section of her bed.

When Georgia had settled into the chair, Melanie reached out, and Georgia took her hand.

"Honey," Georgia said softly, "I'm not going to be able to stay here too long tonight. The nurses won't let me. I know you have a lot to talk to me about, and I have a lot to talk to you about, but I think we're both going to have to wait until tomorrow."

Melanie weakly shook her head. "All I do is rest. And there's no difference between night and day here anyway. It's important."

"Okay," Georgia said. She'd deal with the nurses when she had to. Maybe Milt could explain to them that the best thing for Melanie right now was to let her talk to Georgia.

"You have to let me tell you this without interrupting me, understand?"

"Yes, ma'am," Georgia answered gently, "I understand. Are there any other ground rules you'd like to cover before we begin this interview?"

"Yes," Melanie said, and Georgia understood that even the most tender of teasing was to be suspended. "I'm not going to be able to tell you everything in order. I'm going to skip around, but if you let me, I think I can explain it all to you. Just please don't make any judgments until I've finished."

"Have I ever?"

Melanie closed her eyes a moment, and when she opened them she said, "I don't think so, but if you did, you kept them to yourself. I guess that's the most I can ask of you now."

She waited a moment for a response from Georgia, and when one didn't follow, she took a deep breath and glanced up at the heart monitor. "Everything I've told you about myself is the truth. It's the stuff I left out that might be a problem. And now I have to try to fill in the gaps so that I can make you understand, okay?"

"Okay."

"I told you that I left home because my sister Ellen Louise took me with her to this great new life she'd found in Dallas. Like I said, that's the truth, but there's much more to it, and it's ugly."

Several times in the next hour, a nurse peeked into the room to find Melanie speaking softly. A quick perusal of the monitors assured the nurse that Melanie's vital signs remained stable. Her visitor was listening intently, and it was obvious that to interrupt this conversation was not in her patient's best interest.

**

September 1958

Cummings, Oklahoma, like every other small town, charted its existence by the local school calendar. This was particularly evident in September, when the entire community would adjust its schedule to accommodate the change in pace. Stores opened earlier and closed later, adjusting their inventory to meet the demands for school supplies and clothing. Library hours increased; even the churches added services to accommodate the parents who considered the summer solstice a divine decree to inculcate their progeny with a fresh dose of the fear of God.

Melanie Brownlee was one of the many who spent untold hours kneeling in church while the minister lashed out at unrepentant sinners and warned of the damnation awaiting them. Members of the congrega-

tion were allowed the opportunity to come forward and give testimony as to the power of Christ in their lives. Everyone was keenly aware that gossip and condemnation were the only real diversions available to those who lived in Cummings, Oklahoma, and so there was never a hint of any kind of impropriety in any of these accounts. They were a litany of mundane and inane events, usually overstated to give the attestant a chance to perform before the congregation.

On this Sunday morning, the day before she would enter seventh grade, Melanie had been studying the smudges on the windowpanes of the upper half of the church walls, trying to visualize a western scene with cactus-shaped rain streaks and smudged silhouettes of horses and cattle. Bea Aldridge was trying to get to the aisle, and Melanie had to stand up to let her by. Bea weighed over two hundred pounds. She wobbled up to the podium, wiping the sweat off her forehead with the back of her hand, which she dried on the skirt of her red-and-white polka dot dress.

Bea had come forward, she announced, to tell everyone that her cow had gotten out of the barn this past Tuesday. A detailed narrative of how she and her husband had tried and then succeeded in recapturing the animal was followed by another ten minutes of how her patience and determination were based on her faith in Jesus Christ. Hallelujah and praise the Lord!

Melanie felt someone staring at her from across the aisle. Johnny Crabtree was crossing his eyes and lip-synching with Bea Aldridge. Melanie squelched her giggle. The Crabtrees lived about a quarter mile down the road from Melanie's house. Johnny and his brother, Charlie, were a year older and a year younger than twelve-year-old Melanie. The three of them were great pals, always meeting up after they did chores and homework, occasionally in the boys' backyard, but most of the time behind the Brownlee house, out in the barn. It really wasn't a barn—more like a two-story garage. The kids would climb up into the loft and tell ghost stories or arm and leg wrestle, Indian style. Melanie could hold her own with younger Charlie, but Johnny had been stronger than her for about a year.

That last Sunday evening of summer, after several hours in church and an afternoon of back-to-school picnics and festivities, Johnny and

Charlie had met up with Melanie at the Brownlee barn. Just after sundown, Melanie's father, whose afternoon and early evening had been lubricated by many cans of beer and an equal number of shots of bourbon, came out and told the boys to go home. They jumped down out of the loft, said a quick good-night, and sprinted off.

As Melanie was coming down the ladder, her father growled, "Get back up there. You and me are gonna have a talk."

Melanie climbed back into the rafters, and he followed her. She could smell the liquor on his breath. When he drank he would often stare at her for long periods of time, and if she tried to leave the room, he would order her to stay. She never knew what he was thinking.

Now his voice came on sweet-and-sour breath. "What are you doing up here with those boys?"

"Nothing, just talking."

He leaned forward and put his hand on her crotch. "Nothing like this?"

"No." Melanie tried to scoot backward, away from his grasp, but the wall was right behind her.

He put his other hand on her breast. "Or this?" he hissed, pinning her back against the rough wooden planks.

"No," she said again, choking on the terror that blended with his rank body odor and whisky breath.

"I don't believe you. Your cunt is just about the same size as your tits. That's a lot to offer a boy." Both hands squeezed what they were covering. "You can make boys do just about anything for a chance at getting at these." The pain shot through Melanie's chest and she rasped loudly to pull in air.

"Shut up!" he snarled. Then, in a quick, violent motion, he ripped open the fly in her jeans, reached into her underpants, and slid a finger inside her. She gasped again, and this time he covered her mouth with his own, jabbing with his tongue. Then the finger was out of her, and he yanked down the jeans and tore off her panties. He swung his leg over her then put his finger back into her, pushing it in farther and farther.

"Anything ever been in here before?" The finger came out again, and he unzipped his fly and then jabbed into her with his penis.

It happened very slowly, and Melanie thought that this would be her eternity. When Melanie was sure she was dying and on her way to hell, his breathing became a hissing storm of pants and groans and then quieted down again. He pulled out of her and began to tuck himself away.

"You stay here, understand," he said as he zipped up his fly. The threat was clear in his tone of voice. He climbed down the ladder and walked out of the barn. She lay there, curled up in the dust and debris for the rest of the night. She fell in and out of horrifying dreams until sun streamed through the holes in the roof. There was blood on her legs, and she burned down low, inside.

"Get up, you lazy bones! Just because you fell asleep out here last night doesn't mean you get to stay up there all morning." It was her older sister, Marion. "Daddy told us how you begged him to let you sleep out here. Now it's time to get ready for school."

Melanie climbed down. "I started my period," she mumbled and hurried into the house, praying that the bathroom was free. Miraculously, it was.

The following Saturday, Harmon Brownlee ordered Melanie to go with him to the grocery store. He raped her again, this time in his truck. She tried to stay away from him, but he always found a way to corner her. Never did it occur to her to tell someone or to resist. She was being chastised, although for exactly what was never clear. She only knew that her father used this method of punishment because it worked so well.

**

Careful not to disturb any of the tubes and wires that were attached to so many different parts of Melanie's body, Georgia gently embraced her friend. Neither of them had spoken for some time. Georgia rested her head on the pillow next to Melanie's arm, and she could smell the adhesive tape that held the IV tubes in place. Melanie lay perfectly still, eyes closed, breathing quietly.

"Rest," Georgia whispered. "You must be very tired now."

Melanie nodded and closed her eyes. Across the room, a nurse opened the door and looked in. "Happy New Year," she said softly. "We're a half hour into nineteen ninety-eight. I think visiting hours are just about over."

"Just a few more minutes, please," Melanie whispered. "If I can have a few more minutes then I'll rest better. Please."

The nurse nodded, put up five fingers to define how much more time she'd allow Georgia to stay, and left the room again.

"Let me get all of this out," Melanie pleaded. "Be patient while I try to make you understand."

"I'll be patient."

Melanie took in a breath, tried again vainly to clear her throat then began to speak in a low, raspy voice.

"The man I just told you about, the one who raped me over and over...he wasn't my real father. When I was a little girl, I thought he was my father, but he wasn't. He told me."

Melanie ran her tongue over her dry, cracked lips, and Georgia held a cup of water with a straw up to her mouth so she could take a sip. Melanie tried clearing her throat again.

"He said he'd met and married his first wife—he never used her name—in Brooklyn, right before he was shipped overseas. She had joined him in Germany soon after, and that was when she told him she could never have children. They adopted me and came back to the States. But she didn't last three months in Cummings. One day he came home from working in the gas station to find that she had packed all of her clothes and disappeared. I had been left at a neighbor's. He remarried within the year to a woman with four children whose first husband had died in a car wreck. Then, in the next eight years, the rest of my stepsisters and brothers were born.

"He gave me a picture of a pretty German woman who he said was my mother. She had sold her baby to him and his wife. She told them that the baby's real father was an army officer."

Georgia asked, "Do you still have the picture of your real mother?"

"Yes."

Georgia reached into her purse and pulled out the framed photo that she had taken from Melanie's apartment. "Is this it?"

Melanie gazed at the photo. "Yes. Why do you have it?"

"Because when I went back to your apartment, I saw it sitting on your desk. I had seen a picture of this same woman before, and I decided to bring it back here to ask you about it, but by then you were in surgery."

"First let me finish, please," Melanie said. "Telling you all this is hard. Please hold my hand."

Georgia slipped her hand into Melanie's.

"I've spent my entire life since I left Oklahoma trying to find out who my parents really are. Remember I told you I went to Germany? That's why. I also went back to Cummings. But Harmon had died in nineteen eighty-six, and his widow, Judith—she was really my second stepmother—told me she knew nothing about Harmon's first marriage or my origins. She had married Harmon to replace the father of her own children. I was some adopted stray that my stepfather had brought into their marriage to be tolerated and accepted as part of the bargain. I was cared for mostly by one of my older stepsisters. Judith never seemed to have enough time or energy left over to give me any special attention. When I left home, I never missed her the way I did my sisters. Judith did say that some woman had come asking questions about me, but that had been several years before. I thought maybe that had been Harmon's first wife, but Judith had thrown away the address and telephone number."

Melanie's eyes opened then closed slowly. "When Jacob died and I got all this money, I hired an investigation firm to track down

Harmon's first wife. That was a dead end. But they did get some leads about German children adopted by American military personnel in the early sixties. I went to Germany and hired a German investigator who…"

The door was pushed open by the nurse, but when she saw the pleading in Melanie's eyes, she shook her head resignedly, gave another five-minute signal, and left again.

"I'm running out of steam, so I'll get to the part about you." She squeezed Georgia's hand just slightly, but it seemed to take a tremendous effort. "I tipped Tracie, the secretary in the poker room, to let me know when you made reservations to come back to Vegas. That was why I was in the Mirage that night when you ran into Jules and me at the blackjack table. Actually my meeting Jules was really a coincidence—a shitty one, it turns out. But Jules introduced me to Phillip Vance, which turned out to be another connection to you. And then I got cold feet. I couldn't just tell you that I thought we could be half sisters. I wanted to make you cared about me before you knew that, and I wanted to be as sure as possible that I was right about our connection."

Crystal tears rolled over the sharp angles of Melanie's cheekbones and then dripped off the side of her face. Georgia reached for a tissue and gently blotted the wetness.

Melanie smiled weakly. "Thank you. Just please hear me out. I went into your office during the party in Creste Verde hoping to find some evidence that you were part of the family I had been searching for. I found that little picture of you under the Christmas tree in a storage box. Somehow I thought that when I gave it back to you, you would understand how much I wanted to be connected to you.

"The irony is that I had no idea how to reach out to another woman, and I was stumbling all over the place trying to make it happen. And then you made it so easy for me. Now is that connection strong enough to withstand what I'm telling you, that I have taken advantage of the goodness that is at the core of you? The truth is I didn't really want to be your half sister. I wanted to be you." Melanie's voice was a soft, confessing sigh. "I still want to be you."

Melanie seemed to drift off, and Georgia sat by her quietly while she processed all that Melanie had just told her and combined it with what she had heard from Zivah.

"Melanie, listen to me now," Georgia spoke urgently. Melanie didn't open her eyes, but Georgia knew she was listening. "The picture I brought from your apartment is of the same young woman who I had seen in a photo at Zivah's apartment. That young woman is Zivah. Zivah is your mother."

Melanie's eyes opened wide just as the nurse opened the door again. "Zivah," Melanie murmured. "Zivah from the poker room?"

"She's out in the waiting room with Milt," Georgia said.

"The waiting room? Milt?" Melanie repeated, obviously struggling to make some sense out of what Georgia was saying as she fought the exhaustion that was overwhelming her consciousness.

Georgia looked up at the nurse, who nodded and went out into the hall. A moment later Zivah came in, walking stiffly. Milt waited at the door.

"Happy New Year, meine liebchen," Zivah said.

Melanie looked up at Zivah. She whispered as her eyes closed again. "Mama?"

Georgia and Milt left the room.

Chapter 34

February 1999

In the two months since that New Year's Eve at the hospital, Melanie's recovery had been erratic and disappointing. The pacemaker was barely adequate, and there had been several frightening episodes that ended with Melanie back in the hospital. Each time she was stabilized with medication, but there didn't seem to be a permanent solution to her body's inability to keep a steady and efficient heart rate. The damage from the first massive heart attack caused by the cocaine overdose was irreversible, and whatever status quo Melanie's system had attained since then had been diminished and compromised by the second coronary in late December.

On a late Sunday afternoon at the end February, Zivah opened the front door of Melanie's apartment, and the luscious aroma of baking pastry wafted out into the hallway.

"Come in, come in," Zivah said, ushering Georgia and Milt into the entry. "Dinner is cooking, and Melanie is in the living room." She smoothed out the bright floral-print apron that covered her plain navy-blue shirt-dress then patted the bun of silver hair that was pinned on the top of her head.

"Come in, come in," Zivah said again. "What would you like: wine, beer, coffee, juice?"

Zivah had established herself as chief cook, nurse and taskmaster of Melanie's convalescence, and Georgia had kept her suspicions about Zivah to herself. When Melanie was stronger, there would be time to deal with Georgia's speculations of who else Zivah might be.

But Melanie's condition had been a series of crises, and the opportunity had not appeared. So far Georgia had controlled her fears by putting them into one of those files that she had always so efficiently tucked away in the depths of her mind.

Now, as Georgia watched Zivah bustle off, the malevolent and menacing memories of Hannah peeked out from their hidden corner. If Zivah truly had been the Hannah of Georgia's nightmare memories then could she have transmuted from wicked witch to fairy godmother? Was it possible that the sweet little old lady who could produce these delectable kitchen smells had once been so evil? Several times over the last few months, Georgia had thought about taking the old, frayed snapshot of Hannah to a photo lab to be enlarged, but it was still in her wallet.

Milt was looking at her curiously. "Did you just make a quick mind trip to Bermuda?" he asked, grinning. "You seem to have left the building for a minute."

"I guess I did," Georgia said, shaking her head slightly in an effort to return to the here and now.

"I'll look forward to a more comprehensive report on your travels at a later date," Milt said, kissing her on the forehead. "Meanwhile I'll get drinks and you go see Melanie."

Georgia went into the living room, where the last notion of late-afternoon sunshine barely lit the scene. Melanie slowly and gingerly stood up and turned on the recessed lighting. She was wearing the same deep-blue velour jogging suit she had been when Georgia had come to this apartment for the first time. Now Melanie's almost ethereal pallor had dimmed even more. Her heart condition had taken a noticeable toll. The graceful angles that had defined her exquisite face had become sharp and abrupt. The amazing eyes were still alive with their glints of precious ore, but they had retreated into caverns in her skull and were surrounded by dusky shadows that no amount of concealer could hide. Melanie's hair had been trimmed to a feathery bristle of soft browns and silver grays, and now only the tips retained any remnants of the golden-blond highlights that she had applied right before the holidays.

The two women embraced, and out of the corner of her eye, Georgia saw Milt come into the room and then quietly pivot and leave again.

"How pretty you look," Melanie said, eyeing Georgia's soft coral cashmere sweater and slacks. "And look at how your earrings match. I've always loved jade in that pinky-orange tone." Then Melanie gave Georgia a gentle squeeze and said, "Time for me to sit down again. This female bonding drill takes a lot of my energy."

Melanie eased herself back into the soft gray sofa cushions and held out her hand for Georgia, who sat down very close to her. Georgia put her arm around the much-too-bony shoulders of her friend. They both sat gazing out at the lights of Las Vegas, which had begun their early evening evolution toward brilliance.

"Who wants to go first?" Melanie said. "I know you've been a little preoccupied with your new business, and I know you had to be in California a lot dealing with all the legal stuff, but I've missed you, even though we talk on the phone. I was hoping maybe now you had something more optimistic to report than I do. Should I give you the latest on my medical condition, or do you want to start with your legal situation?"

"Neither. Let's talk about what's best in our lives right now."

Melanie smiled and said dryly, "Then I don't have much to say."

"Fine, then I'll do the talking for both of us."

Melanie's eyes filled with tears. "Georgia, there's probably not much left in my life, both of time and substance, but you're right: what there is matters." She closed her eyes, and teardrops rolled down her face.

Georgia reached over and gently wiped them away with her fingers. "Is this a pity party?" she asked tenderly. "Are we going to recreate a scene from *Beaches* or *Terms of Endearment*? I don't think so."

"I'm scared," Melanie said in sparse, whispered words. "I'm not ready to stop living."

Georgia started to say something, but Melanie gently placed a finger on Georgia's mouth. "Wait, let me finish, please. It's not that I'm afraid to die; it's just that I can't imagine not living the kind of life that I've always had. You know the kind that takes strength and energy and where I make the decisions."

Georgia thought again of a frightened little girl. "You don't have…"

"Please just listen for another minute. I wake up each morning knowing there are only a certain small number of days remaining to me, and that gives me a new perspective on everything. It's easier to measure things when you know you will not be part of them for long. It's like I have one up on everyone else. I'm becoming an observer more than a participant, and amazingly with that certainty comes some sense of peace, but it doesn't seem to be enough."

She pointed toward a stack of paperbacks, pamphlets and magazines that lay next to the coffee table. "I know that depression is often a side effect of both the experience as well as the treatment for heart disease. I've read all about it, and I've talked to doctors and therapists about it. I understand it; I just don't know if I can tolerate it. You see, I survived the crap in my life because I never did have to deal with real depression. Unhappiness, disappointment, anger, fear—yes, plenty, but not depression. And that seems to be what this is called, this vacuum of energy, not just physical energy but spiritual energy. Do you know what I mean?"

Georgia smiled sadly. "Yes," she said, "yes, I do."

They sat quietly for a few minutes as busy kitchen sounds were delivered to the living room on the same current of savory fragrances that had met Georgia and Milt at the front door.

And wafting in with those delicious aromas came hope. Could Georgia possibly know the safety and security that she remembered as a young child? If Melanie was able to trust in Georgia, to whisper her deepest secrets and fears, could Georgia do the same?

"Mmm," Georgia breathed. "Those smells remind me of my grandmother's apartment in New York."

"Zivah is a pretty good cook," Melanie said. "Even though I rarely have much of an appetite, I have to admit that everything she makes is tasty. She's really been wonderful about everything. I know how very lucky I am to have finally found her. I just wish it had been sooner."

"Actually she found you."

Melanie's gaze drifted out the wall-to-wall window for a moment, and then she turned to look directly at Georgia.

"She did find me!" she said as though the fact had just sunk in for the first time. "All that time I was searching for her and my father and then fixating on making you a sister; all that time she was looking for me. And when she found me, she waited patiently for the right time to tell me. You know, I haven't had the chance to really think about that; I've been so preoccupied with my physical problems."

Melanie's eyes widened in realization. "My real mother found me," she said in amazement. "My *real* mother. And I'm her only little girl, and she's been telling me how much I mean to her, and how for so many years she was too frightened to make herself known to me. And I've been only half hearing her, nodding acknowledgment but hardly paying attention."

Melanie slowly shook her head in awe. "My God," she whispered. She smiled and closed her eyes.

After a moment she said, "You know, there's some movie about an alien who can appear to be a normal human being, but when her powers are reduced, her ugly alien form begins to emerge from the beautiful human exterior, and she repulses the humans she's come to care for. I was so afraid the same thing would happen to me and you. That when you began to see the ugliness that I kept inside of me you'd be repulsed. I couldn't stand that. And then I had the chance to make a difference in your life. I could show you how much I love you, and how ugly I was inside would not matter. I could make a donation to keep you from harm."

Georgia tilted her head, squinting in an effort to grasp what Melanie was telling her. "What kind of donation? What kind of harm?" Georgia asked.

The doorbell chimed, and Milt called out, "I'll get it!"

Melanie smiled and said, "To be continued," as she wiped the tears from her face with the back of her hand. Georgia pulled Kleenex out of her purse. She needed some as much as Melanie did.

They heard several voices greeting each other simultaneously. Phillip and Livy Vance had arrived. Months ago, after the terrifying ordeal of Livy's disappearance, Phillip had acquiesced to Livy's wish to have Zivah back as her friend. Since then, although Zivah spent most of her time caring for Melanie, she had invited the father and daughter over several times. All the vicious accusations Phillip had made to Georgia about Zivah's background seemed to have been nullified. Or at least that seemed to be why Phillip had allowed a friendship between his daughter and the old woman to reemerge.

Now Livy, dressed in an Empyrean sweat shirt that ended below her knees and a baseball cap to match, skipped into the room and plopped herself between Melanie and Georgia, who both had to shift quickly to make room for her.

"Hi," she said, twisting her head back and forth to look at both women while she adjusted her dark-green tights.

"Hi, yourself," Melanie and Georgia said in unison, and all three of them giggled.

The two women made eye contact over the child's crown of curly hair. Messages were sent and received, no words needed. Milt came into the room pushing a small wheeled bar, which held glasses, a pitcher of cranberry juice and a bucket of ice. Phillip followed with a bottle of wine and a corkscrew.

"Was that a private joke?" Phillip asked.

"Yes," Livy informed him. "It was a private joke between three best friends. We are best friends, aren't we?" she asked, pivoting her head between Georgia and Melanie again.

"Best, best friends," Melanie confirmed.

"More like sisters in crime," Milt added as he waited for Phillip to open the bottle of wine.

"More like sisters in our hearts," Georgia said, reaching her arm out to encompass both Livy and Melanie.

"And what am I, the chopped liver that delivers the piroshki?" Zivah had come into the room carrying a tray of savory little meat turnovers.

"No, Zivah," Melanie said in a light but very loving tone. "You are the top banana." Everyone laughed again, and then drinks were poured and the tray of warm, fragrant turnovers was passed around.

Georgia looked out over the city. The sun had finally set, and millions of rolling watts of brilliant color had overwhelmed the dusk, which dissipates very quickly in the electrified canyon of Las Vegas Boulevard. Melanie raised her arm to make a toast, and Georgia saw her reflection in the wide glass window. Melanie seemed to be floating out over the volcano in front of the Mirage.

"Here's to us," Melanie said. "Here's to love and friendship and always filling two pair on the river."

"Better yet," Milt proclaimed, "here's to having 'The Nuts' and never having to wait for the river card."

Several voices responded simultaneously. "I'll drink to that!" "Shalom! "To the river!"

Livy laid her small hand on Georgia's arm. "Will you teach me to play poker like you do?"

Georgia looked at Livy for a moment, not sure how to respond, and before she could decide, Zivah spoke up. "Livy, Livy, mein liebchen, why do you want to learn to play that silly game?"

"Because you play it, and Daddy, and Georgia, and Milt, and Melanie too. You all play poker."

"Not so much for me right now," Zivah said. Her smile was enigmatic. "Ah yes, I found out I really liked the poker when I came to Las Vegas, but it is not so important. And my Melanie does not so much enjoy it. Yes, that is true, Melanie?"

"That is true," Melanie repeated, reaching for her mother's hand. "The game really isn't for me."

Then the old woman pursed her lips and shook her head angrily as another thought occurred to her. "And it is a good thing for that Jules Palentine that...that..." Obviously Zivah could not think of a phrase in English strong enough to express her contempt. "He should better stay out of my way," she finally mumbled.

Jules had stayed clear of them all. Obviously he must have been concerned about being charged with assault, and Zivah had spoken once or twice about suing him, but her daughter's condition was paramount, and Melanie had made it clear that any kind of legal action would be more than she could handle. Punishing Jules didn't matter to Melanie.

Georgia had been gently combing her fingers through the soft, curly strands of Livy's hair. She looked up to discover Milt's gaze and the amazing joy it brought her.

"Livy," she said, steering the subject away from the offensive Jules Palentine, "playing cards should be for fun, not for making money. You'll find lots of things to have fun with. Playing cards doesn't necessarily have to be one of them."

"But it could be," Livy insisted. "You have fun playing cards, and I know you make a lot of money because once when Wilbur and I walked past the poker room, I saw all the chips piled in front of you. And besides, I already know a lot about poker. I know what beats what. Wanna see?" She began reciting in a singsong voice. "High card, one pair, two pair, three of a kind, straight, flush, full house, four of a kind, straight flush."

"Excellent, Olivia," Phillip said with a fatherly pride.

Georgia's thoughts drifted off again while the discussion of Livy's future card-playing career continued among the others. So many profound changes had occurred in Georgia's life lately. How much had playing poker had to do with those changes? Had she been on the brink of compulsive gambling? No, she corrected herself, not on the brink; the truth was she'd gone over the brink, and the consequences had been harsh. Because of Jeff's vindictiveness, her ex-partner, Andrea, had been unable to hide the fact that the money in the business account had gone missing for a few days. There had been an investigation, and even though all the money was back in place, the foundation had threatened to sue Georgia for embezzlement.

For weeks Georgia had faced the possibility of being indicted for grand larceny. She had stayed in Los Angeles, spending her days meeting with attorneys, packing up the household, putting items into storage for Sonnie and Mike to claim some day when they had their own homes. Georgia wanted none of it. She would start over again in Las Vegas, if she got the chance to start over at all. But then, possibly, there would be no need for any furnishings or accouterment if her next permanent home was a prison cell.

In order to replace the funds, she'd written a check, delivered it to the bank, and, miraculously, it had cleared before Jeff could put a freeze on their joint money market account. He'd been furious, but then he was always furious lately, and—most amazing of all marvels—he couldn't frighten her anymore. Not that there weren't a dozen other perils to replace Jeff's threats.

Andrea had called her. "Explain this to me," had been her greeting when Georgia answered the phone. "First you tell me that you borrowed five hundred thousand dollars from the foundation account, and when I call to check on the balance, I'm told the account has over a million dollars in it."

"A million?" Georgia heard herself echo the number.

"A million," Andrea repeated. "Are we playing Monopoly here? Is this a bank error? Should I proceed past 'go' and collect another two hundred dollars? Or is this some sort of money laundering scheme? Please, Georgia, I know I told you that I didn't need any details, but I guess I do."

Georgia still was unable to process this data. How did another $500,000 get into that account?

"I...I, uh, I don't know either," was all she could say.

"Right, you don't know either," Andrea had said sarcastically. "Well, now there's half a million in there that I can't account for. What am I supposed to do with it, donate it to charity?"

That conversation with Andrea had taken place over a month ago. Georgia had agreed with Andrea, who had decided not to touch the mysterious half a million dollars until it could be accounted for.

Suddenly it all made sense. Melanie had said, "I could make a donation to keep you from harm."

Georgia slapped her hand on the arm of the sofa. "A donation!" she said out loud.

All conversation came to a halt as everyone stared at Georgia.

"What donation?" Milt and Zivah had asked the question simultaneously. Georgia looked at Melanie, who was smiling like a shy Cheshire cat.

Chapter 35

April 1999

It had been more than four months since Georgia had sat down at a poker table. In that time she had run the full gamut of fear, doubt, panic and depression—not necessarily in that order. Then, miraculously, there had been some relief, now even optimism. The Caroline Foster Foundation had decided to drop the matter of the temporarily missing money when it was ascertained that the anonymous tip about the possible embezzlement of funds turned out to be unsubstantiated. Bank records showed that the withdrawal had been some sort of glitch in the system because money had been withdrawn and redeposited within a four-hour period. Added to that, the fund-raiser itself had been an astounding success, exceeding the estimated profit by almost 20 percent, not to mention the separate half-million-dollar donation from Melanie Nallis.

Gerald Gould, Georgia's attorney, sat behind his desk, drumming his fingers on the parchment blotter, making absolutely no effort to control the scowl on his face. Georgia sat across from him, gazing down at the one and only ring that she wore, a small faceted garnet set in gold. It had been Grandma Genya's. Finally Georgia looked up. The scowl was still in place, but in his eyes she saw the warmth and friendship that had developed between client and attorney.

She spoke calmly and gently. "You could not have been more efficient in representing my interests in the divorce settlement, Gerald.

And you know how much I appreciate your patience. I know we didn't always agree on the arrangements."

Gerald's expression melted into a fond smile, and he took in a deep, resigned sigh. "Now there's an understatement—the 'didn't always agree' part, I mean. Let's see," he said, leaning back in his chair, "we were doing fine with dividing the assets, and then you started giving away chunks of your share like too much chocolate dessert. You know, Jeff was entitled to only half of the five hundred thousand you put into your business account because it was deposited before the divorce. And yet you insisted that he get all of it from your share of the settlement."

Georgia nodded, closing her eyes to indicate that she appreciated the attorney-client privilege that allowed her to tell Gerald about replacing the money she had *borrowed*. She had also paid off all the credit cards and replenished her mother's savings account. Her engagement ring and wedding band were in the bank safe deposit. Maybe Mike or Sonnie would want them one day.

Gerald was still counting on his fingers. "So he gets an extra quarter mil then you bring me that jewel case, which I'm supposed to deliver to Jeff. Talk about giving away the family jewels! Christ, Georgia, how much was all that stuff worth? Another half million at least."

The dinner ring, a four-carat emerald with the dozen ruby baguettesthat surrounded it, had been presented to her to commemorate the first year that Jeff's firm had been listed in the Fortune 500. The band of one-carat diamonds had arrived when Jeff closed a $100,000,000 deal, which happened six months *after* their twenty-fifth anniversary. And then of course there were the pearls—"the funeral pearls," Georgia had dubbed them—the ones that had been bought in Hong Kong.

"It's not important," Georgia said. "I always thought of those pieces as Jeff's possessions anyway. He never really *gave* them to me. It was more like he loaned them to me and I was to display them, like the stars do for Cartier and Harry Winston at the Academy Awards."

"Well, it sure frosts my ass when I think of the lack of grace your ex-husband displayed when he got that incredible, undeserved windfall of cash and gems."

Georgia shook her head again. "I don't care how Jeff reacted. What I decided had nothing to do with his gratitude or his well-being. It was really about ridding myself of any connection whatsoever to the man. Now I'm free of him in every way. Anyway, I never would have chosen any of those pieces if I'd been given the chance, which I never was."

Once everything had been settled, there was some money left to start another business, if she was very careful. She'd done her homework and determined that there were many casino corporations in Vegas that would jump at the chance to get positive publicity from sponsoring charity events. Georgia would offer the means to accomplish this.

For weeks Georgia and Milt had researched office locations, spent evenings filling out forms for a business license and developing a publicity portfolio to introduce their services to the public relations directors of the various casinos. Now, on a late Friday afternoon, they sat in milky-white leather swivel chairs, facing each other across a broad expanse of faux alabaster that comprised a very contemporary version of a partner's desk. The office, the largest in a suite of four rooms that took up a quarter of the tenth floor of the newest high-rise office building on Howard Hughes Parkway, was modest but elegant.

A receptionist sat in the foyer by the elevator, and two secretaries shared one of the rooms. Assistants for the nuts-and-bolts operation of the business would be hired as the client base grew. Meanwhile phones rang, faxes hummed and computers purred. Business was booming.

Georgia had just hung up the phone. She massaged her earlobe before replacing the earring that had been removed when the call came in.

"It seems to be all nailed down," she said. "Opening night of the Empyrean will be used to benefit Habitat for Humanity."

"Then we both deserve a treat," Milt said, swinging his feet from the desk. "I say we head for the Bellagio poker room. It's time we checked it out."

"I'm not sure I'm ready to play poker again. It got kind of out of hand, you know. Maybe I should just stay away."

She stood up and walked over to the window, looking out to the Strip. Milt came up behind.

"I knew we'd have to get back to the subject of poker sooner or later," she said hesitantly. "It's been easy to postpone it since we've been so busy."

Now with the lights of the Strip shimmering through the plate glass window, she leaned back into him, and he wrapped his arms around her.

"Playing poker didn't get you in trouble," he said softly. "In fact, the way I see it, you and I wouldn't be standing here having this conversation if it weren't for poker."

She and Milt were both cautious about committing to a long-term relationship, but their feelings for each other were hard to deny. They spent a great part of every day and many nights together. Nevertheless, Georgia had been reluctant about a full-time domestic arrangement, and when she had rented an apartment just two floors below Melanie's, Milt understood that he was welcome as a friend and lover but not yet as a roommate. Maybe eventually they could work something like that out, but for now Georgia needed the space, both residentially as well as emotionally.

Georgia continued to stare out the window. "You're half right about that," she said, chuckling softly. "I'd rather be here with you than any place in the world, but that doesn't mean that I'm not still in trouble and that playing poker is not at the root of it."

"Not so," Milt replied. "You were already in that world of trouble before you even started playing poker in Vegas, and one way or another, you were going to have to face up to it and get yourself out of it. I'm just glad some of it happened in the Mirage poker room, where I could get involved."

Gently he turned her around to face him. "Georgia, you are okay," he said, pronouncing each word separately and emphatically. "Let yourself off the hook. You can play again. I know how much you want to."

Georgia looked as if she belonged at Bellagio. She wore the Christmas open house outfit, all white silk and sparkling crystal. The red-and-green dinner ring was missing, but she was quite content with a little bit of costume jewelry that added sparkle to her wrists. On her, she was pretty sure, it looked real anyway.

Georgia let the valet open her car door.

I've been on this very spot before. How close am I right now to where our room was when the Dunes still occupied this corner of Flamingo and Las Vegas Boulevard, and Jeff and I had to walk past the kitchen to get to the casino?

Steve Wynn had imploded the Dunes in 1993, spent another year leveling and grading the huge property, and then two more erecting this extravagant and improvident palace. Georgia saw a parallel in her own existence, which had also been imploded, and more than one tractor had rumbled in to level her playing field, and several of life's backhoes had shoved the landscape of her existence in disparate directions.

Would she ever end up as complete, as ensconced in the terra firma as Bellagio?

She smiled to herself. *Enough of these inept metaphors.* She slid her arm through Milt's as they walked toward the main lobby.

Now she focused on the opulent surroundings as she and Milt entered through the imposing etched-glass revolving door, moving under the massive fixture that crowned the entry. Hundreds of hand-blown glass blossoms in soft magical hues had been assembled into a vast, abstract chandelier.

She and Milt continued to stroll arm in arm as they made their way through acres of marble, passing billowing awnings positioned over blackjack and craps tables. With some irony, she remembered how the crowds at the Mirage had seemed to add to the lush ambience, the sense that they were part of the setting. Here at Bellagio, they seemed superfluous, even bothersome. Their numbers, the entire fanny-packed, Bermuda-shorted and sneakered multitude, obstructed the vast panoramic sweep of the phenomenal architecture as well as impeded the close-up scrutiny of the intricate details like the exquisite mosaic floors.

Less than half an hour later, seated in an elegant, ergonomic chair, which could be adjusted to her own proportions, Georgia looked around the poker room as the dealer shuffled a brand-new deck of cards. Not much had changed except the scenery. The Bellagio poker room was large and airy, posh, glamorous and state of the art. But it still was merely another compass point on the same infinite ocean. Some days might be stormier or rougher than others, and she'd had her share of storms at sea, but as Mr. Kruikshank had asserted, the tides of chips continued to ebb and flow with never-ending regularity.

Marsha seemed delighted when Georgia had appeared minutes before. The old woman murmured about how much Georgia had been missed, and this seemed to be confirmed by the number of people who came by the fifteen-thirty stud table to express their own version of the same sentiment. Marsha poked Georgia's arm when she saw Ishiro Zenri and Roxanne Roiballe, who still dominated the high-limit games, waving their greetings from the posh top section.

"So go say hello to your high-roller friends," Marsha urged.

Georgia waved back but didn't get up. "I'd rather stay here with you."

"You are such a darling person," Marsha cooed, obviously thrilled to have reached celebrity status as a friend of Georgia Cates. Everyone was watching them.

Edward Patrone nodded in their direction as he left his office and walked toward the high-limit tables, where Ishiro Zenri sat, inscrutable as ever. But Mindy Cameron, in red spandex biker shorts with a halter top and blazer to match, was massaging the shoulders of a man that Georgia did not recognize.

"Who's that?" Georgia asked Marsha, indicating the recipient of Mindy's services.

"Don't you recognize him?" Marsha chuckled. "Amazing what a little plastic surgery and a month on a fat farm can do for you."

Georgia looked again. Under a freshly cultivated crop of wavy frosted-blond hair was the much thinner but still homely face of Brady Cranston. Mindy saw Georgia looking in her direction, waved at her, kissed Brady on the top of his head, and rushed over to throw her arms around Georgia.

"I'm so glad to see you!" Mindy squealed. "I heard you started a new business. Everyone said you were too busy to play poker anymore. I knew it couldn't be true. You look wonderful. Can we have coffee or something? I've got so much to tell you about!"

"Sure, coffee would be great sometime," Georgia replied.

Too vague? But the last thing she wanted to do was listen to more of Mindy's escapades.

"Great!" Mindy had not picked up on Georgia's tepid response. "Call me," she said and headed back toward Cranston.

"So now let me fill you in on all the gossip," Marsha said. "You've been gone a long time. There's lots to tell."

"Some of it is pretty obvious," Georgia said archly as she watched Mindy return to ministering to Brady Cranston. "But tell me all the good stuff." Georgia grinned.

"Yes, yes," Marsha mumbled as she peeked at the two hole cards that had just been dealt to her. "After this hand." She flipped six redbirds, thirty dollars, into the pot, reraising the opening raise. Georgia folded and watched as with bet after bet, Marsha built a hefty pot with the last of her stack of chips, which she lost when her rolled-up tens were cracked by a small heart flush at the river.

"The river again," Marsha murmured as her eyes filled with tears. She stood up unsteadily and tottered out of the room. Georgia followed her and caught up just as they entered the ladies' room.

"Are you okay?" Georgia gently put her hand on Marsha's arm.

"I'm fine," Marsha managed. "But I can't play anymore today."

Georgia knew the only reason Marsha would leave the game this early in the evening was because she had no more money. "Do you need a small loan?"

"I still owe you two hundred dollars, but yes," the older woman whispered. "I don't know when I can pay you back."

"That's okay, no hurry." She pulled three one-hundred-dollar bills out of her wallet.

Marsha took them without making eye contact. "Thank you," was all she said as she disappeared into a stall.

That night Georgia lost fifteen hundred dollars. After getting stuck five hundred at fifteen-thirty, she moved to thirty-sixty. When a rack of ten-dollar chips, one thousand dollars, disappeared, she stood up and walked out into the sports book. Milt had been keeping an eye on her and got up from a ten-twenty game but left his chips on the table.

"We don't have to leave yet," Georgia said, leaning against one of the huge, luscious leather chairs that brought a luxurious Old World ambience to the sports book. "You seem to be doing okay. I'll just take a walk around the casino. When I get back, I'll either sit and watch you play or, if you're ready by then, we can go."

"We can go now," Milt said gently.

"'No," Georgia said a bit more emphatically than she meant to. "I just want to walk around for a while."

"Are you sure? You look pretty upset."

Georgia's eyes filled with tears. "I can't let this happen again."

"Let what happen again?" he asked, putting his hands on her shoulders.

"If I'm going to have any chance of adding poker back into my life, I'm going to have to stick to very strict loss limits, and fifteen hundred dollars a session is not possible."

He nodded as he put both arms around her and gently patted her back.

"You're right," he said softly. "And I know you have to work that out for yourself. But let's take that walk together to valet." He kissed her on the forehead and went back into the poker room to cash his chips.

It was almost three in the morning when she and Milt got back to her apartment. She told him she needed to sleep alone that night, and she took two sleeping pills when he left. She woke up six hours later, determined to go back to the poker table, play tight and solid, wait for the rushes, use efficient money management and get even. The next evening she won back half of what she lost the night before, but within the month, she had lost twenty-four thousand dollars.

At first she was able to separate the two elements that were provoking the continual epiphanies in her life. During the day, she was the consummate businesswoman, organized, poised, savvy and efficient. She had convinced five major casinos to establish a charity, which would be funded partly from the money cleaned out of the fountains and ornamental pools that were the universal components of every theme and decor from the lake in front of Bellagio to the lagoons of the Mirage and Treasure Island. Caesar's Palace had dozens of classic Roman fountains, and soon enough, the Empyrean's tremendous twin waterfalls would cascade from thirty floors above the entrance into lush tropical pools. Several other casinos had already indicated their interest in joining the Fountains of Miracles project, including the Venetian, which was due to open soon, with its not-so-diminutive version of the Grand Canal.

At night she was a poker player running bad, night after night after night. The cards she was dealt seemed to taunt her. A pocket pair of kings would never improve or ace, king and queen of spades would be followed by the five of diamonds and then, when against her better judgment she'd take off another card, she'd get something like the eight of hearts. Beginning hands that showed promise would cost her lots of chips until the river, which was almost always a disappointment. Time after time, her heartbeat would speed up with the anticipation of winning a pot; then when a higher flush would beat hers, or sevens full would overpower her ace-high straight, she felt the painful ache as her heart processed the disappointment.

Milt had told her more than once, "Never let them see you suffer." At least that part she had down pat; in fact, she could get an Academy

Award nomination. She was the expert, flawless in her demeanor, obviously unconcerned with the loss, and never worried about the money.

"Nice hand," she'd say when the dork in the eight seat drew out on her, beating her trip jacks with a nine-high straight. *Nice hand... bullshit.*

Once in a while she'd book a small win and then convince herself that the trend had been reversed. It never lasted more than a session or two at the most, and the losses far exceeded even the best of wins. Her poker playing was ruled by math, but no longer was it the calculation of the odds of completing a good hand that would win a specific pot. Instead, the only number that her brain continually computed was how much she had lost and how much she had to win to just get even, and those numbers grew most days and were barely diminished on the others.

She tried staying away, but the knowledge that she had maxed out her credit cards again—and now they were in her name only—kept her in constant turmoil. She had to return to the poker table. She had to try to get even. Sleep was sacrificed, and soon the demarcation between business and gaming began to blur, as did her ability to concentrate and make rational choices. She had made several withdrawals from the business account, not so much that she couldn't easily explain it away, but she was stealing again; she knew that.

She couldn't discuss it with Melanie—too much stress for her friend. Besides, Melanie had not had enough experience with poker to understand. No one could understand. Talking it over with Milt never seemed to accomplish much. If Georgia was hoping that he would tell her what to do, she was always disappointed.

"I have much more faith in you than you do in yourself," he said. "You can play your way out of trouble. You'll get through this, but it's going to have to be your own way. You'll figure this out, I know you will. Many players, surely all of the really good ones, have gone through this kind of thing. It's part of playing serious poker, I've told you that before. You've got to keep the big picture in mind," he said. "Right now it's just a streak, a bad run. And if you stick to your game, like you know how, and not go on tilt, the rushes will come again."

She knew all this, and yet the pattern of desperate, reckless play continued. Why couldn't she at least stick to lower limits like ten-twenty or even five-ten? Milt did, but Milt didn't have thousands and thousands in debts. Now when she sat in a game, her goal was to get even, and the larger the pots, the quicker that would happen. Or the more she'd lose.

Her concentration evaporated. She was running bad, and she was playing worse. The freedom that she had fought so hard to win was feeding on itself and would destroy her. She had to get control; there would be nothing ahead but disaster unless she got things under control.

So don't play poker anymore, she told herself. She played every day and faithfully, painfully recorded her minuscule wins and enormous losses.

One evening at the end of April, as Georgia sat in a forty-eighty game, the rush finally arrived. By midnight she had won almost ten thousand dollars and moved up to seventy-five/one-fifty. The rush continued. And now she was in the right place at the right time with every deal of the cards. Big pairs held up, no improvement necessary, or two pairs, straight and flush draws unfailingly blossomed into the winning hand. By three in the morning she had won enough money to replace everything she had taken from the business account. By six, she had amassed a profit above and beyond all that she'd lost in the last several weeks. She was a winner again and in control.

She played until nine in the morning. On her way home, she deposited forty-seven thousand dollars in her private account and eight thousand in the business account, which replaced everything that she had *borrowed*. When she got home, she sat at her desk for an hour, calling credit card companies, confirming balances, getting addresses and writing checks. A little before ten in the morning, she delivered a packet of envelopes to the doorman, who promised to give them to the postman.

Everything was paid off, and she had a ten-thousand-dollar stash. Now she could go back to middle limits and play poker for what she knew were the right reasons. No more desperation, no more crisis. Only control, only discipline. *Pot's right.*

She slept the rest of the day and all that night, soundly. When she woke, it was with that delicious sense that all was well with her world.

Georgia and Milt pulled under the elegant marquee of Bellagio's north entrance. She was very aware that an equanimity had settled upon her, like a filmy cape, shielding her from the cold, but at the same time easily blown off by any strong wind. She could consider herself a front runner, a contender in life's tournament, but was it only because she had been a winner at the poker table?

Milt leaned over and kissed her lightly, interrupting her thoughts. "You go off for another quick trip to Bermuda again?" he asked with his characteristic crooked smile.

"Just thinking," she said.

"Told you so," he said smugly as Georgia got out of the car.

"Told me what? What did you tell me?" Georgia asked as they made their way past shops like Hermès, Tiffany's and Fred Leighton, the most opulent minimall in America, right there at the north entrance of Bellagio.

Milt didn't answer for a minute, just grinned. When they passed by the Sports Book Bar, Milt leaned toward Georgia, playfully nudging her as he intoned, teasing, "Told you your losing streak would pass. Told you you'd get through the bad run. Told you you're a winner."

Then more earnestly he repeated, "Georgia, you're a winner. No matter how hard you try to deny it, the sooner you understand that, the better for both of us."

Was he right? Had she mastered the poker demons? Had she prevailed once again? Could she make it a permanent thing, or was she destined to spend the rest of her life digging holes and clambering out of them, only to begin excavation on yet another crater? Her business account had been replenished, her credit cards paid off, and she had her poker stash. Like other successful poker players, she too had the bankroll that cushioned the losses and fortified the wins.

She smiled, gently bumping him as he had just done to her. "You better be right," she said, "about me being a winner. Otherwise you'd be stuck with a loser."

"Never," he said, pulling her to him, kissing the top of her head.

The first person in the poker room to greet them was Zivah. The older woman was dressed in a gray tailored knit suit. Her silver hair had been trimmed and was very becoming, soft and stylish.

"Melanie is asleep so early, and the nurse is staying until I go back. So I come and see this fancy-shmancy Bellagio for myself," she said as though an explanation was certainly the first order of business.

Georgia merely nodded in reply as an unwonted, eerie, curly feeling invaded the pit of her stomach.

"I go to the bathroom," Zivah announced as she moved away.

Georgia and Milt put their names on waiting lists then sat down at an empty table. The Bellagio poker room spread mostly higher-limit games, and after a short wait, Georgia settled into a twenty-forty stud game. She had brought one thousand dollars in cash, and that was all she would leave if it wasn't her night, but it was. Everything worked in her favor, including her own combination of savvy, instinct, card reading and player analysis. Not only did she win with aces full, but several times she scooped pots over a thousand dollars by calling on the river with one pair. Everything was working.

About eleven, Mr. Kruikshank, dressed like a stevedore again, the knit cap pulled down low on his forehead, came up to her table, waited until she had finished a hand then knelt down beside her.

"Did you hear about Marsha?" he asked in a way that could only portend bad news.

"What? What happened to Marsha?" Georgia asked, adrenaline immediately speeding up her heartbeat.

"She's dead. Pretty sure it's suicide." The words came from just one corner of his mouth as he looked around the room warily. "Sleeping pills." Now he spoke with as little lip movement as he could. "Gotta be careful," he said. "A lot more people than you think can read lips."

"When did this happen?" Georgia stood up quickly, leaning her hands on the table rail to control a trace of dizziness.

"Don't know," Kruikshank answered. "Just heard about it."

Georgia tossed her head slightly, trying to rid herself of the murky haze that had become all too familiar as her mind struggled to absorb yet another shock.

Sure, Marsha had some money problems, but it was all within reason, wasn't it? There was ultimately a solution to any problem, wasn't there? The suicide part must be just rumor. No one could be as cheerful as Marsha always was and also be contemplating suicide. No one could completely hide that much pain and anguish. No one could be so lost and without hope and still manage to seem connected to humanity and reality. Could they?

Mr. Kruikshank was shaking his head at Georgia, and she wondered for a moment if he was reading her mind and responding to the questions that were whirling through it. But then she realized that he was just waiting for her reply to his news and seemed disappointed when she didn't.

Georgia saw Zivah coming toward her. "Such a look you have," Zivah said, reaching for Georgia's hand. Thin, dry fingers squeezed the bands of pale flesh where Georgia's rings used to be. Zivah gently massaged the base of Georgia's fingers.

Georgia wrenched her hand away, not caring about the propriety, or lack thereof, but instead wondering why the air had become so heavy, why she was having trouble breathing, why her heart was not just beating fast but pounding, why she was feeling more and more dizzy.

"Ach, Georgia," Zivah continued, "all those beautiful diamonds. Do you miss them? Your pretty hands are so bare without them."

Mr. Kruikshank leaned toward Zivah and imparted the same news he had just given to Georgia. "Marsha is dead, probably suicide," he repeated.

"Ach, how terrible." Zivah clucked sad sounds with her tongue. "Poor Marsha, such a sweet lady. Why would she do such a thing?"

Georgia tried to move away from Zivah, but the bony old fingers reached out and snagged her wrist in an unbelievably strong grip. "Georgia, liebchen, are you so much upset?" Zivah asked solicitously.

Georgia pulled more firmly, but still Zivah kept hold until Georgia yanked her arm away.

"I have to leave," Georgia gulped. She grabbed up her chips and hurried to the cashier's window.

Good little girls can get hurt!

With trembling hands, she placed her chips and bills on the counter. Zivah and Mr. Kruikshank had come up behind her as she waited to be cashed out.

Zivah was still clucking. "Such terrible news about Marsha," she said.

Kruikshank, eyes down as though he was participating in a prayer, nodded.

Zivah tried to step in even closer. "Georgia?"

Georgia grabbed a rubber band from a container on the counter, snapped it around the pile of bills that had just been counted out to her, pivoted, and rushed out of the room. Her head pounded; her heart hammered. She walked faster.

And *if good little girls can get hurt, if Katherina could have fingers chopped off or Alexandra could be trapped in a suffocating box then imagine what happened to bad little girls—little girls who embezzled money and got off the hook and then did the same thing again and almost got away with it for a second time.*

Stuffing the wad of bills she'd gotten from the cashier down into her purse, she rushed toward the main entrance, across the frozen lake of Bellagio floor tiles, under the omnipotent scrutiny of the surveillance cameras, out through the massive rotating doors.

Her survival did not depend on how much money she had now or how much she had lost or won at the poker table. The photograph that had been hiding in the folds of her wallet was torn into pieces and thrown away, along with her suspicions about her childhood tormenter. No need for either one of them.

Then she was in the cab.

"Lady, what do you wanna do?"

The pulsing, brilliant scenery...only in Las Vegas.

"You lost?"

Lost money? Unable to find her way home? Lost in time and space...still abandoned...within herself?

"I have to go back to Bellagio."

Then she was back on the sidewalk, her feet touching the cement in perfect rhythm, leg muscles harmonizing with gravity, lungs filling, heart pumping, a living, breathing, highly functional member of the human race.

With an exhilarating sense of triumph, Georgia strode back through the entrance to Bellagio. She could deal with anything now. Anything. As she approached the poker room, she spotted Milt walking toward her with an urgency that immediately set off new spasms of alarm. She could deal with anything, she reminded herself, and somehow she was sure that she was about to be tested again.

Milt grabbed her arm, putting his other hand on the small of her back as if he was prepared to support her when she collapsed.

"Georgia," he started hoarsely. "Georgia..." he repeated then cleared his throat and began again. "Honey, we have to leave right now. Melanie is back in the hospital, and it's not good."

No little curly feelings this time. Georgia felt the fear swell in her chest, pushing on her lungs, keeping her from breathing.

"What's not good?" she managed to get out, but she knew. Milt looked at her but said no more.

Georgia lost all confidence that her legs, which had just performed so well when she returned to the Bellagio moments ago, would hold up as they rushed to the north entrance. Milt never let go of her arm and kept the pressure of his other hand on her back. She needed all the help he could give her at this point. Milt told the valet they had an emergency; no time to get his car, just hail a cab.

They pulled up in front of the hospital ten minutes later. No one had spoken once Milt had told the cabby where to go. Georgia had forced her mind into standby mode. For the second time in less than fifteen minutes, she was back in a cab, this time with a very specific destination. What would happen when they arrived was more than she had the strength to think about. Standby mode was the best she could do at this time.

Milt had already paid the driver before they stopped, and he was out of the cab before Georgia, arms ready to support her again as they hurried into the lobby.

They were too late.

Georgia watched Milt ask about Melanie. The receptionist tapped on her computer keys for only a moment then looked up at Milt and shook her head. "Are you relatives?" she asked.

"Good friends," Milt murmured.

"You'll have to wait down here," she said gently.

A dozen or so people sat in the large, softly lit lobby, a few quietly talking together, several sitting alone, separated from each other by side tables and magazine racks, isolated by their individual boredom, worry or grief.

Georgia and Milt sat on a soft sofa, part of a grouping of furniture surrounding a tiny desert garden with a marble statue of a child cradling a dove in her hands. Georgia studied the sculpture, noting the curls around the little girl's forehead and the details of her small fingers, forming a nest for the dove. *Perfect fingers.* Milt sat next to her but said nothing.

Across the lobby, the elevator doors opened, and a young woman in scrubs, a mask cuffed around her neck like an ascot, pushed out a wheelchair. Zivah sat in it, gripping the arms, her head jerking from side to side until she spotted Milt and Georgia. She said something to the woman who stood behind her wheelchair and was wheeled toward them. Before they were near enough for an appropriate voice level, Zivah announced, in a voice implausibly strong and vibrant, "Melanie is dead."

Zivah surveyed the room, seeming to get some ugly compensation from the shock that radiated through all the people in the lobby who had heard her words. No one was prepared for the announcement. The mask of composure of each of them had been yanked away, revealing raw emotion. Zivah studying each face in turn, first the several strangers who happened to be near enough to hear Zivah's cold, virulent announcement, then Milt, and finally her gaze settled on Georgia.

Georgia looked into the murky gray eyes of the old woman. There was nothing to be frightened of. Georgia had known Melanie was gone. Whatever her link had been to Melanie, it had not been strong enough to keep her alive. At the same time that Georgia had been resisting the pull of some existential power that could snatch her from humanity and hurtle her into oblivion, Melanie had been struggling as well. The essential truth was that no matter how hard either woman had tried to grasp hold of the other in an effort to survive the desolation of separateness, they had both been alone, and, for Melanie, it had been the last moments of her life.

Georgia spoke slowly, clearly, calmly. "I am sorry for your loss, Zivah." She didn't need to voice the rest of her thoughts.

Melanie is gone. Your fear, your pain, your guilt are yours alone to cope with, and I wish that before you die, you can find serenity. I have to search for my own.

Georgia turned her back on Zivah and walked to the elevator. Moments later, Milt was by her side. They stepped in and turned around to face the old woman as the doors slid closed.

Alexandra
A novel by Georgia Kassov Cates

October 1950

Alexandra listened as the conversation between Hannah and Kurt floated back and forth just above her head. She couldn't keep up with their rolling, guttural German, and she knew better than to ask. But it had something to do with the big news that Daddy had told her yesterday.

The Kassovs were going back to the States! That's what her daddy had told her. They would drive to Bremerhaven and get on another big ship, but this time all three of them, Alexandra, Mommy and Daddy, would sail off to sea together. They would be leaving their big house in Erlangen at the end of the month and would be at sea for Halloween.

She'd miss the big party at the officers' club, but Daddy promised her that Halloween at sea would be great fun. She told her daddy how excited she was to see Grandma Genya and Aunt Rya again and go to Radio City Music Hall and Rockefeller Center and the park on Riverside Drive.

But Alexandra didn't tell her daddy that the most important thing about going back to America was not about what was waiting for her on the other side of the Atlantic but that Hannah would stay on this side of that great big ocean, thousands and thousands of miles away from her. Then Alexandra would not have to worry about making Hannah angry anymore. And even Lotte, who didn't get mad at her much but didn't really didn't pay much attention to her at all; she wouldn't miss her too much either. Sure, her mommy got mad and yelled sometimes, but then, after a while, she'd forget why she was mad. So no one would ever lock her in her room again or make her get in the dumbwaiter when she really, really didn't want to.

Daddy had said that Hannah didn't have the right papers to come to America, and he could not help her get them. He had started to explain this to Alexandra, but she had interrupted him to say that it was okay that Hannah was not coming with them.

Mommy and Daddy had just left this morning for one more quick trip to Paris. Now she was on her way to Hannah's apartment, strolling through the bustling streets of Erlangen. Even though Alexandra would have preferred to be with old, boring Lotte, Hannah had offered to take her, giving Lotte the night off.

They'd stopped at a sausage stand and bought knockwurst, fresh, crunchy rolls, beers for Hannah and Kurt, and a Coca Cola for her. After they had eaten their lunch at Hannah's small kitchen table, Alexandra was told that she must take a nap.

She climbed onto Hannah's bed, which was even wider than her parents' and took up more than half of the small, one-room flat.

Alexandra arranged the pillows so that she could cuddle into a soft and cozy nest. Hannah and Kurt sat at the small kitchen table, a bottle of schnapps between them. They drank and smoked the same cigarette, passing it back and forth. Tummy full and lulled by the soft music coming from the radio, Alexandra soon fell asleep.

She awoke when Hannah lay down next to her. Kurt sat at the edge of the bed and watched as Hannah gently undressed her. Alexandra began to protest, but Hannah hushed her. Soon Kurt began to remove Hannah's clothes. Soft, soothing words assured the child that this was a beautiful way for people to show love for each other. Alexandra lay between them, becoming hypnotized by the sensation of her skin being caressed by gentle fingertips. She had always loved having her back tickled.

When Hannah suggested that Alexandra help Kurt undress, the child, who had been drifting on a soft, warm sea of half sleep, roused herself and did her best to tug on his shirt sleeves and pant legs as he removed his clothes.

"It will be easier to make each other feel good if our clothes are not in the way," whispered Hannah.

Soon Hannah and Kurt began to squirm, breathing harder and making noises without words. The caressing continued, although not as gently. Hannah lay on her back and pulled Alexandra in front of her, between her legs.

Hannah's words came out in a rush of breath as she firmly held Alexandra's head against her stomach. "Jetzt, Kurt, jetzt!"

Kurt sat up again, his words muffled. "Nein! Nein!"

Hannah's voice was like a dog growling. "Jetzt!"

"What do you want him to do?" Alexandra asked. She knew that "jetzt" meant "now." Now what? What was Kurt supposed to do?

Kurt looked as if he was going to cry, but he bent down, his knees straddling both Hannah and Alexandra, his body supported by his elbows, which were on either side of Alexandra's head.

He leaned into her, and Alexandra felt a strange object between her legs. Again she started to ask what was happening, just as Hannah grabbed her arm and heaved her off to the side, like a rag doll.

Alexandra lay next to the wall, pulling a pillow close to her. She watched as Hannah and Kurt wrapped themselves in each other's bodies. Hannah's mouth found a place between Kurt's legs, and strange noises came from his throat, getting louder and louder. Suddenly Hannah pulled her head up. She turned to grab Alexandra's arm, yanking her back. This time Hannah crouched on her knees, holding Alexandra firmly in front of her.

"Jetzt!"

Breathing as though he had just run up a lot of stairs, and whimpering at the same time, Kurt took hold of Alexandra's ankles, pushing them back toward her, bending her knees and leaning in between. That same strange, blunt thing bumped up against her again.

"Stop," she pleaded. "I don't like that."

"Shut up!" Hannah's voice was vicious.

Alexandra began to turn from side to side in an attempt to escape from Hannah's grasp and that uncomfortable feeling down there. Alexandra's arm was wrenched under her body.

"You're hurting me," she cried.

"Then stay still!"

Sobs from Kurt. Then in English, "I can't! I can't!"

Alexandra's arm was released, and with overwhelming relief she was able to scoot away. Hannah reached over to a drawer in the table next to the bed, retrieving something that she quickly placed behind her. Then she clamped her hand around Alexandra's arm again, dragging her back to the middle of the bed.

Hannah's command: "Hold her down!"

Kurt pinned Alexandra's shoulders down. One of her legs was trapped under Hannah. Something very cold and hard made contact with her, and this time it did not merely bump up against her; it was finding a way inside of her. Slowly it was pushing into a place that she had never felt before. It hurt. When she tried to cry out, Kurt's mouth covered hers, and her screams were stifled. The pain grew as the thing thrust farther inside her. Her attempts to twist away were useless; the thing moved with her.

"How does it feel, mein liebling?" Hannah's words came between heaving breaths. "Do you love it as much as I do? No? Ah, you will someday, you will. Now I'm loving it. This is for me!"

The pain spiraled into Alexandra's stomach, and she knew that the thing was going to tear her open. And then it was coming out. But as it did, it was pulling all of her insides with it. With a final excruciating suction, it was gone. The devastating pain let up and was replaced by aching and stinging. She inhaled a deep breath. She would not die from the aching and stinging.

A moment later she was lifted into the air and flipped onto her stomach. One large hand held her head down. Her legs were shoved upward so that her knees were under her, and she was being entered again in a different place. This time the pain was instantaneous. She screamed. Nothing was supposed to go in this way! Instinct and reflex battled against reality. This was a place for pushing things out of the body only. The thing inside her became burning hot and sent shock waves up her spine and down her legs. And she could feel herself growing bigger. She became the size of the whole room because the pain reached from wall to wall and yet was all within her body. This time, as she cried out, her mouth and nose were covered. This was dying. She could not breathe, and the pain would soon destroy her.

Instinctively she grabbed at the hand that was suffocating her. She could not budge it, and yet in the next moment it slid off her nose but stayed clamped over her mouth. She sucked in some air, and as the oxygen cleared her brain, the pain at the other end of her body intensified.

It had to stop! When was she going to die? It would stop when she died. It could not hurt like this in heaven. Grandma Genya had told her that when people die, they go to Jesus. Could Jesus see her now? Was he waiting for her? The only way to stop this pain was to die. Why was it taking so long? What had she done to be punished so? Why was Hannah punishing her? What was the bad thing that she had done? It must be taking so long because of how bad she'd been. Jesus wouldn't want her. If Hannah had to punish her this much then Jesus would punish her too. If she was this bad, maybe the punishment was that the pain would never stop.

Epilogue

November 15, 1999

Normal. That's all Georgia wanted. Definition of normal? That was not so easy. So maybe it was more about peace of mind. No, that wasn't it. Her mind would never be "at peace" until she was dead. A sense of well-being. Was that it? But there was such a fine line between self-awareness and a sense of well-being. So was it about her self-identity? She'd been stumbling around with that all her life. What she needed to do was give up on that.

She reminded herself for the millionth time. She was who she was. *Move on already. Just live life.*

Answers. That's what she wanted. But what were the questions? And which questions mattered? *Again, move on already. Just live.*

She'd been staring at her computer screen for so long that the power feature had sent it to "screen saver" and then to "sleep mode." The screen was black. She nudged the mouse, which brought up her private inbox. E-mails from every member of her immediate family were interspersed with confirmations from the restaurant, the florist, the cake maker, the printer, and Saks. Wedding plans.

So here she was, moving on. Milt had convinced her in September, when they had taken a week's vacation at the Four Seasons on Kona. His proposal had been official and very romantic. They sat at a table set for two on the beach with a classical trio stationed just far enough away to send their music across the sand but not interfere with their privacy. The discreet waitstaff served cocktails and hors d'oeuvres and then disappeared. Just as a sea turtle began its journey out of the surf, Milt brought out a small box from his trouser pocket and placed it in front of her.

"I love you," he said. His voice was shaky, and he cleared his throat then took in a deep breath and continued. "You know that. And my definition of love in this context means I want to spend the rest of our lives together. So, officially, Georgia Kassov Cates, will you marry me?"

She grinned. "This is how you ask me? On a beach at sunset in Kona? Is this the best you can do?"

"Open the box," he said, grinning back.

"What if I don't like it?"

"The box? I don't care, and you don't even know what's in it. Maybe it's a Tic Tac because you have bad breath."

Not a Tic Tac.

She recognized the ring right away. A two-carat yellow sapphire set in three tiers of platinum, each layer comprised of dozens of tiny diamond baguettes. She had admired it for months, stopping each time she walked to the Bellagio north valet to study the ring in the display window of Fred Leighton.

"Was I that obvious?" She looked up at Milt, eyes filled with happy tears.

"Yeah, you pretty much were," he answered.

So now the wedding was two days away, and everyone from out of town would begin arriving tomorrow. Her mother's plane landed first, and Georgia had arranged for a driver to take her directly to Bellagio's check-in. Sonnie, Mike and his girlfriend, Krista and were driving in from Creste Verde and promised to get in town in time to get settled into rooms at the Hard Rock before they met everyone for dinner. She'd reserved two rooms for the three of them and would not ask questions as to who shared and who didn't. Andrea, Georgia's ex-business partner, and her husband, Eric, would round out the out-of-town guest list.

EPILOGUE

The "locals" list, which included Milt's sister, plus her husband and kids, was short because she and Milt had agreed that even though they both wanted to celebrate their marriage in style and elegance, this wedding was for them and those they cared most about.

Phillip, although he adored his daughter and tried to be the best father possible, was still mostly focused on opening the Empyrean Hotel and Casino and seemed grateful for the affection and care that Georgia provided for his daughter. She and Livy met regularly for lunch or an appropriate show, even staying in touch when Phillip took Livy off on his various business trips. She had kept her promise to Livy, and the astoundingly intelligent child had come to understand and accept that Georgia could only be her friend. Father and daughter would both be at the wedding.

Months had passed since Melanie's death, and Milt had patiently waited as Georgia grieved. There had been no funeral, no memorial service, only hours of solitude as she had come to terms with the reality that Melanie was gone and so was any hope that Georgia could share her childhood burdens with a trusted friend.

When Melanie had sought her out, had parsed out her own layered life story, Georgia had begun to hope that the relationship would become mutual, but there hadn't been time.

The irony had been that Melanie had told Georgia everything and then was gone. The miracle had been that Milt had turned out to be the one who could be trusted and that Georgia had understood that in time.

Zivah had legally been able to claim Melanie's body and have it shipped away. An attorney had called Georgia the day after Melanie died. He was representing Zivah and wanted to meet to discuss any claims that Georgia may have had against Melanie's estate. Georgia had immediately assured him that she wanted nothing, and she'd not heard from Zivah or her representative again. Melanie's apartment had been emptied, the contents packed up and shipped away. Georgia never tried to find out where everything went. It didn't matter.

And writing the conclusion of her novel, *Alexandra*, didn't matter either, at least not for the foreseeable future which was all about wedding plans. And that was plenty for right now.

Joan Destino spent her childhood in various parts of the United States and Europe. After high school and college in New England, she taught school in Boston while her husband attended law school.

In the early seventies, she moved to San Marino, California, where she raised her family. Living fulltime in Las Vegas since 2004, Destino currently plays both cash and tournament poker.

Author Photo: Optionzphotography.com

Joandestino.com

Made in the USA
Lexington, KY
16 July 2014